BARBARA DELINSKY

Secret Promises

HARLEQUIN® HQN™

ISBN-13: 978-0-373-77915-4

Secret Promises

Copyright © 2014 by Harlequin Books S.A.

Recycling programs for this product may not exist in your area.

The publisher acknowledges the copyright holder of the individual works as follows:

Crossed Hearts
Copyright © 1987 as Twelve Across by Barbara Delinsky
Copyright © 2014 as Crossed Hearts by Barbara Delinsky

Threats and Promises
Copyright © 1985 by Barbara Delinsky

This edition published by arrangement with Harlequin Books S.A.

For questions and comments about the quality of this book, please contact us at CustomerService@Harlequin.com.

® and TM are trademarks of Harlequin Enterprises Limited or its corporate affiliates. Trademarks indicated with ® are registered in the United States Patent and Trademark Office, the Canadian Intellectual Property Office and in other countries.

Printed in U.S.A.

CONTENTS

CROSSED HEARTS

first published as *Twelve Across* in 1987

CHAPTER ONE

LEAH GATES MADE a final fold in the blue foil paper, then studied her creation in dismay. "This does not look like a roadrunner," she whispered to the woman at the table beside her.

Victoria Lesser, who'd been diligently folding a pelican, shifted her attention to her friend's work. "Sure, it does," she whispered back. "It's a roadrunner."

"And I'm a groundhog." Leah raised large, round glasses from the bridge of her nose in the hope that a myopic view would improve the image. It didn't. She dropped the frames back into place.

"It's a roadrunner," Victoria repeated.

"You're squinting."

"It looks like a roadrunner."

"It looks like a conglomeration of pointed paper prongs."

Lifting the fragile item, Victoria turned it from side to side. She had to agree with Leah's assessment, though she was far too tactful to say so. "Did you get the stretched bird base right?"

"I thought so."

"And the book fold and the mountain fold?"

"As far as I know."

"Then there must be some problem with the rabbit-ear fold."

"I think the problem's with me."

"Nuh-uh."

"Then with you," Leah scolded in the same hushed whisper. "It was your idea to take an origami course. How do I let myself get talked into these things?"

"Very easily. You love them as much as I do. Besides, you're a puzzle solver, and what's origami but a puzzle in paper? You've done fine up to now. So today's an off day."

"That's an understatement," Leah muttered.

"Ladies?" came a call from the front of the room. Both Leah and Victoria looked up to find the instructor's reproving stare homing in on them over the heads of the other students. "I believe we're ready to start on the frog base. Are there any final questions on the stretched bird base?"

Leah quickly shook her head, then bit her lip against a moan of despair. The frog base?

Victoria simply sat with a gentle smile on her face. By the time the class had ended, though, the smile had faded. Taking Leah by the arm, she ushered her toward the door. "Come on," she said softly. "Let's get some coffee."

When they were seated in a small coffee shop on Third Avenue, Victoria wasted no time in speaking her mind. "Something's bothering you. Out with it."

Leah set her glasses on the table. They'd fogged up the instant she'd come in from the cold, and long-time experience told her they'd be useless for several minutes. The oversize fuchsia sweater Victoria wore was more than bright enough to be seen by the weakest of eyes, however, and above the sweater was the gentlest of expressions. It was toward these that Leah sent a sheepish look. "My frog base stunk, too, huh?"

"Your mind wasn't on it. Your attention's been else- where all night. Where, if I may be so bold as to ask?"

Leah had to laugh at that. In the year she'd known Victoria Lesser, the woman had on occasion been far bolder. But not once had Leah minded. What might have been considered intrusive in others was caring in Victoria. She was compassionate, down-to-earth and insightful, and had such a remarkably positive view of the world that time spent with her was always uplifting.

"Guess," Leah invited with a wry half grin.

"Well, I know your mind's not on your marriage, because that's been over and done for two years now. And I know it's not on a man, because despite my own considerable—" she drawled the word pointedly "—efforts to fix you up, you refuse to date. And I doubt it's on your work, because crosswords are in as much of a demand as ever, and because just last week you told me that your contract's been renewed. Which leaves your apartment." Victoria knew how much Leah adored the loft she'd lived in since her divorce. "Is your land- lord raising the rent?"

"Worse."

"Oh-oh. He's talking condo conversion."

"He's *decided* condo conversion."

"Oh, sweetheart. Mucho?"

"Mucho mucho."

"When's it happening?"

"Too soon." Idly Leah strummed the rim of her glasses, then, as though recalling their purpose, slipped them back onto her nose. "I can look for another place, but I doubt I'll find one half as nice. Waterfront build- ings are hot, and most of them have already gone condo. Even if there were a vacancy in one of the few remain- ing rentals, I doubt I could afford it."

"Thank you, New York."

"Mmm." Seeking to warm her chilled fingers, Leah wrapped her hands around her coffee cup. "Prices have gone sky-high in the two years since I rented the loft. The only reason I got it at a reasonable rate in the first place was that I was willing to fix it up myself. It was a mess when I first saw it, but the view was…ineffable."

"Ineffable?"

"Indescribable. It isn't fair, Victoria. For weeks I scraped walls and ceilings, sanded, painted, and now someone else will reap the fruits of my labor." She gave a frustrated growl. "I had a feeling this was coming, but that doesn't make it any easier to take."

Victoria's heart went out to this woman who'd become such a special friend. They'd met the year before in the public library and had hit it off from the start. Victoria had enjoyed Leah's subtle wit and soft-spoken manner. Though at the age of thirty-three Leah was twenty years younger, they shared an interest in things new and different. They'd gone to the theater together, tried out newly opened restaurants together, taken classes not only in origami but in papier-mâché, conversational Russian and ballet.

Victoria had come to know Leah well. She'd learned that Leah had been badly burned by an unhappy marriage and that behind the urban adventuress was a basically shy woman. She also saw that Leah had constructed a very tidy and self-contained shell for herself, and that within that shell was a world of loneliness and vulnerability. Losing the apartment she loved would feed that vulnerability.

"You know," Victoria ventured, "I'd be more than happy to loan you the down payment on that condo—"

The hand Leah pressed over hers cut off her words. "I can't take your money."

"But I have it. More than enough—"

"It's not my way, Victoria. I wouldn't be comfortable. And it's not as much a matter of principle as it is the amount of money involved. If I had to make loan payments to you on top of mortgage payments to the bank, I'd be house-poor. Another few years... That's all I'd have needed to save for the down payment myself." It might have taken less if she'd been more frugal, but Leah lived comfortably and enjoyed it. She took pleasure in splurging on an exquisite hand-knit sweater, a pair of imported shoes, a piece of original art. She reasoned that she'd earned them. But a bank wouldn't take them as collateral. "Unfortunately I don't have another few years."

"You wouldn't have to pay me back right away."

"That's bad business."

"So? It's my money, my business—"

"And our friendship. I'd feel awkward taking advantage of it."

"I'm the one who's made the offer. There'd be no taking advantage involved."

But Leah was shaking her head. "Thanks, but I can't. I just can't."

Victoria opened her mouth to speak, then paused. She'd been about to suggest that Richard might help. Given the fact that Leah had been married to him once and that she had no other family, it seemed the only other option. He had money. Unfortunately he also had a new wife and a child. Victoria knew that Leah's pride wouldn't allow her to ask him for a thing. "What will you do?"

"Look for another place, I guess. If I have to settle for something less exciting, so be it."

"Are you sure you want to stay in the city? Seems to me you could get a super place somewhere farther out."

Leah considered that idea. "But I like the city."

"You're used to the city. You've lived here all your life. Maybe it's time for a change."

"I don't know—"

"It'd be good for you, sweetheart. New scenery, new people, new stores, new courses—"

"Are you trying to get rid of me?"

"And lose my companion in whimsy? Of course not! But I'd be selfish if I didn't encourage you to spread your wings a little. One part of you loves new experiences. The other part avoids them. But you're young, Leah. You have so much living to do."

"What better place to do it than here? I mean, if New York isn't multifarious—"

"Leah, please."

"Diverse, as in filled with opportunities, okay? If New York isn't that, what place is?"

"Just about any place. Perhaps it'd be a different kind of experience…" The wheels in Victoria's mind were beginning to turn. "You know, there's another possibility entirely. If you were willing to shift gears, if you were game…" She shook her head. "No. Maybe not."

"What?"

"It'd be too much. Forget I mentioned it."

"You haven't mentioned anything," Leah pointed out in her quiet way. But she was curious, just as she was sure Victoria had intended. "What were you thinking of?"

It was a minute before Victoria answered, and the delay wasn't all for effect. She hated to be devious with

someone she adored as much as she did Leah. And yet…
and yet…it could possibly work. Hadn't a little devious-
ness brought two other good friends of hers together?

"I have a place. It's pretty secluded."

"The island in Maine?"

"There's that, but it wasn't what I had in mind." The
island was totally secluded. She didn't want Leah to be
alone; that would defeat the purpose. "I have a cabin in
New Hampshire. Arthur bought it years ago as a hunting lodge. I've been up several times since he died,
but it's a little too quiet for me." She shook her head
again. "No. It'd be too quiet for you, too. You're used
to the city."

"Tell me more."

"You like the city."

"Tell me, Victoria."

Again Victoria paused, this time entirely for effect.
"It's in the middle of the woods, and it's small," she
said with caution.

"Go on."

"We're talking mountain retreat here."

"Yes."

"There are two rooms—a living area and a bedroom.
The nearest town is three miles away. You'd hate it,
Leah."

But Leah wasn't so sure. She was intimidated by the
idea of moving to a suburban neighborhood, but something rustic… It was a new thought, suddenly worth
considering. "I don't know as I could buy it."

"It's not for sale," Victoria said quickly. "But I could
easily loan—"

"Rent. It'd have to be a rental."

"Okay. I could easily rent it to you for a little while.

That's all you'd need to decide whether you can live outside New York. You could view it as a trial run."

"Are there people nearby?"

"In the town, yes. Not many, mind you, and they're quiet, private types."

So much the better, Leah thought. She didn't care to cope with throngs of new faces. "That's okay. I could do my work at a mountain cabin without any problem, and if I had books and a tape deck—"

"There's a community of artists about fifteen miles from the mountain. You once mentioned wanting to learn how to weave. You'd have the perfect opportunity for that." Victoria considered mentioning Garrick, then ruled against it for the time being. Leah was smiling; she obviously liked what she'd heard so far. It seemed that reverse psychology was the way to go. "It's not New York," she reminded her friend gently.

"I know."

"It'd be a total change."

"I know."

"A few minutes ago you said you didn't want to leave New York."

"But my apartment's being stolen from under me, so some change is inevitable."

"You could still look for another apartment."

"I could."

"Or move to the suburbs."

Leah's firm head shake sent thick black hair shimmering along the crew neckline of her sweater.

"I want you to think about this, Leah. It'd be a pretty drastic step."

"True, but not an irrevocable one. If I'm climbing the walls after a week, I can turn around and come back. I really wouldn't be any worse off than I am now, would

I?" She didn't wait for Victoria to answer. She was feeling more enthused than she had since she'd learned she was losing her loft. "Tell me more about the cabin itself. Is it primitive?"

Victoria laughed. "If you'd had a chance to know Arthur, you'd have the answer to that. Arthur Lesser never did anything primitive. For that matter, you know me. I'm not exactly the rough-it-in-the-wild type, am I?"

Leah had spent time in Victoria's Park Avenue co-op. It was spacious, stylish, sumptuous. She'd also seen her plush summer place in the Hamptons. But neither Manhattan nor Long Island was a secluded mountain in New Hampshire, and for all her wealth, Victoria wasn't snobbish. She was just enough of a nonconformist to survive for a stretch on the bare basics.

Leah, who'd never had the kind of wealth that inspired total nonconformity, liked to go into things with her eyes open. "Is the cabin well equipped?"

"When last I saw it, it was," Victoria said with an innocence that concealed a multitude of sins. "Don't make a decision now, sweetheart. Think about it for a bit. If you decide to go up there, you'd have to store your furniture. I don't know how you feel about that."

"It shouldn't be difficult."

"It'd be a pain in the neck."

"Being ousted from my apartment is a pain in the neck. If movers have to come in, what difference does it make where they take my things? Besides, if I hate it in New Hampshire, I won't have to worry about my furniture while I look around back here for a place to live."

"The green room's yours if you want it."

Leah grinned. While she'd never have taken a monetary loan, the use of that beautiful room in Victoria's apartment, where she'd already spent a night or two on occasion, was a security blanket she'd welcome. "I was hoping you'd say that."

"Well, you'd better remember it. I'd never forgive myself if, after I talked you into it, you hated the mountains and then didn't have anywhere to turn." Actually, Victoria was more worried that Leah would be the one without forgiveness. But it was a risk worth taking. Victoria had gone with her instincts where Deirdre and Neil Hersey were concerned, and things couldn't have worked out better. Now here was Leah—tall and slender, adorable with her glossy black page boy and bangs, and her huge round glasses with thin red frames. If Leah could meet Garrick...

"I'll take it," Leah was saying.

"The green room? Of course you will."

"No, the cabin. I'll take the cabin." Leah wasn't an impulsive person, but she did know her own mind. When something appealed to her, she saw no point in waffling. Victoria's mountain retreat sounded like a perfect solution to the problem she'd been grappling with for seventy-two hours straight. It would afford her the time to think things through and decide where to go from there. "Just tell me how much you want for rent."

Victoria brushed the matter aside with the graceful wave of one hand. "No rush on that. We can discuss it later."

"I'm paying rent, Victoria. If you don't let me, the deal's off."

"I agreed that you could pay rent, sweetheart. It's just that I have no idea how much to charge. Why don't you see what shape things are in when you get there? Then you can pay me whatever you think the place merits."

"I'd rather pay you in advance."

"And I'd rather wait."

"You're being pertinacious."

Victoria wasn't sure what "pertinacious" meant, but she could guess. "That's right."

"Fine. I'll wait as you've asked, but so help me, Victoria, if you return my check—"

"I won't," Victoria said, fully confident that it wouldn't come to that. "Have faith, Leah. Have faith."

LEAH HAD FAITH. It grew day by day, along with her enthusiasm. She surprised herself at times, because she truly was a dyed-in-the-wool urbanite. Yet something about an abrupt change in life-style appealed to her for the very first time. She wondered if it had something to do with her age; perhaps the thirties brought boldness. Or desperation. No, she didn't want to think that. Perhaps she was simply staging a belated rebellion against the way of life she'd known from birth.

It had been years since she'd taken a vacation, much less one to a remote spot. She remembered short jaunts to Cape Cod with her parents when she'd been a child, and *remote* had consisted of isolated sand dunes and sunrise sails. The trips she'd taken with her husband had never been remote in any sense. Inevitably they'd been tied to his work, and she'd found them far from relaxing. Richard had been constantly *on,* which wouldn't have bothered her if he hadn't been so fussy about how she looked and behaved when she was by his side. Not that she'd given him cause for complaint; she'd been born and bred in the urban arena and knew how to play its games when necessary. Unfortunately Richard's games had incorporated rules she hadn't anticipated.

But Leah wasn't thinking about Richard on the day in late March when she left Manhattan. She was thinking of the gut instinct that told her she was doing the right thing. And she was thinking of the farewell dinner Victoria had insisted on treating her to the night before.

They'd spent the better part of the meal chatting about incidentals. Only when they'd reached dessert did they get around to the nitty-gritty. "You're all set to go, then?"

"You bet."

Victoria had had many a qualm in the three weeks since she'd suggested the plan, and in truth, she was feeling a little like a weasel. It was fine and dandy, she knew, to say that she had Leah's best interests at heart. She was still being manipulative, and Leah was bound to be angry when she discovered the fact. "Are you sure you want to go through with this?"

"Uh-huh."

"There isn't any air-conditioning."

"In the mountains? I should hope not."

"Or phone."

"So you've told me," Leah said with a smile. "Twice. I'll give you a call from town once I'm settled."

Victoria wasn't sure whether to look forward to that or not. "Did the storage people get all your furniture?"

"This morning."

"My Lord, that means the bed, too! Where will you sleep tonight?"

"On the floor. And no, I don't want the green room. I've about had it with packing. Everything's ready to go from my place. All I'll have to do in the morning is load up the car and take off."

A night on the bare floor. Victoria felt guiltier than ever, but she knew a stubborn expression when she saw one. "Is the car okay?"

It was a demo Volkswagen Golf that Leah had bought from a dealer three days before. "The car is fine."

"Can you drive it?"

"Sure can."

"You haven't driven in years, Leah."

"It's like riding a bike—you never forget how. Isn't that what you told me two weeks ago? Come on, Victoria. It's not like you to be a worrywart."

She was right. Still, Victoria felt uncomfortable. With Deirdre and Neil, there had been a single phone call from each and they'd been on their way. With Leah it had meant three weeks of deception, which seemed to make the crime that much greater.

But what was done was done. Leah's mind was set. Her arrangements were made. She was going.

Taking a deep breath, Victoria produced first a reassuring smile, then two envelopes from her purse. "Directions to the cabin," she said, handing over the top one. "I had my secretary type them up, and they're quite detailed." Cautiously she watched Leah remove the paper and scan it. She knew the exact moment Leah reached the instructions on the bottom, and responded to her frown by explaining, "Garrick Rodenhiser is a trapper. His cabin is several miles from mine by car, but there's an old logging trail through the woods that will get you there on foot in no time. In case of emergency you're to contact him. He's a good man. He'll help you in any way he can."

"Goodness," Leah murmured distractedly as she reread the directions, "you sound as though you expect trouble."

"Nonsense. But I do trust Garrick. When I'm up there alone myself, it's a comfort knowing he's around."

"Well—" Leah folded the paper and returned it to the envelope "—I'm sure I'll be fine."

"So you will be," Victoria declared, holding out the second envelope. "For Garrick. Deliver it for me?"

Leah took it, then turned it over and over. It was sealed and opaque, with the trapper's name written on the front in Victoria's elegant script. "A love letter?" she teased, tapping the tip of the envelope against her nose. "Somehow I can't imagine you with a craggy old trapper."

"Craggy old trappers can be very nice."

"Are there lots of them up there?"

"A few."

"Don't they smell?"

Victoria laughed. "That's precious, Leah."

"They don't?"

"Not badly."

"Oh. Okay. Well, that's good. Y'know, this trip could well be educational."

That was, in many ways, how Leah thought of it as she worked her way through the midtown traffic. The car was packed to the hilt with clothing and other essentials, boxes of books, a tape deck and three cases of cassettes, plus sundry supplies. She had dozens of plans, projects to keep her busy over and above the crossword puzzles she intended to create.

Filling her mind with these prospects was in part a defense mechanism, she knew, and it was successful only to a point. There remained a certain wistfulness in leaving the loft where she'd been independent for the first time in her life, saying goodbye to the little man at the corner kiosk from whom she'd bought the *Times* each day, bidding a silent farewell to the theaters and restaurants and museums she wouldn't be visiting for a while.

The exhaust fumes that surrounded her were as

familiar as the traffic. Not so the sense of nostalgia
that assailed her as she navigated the Golf through the
streets. She'd loved New York from the time she'd been
old enough to appreciate it as a city. Her parents' apartment had been modest by New York standards, but Central Park had been free to all, as had Fifth Avenue,
Rockefeller Center and Washington Square.

Memories. A few close friends. The kind of anonymity she liked. Such was New York. But they'd all
be there when she returned. Determinedly squaring her
shoulders, she thrust off sentimentality in favor of prac-
ticality, which at the moment meant avoiding swerving
taxis and swarming pedestrians as she headed toward
the East River.

Traffic was surprisingly heavy for ten in the morning, and Leah was the kind of driver others either loved
or hated. When in doubt she yielded the road, which
meant grins on the faces of those who cut her off and
impatient honks from those behind her. She was relieved to leave the concrete jungle behind and start
north on the thruway.

It was a sunny day, mild for March, a good omen,
she decided. Though she'd brought heavier clothes with
her, she was glad she'd worn a pair of lightweight knit
pants and a loose cashmere sweater for the drive. She
was comfortable and increasingly relaxed as she coasted
in the limbo between city and country.

By the time she reached the outskirts of Boston, it
was two o'clock and she was famished. As eager to
stretch as to eat, she pulled into a Burger King on the
turnpike and climbed from the car, pausing only to grab
for her jacket before heading for the restaurant. The sun
was lost behind cloud cover that had gathered since
she'd reached the Massachusetts border, and the air had

grown chilly. Knowing that she had another three hours of driving before her, and desperately wanting to reach the cabin before dark, she gulped down a burger and a Coke, used the rest rooms, then was quickly on her way again.

The sky darkened progressively. With the New Hampshire border came a light drizzle. So much for good omens, she mused silently as she turned one switch after another until at last she hit paydirt with the windshield wipers. Within half an hour she set them to swishing double time.

It was pouring. Dark, gloomy, cold and wet. Leah thanked her lucky stars that she'd read the directions so many times before she'd left, because she loathed the idea of pulling over to the side of the road even for the briefest of moments. With the typed words neatly etched in her brain, she was able to devote her full concentration to driving.

And driving demanded it. She eased up on the gas, but even then had to struggle to see the road through the torrent. Lane markers were badly blurred. The back spray from passing cars made the already poor visibility worse. She breathed a sigh of relief when she found her turnoff, then tensed up again when the sudden sparsity of other cars meant the absence of taillights as guides.

But she drove on. She passed a restaurant and briefly considered taking shelter until the storm was spent, but decided that it would be far worse to have to negotiate strange roads—and a lonesome cabin—in the dark later. She passed a dingy motel and toyed with the idea of taking a room for the night, but decided that she really did want to be in the cabin. Having left behind the life she'd always known, she was feeling unsettled; spending the night in a fleabag motel wouldn't help.

What would help, she decided grimly, would be an end to the rain. And a little sun peeking through the clouds. And several extra hours of daylight.

None of those happened. The rain did lessen to a steady downpour, but the sky grew darker and darker as daylight began to wane. The fiddling she'd done earlier in search of the wipers paid off; she knew just what to press to turn on the headlights.

When she passed through the small town Victoria had mentioned, she was elated. Elation faded in an instant, though, when she took the prescribed turn past the post office and saw what lay ahead.

A narrow, twisting road, barely wide enough for two cars. No streetlamps. No center line. No directional signs.

Leah sat ramrod straight at the wheel. Her knuckles were white, her eyes straining to delineate the rain-spattered landscape ahead. Too late she realized that she hadn't checked the odometer when she'd passed the post office. One-point-nine miles to the turnoff, her instructions said. How far had she gone? All but creeping along the uphill grade, she searched for the triangular boulder backed by a stand of twisted birch that would mark the start of Victoria's road.

It was just another puzzle, Leah told herself. She loved puzzles.

She hated this one. If she missed the road… But she didn't want to miss the road. One-point-nine miles at fifteen miles an hour…eight minutes… How long had she been driving since she'd left the town?

Just when she was about to stop and return to the post office to take an odometer reading, she saw a triangular boulder backed by a stand of twisted birch. And a road. Vaguely.

It was with mixed feelings that she made the turn, for not only was she suddenly on rutted dirt, but forested growth closed in on her, slapping the sides of the car. In her anxious state it sounded clearly hostile.

She began to speak to herself, albeit silently. *This is God's land, Leah. The wild and woolly outdoors. Picture it in the bright sunshine. You'll love it.*

The car bumped and jerked along, jolting her up and down and from side to side. One of the tires began to spin and she caught her breath, barely releasing it when the car surged onward and upward. The words she spoke to herself grew more beseechful. *Just a little farther, Leah. You're almost there. Come on, Golf, don't fade on me now.*

Her progress was agonizingly slow, made all the more so by the steepening pitch as the road climbed the hill. The Golf didn't falter, but when it wasn't jouncing, it slid pitifully from one side to the other, even back when she took her foot from the gas to better weather the ruts. She wished she'd had the foresight to rent a Jeep, if not a Sherman tank. It was all she could do to hold the steering wheel steady. It was all she could do to see the road.

Leah was frightened. Darkness was closing in from every angle, leaving her high beams as a beacon to nowhere. When they picked up an expanse of water directly in her path, she slammed on the brakes. The car fishtailed in the mud, then came to a stop, its sudden stillness compensated for by the racing of her pulse.

A little voice inside her screamed, *Turn back! Turn back!* But she couldn't turn. She was hemmed in on both sides by the woods.

She stared at the water before her. Beneath the pelting rain, it undulated as a living thing. But it was only a puddle, she told herself. Victoria would have mentioned a stream, and there was no sign of a bridge, washed out or otherwise.

Cautiously she stepped on the gas. Yard by yard, the car stole forward. She tried not to think about how high the water might be on the hubcaps. She tried not to think about the prospect of brake damage or stalling. She tried not to think about what creatures of the wild might be lurking beneath the rain-swollen depths. She kept as steady a foot on the gas pedal as possible and released a short sigh of relief when she reached high ground once again.

There were other puddles and ruts and thick beds of mud, but then the road widened. Heart pounding, she squinted through the windshield as she pushed on the accelerator. The cabin had to be ahead. *Please, God, let it be ahead.*

All at once, with terrifying abruptness, the road seemed to disappear. She'd barely had time to jerk her foot to the brake, when the car careened over a rise and began a downward slide. After a harrowing aeon, it came to rest in a deep pocket of sludge.

Shaking all over, Leah closed her eyes for a minute. She took one tremulous breath, then another, then opened her eyes and looked ahead. What she saw took her breath away completely.

For three weeks she'd been picturing a compact and charming log cabin. A chimney would rise from one side; windows would flank the front door. Nestled in the woods, the cabin would be the epitome of a snug country haven.

Instead it was the epitome of ruin. She blinked, convinced that she was hallucinating. Before her lay the charred remains of what might indeed have once been a snug and charming cabin. Now only the chimney was standing.

"Oh, Lord," she wailed, her cry nearly drowned out by the thunder of rain on the roof of the car, "what *happened?*"

Unfortunately what had happened was obvious. There had been a fire. But when? And why hadn't Victoria been notified?

The moan that followed bore equal parts disappointment, fatigue and anxiety. In the confines of the car it had such an eerie edge that Leah knew she had to get back to civilization and fast. At that moment even the thought of spending the night in a fleabag motel held appeal.

She stepped on the gas and the front wheels spun. She shifted into reverse and hit the gas again, but the car didn't budge. Into drive...into reverse...she repeated the cycle a dozen times, uselessly. Not only was she not getting back to civilization she wasn't getting *anywhere,* at least, not in the Golf.

Dropping her head to the steering wheel, she took several shuddering breaths. Leah Gates didn't panic. She hadn't done so when her parents had died. She hadn't done so when her babies had died. She hadn't done so when her husband had pronounced her unfit as a wife and left her.

What she had done in each of those situations was cry until her grief was spent, then pick herself up and restructure her dreams. In essence, that was what she had to do now. There wasn't time to give vent to tears, but a definite restructuring of plans was in order.

She couldn't spend the night in the car. She couldn't get back to town. Help wasn't about to come to her, so...

Fishing the paper with the typed directions from her

purse, she turned on the overhead light and read at the bottom of the page the lines that she'd merely skimmed before. True, she'd promised Victoria that she'd deliver the letter to the trapper, Garrick Rodenhiser, but she'd assumed she'd do it at her leisure. Certainly not in the dark of night—or in the midst of a storm.

But seeking out the trapper seemed her only hope of rescue. It was pouring and very dark. She had neither flashlight, umbrella nor rain poncho handy. She'd just have to make a dash for it. Hadn't she done the same often enough in New York when a sudden downpour soaked the streets?

Diligently she reread the directions to the trapper's cabin. Peering through the windshield, she located the break in the woods behind and to the left of the chimney. Without dwelling on the darkness ahead, she tucked the paper back in her purse, dropped the purse to the floor, turned off the lights, then the engine. After pocketing the keys, she took a deep breath, swung open the door and stepped out into the rain.

Her feet promptly sank six inches into mud. Dumbly she stared down at where her ankles should have been. Equally as dumbly she tugged at one foot, which emerged minus its shoe. She stuck her foot back into the mud, rooted around until she'd located the shoe and squished her foot inside, then drew the whole thing up toe first.

After tottering for a second, she lunged onto what she hoped was firmer ground. It was, though this time her other foot came up shoeless. Legs wide apart, she repeated the procedure of retrieving her shoe, then scrambled ahead.

She didn't think about the fact that the comfortable leather flats she'd loved were no doubt ruined. She didn't think about her stockings or her pants or, for that matter, the rest of her clothes, which were already drenched. And assuming that it would be a quick trip to the trapper's cabin, then a quick one back with help, she didn't think once about locking the car. As quickly as she could she ran around the ruins of Victoria's cabin and plunged on into the woods.

An old logging trail, Victoria had called it. Leah could believe that. No car could have fit through, for subsequent years of woodland growth had narrowed it greatly. But it was visible, and for that she was grateful.

It was also wet, and in places nearly as muddy as what she'd so precipitously stepped into from her car. As hastily as she could, she slogged through, only to find her feet mired again a few steps later.

As the minutes passed, she found it harder to will away the discomfort she felt. It occurred to her on a slightly hysterical note that dashing across Manhattan in the rain had never been like this. She was cold and wet. Her clothes clung to her body, providing little if any protection. Her hair was soaked; her bangs dripped into her eyes behind glasses whose lenses were streaked. Tension and the effort of wading through mud made her entire body ache.

Worse, there was no sign of a cabin ahead, or of anything else remotely human. For the first time since her car had become stuck she realized exactly how alone and vulnerable she was. Garrick Rodenhiser was a trapper, which meant that there were animals about. The thought that they might hunt humans in the rain sent shivers through her limbs, over and above those caused by the cold night air. Then she slipped in the mud and lost her balance, falling to the ground with a sharp cry.

Sheer terror had her on her feet in an instant, and she whimpered as she struggled on.

Several more times Leah lost a shoe and would have left it if the thought of walking in her sheer-stockinged feet hadn't been far worse than the slimness of the once fine leather. Twice more she fell, crying out in pain the second time when her thigh connected with something sharp. Not caring to consider what it might have been, she limped on. Hopping, sliding, scrambling for a foot-hold at times, she grew colder, wetter and muddier.

At one point pure exhaustion brought her to a stand-still. Her arms and legs were stiff; her insides trembled; her breath came in short, sharp gasps. She had to go on, she told herself, but it was another minute before her limbs would listen. And then it was only because the pain of movement was preferable to the psychological agony of inaction.

When she heard sounds beyond the rain, her panic grew. Glancing blindly behind her, she ricocheted off a tree and spun around, barely saving herself from yet another fall. She was sure she was crying, because she'd never been so frightened in her life, but she couldn't distinguish tears from raindrops.

A world of doubts crowded in on her. How much far-ther could she push her protesting limbs? How could she be sure that the trapper's cabin still existed? What if Garrick Rodenhiser simply wasn't there? *What would she do then?*

Nearing the point of despair, Leah didn't see the cabin until she was practically on top of it. She stumbled and fell, but on a path of flat stones this time. Shoving up her glasses with the back of one cold, stiff hand, she peered through the rain at the dark structure before her. After a frantic few seconds' search, she spotted the sliver of light that escaped through the shutters. It was the sweetest sight she'd ever seen.

Pushing herself upright, she staggered the final distance and all but crawled up the few short steps to the cabin's door. Beneath the overhang of the porch she was out of the rain, but her teeth were chattering, and her legs abruptly refused to hold her any longer. Sliding down on her bottom close by the door, she mustered the last of her strength to bang her elbow against the wood. Then she wrapped her arms around her middle and tried to hold herself together.

When a minute passed and nothing happened, her misery grew. The cold air of night gusted past her, chilling her wet clothing even more. She tapped more feebly on the wood, but it must have done the trick, for within seconds the door opened. Weakly she raised her eyes. Through wet glasses she could make out a huge form silhouetted in the doorway. Behind it was sanctuary.

"I…" she began, "I…"

The mighty figure didn't move.

"I am…I need…" Her voice was thready, severely impeded by the chill that had reduced her to a shivering mass.

Slowly, cautiously, the giant lowered itself to its haunches. Leah knew it was human. It moved like a human. It had hands like a human. She could only pray that it had the heart of a human.

"Victoria sent me," she whispered. "I'm so cold."

CHAPTER TWO

GARRICK RODENHISER WOULD have laughed had the huddled figure before him been less pathetic. Victoria wouldn't have sent him a woman; she knew that he valued his privacy too much. And she respected that, which was one of the reasons they'd become friends.

But the figure on his doorstep was indeed pathetic. She was soaking wet, covered with mud and, from the way she was quaking, looked to be chilled to the bone. Of course, the quaking could be from fear, he mused, and if she was handing him a line, she had due cause for fear.

Still, he wasn't an ogre. Regardless of what had brought her here, he couldn't close his door and leave her to the storm.

"Come inside," he said as he closed a hand around her upper arm and started to help her up.

She tried to pull away, whispering a frantic, "I'm filthy!"

The tightening of his fingers was his only response. Leah didn't protest further. Her legs were stiff and sore; she wasn't sure she'd have made it up on her own. His hand fell away, though, the instant she was standing, and he stood back for her to precede him into the cabin.

She took three steps into the warmth, then stopped. Behind her the door closed. Before her the fire blazed. Beneath her was a rapidly spreading puddle of mud.

Removing her glasses, she started to wipe them on her jacket, only to realize after several swipes that it wouldn't help. Glasses dangling, she looked helplessly around.

"Not exactly dressed for the weather, are you?" the trapper asked.

His voice was deep, faintly gravelly. Leah's eyes shot to his face. Though his features were fuzzy, his immense size was not. It had been one thing for him to tower over her when she'd been collapsed on the porch; now she was standing, all five-seven of her. He had to be close to six-four, and was strapping to boot. She wondered if she should fear him.

"Are you Garrick Rodenhiser?" Her voice sounded odd. It was hoarse and as shaky as the rest of her.

He nodded.

She noted that he was dressed darkly and that he was bearded, but if he was who he said, then he was a friend of Victoria's, and she was safe.

"I need help," she croaked, forcing the words out with great effort. "My car got stuck in the mud—"

"You need a shower," Garrick interrupted. He strode to the far side of the room—the large and only room of the cabin—where he opened a closet and drew out several clean towels. Though he didn't know who his guest was, she was not only trembling like a leaf, she was also making a mess on his floor. The sooner she was clean and warm, the sooner she could explain her presence.

Flipping on the bathroom light, he tossed the towels onto the counter by the sink, then gestured for Leah to come. When she didn't move, he gestured again. "There's plenty of hot water. And soap and shampoo."

Leah looked down at her clothes. They were nearly

unrecognizable as those she'd put on that morning. "It wasn't like this in the movie," she cried weakly.

Garrick stiffened, wondering if he was being set up. "Excuse me?"

"*Romancing the Stone*. They went through rain and mud, but their clothes came out looking clean."

He hadn't seen a movie in four years, and whether or not her remark was innocent remained to be seen. "You'd better take them off."

"But I don't have any others." Her body shook; her teeth clicked together between words. "They're in my car."

Garrick set off for the side of the room, where a huge bed shared the wall with a low dresser. He opened one drawer after another, finally returning to toss a pile of neatly folded clothes into the bathroom by the towels.

This time when he gestured, Leah moved. Her gait was stilted, though, and before she'd reached the bathroom, she was stopped by a raspy inquiry.

"What happened to your leg?"

She shot a glance at her thigh and swallowed hard. Not even the coating of mud on her pants could hide the fact that they were torn and she was bleeding. "I fell."

"What did you hit?"

"Something sharp." Rooted to the spot by curiosity as much as fatigue, she watched Garrick head for the part of the room that served as a kitchen, open a cabinet and set a large first-aid kit on the counter. He rummaged through and came up with a bottle of disinfectant and bandaging material, which he then added to the gathering pile in the bathroom.

"Take your shower," he instructed. "I'll make coffee."

"Brandy, I need brandy," she blurted out.

"Sorry. No brandy."

"Whiskey?" she asked more meekly. Didn't all woodsmen drink, preferably the potent, homemade stuff?

"Sorry."

"Anything?" she whispered.

Garrick shook his head. He almost wished he did have something strong. Despite the warmth of the cabin, the woman before him continued to tremble. If she'd trekked through the forest for any distance—and from the look of her she had—she was probably feeling the aftereffects of shock. But he didn't have anything remotely alcoholic to drink. He hadn't so much as looked at a bottle since he'd left California.

"Then hot coffee would…be lovely." She tried to smile, but her face wouldn't work. Nor were her legs eager to function in any trained manner. They protested when she forced them to carry her to the bathroom. She was feeling achier by the minute.

With the tip of one grimy finger, she closed the bathroom door. What she really wanted was a bath, but she quickly saw that there wasn't a tub. The bathroom was large, though, surprisingly modern, bright, clean and well equipped.

"There's a heat lamp," Garrick called from the other side of the door.

She found the switch and turned it on, determinedly avoiding the mirror in the process. Setting her glasses by the sink, she opened the door of the oversize shower stall and turned on the water. The minute it was hot, she stepped in, clothes and all.

It was heaven, sheer heaven. Hot water rained down on her head, spilling over the rest of her in a cascade of instant warmth. She didn't know how long she stood there without moving, nor did she care. Garrick had offered plenty of hot water, and despite the fact that she'd never been one to be selfish or greedy, she planned to take advantage of every drop. These were extenuating circumstances, she reasoned. After the ordeal she'd been through, her body deserved a little pampering.

Moreover, standing under the shower was as much of a limbo as the highway driving had been earlier. She knew that once she emerged, she was going to have to face a future that was as mucked up as her clothes. She wasn't looking forward to it.

Gradually the numbness in her hands and feet wore off. Slowly, and with distaste, she began to strip off her things. When every last item lay in a pile in a corner of the stall, she went to work with soap and shampoo, lathering, rinsing, lathering, rinsing, continuing the process far longer than was necessary, almost obsessive in her need to rid herself of the mud that was synonymous with terror.

By the time she turned off the water, the ache in her limbs had given way to a pervasive tiredness. More than anything at that moment she craved a soft chair, if not a sofa or, better yet, a bed. But there was work to be done first. Emerging from the shower, she wrapped one towel around her hair, then began to dry herself with another. When she inadvertently ran the towel over her thigh, she gasped. Fumbling for her glasses, she rinsed and dried them, then shakily fit them onto her nose.

She almost wished she hadn't. Her outer thigh bore a deep, three-inch gash that was ugly enough to make her stomach turn. Straightening, she closed her eyes, pressed a hand to her middle and took several deep breaths. Then, postponing another look for as long as possible, she reached for the clothes Garrick had left.

Beggars couldn't be choosers, which was why she
thought no evil of the gray thermal top she pulled on
and the green flannel shirt she layered over it. The thermal top hit her upper thigh; the shirt was even longer.
The warmth of both was welcome.

Tucking the tails beneath her, she lowered herself to
the closed commode. Working quickly, lest she lose her
nerve, she opened the bottle of disinfectant, poured a
liberal amount on a corner of the towel and pressed it
firmly to the gash.

White-hot pain shot through her leg. Crying aloud,
she tore the towel away. At the same time, her other
hand went boneless, releasing its grip on the bottle,
which fell to the floor and shattered.

Garrick, who'd been standing pensively before the
fire, jerked up his head when he heard her cry. Within
seconds he'd crossed the floor and burst into the bathroom.

Leah's hands were fisted on her knees, and she was
rocking back and forth, waiting for the stinging in her
leg to subside. Her gaze flew to his. "I didn't think it
would hurt so much," she whispered.

His grip tightened on the doorknob, and for a split
second he considered retreating. It had been more than
four years since he'd seen legs like those—long and
slender, living silk the color of cream. His eyes were
riveted to them, while his heart yawed. He told himself
to turn and run—until he caught sight of the red gouge
marring that silk and knew he wasn't going anywhere.

Squatting before her, he took the towel from where
it lay across her lap and dabbed at the area around the
cut. The color of the antiseptic was distinct on the corner of the towel she'd used. He reversed the terry cloth
and flicked her a glance.

"Hold on."

With a gentle dabbing motion, he applied whatever disinfectant was left on the towel to her cut. She sucked in her breath and splayed one hand tightly over the top of her thigh to hold it still. Even then her leg was shaking badly by the time Garrick reached for the bandages.

"I can do it," she breathed. Beads of sweat had broken out on her nose, causing her glasses to slip. Her fingers trembled when she shoved them up, but she was feeling foolish about the broken bottle and needed desperately to show her grit.

She might as well not have spoken. Garrick proceeded to cover the wound with a large piece of gauze and strap it in place with adhesive tape. When that was done, he carefully collected the largest pieces of broken glass and set them on the counter.

He looked at her then, eyes skimming her pale features before coming to rest on her temple. Taking a fresh piece of gauze, he dipped it into the small amount of liquid left in the bottom quarter of the bottle and, with the same gentle dabbing, disinfected the cluster of scratches he'd found.

Leah hadn't been aware of their existence. She vaguely recalled reeling off a tree, but surface scratches had been the least of her worries when the rest of her had been so cold and sore. Even now the scratches were quickly forgotten, because Garrick had turned his attention to her hand that had remained in a fist throughout the procedure. She held her breath when he reached for it.

Without asking himself why or to what end, he slowly and carefully unclenched her fingers, then stared at the purple crescents her short nails had left on her palm. They were a testament to the kind of self-control he admired; even when he brushed his thumb across them, willing them away, they remained. Cradling her hand in his far larger one, he raised his eyes to hers.

She wasn't prepared for their luminous force. They penetrated her, warmed her, frightened her in ways she didn't understand. Hazel depths spoke of loneliness; silver flecks spoke of need. They reached out and enveloped her, demanding nothing, demanding everything.

It was an incredible moment.

Of all the new experiences she'd had that day, this was the most stunning. For Garrick Rodenhiser wasn't the grizzled old trapper she'd assumed she'd find in a rustic cabin in the woods. He was a man in his prime, and the only scents emanating from him had to do with wood smoke and maleness.

At that most improbable and unexpected time, she was drawn to him.

Unable to cope with the idea of being drawn to anyone, least of all a total stranger, she looked away. But she wasn't the only one stunned by the brief visual interlude. Garrick, too, was pricked by new and unbidden emotions.

Abruptly releasing her hand, he stood. "Don't touch the glass," he ordered gruffly. "I'll take care of it when you're done." Turning on his heel, he left the bathroom and strode back to the hearth. He was still there, bent over the mantel with his forearms on the rough wood and his forehead on his arms, when he heard the sound of the bathroom door opening sometime later.

With measured movements he straightened and turned, fully prepared to commence his inquisition. This woman, whoever she was, was trespassing on his turf. He didn't like uninvited visitors. He didn't like anything remotely resembling a threat to his peace.

He hadn't counted on what he'd see, much less what he'd feel when he saw it. If he'd thought he'd gained control of his senses during those few minutes alone, he'd been mistaken. Now, looking at this woman about whom he knew absolutely nothing, he was shaken by the same desire that had shocked his system earlier.

Strangely, if that desire had been physical, he'd have felt less threatened. Hormonal needs were understand-able, acceptable, easily slaked.

But what he felt went beyond the physical. It had first sparked when he'd barged into the bathroom and seen legs that were feminine, ivory, sleek and exposed. There had been nothing seductive about the way they'd trem-bled, but he'd been disturbed anyway. He had thought of a doe he'd encountered in the woods; the animal had stared at him, motionless save for the faint tremor in her hind legs that betrayed an elemental fear. He'd been frustrated then, unable to assure the doe that he'd never harm her. He was frustrated now because the woman seemed equally as defenseless, and while he might have assured her, he wasn't able to form the words.

The desire he felt had grown during his ministra-tions, when his fingers had brushed her thigh and found it to be warmed from the shower and smooth, so smooth. Very definitely human and alive. A member of his own species. At that moment, he'd felt an instinc-tive need for assurance from her that he was every bit as human and alive.

When he'd cupped her hand in his, he'd felt the odd-est urge to guard her well. Fragility, the need for pro-tection, a primal plea for closeness...he'd been unable to deny the feelings, though they shocked him.

And when he'd searched her eyes, he'd found them as startled as his own must have been.

He wasn't sure if he believed she was genuine; he'd known too many quality actors in his day to take anything at face value. What he couldn't ignore, though, were his own feelings, for they said something about himself that he didn't want to know.

Those feelings hit him full force as he stared at her. It wasn't that she was beautiful. Her black hair, clean now and unturbaned, was damp and straight, falling just shy of her collarbone, save for the bangs that covered her brow. Her features were average, her face dominated by the owl-eyed glasses that perched on her nose. No, she wasn't beautiful, and certainly not sexy wearing his shirt and long johns. But her pallor did something to him, as did the slight forward curve of her shoulders as she wrapped her arms around her waist.

She was the image of vulnerability, and watching her, he felt vulnerable himself. He wanted to hold her, that was all, just to hold her. He couldn't understand it, didn't want to admit it, but it was so.

"I'm not sure what to do with my clothes," she said. Her eyes registered bewilderment, though her voice was calm. "I rinsed them out as best I could. Is there somewhere I can hang them to dry?"

Garrick was grateful for the mundaneness of the question, which allowed him to sidestep those deeper thoughts. "You'd better put them through a real wash first. Over there." He inclined his head toward the kitchen area.

Through clean, dry glasses, Leah saw what she hadn't been physically or emotionally capable of seeing earlier. A washer-dryer combo stood beyond the sink, not far from a dishwasher and a microwave oven. Modern kitchen, modern bathroom—Garrick Rodenhiser, it seemed, roughed it only to a point.

Ducking back into the bathroom, she retrieved her clothes and put them into the washer with a generous amount of detergent. Once the machine was running, she eyed the coffeemaker and its fresh, steaming pot.

"Help yourself," Garrick said. Resuming his silence, he watched her open one cabinet after another until she'd found a mug.

"Will you have some?" she asked without turning.

"No."

Her hand trembled as she poured the coffee, and even the small movement had repercussions in the tension-weary muscles of her shoulders. Cup in hand, she padded barefoot across the floor to peer through the small opening between the shutters that served as drapes. She couldn't see much of anything, but the steady beat of rain on the roof told her what she wanted to know.

Straightening, she turned to face Garrick. "Is there any chance of getting to my car tonight?"

"No."

His single word was a confirmation of what she'd already suspected. There seemed no point in railing against what neither of them could change. "Do you mind if I sit by your fire?"

He stepped aside in silent invitation.

The wide oak planks were warm under her bare feet as she crossed to the hearth. Lowering herself to the small rag rug with more fatigue than finesse, she tucked her legs under her, pressed her arms to her sides and cupped the coffee with both hands.

The flames danced low and gently, and would have been soothing had she been capable of being soothed. But sitting before them, relatively warm and safe for the first time in hours, she saw all too clearly what she faced tonight. She was here for the night; she knew that

much. The storm continued. Her car wouldn't move.
She was going nowhere until morning. But what then?

Even once her car was freed, she had nowhere to go.
Victoria's cabin was gone, and with it the plans she'd
spent the past three weeks making. It had all seemed so
simple; now nothing was simple. She could look around
for another country cabin to rent, but she didn't know
where to begin. She could take a room at an inn, but her
supply of money was far from endless. She could return to New York, but something about that smacked of
defeat—or so she told herself when she found no other
excuse for her hesitancy to take that particular option.

If she'd felt unsettled during the drive north, now
she felt thoroughly disoriented. Not even at her lowest
points in the past had she been without a home.

Behind her, the sofa springs creaked. Garrick. With
her glasses on, she'd seen far more than details of the
cabin. She'd also seen that Garrick Rodenhiser was ex-
traordinarily handsome. The bulk that had originally
impressed her was concentrated in his upper body, in
the well-developed shoulders and back defined by a
thick black turtleneck. Dark gray corduroys molded
a lean pair of hips and long, powerful legs. He was
bearded, yes, but twenty-twenty vision revealed that
beard to be closely trimmed. And though his hair was
on the long side, it, too, was far from unruly and was
an attractive dark blond shot through with silver.

His nose was straight, his lips thin and masculine.
His skin was stretched over high cheekbones, but his
eyes were what held the true force of his being. Sil-
very hazel, they were alive with questions unasked and
thoughts unspoken.

Had Leah been a gambler, she'd have bet that Garrick was a transplant. He simply didn't fit the image of

a trapper. There were the amenities in the cabin, for one thing, which spoke of a certain sophistication. There was also his speech; though his words were few and far between, his enunciation was cultured. And his eyes— those eyes—held a worldly look, realistic, cynical, simultaneously knowing and inquisitive.

She wondered where he'd come from and what had brought him here. She wondered what he thought of her arrival and of the fact that she'd be spending the night. She wondered what kind of a man he was where women were concerned, and whether the need she'd sensed in him went as deep as, in that fleeting moment in the bathroom, it had seemed.

Garrick was wondering similar things. In his forty years, he'd had more women than he cared to count. From the age of fourteen he'd been aware of himself as a man. Increasingly his ego and his groin had been rivals in his search for and conquest of women. As the years had passed, quantity had countermanded quality; he'd laid anything feminine, indiscriminately and often with little care. He'd used and been used, and the sexual skill in which he'd once taken pride had been reduced to a physical act that was shallow and hurtful. It had reflected the rest of his life too well.

All that had ended four years ago. When he'd first come to New Hampshire, he'd stayed celibate. He hadn't yearned, hadn't wanted. He'd lived within well-defined walls, unsure of himself, distrusting his emotions and motivations. During those early months his sole goal had been to forge out an existence as a human being.

Gradually, the day-to-day course of his life had fallen into place. He'd had the occasional woman since then, though not out of any gut-wrenching desire as much as the simple need to assure himself that he was male

and normal. Rarely had he seen the same woman twice.
Never had he brought one to his home.

But one was here now. He hadn't asked for her. In
fact, he wanted her gone as soon as possible. Yet even as
he studied her, as he watched her stare into the fire, take
an occasional sip of coffee, flex her arms around herself
protectively, he felt an intense need for human contact.

He wondered if the need was indicative of a new
stage in his redevelopment, if he'd reached the point of
being comfortable with himself and was now ready to
share himself with others.

To share. To *learn* to share. He'd always been self-
centered, and to an extent, the life he'd built here rein-
forced that. He did what he wanted when he wanted.
He wasn't sure if he was capable of changing that, or if
he wanted to change it. He wasn't sure if he was ready
to venture into something new.

Still, there was the small voice of need that cried out
when he looked at her....

"What's your name?"

His voice came so unexpectedly that Leah jumped.
Her head shot around, eyes wide as they met his. "Leah
Gates."

"You're a friend of Victoria's?"

"Yes."

He shifted his gaze to the flames. Only when she
had absorbed the dismissal and turned back to the fire
herself did he look at her again.

Leah Gates. A friend of Victoria's. His mind conjured up several possibilities, none of which was entirely
reassuring. She could indeed be a friend of Victoria's,
an acquaintance who'd somehow learned of his existence and had decided, for whatever her reasons, to seek
him out. On the other hand she could be lying outright,

using Victoria's name to get the story that no one else had been able to get. Or she could be telling the truth, which left the monumental question of why Victoria would have sent her to him.

Only two facts were clear. The first was that he was stuck with her; she wasn't going anywhere for a while. The second was that she'd been through a minor ordeal getting here and that, even as she sat before the fire, she'd begun to tremble again.

Pushing himself from the sofa, he went for the spare quilt that lay neatly folded on the end of the bed. He shook it out as he returned to the fire, then draped it lightly over her shoulders. She sent him a brief but silent word of thanks before tugging it closely around her.

This time when he sank onto the sofa it was with a vague sense of satisfaction. He ignored it at first, but it lingered, and at length he deigned to consider it. He'd never been one to give. His life—that life—had been ruled by selfishness and egotism. That as small a gesture as offering a quilt should please him was interesting…encouraging…puzzling.

As the evening passed, the only sounds in the cabin were the crackle of the fire and the echo of the rain. From time to time Garrick added another log to the grate, and after a bit, Leah curled onto her side beneath the quilt. He knew the very moment she fell asleep, for the fingers that clutched the quilt so tightly relaxed and her breathing grew steady.

Watching her sleep, he felt it again, the need to hold and be held, the need to protect. His fertile mind created a scenario in which Leah was a lost soul with no ties to the past, no plans for the future, no need beyond that of a little human warmth. It was a dream, of course, but it reflected what he hadn't glimpsed about himself until tonight. He didn't think he liked it, because it meant that something was lacking in the life he'd so painstakingly shaped for himself, but it was there, and it had a sudden and odd kind of power.

Rising silently from the sofa this time, he got down on his haunches beside her. Her face was half-hidden, so he eased the quilt down to her chin, studying features lit only by the dying embers in the hearth. She looked totally guileless; he wished he could believe that she was.

Unable to help himself, he touched the back of his fingers to her cheek. Her skin was soft and unblemished, warmed by the fire, faintly flushed. Dry now, her hair was thick. The bangs that covered her brow made her features look all the more delicate. She wasn't beautiful or sexy, but he had to give her pretty. If only he could give her innocent.

It wouldn't hurt to pretend for one night, would it?

Careful not to disturb her, he gently slid his arms beneath her and, quilt and all, carried her to his bed. When she was safely tucked into one side, he crossed to the other, stripped down to his underwear and stretched out beneath the sheets.

Lying flat on his back, he tipped his head her way. The black gloss of her hair was all he could see above the quilt, but the series of lumps beneath it suggested far more. She wasn't curvaceous. Her drenched clothes had clung to a slender body. And she wasn't heavy. He knew; he'd carried her. Still, even when she'd been covered with mud and soaked, he'd known she was a woman.

Eyes rising to the darkened rafters, he shifted once, paused, then shifted again. With each shift, he inched closer to her. He couldn't feel her warmth, couldn't smell her scent. Multiple layers of bedclothes, plus a safe twelve inches of space prevented that. But he knew she was there, and in the dark, where no one could see or know, he smiled.

LEAH AWOKE THE next morning to the smell of fresh coffee and the sizzle of bacon. She was frowning even before she'd opened her eyes, because she didn't understand who would be in her apartment, much less making breakfast. Then the events of the day before returned to her, and her eyes flew open. Last she remembered she'd been lying in front of the fire. Now she was in a bed. But there was only one bed in Garrick's cabin.

Garrick. Her head spun around and she saw a blurred form before the stove. Moments later, with her glasses firmly in place, she confirmed the identity of that form.

It took her a minute to free herself from the cocoon of quilts and another minute to push herself up and drop her feet to the floor. In the process she was scolded by every sore muscle in her body. Gritting back a moan, she rose from the bed and limped into the bathroom.

By the time she'd washed up and combed her hair, she was contemplating sneaking back to bed. She ached all over, she looked like hell, and from the sounds of it, the rain hadn't let up. Going out in the storm, even in daylight, was a dismal thought.

But she couldn't sneak back to bed because the bed wasn't hers. And he'd seen her get up. And she had decisions to make.

Garrick had just set two plates of food on the small table, when she hesitantly approached. His keen glance took in her pale skin and the gingerliness of her movements. "Sit," he commanded, refusing to be touched. He'd had his one night of pretending and resented the fact that it had left him wanting. Now morning had come, and he needed some answers.

Leah sat—and proceeded, with no encouragement at all, to consume an indeterminate number of scrambled eggs, four rashers of bacon, two corn muffins, a large glass of orange juice and a cup of coffee. She was working on a second cup, when she realized what she'd done. Peering sheepishly over the rim of the cup, she murmured, "Sorry about that. I guess I was hungry."

"No dinner last night?"

"No dinner." It must have been close to eight o'clock when she'd finally stumbled to his door. Not once had she thought of food, even when she'd passed the stove en route to the washing machine. With an intake of breath at the memory, she started to get up. "I left my clothes in the washer—"

"They're dry." He'd switched them into the dryer after she'd fallen asleep. "All except the sweater. I hung it up. Don't think it should have been washed, being cashmere."

He'd drawled the last with a hint of sarcasm, but Leah was feeling too self-conscious to catch it. She hadn't had anyone tend to her in years. That Garrick should be doing it—a total stranger handling her clothes, her underthings—was disturbing. Even worse, he'd carried her to his bed, and she'd slept there with him. Granted, she'd been oblivious to it all, but in the light of day she was far from oblivious to the air of potent masculinity he projected. He looked unbelievably rugged, yet unconscionably civilized. Fresh from the shower, his hair was damp. In a hunter green turtleneck and tan cords that matched the color of his hair and beard, he was gorgeous.

"It was probably ruined long before I put it in the

washer," she murmured breathily, then darted an awkward glance toward the window. "How long do you think the rain will last?"

"Days."

She caught his gaze and forced a laugh. "Thanks." When she saw no sign of a returning smile, her own faded. "You're serious, aren't you." It wasn't a question.

"Very."

"But I need my car."

"Where is it?"

"At Victoria's cabin."

"Why?"

"Why do I need it?" She'd have thought that would be obvious.

"Why is it at Victoria's?"

In a rush, Leah remembered how little she and Garrick had spoken the night before. "Because she was renting the cabin to me, only when I got there, I saw that it was nothing but—" She didn't finish, because Garrick was eyeing her challengingly. That, combined with the way he was sitting—leaning far back in his chair with one hand on his thigh and the other toying with his mug—evoked an illusion of menace. At least, she hoped it was only an illusion.

"You said that Victoria sent you to me," he reminded her tightly.

"That's right."

"In what context?"

The nervousness Leah was feeling caused her words to tumble out with uncharacteristic speed. "She said that if I had a problem, you'd be able to help. And I have a problem. The cabin's burned down, my car is stuck in the mud, I have to find somewhere to stay because my apartment's gone—"

"Victoria sent you to stay in the cabin," he stated, seeming to weigh the words.

Leah didn't like his tone. "Is there a problem with that?"

"Yes."

"What is it?"

He didn't blink an eye. "Victoria's cabin burned three months ago."

For a minute she said nothing. Then she asked very quietly, "What?"

"The cabin burned three months ago."

"That can't be."

"It is."

If it had been three days ago, Leah might have understood. With a stretch of the imagination, she might even have believed three weeks. After all, no one was living at the cabin. To her knowledge Garrick wasn't its caretaker. But three *months?* Surely someone would have been by during that time. "You're telling me that the cabin burned three months ago and that Victoria wasn't told?"

"I'm telling you that the cabin burned three months ago."

"Why wasn't Victoria *told?*" Leah demanded impatiently.

"She was."

Her anger rose. "I don't believe you."

Garrick was staring at her straight and hard. "I called her myself, then gave the insurance people a tour."

"Call her now. We'll see what she knows."

"I don't have a phone."

Given the other modern amenities in the cabin, Leah couldn't believe there was no phone. She looked around a little frantically for an instrument that would connect her with the outside world but saw nothing remotely resembling one. Then she remembered Victoria saying that she didn't have a phone at her cabin, either.

Why would she have said that, if she'd known that she didn't have a *cabin?*

"She didn't know about the fire," Leah insisted.

"She did."

"You're lying."

"I don't lie."

"You have to be lying," she declared, but her voice had risen in pitch. "Because if you're not, the implication is that Victoria sent me up here knowing full well that I wouldn't be able to stay. And that's preposterous."

The coffee cup began to shake in her hand. She set it on the table and wrapped her arms around her waist in a gesture Garrick had seen her make before. It suggested distress, but whether that distress was legitimate remained to be seen.

He said nothing, simply stared at the confusion that clouded her eyes.

"She wouldn't do that," Leah whispered pleadingly, wanting, needing to believe it. "For three weeks she's been listening to me—helping me—make plans. I stored all my furniture, notified the electric company, the phone company, my friends. Victoria personally gave me a set of typed directions and sat by while I read them. She wouldn't have gone to the effort—or let me go to the effort—if she'd known the cabin was useless."

Garrick, too, was finding it hard to believe, but it was Leah's story rather than Victoria's alleged behavior that evoked his skepticism. Yes, Leah looked confused, but perhaps that was part of the act. If she'd set out to find him, she'd done it. She was in his cabin, wearing his clothing, eating his food, drinking his coffee. She'd even spent the night in his bed, albeit innocently. If she wanted a scoop on Greg Reynolds, she'd positioned herself well.

"Who are you?" he asked.

Her head shot up. "I told you. Leah Gates."

"Where are you from?"

"New York."

"I don't suppose you happen to work for a newspaper," he commented, fully expecting an immediate denial. He was momentarily surprised when her eyes lit up.

"How did you know?"

He grunted.

She didn't know what to make of that, any more than she knew what to make of the fact that his lips were set tautly, almost angrily, within the confines of his beard.

"Have you seen my name?" she asked. If he was a crossword addict, as were so many of her fans, her name would have rung a bell.

"I don't read papers."

"Then you've seen one of my books?"

"You write books, too?" he barked.

His question and its tone had her thoroughly perplexed. "I compose crossword puzzles. They appear in a small weekly paper, but I've had several full books of puzzles published."

Crossword puzzles? A likely story. Still, if she was a reporter, she couldn't be an actress—which didn't explain why her words sounded so sincere. "Why were you moving up here?" he asked in a more tempered tone of voice.

"I lost my apartment and I wasn't sure where to go, so Victoria suggested I rent her cabin for a while until

I decided." She dropped a frowning gaze to the table as she mumbled, "It seemed like a good idea at the time."

Garrick said nothing.

In the ensuing silence, Leah reran the past few minutes of conversation in her mind. Then, slowly, her eyes rose. "You don't believe what I'm saying. Why not?"

He hadn't expected such forthrightness, and when she looked at him that way, all honesty and vulnerability, he was the one confused. He couldn't tell her the truth. After staunchly guarding his identity for four years, he wasn't about to blow it by making an accusation that revealed all.

So he lifted one shoulder in a negligent shrug. "It's not often that a woman chooses to live up here alone. I take it you are alone."

She hesitated before offering a tentative, "Yes."

Good Lord, could she have a photographer stashed somewhere about? "*Are* you?"

"Yes!"

"Then why the pause?"

Leah's eyes flashed. She wasn't used to having her integrity questioned. "When you've spent your entire life in New York, you think twice about giving a man certain information. It's instinct."

"It's distrust."

"Then we're even!"

"But you did answer me."

"Victoria said you were a friend. I trust her judgment. She even gave me a letter to deliver to you."

He extended one large hand, palm up, in invitation. The smug twist of his lips only heightened her defensiveness.

"If it were on me, you'd have had it by now," she

cried. "It's in my car, along with my purse and every-thing else I own in the world."

"Except for your furniture," he remarked, dropping his hand back to his thigh.

She made a little sound of defeat. "Yes."

"And you can't get to your car. You may not be able to get there for days. You're stuck here with me."

Leah shook her head, willing away that prospect. It wasn't that Garrick was repulsive; indeed, the opposite was true. But while there was a side to him that was gentle and considerate, there was another more cynical side, and that frightened her. "I'll get to my car later."

"Unless the rain lets up, you're not going anywhere."

"I have to get to my car."

"How?"

"The same way I got here. If you won't drive me, I'll walk."

"It's not that I *won't* drive you, Leah," he said, using her name for the first time. "It's that I *can't*. You've ar-rived up here at the onset of mud season, and during mud season, no one moves! The sturdiest of vehicles is useless. The roads are impassable." Arching a brow, he stroked his bearded jaw with his knuckles. "Tell me. What was it like driving the road to Victoria's cabin last night?"

"Hell."

"And walking from Victoria's to mine?"

The look she sent him was eloquent.

"Well, it'll be worse today and even worse tomor-row. At this time of year, snow melts from the upper mountain and drains down over ground that is already thawing and soggy. When the rain comes, forget it."

But Leah didn't want to. "Maybe if we walk back to the car and I get behind the wheel and you push—"

"I'm neither a bulldozer nor a tow truck, and let me tell you, I'm not even sure one of those would do the trick. I've seen off-road vehicles get stuck on roads far less steep than the ones on this hill."

"It's worth a try."

"It isn't."

"Victoria said you'd help me."

"I am. I'm offering you a place to stay."

"But I can't stay here!"

"You don't have much choice."

"You can't *want* me to stay here!"

"I don't have much choice."

With a helpless little moan, Leah rose from the table and went to stare bleakly out the window. He was right, she supposed. She didn't have much choice. She could go out in the rain and trek back to her car, but if what he said was true—and he'd certainly be in a position to know—she'd simply find herself back on his doorstep, wet, muddy, exhausted and humiliated.

This wasn't at all what she'd had in mind when she'd left New York!

CHAPTER THREE

THE CLATTER OF pans in the sink brought Leah from her self-indulgent funk a short time later. Feeling instantly contrite, she returned to the kitchen. Garrick had already loaded the dishwasher; taking a towel, she began to dry the pans as he washed them.

They worked in silence. When the last skillet had been put away, she folded the towel and placed it neatly on the counter. "I'm sorry," she said quietly. She didn't look at Garrick, who was wiping down the sink. "I must have sounded ungrateful, and I'm not. I appreciate what you're doing." Pausing, she searched for suitably tactful words. "It's just that this isn't quite what I'd planned."

"What had you planned?"

"Sunshine and fresh air. A cabin all to myself. Plenty of time to work and read and walk in the woods. And cook—" She looked up in alarm at the thought. "I have food in the car! It'll spoil if I don't get it refrigerated!"

"It's cold outside."

"Cold enough?"

"Depends on what kind of food you have."

She would have listed off an inventory had there been any point. But there wasn't, so she simply let out a breath of resignation. He'd made it clear that she couldn't get to her car. Whatever spoiled would spoil.

Tugging the lapels of the flannel shirt more tightly around her, she sent him a pleading glance. "This is the first time I've even thought of living outside New York, and to have things go wrong is upsetting. I still can't understand why Victoria offered me the cabin."

Garrick was beginning to entertain one particularly grating suspicion. Eyes dark, he set the dishrag aside and retreated to the living room. The sofa took his weight with multiple creaks of protest, but the protests in his mind were even louder.

Leah remained where she was for several minutes, waiting for him to speak. He was clearly upset; his brooding slouch was as much a giveaway as the low shelving of his brows. And he had a right to be upset, she told herself. No man who'd chosen to live alone on a secluded mountainside deserved to have that seclusion violated.

Studying him, taking in the power that radiated from even his idle body, she wondered why he'd chosen the life he had. He wasn't an avid conversationalist. But, then, neither was she, yet she'd functioned well in the city. He'd left it—at least, that was what she assumed, though perhaps it was an ingrained snobbishness telling her that the cultured ring to his speech and his fondness for certain luxuries were urban-born. In any case, she couldn't believe that a simple housing problem such as the one she'd faced had sent him into exile. For that matter, he didn't look as though he were in exile at all; he looked as though he were here to stay.

Leah took advantage of his continued distraction to examine the cabin in its entirety. A large, rectangular room with the fireplace and bed on opposite sides, it had a kitchen spread along part of the back wall, leaving space for the bathroom and what looked to be a closet. Large windows flanked the front door. Sandwiched between door, windows, furniture and appliances were bookshelves—a small one here, a larger one there, each and every one brimming with books.

They explained, in part, what Garrick Rodenhiser did with his time. He wasn't reading now, though. He was sitting as he'd been before, staring at the ashes in the hearth. While moments before he'd been brooding, his profile had mellowed to something she couldn't quite define. Loneliness? Sorrow? Confusion?

Or was she simply putting a name to her own feelings?

Unwilling to believe that, despite the clenching of her heart at the sight of Garrick, she looked desperately around for something to do. Her eye fell on the bed, still mussed from the night they'd spent. Crossing the room, she straightened the sheets and quilt, then folded the spare one he'd wrapped around her and set it at the foot of the bed.

What else? She scanned the cabin again, but there was little that needed attention. Everything was neat, clean, organized.

At a loss, she walked quietly to the window. The woods were gray, shrouded in fog, drenched in rain. The bleakness of the scene only emphasized the strange emptiness she felt.

Garrick's deep voice came out of the blue. "What, exactly, is your relationship to Victoria?"

Startled, Leah half turned to find herself the object of his grim scrutiny. "We're friends."

"You've said that. When did you meet?"

"Last year."

"Where?"

"The public library. Victoria was researching the aborigines of New Zealand. We literally bumped into each other."

His expression turned wry, then softened into a reluctant smile. "The aborigines of New Zealand—that does sound like Victoria. Is she going back to school in anthropology?"

"Not exactly," Leah answered, but she had to force herself to think, because his smile—lean lips curving upward between mustache and beard, the flash of even, white teeth—momentarily absorbed her. "She is, uh, she was fascinated by an article she'd read about the Maori, so she decided to visit. She was preparing for the trip when I met her."

"Did she get there?"

"To New Zealand? What do you think?"

Garrick thought yes, and his eyes said as much, but his mind returned quickly to Leah. "Why were you at the library?"

"I often work there—sometimes doing research for puzzles, sometimes just for the change of scenery."

"So you and Victoria became friends. How old are you?"

"Thirty-three."

He pushed out his lips in surprise. "I'd have given you twenty-eight or twenty-nine—" the lips straightened "—but even at thirty-three, there's quite a gap between you."

"But there isn't," Leah returned with quiet vehemence, even wonder. "That's what's so great about Victoria. She's positively…positively amaranthine."

"Amaranthine?"

"Unfading, undying, timeless. Her bio may list her as fifty-three, but she has the body of a forty-year-old, the mind of a thirty-year-old, the enthusiasm of a twenty-year-old and the heart of a child."

The description was one Garrick might have made,

though he'd never have been able to express it as well.
At the height of his career he'd been a master techni-
cian, able to deliver lines from a script with precisely
the feeling the director wanted. But no amount of arrogance—and he'd had more than his share—could have
made him try to write that script himself.

So Leah did know Victoria, and well. That ruled out
one possible lie but left open another. Even knowing
that she would compromise her friendship with Victoria, Leah might have taken it upon herself to find and
interview the man who'd once been the heartthrob of
every woman between the ages of sixteen and sixty-
five. Every woman who watched television, that is. Did
Leah watch television? Even if she'd come here in total
innocence, wouldn't she recognize him?

Shifting his gaze back to the hearth, Garrick lapsed
into silence once again. He was recalling how worried
he'd been when he'd first arrived in New Hampshire.
Each time he'd gone into town for supplies, he'd kept
his head down, his eyes averted. Each time he'd waited
in dread for telling whispers, tiny squeals, the thrust of
pen and paper under his nose.

In fact, he'd looked different from the man who'd
graced the television screens of America on a weekly
basis for seven years running. His hair was longer, less
perfectly styled, and he'd stopped rinsing out the sprin-
kles of silver that once upon a time he'd been sure would
detract from his appeal.

The beard had made a difference, too, but in those
early months he'd worried that sharp eyes would see
through it to the jaw about which critics had raved. He'd
dressed without distinction, wearing the oldest clothes
he'd had. Above all, he'd prayed that the mere improb-
ability of a one-time megastar living on a mountain-

side in the middle of nowhere would shield him from discovery.

With the passing of time—during which he wasn't recognized—he'd gained confidence. He made eye contact. He held his head higher.

Body language. A fascinating thing. He wasn't innocent enough to think that the recognition factor alone had determined the set of his head. No, he'd held his head higher because he felt better about himself. He was learning to live with nature, learning to provide for himself, learning to respect himself as a clean-living human being.

Buoyed by that confidence, he turned to Leah. "You've come to know Victoria well in a year. You must have spent a lot of time with her."

Leah, who'd eyed him steadily during his latest bout of silence, was more prepared for its end this time. "I did."

"Socially?"

"If you're asking whether I went to her parties, the answer is no."

"Are you married?"

"No."

"Have you ever been?" It wasn't crucial to the point of his investigation, but he was curious.

"Yes."

"Divorced?"

She nodded.

"Recently?"

"It's been final for two years."

"Do you date?"

"Do you?"

"I'm asking the questions."

"That's obvious, but I'd like to know why. I'm beginning to feel like I'm on a hot seat."

She sounded hurt. She looked hurt. Garrick surprised himself by feeling remorse, but he was too close to the answer he sought to give up. He did make an effort to soften his tone. "Bear with me. There's a point to all this."

"Mmm. To make me turn tail and run. Believe me, I would if I could. I know that you don't like the idea of a stranger invading your home, but you're a stranger to me, too, and I'm not so much an invader as a refugee, and if you think I like feeling like a refugee, you're nuts..." Her voice faded as her eyes began to skip around the cabin. "Paper and pencil?"

Garrick was nonplussed. "What—"

"If I don't write it down, I'll forget."

"Write what down?"

"The idea—nuts, nutty, nutty as a fruitcake, having bats in one's belfry. Perfect for a theme puzzle." She was moving her hand, simulating a scribble. "Paper?"

Bemused, Garrick cocked his head toward the kitchen. "Second drawer to the left of the sink."

Within seconds, she was jotting down the phrases she'd spoken aloud, adding several others to the list before she'd straightened. Tearing off the sheet, she folded it and tucked it into her breast pocket, returned the pad and pen to the drawer, then sent him a winsome smile. "Where were we?"

Garrick didn't try to fight the warm feeling that settled in his chest. "Do you do that a lot?"

"Write down ideas? Uh-huh."

"You really do make crossword puzzles?"

"You didn't believe me about that, either?"

He moved his head in a way that could have been

positive, negative or sheepish. "I've never really thought about people doing it."

"Someone has to."

He considered that for a minute, uttered a quiet, "True," then withdrew into his private world again.

Wondering how long he'd be gone this time, Leah walked softly toward the bookshelf nearest her. Its shelves had a wide array of volumes, mostly works of fiction that had been on bestselling lists in recent years. The books were predominantly hardbacked, their paper sheaths worn where they'd been held. Both facts were revealing. Not only did Garrick read everything he bought, but he bought the latest and most expensive, rather than waiting for cheaper mass market editions.

He wasn't a pauper, that was for sure. Leah wondered where he got the money.

"It must be difficult," came his husky voice. "Finding the right words that will fit together, coming up with witty clues."

It took Leah a minute to realize that he was talking about crossword puzzles. She had to smile. He faded in and out, but the train of his thought ran along a continuous track. "It is a challenge," she admitted.

"I'd never be able to do it."

"That's okay. I'd never be able to lay traps, catch animals and gut them." She'd offered the words in innocence and was appalled at how critical they sounded. Turning to qualify them, she lost out to Garrick's quicker tongue.

"Is that what Victoria told you I do?"

"She said you were a trapper," Leah answered with greater deference, then added meekly, "I'm afraid the elaboration was my own."

His expression was guarded. "What else did Victoria say about me?"

"Only what I told you before—that you were a friend and could be trusted. To be honest, I was expecting someone a little—" she shifted a shoulder "—different."

He raised one eyebrow in question.

"Older. Craggier." Blushing, she looked off across the room. "When Victoria handed me that envelope, I asked her if it was a love letter."

"How do you know it wasn't?" Garrick asked evenly.

Come to think of it, Leah didn't know. She recalled Victoria saying something vague about craggy old trappers being nice, but the answer had been far from definitive. Her eyes went wide behind her glasses.

To her surprise, he chuckled. "It wasn't. We're just friends." His expression sobered. Propping his elbow on the sofa arm, he pressed his knuckles to his upper lip and mustache. Leah was preparing for another silent spell, when he murmured a muffled, "Until now."

"What do you mean?"

He dropped his hand and took a breath. "Her sending you here. It's beginning to smack of something deliberate."

Leah searched his face for further thoughts. When he didn't answer immediately, she prodded. "I'm listening."

"You said that you never went to Victoria's parties. Did you see her in other social contexts?"

"We went out to dinner often."

"As a foursome—with men?"

"No."

"Did she ever comment on that?"

"She didn't have to. I know that she has male friends, but she loved Arthur very much and has no desire to remarry. She's never at a loss for an escort when the occasion calls for it."

"How about you? *Do* you date?" he asked, repeating the question that had sparked earlier resistance.

Leah answered in a tone that was firm and final. "Not when I can help it."

He was unfazed by her resolve, because he was getting closer to his goal. "Did Victoria have anything to say about that?"

"Oh, yes. She thought I was…working with less than a full deck." Leah grinned at the phrase she had written down moments before, but the grin didn't last. "She was forever trying to fix me up, and I was forever refusing."

Garrick nodded and pressed his lips together, then slid farther down on the sofa, until his thick hair rose against its back. For several more minutes he was lost in thought. Eventually he took a deep breath and raised disheartened eyes to the rafters. "That," he said, "was what I was afraid of."

Not having been privy to his thoughts, Leah didn't follow. "What do you mean?"

"She's done the same to me more than once."

"Done what?"

"Tried to fix me up." He held up a hand. "Granted, it's more difficult up here, but that didn't stop her. She's convinced that anyone who hasn't experienced what she had with Arthur is missing out on life's bounty." His eyes sought Leah's, and he hesitated for a long moment before speaking. "Do you see what I'm getting at?"

With dawning horror, Leah did see. "She did it on purpose."

"Looks that way."

"She didn't tell me about the fire, but she did tell me about you."

"Right."

Closing her eyes, Leah fought a rising anger. "She was so cavalier about my paying rent, wouldn't accept anything beforehand, told me to send her whatever I thought the place was worth."

"Clever."

"When I asked if the cabin was well equipped, her exact words were, 'When last I saw it, it was.'"

"True enough."

"No wonder she was edgy."

"Victoria? Edgy?"

"Unusual, I know, but she was. I chalked it up to a latent maternal instinct." She rolled her eyes. "Boy, was I wrong. It was guilt, pure guilt. She actually had the gall to remind me that I wouldn't have air-conditioning or a phone, the snake." Muttering the last under her breath, Leah turned her back on Garrick and crossed her arms over her breasts.

That was the moment he came to believe that everything she'd told him was the truth. Had she started to shout and pace the floor in anger, he would have wondered. That would have smelled of a script, a soap-opera reaction, lacking subtlety.

But she wasn't shouting or pacing. Her anger was betrayed only by quickened breathing and the rigidity of her stance. From the little he'd seen of her, he'd judged her to be restrained where her emotions were concerned. Her reaction now was consistent with that impression.

Strangely, Garrick's own anger was less acute than he would have expected. If he'd known beforehand what Victoria had planned, he'd have hit the roof. But he hadn't known, and Leah was already here, and there was something about her self-contained distress that tugged at his heart.

Almost before his eyes, that distress turned to mortification. Cheeks a bright red, she cast a harried glance over her shoulder.

"I'm sorry. She had no right to foist me on you."

"It wasn't your fault—"

"But you shouldn't have to be stuck with me."

"It goes two ways. You're stuck with me, too."

"I could have done worse."

"So could I."

Unsure of what to make of his agreeable tone, Leah turned back to the bookshelf. It was then that the full measure of her predicament hit her. She and Garrick had been thrust together for what Victoria had intended to be a romantic spell. But if Victoria had hoped for love at first sight, she was going to be disappointed. Leah didn't believe in love at first sight. She wasn't even sure if she believed in love, since it had brought her pain once before, but that was neither here nor there. She didn't know Garrick Rodenhiser. Talk of love was totally inappropriate.

Attraction at first sight—that, perhaps, was worth considering. She couldn't deny that she found Garrick physically appealing. Not even his sprawling pose could detract from his long-limbed grace. His face, his beard, the sturdiness of his shoulders spoke of ruggedness; she'd have had to be blind not to see it, and dead not to respond.

And that other attraction—the one spawned by the deep, inner feelings that occasionally escaped from his eyes? It baffled her.

"I didn't want this," she murmured to her knotted hands.

From the silence came a quiet, "I know."

"I feel...you must feel...humiliated."

"A little awkward. That's all."

"Here I am in your underwear..."

"You can get dressed if you want."

It was, of course, the wise thing to do. Perhaps, once she was wearing her own clothes again, she'd feel less vulnerable, less exposed....

Crossing to the dryer, she removed her things and folded them over the crook of her elbow. When she reached for her sweater, though, she found it still damp.

"Here." Garrick stood directly behind her, holding out one of his own sweaters. "Clean and dry."

She accepted it with a quiet thanks and made her escape to the bathroom. He was working at the fireplace when she came out. She suddenly realized that though the fire had gone out during the night, the cabin had stayed warm.

"How do you manage for heat and electricity?" she asked, bracing her hands on the back of the sofa.

He added a final log to the arrangement and reached for a match. "There's a generator out back."

"And food? If you can't get to the store in this weather..."

"I stocked up last week." Sitting back on his heels, he watched the flames take hold. "Anyone who's lived through mud season once knows to be prepared. The freezer is full, and the cabinets. I picked up more fresh stuff a couple of days ago, but I'm afraid the bacon we had for breakfast is the last of it for a while."

He'd have had some left for tomorrow if he hadn't had to share. Leah's feelings of guilt remained unexpressed, though; there was nothing more boring than a person who constantly apologized.

Garrick stood and turned to face her, then wished he hadn't. She was wearing his sweater. It was far too large for her, of course, and she'd rolled the sleeves to a proper length, but the way it fell around her shoulders and breasts was far more suggestive than he'd have dreamed. She looked adorable. And unsure.

He gestured toward the sofa. With a tight smile, she took possession of a corner cushion, drew up her knees and tucked her feet beneath her. That was when he caught sight of the tear in her slacks.

"How's the leg?"

"Okay."

"Did you change the dressing?"

"No."

"Have you looked under it?"

"I'd be able to see if something was oozing through the gauze. Nothing is."

She hadn't looked, he decided. Either she was squeamish, or the gash didn't bother her enough to warrant attention. He wanted to know which it was.

Facing her on the sofa, he eased back the torn knit of her slacks.

"It's fine. Really."

But he was quickly tugging at the adhesive and, less quickly, lifting the gauze. "Doesn't look fine," he muttered. "I'll bet it hurts like hell." With cautious fingertips he probed the angry flesh around the wound. Leah's soft intake of breath confirmed his guess. "It probably should have been stitched, but the nearest hospital's sixty miles away. We wouldn't have made it off the mountain."

"It's not bleeding. It'll be okay."

"You'll have a scar."

"What's one more scar?"

He met her eyes. "You have others?"

Oh, yes, but only one was visible to the naked eye. "I had my appendix out when I was twelve."

He imagined the way her stomach would be, smooth and soft, warm, touchable. When the blood that flowed through his veins grew warmer, he tried to imagine the ugly line marring the flesh, but couldn't. Nor, at that moment, could he tear his eyes from hers.

Pain and loneliness. That was what he saw. She blinked once, as though to will the feelings away, but they remained, swelling against her self-restraint.

He saw, heard, felt. He wanted to ask her, to tell her, to share the pain and ease the burden. He wanted to reach out.

But he didn't.

Instead, he rose quickly and strode off, returning moments later with a tube of ointment and fresh bandages. When he'd dressed the injury to his satisfaction, he replaced the first-aid supplies in the cupboard, took a down vest, then a hooded rain jacket from the closet, stepped into a pair of crusty work boots and went out into the storm.

Leah stared after him, belatedly aware that she was trembling. She didn't understand what had happened just then, any more than she'd understood it when it had happened the night before. His eyes had reflected every one of her emotions. Could he know what she felt?

On a more mundane level, she was puzzled by his abrupt departure, mystified as to where he'd be going in the rain. A short time later she had an answer when a distinct and easily recognizable sound joined that of the steady patter on the roof. She went to the window and peered out. He was across the clearing, chopping wood beneath the shelter of a primitive lean-to.

Smiling at the image of the outdoorsman at work, she returned to the sofa. While she directed her eyes to the fire, though, she wasn't as successful with her thoughts. She was wondering how the hands of a woodsman, hands that were callused, fingers that were long and blunt, could be as gentle as they'd been. Richard had never touched her that way, though as her husband, he'd touched her far more intimately.

But there was touching and there was touching, one merely physical, the other emotional, as well. There was something about Garrick…something about Garrick…

Unsettled by her inability to find answers to the myriad questions, she sought diversion in one of the books she'd seen on the shelf. Sheer determination had her surprisingly engrossed in the story when Garrick returned sometime later.

Arms piled high with split logs, he blindly kicked off his boots at the door, deposited the wood in a basket by the hearth, threw back his hood and unbuckled his jacket.

Leah didn't have to ask if the rain had let up. The boots he'd left by the door were covered with mud; his jacket dripped as he shrugged it off.

She returned to her book.

He took up one of his own and sat down.

Briefly she felt the chill he'd brought in. It touched her face, her arm, her leg on the side nearest to him. The fire was warm, though, and the chill soon dissipated.

She read on.

"Do you like it?" he asked after a time.

"It's very well written."

He nodded at that and lowered his eyes to his own book.

Leah had turned several pages before realizing that

he hadn't turned a one. Yet he was concentrating on something....

Craning her neck, she tried to reach the running head at the top of the page. She was beginning to wonder whether she needed a new eyeglass prescription, when he spoke.

"It's Latin."

She smiled. "You're kidding."

"No."

"Are you a Latin scholar?"

"Not yet."

"You're a novice."

"Uh-huh."

Reluctant to disturb him, she returned to her own corner. Studying Latin? That was odd for a trapper, not so odd for a man with a very different past. She would have liked to ask about that past, but she didn't see how she could. He wasn't encouraging conversation. It was bad enough that she was here. The more unobtrusive she was, the better.

Delving into her own book again, she'd read several chapters, when his voice broke the silence.

"Hungry?"

Now that he'd mentioned it... "A little."

"Want some lunch?"

"If I can make it."

"You can't." It was his house, his refrigerator, his food. Given the doubts he'd had about himself since Leah had arrived, he needed to feel in command of something. "Does that mean you won't eat?"

She grimaced. "Got myself into a corner with that one, didn't I?"

"Uh-huh."

"I'll eat."

Trying his best not to smile, Garrick set down his book and went to make lunch. Despite the time he'd spent at the woodshed, he was still annoyed with Victoria. It was difficult, though, to be annoyed with Leah. She was as innocent a pawn in Victoria's game as he was, and, apparently, as uncomfortable with it. But she was a good sport. She conducted herself with dignity. He respected that.

None of the women he'd known in the past would have acceded to as untenable a situation with such grace. Linda Prince would have been livid at the thought of someone isolating her in a secluded cabin. Mona Weston would have been frantic without a direct phone line to her agent. Darcy Hogan would have ransacked his drawers in search of a flattering garment to display her goods. Heather Kane would have screamed at him to stop the rain.

Leah Gates had taken the sweater he offered with gratitude, had found herself a book to read and was keeping to herself.

Which made him all the more curious about her. He wondered what had happened to her marriage and why she didn't date now. He wondered whether she had family, or dreams for the future. He wondered whether the loneliness he saw in her eyes from time to time had to do with the loneliness of this mountainside. Somehow he didn't think so. Somehow he thought the loneliness went deeper. He felt it himself.

Lunch consisted of ham-and-cheese sandwiches on rye. Leah didn't go scurrying for a knife to cut hers in two. She didn't complain about the liberal helping of mayonnaise he'd smeared on out of habit, or about the lettuce and tomato that added bulk and made for a certain sloppiness. She finished every drop of the milk he'd poured without making inane cracks about growing boys and girls or the need for calcium or the marvel of cows. When she'd finished eating, she simply carried both of their plates to the sink, rinsed them and put them in the dishwasher, then returned to the sofa to read.

Midway through a very quiet afternoon, Garrick wasn't concentrating on Latin. He was still thinking of the woman curled in the opposite corner of the sofa. Her legs were tucked beneath her and the book remained open on her lap, but her head had fallen into the crook of the sofa's winged back, and she was sleeping. Silently. Sweetly.

He felt sorry for her. The trip she'd made yesterday— first the drive from New York, then the harrowing hike to his cabin—had exhausted her. He felt a moment's renewed anger toward Victoria for having put her through that ordeal, then realized that Victoria was probably as ignorant of mud season as any other nonnative. Now that he thought of it, she had only been up to the cabin in the best of weather—late spring, summer, early fall.

They'd met for the first time during one of those summer trips, and even then, barely knowing her, he'd asked her why she came at all. She was obviously a city person. She didn't hunt, didn't hike, didn't plant vegetables in a garden behind the cabin. He remembered her response as clearly as if she'd made it yesterday. She had looked him in the eye and told him that the cabin made her feel closer to Arthur. No apology. No bid for sympathy. Just an honest, heartfelt statement of fact that had established the basis of strength and sincerity on which their relationship had bloomed.

Of course, she hadn't been particularly honest in sending Leah to stay in a cabin that didn't exist. He had no doubt, though, that she'd been well-meaning in her desire to get Leah and him together. What puzzled him, irked him, was that she should have known better. He'd fought her in the past. He thought he'd told her enough about himself and his feelings to make himself clear. Why would she think things had changed?

Once upon a time he'd been a city man. He'd lived high and wild. The only things he'd feared in the world had been obscurity and anonymity. Ironically, that very fear had driven him higher and wilder, until he'd destroyed his career and very nearly himself in the process. That was when he'd retreated from the world and sought haven in New Hampshire.

Now he feared everything he'd once prized so dearly. He feared fame because it was fleeting. He feared glory because it was shallow. He feared aggressive crowds because they brought out the worst in human nature, the need for supremacy and domination even on the most mundane of levels.

He'd had it up to his eyeballs with competition. Even after being away from it for four years, he remembered with vile clarity that feeling of itching under the skin, of not being able to sit still and relax for fear someone would overtake him. He couldn't bear the thought of having to be quicker, cruder, more cutthroat than the next. He didn't want to have to worry about how he looked or how he smelled. He didn't want to have to see those younger, more eager actors waiting smugly in the wings for him to falter. And he didn't want the women, clinging like spiders, feeding off him until a sweeter fly came along.

Oh, yes, he knew what he didn't want. He'd made a deliberate intellectual decision when he'd left California. The world of glitz and glamour was behind him, as was the way of life that had had him clawing his way up a swaying ladder. The life he lived here was free of all that. It was simple. It was clean. It was comfortable. It was what he *did* want.

Why, then, did he feel threatened by Leah's presence?

He blinked and realized that she was waking. Rolling slightly, she stretched one leg until the sole of her foot touched his thigh. He felt its warmth and the slight pressure behind it. He saw the way one hand dropped limply to her belly. He watched her turn her head, as though trying to identify the nature of her pillow, then open her eyes with the realization of where she was.

She looked at him. He didn't blink. Slowly, carefully, she drew back her leg and, pushing herself into a seated position, picked up her book and lowered her eyes.

Leah did pose a threat to him, but it wasn't the immediate one of disturbing his peace. She was peaceful herself, quiet, undemanding. No, the threat wasn't a physical one. It was deeply emotional. He looked at her and saw human warmth and companionship—which were the very two things his life lacked. He'd thought he could live without them. Now, for the first time, he wondered.

Leah, too, was pensive. Silently setting her book aside, she went to the window. Rain fell as hard as ever from an endless cloud mass that was heavy and gray. She figured that the rain would last at least through the rest of the day. But even when it stopped—if she'd interpreted Garrick correctly—she wouldn't be immediately on her way. There was the mud to contend with, and if this was mud season, it was possible she'd be here for a while.

Propping her elbows on the window sash, she cupped her chin in her palms and stared out. She could have done worse, she'd told him, and indeed it was so. Garrick Rodenhiser was an easy cabin mate. She was reading, much as she did at home. If she had her dictionaries and thesauruses with her, she could be working much as she did at home. If his pattern of activity on this day was any indication, they could each do their own thing without bothering the other.

The only problem was that he made her think of things she didn't think of when she was at home. He made her think of things she hadn't thought about for years.

Nine years, to be exact. She'd been twenty-four and a graduate student in English when she'd met and married Richard Gates. She'd had dreams then of love and happiness, and she'd been sure that Richard shared them. He was twenty-six when they married and was getting settled in the business world. Or so she'd thought. All too quickly she'd learned that there was nothing "settled" about Richard's view of business. He was on his way to the top, he said, and to get there meant a certain amount of scrambling. It meant temporarily sacrificing a leisurely home life, he said. It meant long days at the office and business trips and parties. Somewhere along the way, love and happiness had been forgotten.

She'd completed her degree but had given up thought of teaching, of course. A working wife hadn't fit into Richard's concept of the corporate life-style. Out of sheer desperation, she'd begun to create crosswords, then had found that she did it well, that she loved it and that there was a ready market for what she composed. Having a career that was part-time and flexible eased some of the frustration she felt.

Perhaps it would have been different if the babies she'd carried had lived. Somehow she doubted it. Richard would have continued on with the work he adored, the business trips and the parties. And why not? He was good at it. There was a charismatic quality to him that drew people right and left. Even aside from the issue of children, she and Richard were in different leagues.

Now, though, she was thinking of love and happiness. She was thinking of the life she'd lived in New York since the divorce. It had seemed fine and comfortable and rewarding...until now.

Garrick affected her. He made her think that there had been something wrong with that single life in New York because it was...single. Seeing him, sitting with him, being touched by those hazel and silver eyes, she sensed what she'd missed. He made her feel lonely. He made her ache for something more than what she'd had.

Was it because she was in a strange place? Was it because her life had been turned upside down? Was it because she didn't know where she was going from here?

He made her think of the future. Yes, she'd probably go back to New York, search for and find another apartment. She'd work; she'd visit friends; she'd go to restaurants and museums and parks. She'd do what she'd always found so comfortable. Why, then, did there seem a certain emptiness to it?

With a sigh of confusion, she returned to the sofa and her book, though she read precious little in the hours that passed. From time to time she felt Garrick's eyes on her. From time to time she looked at him. His presence was both comfort and torment.

He made her feel less alone because he was there, because he'd help her, she knew, if something happened. He made her feel more alone because he was there, because the power of his quiet presence reminded her of everything she'd once wanted and needed.

Garrick went out again late in the afternoon. This time Leah had no clue to his purpose. She wandered around the cabin while he was gone, feeling a restlessness that she couldn't explain any more than she could those other feelings she'd glimpsed.

When he returned, he started making dinner. Once again he refused her offer of help. They ate in silence, occasionally glancing at each other, always looking away when their eyes met. After they'd finished, they returned to the fire. This time, despite the fact that she was without resource books, Leah worked with pad and pencil, sketching out simple puzzles. Garrick whittled.

She wondered where he'd learned to whittle, how he did it, what he was making—but she didn't ask.

He wondered where she started a puzzle, how she got the words to mesh, what she did at an impasse—but he didn't ask.

By ten o'clock she was feeling tired and frustrated and distinctly out of sorts. Crumpling up a piece of paper, on which she'd created nothing worth saving, she tossed it into the dying fire, then took a shower, put on the long underwear that seemed as good a pair of pajamas as any and climbed onto the same side of the bed where she'd slept the night before.

By ten-thirty, Garrick was feeling tired and frustrated and distinctly out of sorts. Flipping his piece of wood, out of which he'd whittled nothing worth saving, into the nearly dead fire, he turned off the lights, stripped down to his underwear and climbed onto his own side of the bed.

He lay on his back, wide-awake. He thought of L.A. and the day, several months before he'd left, that he'd finally tracked down his agent. Timothy Wilder had been avoiding him. Phone calls had gone unanswered;

each time Garrick had shown up at his office, Wilder had been "out." But Garrick had finally located him on the set of a TV movie, where another of Wilder's clients was at work. It hadn't done Garrick any good. Wilder had barely acknowledged him. The director and crew, many of whom he'd worked with in the past, couldn't have been bothered asking how he was. Wilder's client, the star of the show, hadn't given him so much as a glance. And the woman who, six months before, had sworn she adored Garrick, turned her back and walked away. He'd never felt so alone in his life.

Leah, too, lay on her back, wide-awake. She thought of one of the last parties she'd gone to as Richard's wife. It had been a gala charity function, and she'd taken great care to look smashing. Richard hadn't noticed. Nor had any of the others present. For a time, Richard had towed her from group to group, but then he'd left her to exchange inanities with an eighty-year-old matron. She'd never felt so alone in her life.

Garrick shifted his legs, his gaze on the darkened rafters overhead. He thought of the days following his accident, the three long weeks he'd lain in the hospital. No one had visited. No one had sent cards or flowers. No one had called to cheer him up. Though he fully blamed himself for his downfall and knew that he didn't deserve anyone's sympathy, what he would have liked, could have used, was a little solace. A little understanding. A little encouragement. The fact that it never materialized was the final sorrow.

Leah, too, shifted slightly. She thought of the hours she'd lain in the hospital following the loss of her second child. Richard had made the obligatory visits, but she'd come to dread them, for he clearly saw her as a failure. She'd felt like one, too, and though the doctors assured her that there was nothing more she could have possibly done, she'd been distraught. Had her parents been alive, they'd have been by her side. Had she had her own friends, ones who'd cared for her more than they'd cared for appearances, she mightn't have felt so utterly empty. But her parents were dead, and her "friends" were Richard's. Sorrow had been her sole companion.

Garrick took a deep, faintly shuddering breath. He felt Leah beside him, heard the slight irregularity of her own breathing. Slowly, cautiously, he turned his head on the pillow.

The cabin was dark. He couldn't see her. But he heard a soft swish when her head turned toward his.

They lay that way for long moments. Tension strummed between them, a wire of need, vibrating, pulling. Each held back, held back, fought the magnetism drawing them together until, at last, it became too great.

It wasn't a question of one moving first. In a simultaneous turning, their bodies came together as their minds had already done. Their arms wound around each other. Their legs tangled.

And they clung to each other. Silently. Soulfully.

CHAPTER FOUR

LEAH CLOSED HER eyes and greedily immersed herself in Garrick's strength. He was warm and alive, and the way he held her confirmed his own need for the closeness she so badly craved. His face was buried in her hair. His arms trembled as they crushed her to him, but not for a minute did she mind the pressure. Instead her own arms tightened around his neck, and she sighed softly in relief.

And pleasure. His body was a marvel. It was long and firm, accommodating itself to fit her perfectly. Richard had never accommodated himself to fit her either physically or emotionally. The fact that Garrick, who owed her nothing, should do so with such sweetness was a wonder she couldn't begin to analyze.

Not that she tried very hard. She was too busy absorbing the comfort he offered to think of much of anything except prolonging it. One of her legs slid deeper between his. Her fingers wound into his hair and held.

Garrick, too, was inundated with gratifying sensations. He felt Leah from head to toe and drank in her softness as though he'd lived through a drought. In a sense he had. From birth. His parents had been wonderful people, but they'd both been professionals, engrossed in their careers, and they'd had neither time nor warmth to give to their son. Had he been born with the need for physical closeness? Had he been born a toucher? If so, it explained why he'd turned to women from the time he'd had something to offer. Only that hadn't fully satisfied him, either, because even at fourteen he'd been ambitious. He'd been always angling for something bigger and better, never taking stock of what he had, never quite appreciating it.

Until now. Holding Leah Gates in his arms, he felt a measure of fullness that he'd never experienced before. He moved his hands along her spine. He rubbed his thigh against her hip. He inhaled, heightening the pressure of his chest against her breasts.

She needed him. The soft, purring sounds she made from time to time told him so. She needed him, but not because he would be a notch in her belt, or because he could further her career, or because he had money. She didn't know who he was and where he'd been, yet she still needed him. For *him*.

The moan that rumbled from his chest was one of sheer gratitude.

For a long, long time, they lay wrapped in each other's arms. Their closeness was a healing balm, blotting out memories of past pain and sorrow. Nothing existed but the present, and it was so soothing that neither would have thought to disturb it.

Ironically, what disturbed it was the very solace it brought. For with the edge taken off emptiness came a new awareness. It struck Leah gradually—a pleasantly male and musky scent filtering into her nostrils, the thick silk of hair sifting through her fingers, the swell of muscles flexing beneath her arm. On his part, Garrick grew conscious of a clean, womanly fragrance, the gentleness of the curves that his palms rounded, the heat that beckoned daringly close to his loins.

He hadn't been thinking of sex when he'd taken Leah

in his arms. He'd simply wanted to hold her and be held back. He'd wanted, for however fleeting the moments, to binge on the nearness of another human being. But his body was insistent. His heart had begun to beat louder, his blood to course faster, his muscles to grow tighter. He'd never been hit by anything as unexpectedly—or as desperately.

He might have restrained himself if Leah hadn't begun, in wordless ways, to tell him how she wanted him, too. Her hands had slipped down his back and were furrowing beneath his thermal top, gliding upward along his flesh. Her breathing was more shallow. Her breasts swelled against him. He might have called all that simply an extension of the act of holding had it not been for the faint but definitely perceptible arching of her hips.

Or was the arching his? His lower body, with a will of its own, was pressing into her heat, then undulating slowly, then needing even more. He, too, was exploring beneath thermal, only his hands had forayed below Leah's waist and were clenching the firm flare of her bottom, holding her closer, increasing the friction, adding to a hunger that was already explosive.

He had to have her. He had to bury himself in her depths, because he needed that closeness, too, and he was frightened that he'd lose it if he waited.

With hands that shook, he pushed her bottoms to her knees. She squirmed free of them while he lowered his own. Her thigh was already lifting over his when he began his penetration, and by the time he was fully sheathed, she was digging her fingers into his back and sighing softly against his neck.

It was fast and mutual. He stroked deeply and with growing speed. She matched each stroke in pace and ardor. He gasped and quivered. She gulped and shivered. Then they surged against each other a final time, and their bodies erupted into simultaneous spasms. Totally earth-shattering. Endlessly fulfilling. Warm and wet and wonderful.

Garrick's heart thundered long after. His breath came in ragged pants that would have embarrassed him had not Leah been equally as winded. He thought about withdrawing, then thought again, reluctant to leave her when he felt so incredibly contained and content. So he stayed where he was until he began to fear that he was hurting her. But when he made to move away, she clutched him tighter.

"Don't go!" she whispered.

They were the sweetest after-love words he'd ever heard. Not only did they tell him that she savored the continuing contact, they also said something about her feelings toward what they'd just shared.

They reassured him, too. He hadn't performed in a particularly skillful way. He hadn't coaxed her, caressed her, teased her into a state of arousal. He hadn't spoken. He hadn't even kissed her. But she'd been ready.

Because she'd needed him. Because she hadn't had a man in a long time. Because it had been more than sex. And because she, too, had felt its uniqueness.

He didn't say anything when he felt the tremors in her body and realized that she was crying. He spoke with his hands, curving one around her neck to keep her pressed close, using the other to gently stroke her hair. He knew why she was crying, and he felt it, too. But he felt more—a protectiveness that kept his movements steady and soothing until, at length, she cried herself to sleep. Only then did he close his eyes as well.

CONSCIOUSNESS CAME SLOWLY to Leah the next morning. She was first aware of being delightfully warm. Drawing her knees closer, she snuggled beneath the thick quilt. With a lazy yawn, she discovered that she felt rested. And satisfied. Her limbs were relaxed, almost languid, but there was a fullness inside that hadn't been there before.

Then she realized that she was wearing nothing from the waist down, and her eyes opened.

Garrick was sitting on the side of the bed. On her side. He was fully dressed. And he was watching her.

Not quite sure what to say, she simply looked at him.

Gently and with a slight hesitance, he smoothed a strand of dark hair from her cheek and tucked it behind her ear. "Are you okay?"

She nodded.

His voice dropped to a whisper. "I didn't hurt you?"

She shook her head.

"Any regrets?"

She spoke as softly as he had. "No."

"I'm glad." His hand fell back to the quilt. "Hungry?"

"Famished."

"Could you eat some pancakes?"

"Very easily."

A tiny smile broke out on his face. She would have reached for her glasses to better see and enjoy it, but she didn't want to move an inch.

"How 'bout I make a double batch while you get dressed?"

"Sounds fair."

He squeezed her shoulder lightly through the quilt before leaving to fulfill his half of the bargain. Only when she heard busy sounds coming from the kitchen did she pay heed to her half. Rooting around between the sheets, she found and managed to struggle into her thermal bottoms. Once in the bathroom, she showered and dressed, then returned to the main room, where Garrick was adding the last of the pancakes to high stacks on each of two plates.

"Real syrup," she observed after she'd sat down. "This is a luxury."

He watched her dribble it sparingly atop the pancakes, then ordered quietly, "More."

"But it's too good to waste."

"There's no waste if you enjoy it. Besides, this is last year's batch. The new stuff will be along in another month."

Leah turned the plastic container in her hand. It had no label. "Is this local?"

"Very."

"You made it yourself?"

He shook his head. "I don't have the equipment."

"I thought all you had to do was to stick a little spigot in a tree."

"That's true, in a sense. But if you stick one little spigot in one tree, then take the sap you get and boil it down into syrup, you get just about enough to sprinkle on a single pancake."

"Oh."

"Exactly. What you have to do is tap many trees, preferably have long hoses carrying the sap directly to a sugar house, then boil it all in huge vats. There are many people in the area who do it that way. I get my syrup from a family that lives on the other side of town."

"Do they make syrup for a living?"

"They earn some money from it, but not enough to support them. The season's pretty limited."

She nodded in understanding, but her appreciation wasn't as much for the information as for the fact that he'd offered it willingly. Up until now they'd exchanged few words. She realized that, living alone, he wasn't used to talking. Still, while she'd been showering she'd wondered whether there would be awkward silences between them, given what had happened last night. She'd meant what she'd said; she had no regrets. But she hadn't asked him if he did.

From his relaxed manner, she guessed that he didn't, and it pleased her. Turning her attention to her pancakes, she cut off a healthy forkful. Her fork wavered just above the plate, though, and she stared at it.

"Garrick?"

His mouth was full. "Mmm?"

"I just wanted to say...I wanted to tell you...what happened last night...well, I haven't ever done anything like that before."

He swallowed what was in his mouth. "I know."

Her eyes met his. "You do?"

"You were tight. You haven't made love in a long time. Not since your divorce?"

Cheeks pink, she shook her head in affirmation. "I wanted to make sure you knew. I didn't want you to get the wrong impression. I mean, I don't regret for a minute what we did, but I'm not the kind of woman who just jumps into bed with a man."

"I know—"

"But I wasn't sex starved—"

"I know—"

"And it wasn't just because you were there—"

"I know—"

"Because I don't believe in casual affairs—"

"I know—"

Setting down her fork, she curved her fingers against

her bangs. "This is coming out wrong. Now it sounds as though I'm rigidly principled and expect something from you, but that isn't it at all."

"I know. Leah? If you don't eat, the pancakes will get cold."

"I'm not a prude *or* a sex fiend. It's just that last night I needed you—"

"Leah…" He focused pointedly on her plate.

She gave up trying to explain and set to eating. All she could do was hope that he'd understood what she'd been trying to say. She cared what he thought of her, and though part of her was sure he'd known what she'd been feeling last night another part was less confident.

Confidence was something she lacked where relationships with men were concerned. She'd thought she'd known what Richard had wanted, and she'd been wrong. But that was only one of the reasons she'd avoided men since her divorce.

She avoided them because she was independent for the first time in her life and was enjoying it. She avoided them because she always had and always would detest the dating ritual. She avoided them because none of the men she met sparked the slightest romantic interest. And she avoided them because she had a fair idea of what a man had in mind when he asked out a thirty-three-year-old divorcée.

Yes, she cared about what Garrick thought of her, but before that—and more so now than ever—she cared what she thought about herself. She wasn't a tramp. She wasn't out for gratuitous sex. She liked to think of herself as a woman of pride, a selective woman. She liked to think that when she did something, she did it with good reason.

That had been the case in bed last night. From the

first she'd felt an affinity for Garrick. Above and beyond what Victoria had said, her instincts had told her
much about the kind of man he was. He wasn't a play-
boy. Just as he'd known she hadn't made love in a while,
she knew the same about him. There was nothing in
his cabin—no leftover lingerie, no perfume or errant
earrings stuck in a corner of the medicine chest—to
suggest that he'd had a woman here. The urgency with
which he'd entered her and so quickly climaxed was
telling.

Indefinite periods of celibacy notwithstanding, he
was all man, ruggedness incarnate. From the way his
sandy-gray hair fell randomly over his brow, to the way
his beard grew, to his pantherlike gait, to his capac-
ity for chopping and carting wood, he was the kind of
macho hero too often limited to the silver screen.

Macho ended, though, with his looks and carriage.
He was a three-dimensional man, capable of gentleness
and consideration. Those qualities were the ones that
had gotten to her first. They were, ironically, the ones
that had evoked such a tremendous surge of emotion
within her—emotion that had, in the final analysis,
been the reason she'd made love with him.

It hadn't been simply because he was there. If he'd
been cruel or unfeeling, repulsive either physically or
emotionally, she'd never have climbed into his bed,
much less made love with him, regardless of the depth
of her need. No, she'd sought comfort from him because
he was Garrick. He was a man she could probably love,
given the inclination and time.

Of course, she had neither, and thought of the time
brought her back to the present. Swishing the last piece
of pancake around in the remaining drops of syrup, she

brought it to her mouth and ate it, then put down her fork and looked toward the window.

"It's still raining, isn't it?" She'd gotten so used to the sound on the roof that she practically didn't hear it.

Garrick, who'd finished well before her, had his chair braced back on its rear legs. He was nursing the last of his coffee. "Uh-huh."

"No sign of a letup?"

"Nope."

It occurred to her that she wasn't as disappointed about that as she might have been, and she felt guilty. Despite all that had happened, she was still imposing on Garrick. "No hope of getting to my car?" she forced herself to ask.

He shrugged. The front legs of his chair met the floor with a soft thud, and he stood, gathering the dishes together. "I was thinking of making a try later. You'd probably like some other clothes."

He hadn't said anything about freeing the car or getting rid of her. She smiled and, looking down, plucked at the voluminous folds of his sweater. "I don't know. I'm beginning to get used to this. It's comfortable."

Garrick wasn't sure he'd ever get used to how great she looked. When he'd first seen her in it, he'd thought she looked adorable. Now, having had the intense pleasure of being inside her, he thought she looked sexy. That went for the way she looked in his thermal long johns, too. He hadn't thought so at first, but he'd changed his mind, and his body wasn't about to let him change it back.

Taking refuge at the sink, he began to clean up with more energy than was strictly necessary. It helped. By the time he was done, he had his libido in check. He didn't want to frighten Leah or act as though she should pay for her keep by satisfying his every urge. And it wasn't as if his every urge *was* for sex, though after last night, he had a greater inclination toward it than he'd had in years.

Last night…last night had been very, very special. It was sex, but it wasn't. It was so much an emotional act, rather than a physical one, that he didn't have the words to describe it. Yes, if there were to be a repeat, the emotional element would be present, but he knew that there'd be more. He knew that this time he'd want to touch her and kiss her. This time he'd want to explore her body and get to know it as completely as, in some ways, he felt he knew her soul. Her mind, ah, that was another matter. He wanted to get to know it, too, but… probably that wasn't wise. When the ground dried up, she'd be leaving. He didn't want to miss her.

Which was why he reverted into the silence with which he'd grown increasingly comfortable over four years' time. He didn't ask her any of the million questions he had. He told himself he didn't want to know the details of what made Leah Gates tick. If he didn't know it would be easier to pretend that she was shallow and boring. Easier to tell himself, when she was gone, that he was better off without her.

Leah spent the morning much as she had her waking hours the day before. She finished one book and started another. She made frequent notes on a pad of paper when she encountered a word or concept in her reading that would translate into a crossword. She doodled out nonsense puzzles, but the puzzle that commanded her real interest was Garrick.

He was an enigma. She knew that they had at least one need in common, and she knew, in general, the type of man he was. The specifics of his day-to-day life, though, were a mystery, as was his past.

Mentally she'd outlined a crossword puzzle. Garrick's name was blocked in, as were certain other facts pertaining to their relationship, but she needed more information if she hoped to find the words to complete the grid.

It was late morning. They were each sitting in what she'd come to think of as their own little corner of the sofa. Garrick had gone outside for a while, though not to the car, he'd told her when she'd asked. He hadn't elaborated further, and she'd been loath to press. It was his home. He was free to come and go as he pleased. She couldn't help but be curious, though, particularly when he returned after no more than thirty minutes.

After letting him dry off and settle in with his book for a while, she ventured to satisfy her curiosity.

"I hope I'm not keeping you from doing things."

"You're not."

"What would you be doing if I weren't here?"

"On a day like this, not much of anything."

Which was precisely what he was doing now, he mused a tad wryly. He'd gone to the back shed, thinking that working with toothpicks and glue, making progress on the model home he'd been commissioned to make, would be therapeutic. But if the therapy had been intended to take his mind off Leah, it had failed. Even the book that lay open on his lap—a novel he'd purchased the week before—failed to capture him.

Leah broke into his thoughts. "And if it weren't raining?"

"I'd be outside."

"Trapping?"

He shrugged.

"Victoria said you were a trapper."

"I am, but the best part of the trapping season's over for the year."

She let that statement sink in, but it raised more questions than it answered. So a while later, she tried again.

"What do you trap?"

He was crouching before the fire, adding another log to the flames. "Fisher, fox, raccoon."

"You sell the furs?"

He hesitated, wondering if Leah was the crusader type who'd lecture him about the evils of killing animals to provide luxury items for rich people. He decided that there was only one way to find out.

"That's right."

"I've never owned a fur coat."

"Why not?" He turned on his haunches, waiting for the lecture.

"They're too expensive, for one thing. Richard—my ex-husband—thought I should have one, but I kept putting him off. If you walk into a restaurant with a fur, either you're afraid to check it in case it gets stolen, or the management refuses to *let* you check it. In either case, you have to spend the evening worrying about whether your *fruits de mer au chardonnay* will spatter. Besides, I've always thought fur coats to be too showy. And they're heavy. I don't want that kind of weight on my shoulders."

It wasn't quite the answer Garrick had feared, but it was a fearful one nonetheless, for it had given him a glimpse of her life—at least, the one she'd had when she'd been married. Her husband had apparently been well-to-do. They'd gone to fine French restaurants and had kept company with women who *did* worry about spattering sauce on their furs. If he could tell himself that Leah was as turned off by that kind of life-style as he was, he'd feel better. He'd also feel worse, because he'd like her even more.

"I see your point" was all he said, returning to the sofa and lowering his eyes to his book in hopes of ending the conversation. Leah took the hint and said nothing more, but *that* bothered him. If she'd pushed, he might have had something to hold against her. He hated pushy women, and Lord, had he known his share.

Lunchtime came. Halfway through her bologna sandwich, Leah set it down gently. "Did I offend you?"

"Excuse me?"

"When I said that I didn't like fur coats?"

He'd been deep in his own musings, which had gone far beyond fur coats. It took him a minute to return. "You didn't offend me. I don't like them, either."

"No?"

He shook his head.

"Doesn't that take some of the pleasure out of your work?"

"How so?"

"Having someone turn the product of your hard work into something you don't like? I know I'd be devastated if someone used my page of the paper to wrap fish."

"Does anyone?"

"I've never witnessed it personally, but I'm sure it's been done more than once."

"If you see it, what would you do?"

She considered for a minute, then gave a half shrug. "Rationalize, I suppose."

"How?"

"I'd tell myself that I enjoyed creating the puzzle and that I was paid for it, but that...that's the end of my involvement. If it gives someone pleasure to wrap fish in my puzzle—" she hesitated, hating to say the next but knowing she had to "—so be it."

He grinned.

She winced, then murmured sheepishly, "If it gives someone pleasure to wear a fur coat, so be it...." She tucked her hair behind her ear. "Do you enjoy trapping?"

"Yes."

"Why?"

"It takes skill."

"You like the challenge."

"Yes."

"Where did you learn how to do it?"

"A trapper taught me." He stood and reached across the table for her plate. "All done?"

She nodded. "A local trapper?"

"He's dead now." Stacking the plates together, balancing glasses and flatware on top, he carried the lot to the sink. "I thought I'd make a stab at reaching your car. If you tell me what you want, I'll bring back as much as I can."

She rose quickly. "I'll come with you."

"No."

"Two pairs of hands are better than one."

He turned to face her. "Not in this case. If I have to hold you with one arm, I'll have only one left for your things."

"You won't have to hold me."

"Come on, Leah. You've been through that muck once. You know how treacherous it is."

She approached the sink, intent on making her point. "But that was at night. I couldn't see. I didn't know where I was going. My shoes weren't the greatest—"

"What shoes would you wear now?"

"Yours. You must have an old pair of boots lying around."

"Sure. Size twelve."

She was standing directly before him, her face bright with hope. "I could pad them with wool socks."

"You could also pack your feet in cement and try to move, because that's pretty much what it would be like."

"I could do it, Garrick."

"Not fast enough. In case you've forgotten, it's raining out there. The idea is to make the round trip as quickly as possible."

"How long can it take to dash a mile?"

"A mile?" He laughed. "Is that how far you thought you'd gone?"

"It took me forever," she reasoned defensively, then quickly added, "but that was because it was dark and I kept falling."

"Well, it's light now, but you'll fall anyway, because it's slippery as hell out there. I'm used to it." He brushed a forefinger along his mustache. "By the way, Victoria's cabin is just about a third of a mile from here."

"A *third*—" she began in amazement, then turned embarrassment into optimism. "But that's *nothing*. I'll be able to do it."

Garrick looked down at her. Her head was tipped back, her brows arched high in hope. He found himself caught, enchanted by the gentle color on her cheeks, taunted by her moist, slightly parted lips. He wanted to kiss her just then, wanted it so suddenly and so badly that he knew he couldn't do it. He'd bruise her. He'd be settling an argument in the sexist way he'd used in the past but detested now. Worse, he'd be showing a decided lack of control.

Control was what his new life was about. Self-control. No drinking, no smoking, no carousing. No impulsive kisses.

Instead of lowering his mouth to hers, he raised his hands to her shoulders and held them lightly. "I'd rather you stay here, Leah. For your own safety and comfort, if nothing else."

Had he said it any other way or offered any other reason, Leah probably would have continued to argue. But his voice had been like smooth sand in the sun, fine grains of warmth entering her, quieting her, and his expression of concern was new and welcome.

Sucking on her upper lip, she stepped back, then forward again, this time around his large frame. She gave him a gentle nudge at the back of his waist. "Go. I'll clean up."

"You'll have to tell me what you want."

"Let me think for a minute."

While she thought, he built up the fire and pulled on his rain gear. He was just finishing buckling his boots, when she handed him a list of what she'd like and where in her car he could find it. Tucking that list into the pocket of his oilskin slicker, he tugged up the hood, tipped its rim in the facsimile of a salute, then left.

A SHORT TIME LATER, sitting in the driver's seat of the Golf, Garrick drew Victoria's letter from Leah's purse. He held it, turned it, stared at the back flap. He should slit it open, but he didn't want to. He knew that he'd find an enthusiastic recommendation of Leah, and he certainly didn't need that. Leah was doing just fine on her own behalf.

Damn, Victoria!

Stuffing the letter back into the purse, he quickly

collected the things Leah had requested. It was an easy
task, actually. She was very organized. Her note was
even funny.

> Battered Vuitton duffel (a gift, not my style) on
> top of no-name suitcases behind passenger's seat.
> Mickey Mouse bookbag, one across and two down
> from duffel. Large grocery sack behind driver's
> seat. (If sack reeks, scatter contents for animals
> and take black canvas tote bag, riding shotgun,
> instead.)

The sack didn't reek, and he was able to manage the
tote, too. He felt a little foolish with a purse slung over
his shoulder, but it was well hidden by the rest of the
load, and besides, who would see him?

No one did see him, but as he slogged through the
rain heading back toward the cabin, he grew more and
more annoyed. He was peeved at Leah for being so
sweet and alone and comfortable. He was put out with
Victoria for having sent her to him in the first place.
He was riled by the bundles he carried, for they swung
against his sides and made the task of keeping his balance on the slick mud that much harder. He was irritated
with the rain, which trickled up his cuffs and which, if
it hadn't come at all, would have spared him the larger
mess he was in.

Mostly he was angry at life for throwing him a curve
when he least expected or needed it. Things had been
going so well for him. He had his head straight, his pri-
orities set. Then Leah came along, and suddenly he saw
voids where he hadn't seen them before.

He wanted her with a vengeance, and that infuriated
him. She was a threat to the way of life he'd worked so

hard to establish, because he sensed that nothing would be the same when she left. And she would leave. She was city. She was restaurants and theater and Louis Vuitton luggage—even if it *had* been a gift. She wasn't about to fit into his life-style for long. Oh, sure, she found it a novelty now. The leisurely pace and the quiet were a break from her regular routine. But she'd be bored before long. So she'd leave. And he'd be alone again. Only this time he'd mind it.

By the time he reached the cabin he was in a dark mood. After silently depositing his load, he went out again and hiked farther up the mountain, moving quickly, ignoring the rain and cold. He felt a little more in control of himself when he finally turned and began the descent, but even then he bought extra time by going to the shed to work.

It was late when he entered the cabin. Leah had turned on the lights, and the fire was burning brightly. But it wasn't the smell of wood smoke that met him. Shrugging from his wet outerwear, he sniffed the air, then glowered toward the kitchen.

Leah was at the stove. She'd looked up when he'd stomped in, but her attention had quickly returned to whatever it was she was stirring. He didn't recognize the pan as one of his own, though he hadn't been that long from civilization not to recognize it as a wok.

"Chinese?" he warbled. "You're cooking Chinese?"

She sent him a nervous glance. "I'm trying. I just finished taking a course in it, but I haven't really done it on my own. It was one of the things I was going to play with at Victoria's cabin." What was apparently an instruction book lay open on the counter beside her, but Garrick wasn't up for marveling at Leah's industriousness.

"You mean—I was hauling Chinese groceries in that sack?"

"Among other things." Many of which she'd quickly put in the freezer, others of which were refrigerated, a few of which she'd questioned and thrown out.

"And a *wok?* I thought I was bringing you *essentials.*"

She shot him a second, even more nervous glance. He was angry. She had no idea why. "You asked me to tell you what I wanted. These were some of the things."

He looked around for the other bags he'd carried, but they'd apparently been unloaded and stored—somewhere. Planting his hands on his hips, he glared at her. "What else did I cart through the rain?"

His tone was so reminiscent of the imperious one Richard had often used that Leah had to struggle not to cringe. She kept her voice steady, but it was small. "The wok. It was with my books in the Mickey Mouse bag. And some clothes." She spared a fast glance at the faded jeans she'd put on. "I threw out the torn slacks. They were hopeless." She was also wearing a pair of well-worn moccasins that had been in the duffel, but she hadn't changed out of Garrick's sweater. Now she wished she had.

"What was in the black tote? It was heavy as hell."

At that moment, Leah would have given anything to be able to lie. She'd never been good at it; her eyes gave her away. Not that lying would have done any good in this case, since he would learn the truth soon enough.

"A cassette player and tapes," she mumbled.

"A *what?*"

She looked him in the eye and said more clearly, "A cassette player and tapes."

"Oh-ho, no, you don't! You're not going to disturb my peace and quiet with raucous music!"

"It's not raucous."

"Then loud. I didn't come up here to put up with *that*."

Leah knew she should indulge him. After all, it was his cabin and he was doing her a favor by taking her in. But there'd been so much more between them that having him shout at her only raised her hackles. She'd heard enough shouting from Richard. When they divorced, she'd vowed never to be the butt of unreasonable mood swings again.

She'd thought Garrick was different.

"I'll play it softly, or not at all while you're here," she stated firmly, "but if you're gone for hours like you were today, I'll enjoy it any way I want."

"It bothered you that I left you alone, did it?" he demanded.

"It did not! You can go where you want, when you want and for however long you want. But if you're not here, I'll listen to my music. And anyway, in a few days I'll be gone." She took a shaky breath. "I may be invading your privacy, but, don't forget, if it hadn't been for you Victoria would have never sent me up here!"

That took Garrick aback. He hadn't thought of it quite that way, but Leah had a point. For that matter, Leah often had a point and it was usually reasonable. Which made him feel all the more unreasonable.

Wheeling away, he strode off to hang his wet jacket on a hook, then marched back to the dresser by the bed, yanked his turtleneck jersey and heavy wool sweater over his head in one piece, tossed them heedlessly aside and began tugging out drawers in search of a replacement.

Leah's throat went positively dry as she stared after him. All anger was forgotten in the face of his nakedness. Granted, it was only his back, but his cords hung low on his hips, presenting her with a view of skin that was breathtaking. There was nothing burly about his shoulders. They were broad, but every inch was hard flesh over corded sinew. The same was true of his arms and, for that matter, the rest of his torso. There wasn't a spare ounce of fat in sight. His spine bisected symmetrical pockets of muscle that stretched and flexed as he bent over and tore through the drawer. His waist was lean, the skin there smooth. He wasn't tanned, though she guessed that once the spring sun came he would be. He struck her as a man who'd be outside in good weather, shirtless.

Her insides burned, but jerking her eyes back to the contents of the wok, she realized with relief that that was all that had. She set the cover on the shallow pan with a hand that trembled, turned off the propane gas, then lifted the cover from a second pan, one of Garrick's, and checked the rice.

Everything was ready. The food was cooked. The table was set. And Garrick was slouched on the sofa, wearing a battered sweatshirt, taking his sour mood out on the fire.

She debated leaving him alone. She could dish out the food and sit down. Surely he'd see that dinner was on the table and join her. Or would he?

Her approach was quiet and hesitant. "Garrick?"

His mouth rested against a fist. "Mmm?"

"I'm all set. If you're hungry." She pressed her damp palms to her jeans.

"Ydnnvtmakdnnn."

"Excuse me?"

He raised his fist, but his words remained low and begrudging. "You didn't have to make dinner."

"I know."

"What is it, anyway?"

"Braised chicken with black beans."

He didn't take his eyes from the fire. "I haven't had Chinese food in four years. I've always hated it."

Feeling inexplicably hurt, Leah turned away. She wasn't all that hungry herself, all of a sudden, but she had no intention of letting her efforts go to waste. So she prepared a plate for herself, sat down and began to eat.

Out of the corner of her eye she saw Garrick rise from the sofa. He went to the stove, clattered covers and sniffed loudly. She was struggling to swallow a small cube of chicken, when she heard the distinct sounds of food being dished out. The chicken slid down more easily.

Moments later, he took his place across from her. She didn't look up but continued to eat, though she couldn't have described what she was tasting.

"Not bad," Garrick conceded. His normally raspy voice was gruffer than normal. He took another bite, chewed and swallowed. "What's in it?"

"Ginger root, bamboo shoots, scallions, oyster sauce, sherry..."

"Not the kind of stuff that comes in cardboard take-out containers."

"No." She took a minute to concentrate on what she was eating and, to her relief, agreed with his assessment. It was good. She had nothing to be ashamed of, and that mattered to her, where Garrick was concerned. It was the first time she'd cooked for him. As a matter of pride, she'd wanted the results to be highly palatable.

They ate in silence. More than once, Leah had to

bite her tongue to keep from voicing the questions on her mind. She wanted to know why he'd been so angry, what she'd done to cause it. She wanted to know what he had against music. She wanted to know when he'd eaten Chinese food from takeout containers and why he'd developed such an aversion to it. And she wanted to know where he'd been and what he'd been doing four years ago.

He didn't offer any further conversation, though, and she didn't dare start any for fear of setting him off. She liked the Garrick who was quiet and gentle, not the one who brooded darkly, or worse, growled at her.

She had no way of knowing that, at that moment, Garrick was disliking himself. He was disgusted with the way he'd behaved earlier, though his present behavior was only a marginal improvement. But he couldn't seem to help himself. The more he saw of Leah, the more he liked her, and paradoxically, the more he resented her.

Chinese food. The mere words conjured up images of late nights on the set, where dinner was wolfed out of cartons scattered along an endless table at the rear of the studio. He'd barely known what he was eating. His stomach had inevitably been upset long before, and the best he'd been able to do was to wash whatever it was down with swigs of Scotch.

Chinese food. Another image came to mind, this one of a midnight date with a willowy blonde who'd been good enough to pick up the food on her way over to his place. He wouldn't have bothered to pick *her* up. He'd known what she'd wanted and he'd delivered—crudely and with little feeling. The next morning, more than a little hung over, he'd retched at the smell of the food that remained in the cartons.

Chinese food. One last image. He'd been alone. No work, no friends. He'd been high on something or other, and he'd gone to the takeout counter and ordered enough for twelve, supposedly to look as though he were having a party. As though he were still important, still a star. He'd gone home, sat in his garish living room, stared at the leather sofas and the huge bags of food and had bawled like a baby.

"Garrick?"

Leah's voice brought him back. His head shot up just as she passed an envelope across the table. Victoria's letter. He glared at it for a minute before snatching it from her fingers. The legs of his chair scraped against the floor. He crossed the room quickly, slapped the unopened letter onto the top of the dresser, then dropped back into the sofa and resumed his brooding.

Quietly Leah began to clear the table. Her movements were slow, her shoulders slumped in defeat. It wasn't the meal that caused her discouragement; she knew it had been good and that for a time Garrick had enjoyed what he'd eaten. She couldn't even take offense at his brusque departure, because she knew he was hurting. She'd seen his eyes grow distant, seen the pain they'd held. Oh, yes, she knew he was hurting, but she didn't know what to do about it, and that was the cause of her distress. She wanted to reach out, but she was afraid. She felt totally impotent.

When there was nothing left to do in the kitchen, she picked up a book—one of her own—and as unobtrusively as possible slid into her corner of the sofa. She couldn't read, though. She was too aware of Garrick.

An hour passed. He looked at her. "You said there were clothes in the bag I brought."

She glanced down at her jeans, then her moccasins.

"Besides those," he muttered.

"There are others." She knew he was complaining because she'd left on his sweater. She closed her fingers around a handful of the wool. "I'll wash this and your long johns in the morning."

He grunted and looked away. Another period of silence passed. He moved only to feed the fire. She moved only to turn an unread page.

Then his rough voice jagged into her again. I can't believe you sent me for books and tapes. "You'll need more than one change of clothes."

"There were two in the duffel."

"That's not enough if you're stuck here awhile."

"You have a washer. I'll do fine. Besides, I have boots in the duffel. I can always go back to the car—"

"*Boots?* Why in the hell didn't you put them on the other night?"

She drew her elbows in tighter. Strangely, this kind of criticism had been less hurtful coming from Richard. "I didn't think the mud would be so bad."

"You didn't think period. Your car's stuck in pretty good. That took some doing."

"I'm not an expert—with cars *or* mud," she argued, but she was shaking inside. She had no idea why he was harping at her this way. "I was only trying to get out—"

"By grinding the tires in deeper?"

"I was trying my best!"

Again he grunted. Again he looked away. Tension made the air nearly as heavy as her heart.

"You didn't even lock the damn car!" he roared a short time later. "With your purse lying there, and all your supposed worldly possessions, you left the thing open!"

"I was too upset to think about that."

"And you're supposed to be a New Yorker?"

She slammed her book shut. "I've never *had* a car before. What is the *problem,* Garrick? You said yourself that no one moves in this kind of weather. Even if someone could, who in his right mind would be going to a burned out cabin? My things were safe, and if they weren't, they're only *things.*"

He snorted. "You'd probably *give* the rest away, now that you've got your precious books and your tapes and your wok—"

"Damn it, Garrick!" she cried, sliding forward on the sofa. "Why are you doing this to me? I don't tell you how to live, do I? If my books mean more to me than clothes, that's *my* choice." Tears sparkled on her lids but she refused to let them fall. "I may not be like other women in that sense, but it's the way I am. Will it really hurt you if I alternate between two outfits? If I'm clean and I don't smell, why should you be concerned? Am I that awful to look at that I need all kinds of fancy things to make my presence bearable?"

She was on her feet, looking at him with hurt-filled eyes. "You don't want me here. I know that, and because of it, I don't want to be here, either. I never asked to be marooned with you. If I'd known what Victoria was planning, I'd never have left New York!" She was breathing hard, trying to control her temper, but without success. "I'm as independent as you are, and I prize that independence. I've earned it. Do you think it's easy for me to be stuck in an isolated cabin with a sharp-tongued, self-indulgent recluse? Well, it isn't! I took enough abuse from my husband. I don't have to take it from you!"

She started to move away, but turned back as quickly. "And since we've taken off the gloves, let me tell you something else. You have the manners of a *boor!* I didn't have to cook dinner tonight. You've made it clear that you're more than happy doing it. But I wanted to do something for *you,* for a change. I wanted to please you. I wanted to show you that I'm not a wimpy female who needs to be waited on. And what did I get for it? Out-and-out rudeness. You took your sweet time deciding whether you'd privilege me with your company at the table. Then after you shoveled food in your mouth, you stormed off as though I'd committed some unpardonable sin. What did I *do?* Can't you at least tell me that? Or is it beyond your capability to share your thoughts once in a while?"

Through her entire tirade, he didn't move a muscle. Throwing her hands up in a gesture of futility, she turned away. Yanking a nightshirt from the duffel she'd stowed under the bed, she fled to the bathroom. A minute later she was out again, throwing her clothes down on top of the duffel, plopping down on the edge of the bed.

Her breath was ragged and her fingers dug into the quilt with fearsome strength. She was angry. She was hurt. But mostly she was dismayed, because she'd taken both her anger and her hurt out on Garrick. It wasn't like her to do that to anyone. She was normally the most composed of women. Yet she'd disintegrated before Garrick. Garrick. After last night.

She didn't see or hear him until he was standing directly before her. Her eyes focused on his legs. She couldn't look up. She didn't know what to say.

Very slowly, he lowered himself to his haunches. She bowed her head even more, but he raised it with a finger beneath her chin. A gentle finger. Her gaze crept upward.

His eyes held the words of apology that his lips wouldn't form, and that gentle finger became five, touching her cheek with soulful hesitance. Callused fingertips moved falteringly, exploring her cheek, her cheekbone, the straight slope of her nose, her lips.

Her breath caught in her throat, because all the while he was touching her, his eyes were speaking, and the words were so sad and humble and heartfelt that she wanted to cry.

He leaned forward, then hesitated.

She touched her fingertips to the thick brush of his beard in encouragement.

This time when he leaned forward he didn't falter, and the words he spoke so silently were the most meaningful of all.

CHAPTER FIVE

GARRICK KISSED HER. It was the first time their lips had touched, and it wasn't so much the touching itself as its manner that shook Leah to the core. His mouth was artful, capturing hers with a gentleness that spoke of caring, a sweetness that spoke of a deep inner need. He brushed his lips back and forth across her softening flesh, then drew back to look at her again.

His eyes caressed each of her features. Setting her glasses aside, he kissed her eyes, the bridge of her nose, her cheekbone, her temple. By the time he returned to her mouth, her lips were parted. She tipped her head to perfect the fit, welcoming him with rapidly flaring desire.

His enthusiasm matched hers. Oh, he'd fought it. All day and all evening he'd been telling himself that he didn't want this or need it, that it would cause more trouble than it was worth. He'd been telling himself that he had the self-control to resist any and all urgings of the flesh. But then Leah had blown up. She'd given him a piece of her mind, and she'd been right in what she'd said. He'd seen and felt her hurt, and he'd known that urgings of the flesh were but a small part of the attraction he felt for her.

He couldn't fight it any longer, because just as his new life was built on control, it was built on honesty. What he felt for Leah, what he needed from her and with her was too raw, too beautiful to be sullied by ugly behavior or lack of communication. He'd talk. He'd tell her about himself. For now, though, he needed to speak with his body.

Calling on everything he'd ever learned about pleasing a woman, he set to pleasing Leah. His mouth was never still, never rough or forceful, demanding only in the most subtle of ways. He stroked her lips, loved them with his own and with his tongue, worshiped the small teeth that lay behind, then the deeper, warmer, moister recesses that beckoned.

There was nothing calculated in what he did. He might have learned and perfected the technique from and on other women, but what he felt as he pleasured Leah came straight from the heart. And he was pleasuring himself, as well, discovering a goodness he'd never known, realizing yet again that what he'd once thought of as purely physical was emotionally uplifting with Leah. In that sense, he was experiencing a rebirth. His past took on meaning, for it was the groundwork from which he could love Leah completely.

She felt it. She felt the wealth of feeling behind the mouth that revered hers, the tongue that flowed around and against hers, the hands that sifted through her hair with such tenderness. She felt things new and different, things that arrowed into her heart and made her tremble.

"Garrick?" she breathed when his lips left hers for a minute.

"Shhhhh—"

"I'm sorry for yelling—"

He was cupping her head, his breath whispering over her. "We'll talk later. I need you too much now." He kissed her once more, lingeringly, then released her to whip his sweatshirt over his head.

Her palms were on him even before the sweatshirt hit the floor. Palms open, fingers splayed, she ran her hands over his chest, covering every inch in greedy possession. He was warm and firm. A fine mat of hair, its tawny hue made golden by the residual light of the fire, wove a manly pattern over his flesh. She explored the broader patch above his breasts and traced its narrowing to his waist, then dragged her hands upward again until they spanned dual swells of muscle and small, tight nipples rasped against her palms.

The breath he expelled was a shuddering one. He had his eyes closed and his head thrown back. His long fingers closed around her wrists, not to stop her voyage but simply because he needed to hold her, to know that he wasn't imagining her touch. His insides were hot; shafts of fire were shooting toward his loins, and a sheen of perspiration had broken out on his skin, adding to the sensual slide of her hands.

When she rounded his shoulders and began to stroke his back in those same, broad sweeps of discovery, he shakily released the buttons of her nightshirt and pushed the soft fabric down her arms. For a minute he could do nothing but look; the perfection before him all but stopped his breathing. Her breasts were round and full, their tips gilded by the firelight. He touched one. Her nipple was already hard, but grew even more so. Sucking in a breath at the sweet pain, Leah closed her fingers on the smooth flesh at his sides and clung for dear life.

His eyes locked with hers, finding a desire there that was echoed in the shallowness of her breathing. "I want to touch you, Leah. I need to. I need to touch and to taste."

She gave a convulsive swallow, then whispered, "Please!"

Unable to help himself, he smiled. She was so adorable, so sexy, so guileless when it came to this. He had
to kiss her again, and he did, and while his lips held
hers, he touched her breasts. She jerked at the sudden
charge of sensation, but he gentled her with his mouth,
and his work-roughened hands circled her, covered her,
lifted her with care. She never quite got used to his
touch, because each time he moved his palm or finger,
new currents of awareness sizzled through her. When
the pads of his thumbs scored her nipples, soft sounds
of arousal came from deep in her throat, and when fore-
fingers joined thumbs in an erotic rolling, a snowball-
ing need had her squirming restlessly.

Her hands moved with desperation to the waistband
of his cords. His met them there, unsnapping and unzip-
ping, before leaving her to her own devices. He wanted
to touch her more, this time her knees, which were
widespread, allowing him to kneel between them, then
her thighs, which were soft and smooth and quivering.
When her hands slipped beneath the band of his shorts
in search of the point of greatest heat, his surged higher,
similarly seeking and finding the heart of her sex.

Leah's head fell forward, mouth open, teeth braced
on his shoulder. Her hands surrounded him. They measured his length and width, weighed the heaviness beneath. They caressed satin over steel and were rewarded
when he strained harder against her palms. But her mind
was only half there, because Garrick had opened her
and begun to do such intimately arousing things to her
that she could barely breathe, much less think.

She'd never thought of herself as lacking control
where sex was concerned, but she'd never been half
as hot as she was now. She felt herself floating, rising,

and her attempts to rein in were futile. Sandwiching the power of his virility between them, her hands went still.

"Garrick…oh…oh." She sucked in a breath, let it out in a tremulous whisper. "Please…I need…wait."

But just then he took her nipple into his mouth, and it was too late. The brush of his mustache and beard and his gentle sucking snapped the fine thread from which she'd been hanging. Her thighs closed on his hands as her insides exploded, and she could only gasp against his shoulder while she rode out a storm of endless spasms. When they subsided at last, she rolled her face to the crook of his neck.

"I'm sorry…I couldn't hold back…"

Framing her face, he raised it and kissed her. His lips shifted and angled and sucked, never once leaving hers as he bore her gently back on the bed. His hands tugged the nightshirt from her hips, then went to work baring himself. Naked, he lowered his large frame over her.

Leah was ready to take him in, but he had no intention of simply slaking his desire while she lay quiescent and sated. He wanted her hungry again. He wanted her aroused and aching for him, because he knew that if it was so, his own fulfillment would be all the richer.

So he began to touch her anew. Her breasts, her belly, that ultrasensitive spot between her legs—he stimulated and teased, using hands, lips and tongue. And he was doing just fine until she became active herself, finding the places that set him to shaking, stroking them, tormenting them with fingers that were innocent and eager to please.

And Garrick was pleased, though the word seemed a paltry one to describe his feelings. He'd never felt so valued—not just needed, *valued*. Beneath Leah's hands and lips and the sweet waft of her breath, he felt cherished, special and unique. He felt as though she couldn't be doing this with any other man but him.

At that moment, he knew the future would have to take care of itself. He needed her now and for however long she chose to stay with him. If, at the end of that time, he was alone, he knew that he'd have experienced something most men never even approach. He'd have memories of something rare and wonderful, and he'd be a stronger man for it.

Writhing gently beneath him, Leah urged him to her. He grasped her hands, intertwined his fingers with hers and pinned them to the quilt by her shoulders. Poised above her, he watched her face as slowly, slowly he entered her.

Her eyes fell shut and a tiny smile of bliss curved her lips. Then, with a sigh, she lifted her legs and wrapped them tightly around him. "Don't move," she whispered, still smiling in that catlike way that gave him a thrill. "You feel…I feel so…good…full."

"Leah?" he whispered.

Slowly her eyes opened. They were filled with the same love that filled his heart. He knew it was absurd. He and Leah had known each other for only two days, and those under unusual conditions. They hadn't talked much, hadn't shared thoughts of the past or the future, much less the present, but he *did* love her. He'd never felt anything like it before—the driving desire to please a woman, to make her happy in the broadest sense—but he felt that way toward Leah. He felt that he'd willingly sacrifice his quiet to hear her music, his steak and potatoes to eat her Chinese food, his normal efficiency to take her floundering in the mud. He knew that if she asked him to withdraw from her just then, he'd forgo a climax and still feel complete.

She didn't ask him anything of the sort, though. Rather, she began to move her hips and her inner muscles, holding him ever more tightly, taking his breath away. Lifting her head from the pillow, she sought his lips, and he lost track of everything but the intense pleasure of stroking her tongue and drawing it into his mouth. Bowing his back, he withdrew, then thrust forward, withdrew, then thrust forward. With each thrust he went deeper. With each withdrawal, he returned hotter. Finally, with a surge that touched her womb, he stiffened and held, erupting into a release so powerful that he thought he'd die, so glorious that he would have welcomed it.

Only when awareness returned did he realize that Leah, too, was vibrating in the aftermath of climax. Her cheek was pressed to their intertwined hands. Her eyes were shut tightly. Her lips were parted to allow for the soft panting that was sweet music to his ears. He was glad then that he hadn't died, for there was more to come, so much more.

Very gently he slid from her, but before she could protest, he'd nestled her snugly into the crook of his shoulder. One of his arms encircled her back, the other grasped her thigh and drew it over his. His fingers remained in a warm clasp around her knee.

Eyes closed, Leah sighed in contentment. She rubbed her nose against Garrick's chest, inhaling the scent of man and musk and sex that would have been arousing had not she been so thoroughly sated.

"Ahhh, Garrick," she whispered. "So nice…"

"It is, isn't it?" he responded as softly. In the past he would have been reaching for a cigarette. Putting distance between himself and the body next to him. Biding the few obligatory minutes before he could clear whatever woman he was with from his bed. Now, though, the only thing he wanted to do was lie holding Leah. And talk.

"You're spectacular," she said. "Maybe I should yell at you more."

That drew a lazy chuckle from his throat. "Maybe you should. It brings me to my senses."

"I'm not usually the yelling type."

"I'm not usually the brooding type."

"What brought it on?"

He cuffed his chin against the top of her head, knowing that his beard would cushion the gentle blow. "You."

"Is it that difficult having me here?"

"Just the opposite. I like having you here."

"Then why—"

"I like it too much. I thought I had my life all worked out. Then you pop in and upset the apple cart."

"Oh." She took a quick breath. "I know what you mean."

"You do?"

"Mmm. I haven't minded living alone—living without a man. I thought it was the safest thing."

"Did your marriage hurt you that much?"

"Yes."

"You said he abused you. Was it physical?"

"He never beat me. It was more an emotional thing."

"Tell me about him. What was he like?"

Leah thought for a minute, seeking to express her feelings with a minimum of bitterness. "He was good-looking and charming. He could sell an icebox to an Eskimo."

"He was a salesman?"

"Indirectly. He was—is—a top executive in an ad agency. If you want to know what charisma is, you don't have to look farther than Richard. People flock to him. He attracts clients like flies. Lord only knows why he married me."

Garrick gave her a sharp squeeze, but she went on.

"I'm serious. I guess it was the stage he was at when we met. He was just getting started. He needed a wife who looked relatively sophisticated, and when I try, I suppose I do look that. He needed someone who knew the ins and outs of New York, and since I'd lived there all my life, I guess I qualified on that score, too. He needed someone he could manipulate, and I fit the bill."

"You don't strike *me* as being terribly manipulatable," Garrick said with feeling.

She laughed. "How can you say that after what Victoria did?"

"That may be the one exception, and since we were both patsies, we won't count it."

"Well, Richard was able to manipulate me. I wanted to please him. I wanted to make the marriage work."

"Why didn't it?"

"Oh, lots of reasons. Mainly because I couldn't be what Richard wanted."

"Couldn't?"

"That, and wouldn't. I got tired of being told when to be where wearing what. I got tired of feeling that regardless how hard I tried, I didn't measure up."

"What did the guy want?" Garrick barked. The sound reverberated in his chest beneath Leah's ear. Knowing that he was on her side, she didn't mind his anger.

"Perfection."

"None of us is perfect."

"Tell that to Richard."

"Thanks, but I'll pass. He sounds like the kind of guy I avoid."

"You're very wise."

"Either that, or very weak. I haven't quite decided which yet."

Leah shifted, turning her head so that she looked up at him. "You, weak? I don't believe that for a minute. Look at the way you live. It takes strength to do what you do."

"Physical strength, yes."

"No, psychological. To live alone on a mountainside, to be comfortable enough with yourself to live alone—many people can't do that."

It was the perfect opening. He knew he should say something about himself and his past, but the words wouldn't come. He wanted Leah's respect. He feared he'd risk it if she knew where he'd been. "I'm not sure I've done it so well, judging from the way I've latched on to you." Hauling her higher on his chest, he gave her a fierce kiss. But the fierceness mellowed quickly. "You taste so good, Leah," he whispered hoarsely. "You *feel* so good." His hands had begun to glide up and down her body. "You feel so good on top of me."

That was precisely where she was. Her breasts were pillowed by the soft furring of his chest hair. Her thighs, straddling his, knew their sinewed strength. He felt so good beneath her that her body began a slow rocking while her mouth inched over his nose, his cheek and down to the warm, bare skin below his beard.

"You smell good," she whispered against his throat.

Garrick grinned in pure delight. He felt redeemed, almost defiant. He smelled earthy, but Leah liked it. So there, L.A.! Take your Brut and stuff it!

"Garrick?" Her voice was muffled against his chest.

"What is it, love?"

She kept her face buried. "I want you again."

He laughed in continued delight.

"What's so funny?"

"You. You're wonderful."

"Does that mean you want me, too?"

He arched his hips against hers. "What do you think?"

"I think yes, but maybe you think I'm only after your body."

He didn't laugh this time. Instead his long fingers caged her head and gently raised it. His expression was soft and filled with wonder. "What I think is that I'm the luckiest man alive." He didn't say anything else, because his mouth covered hers. His hands spread over her hips, lifting, lowering, until she was fully impaled.

Leah had seldom been in the dominant position, but her desire more than compensated for her lack of experience. He guided her at first, moving her up and down in slow, sure strokes, but then he began caressing her breasts and she let instinct be her guide. She heard the quickening of his breathing and increased rhythm. She felt him lower his head and craned upward so he could reach her breasts with his lips. She sensed when he approached his climax and ground herself more tightly against him. And when he cried out in release, she was with him all the way.

When her heartbeat finally slowed she thought she'd be exhausted, but she wasn't. Her body was sated, but her mind had only begun to hunger. She wanted to talk. It was as though a dam had burst, years of holding in thoughts and questions given way now to a steady flow. She was fearing that Garrick would rather sleep, when his voice drifted over her brow.

"I've never had a woman here before."

They'd slipped between the sheets and were snuggled warmly and closely. "I know," she breathed against his chest.

"I've never had much of anyone here before. Another trapper will stop by once in a while. And buyers come for my furs."

"Is that only in the winter?"

"Pretty much so. I can't trap the good stuff after the middle of January."

"The good stuff—fisher, fox and raccoon?"

"Um-hmm."

"Why not after the middle of January?"

"That's the law, and it makes sense. The furs are thickest in winter, and prime fur draws the best price. But that's secondary to the concept of wildlife management."

"Explain."

"The theory is that hunting and trapping shouldn't be done to exploit the wildlife population, but to control it. Raccoon threaten local cornfields. Beaver threaten the free flow of streams."

"You don't have to justify what you do."

"But it's all part of the explanation. Trapping isn't a free-for-all. At the beginning of each season, the Fish and Game Department issues strict guidelines, in some cases limiting the catch of certain species. For example, I can take only three fisher a year. With roughly eight hundred trappers in the state, three fisher per trapper, the number adds up. If limits aren't set, the population will be endangered."

"How are limits set?"

"The department decides based on information it gets from trappers the previous year. Every catch I make has to be tagged. I tell the department where and when I made the catch, what condition the animal was in and what I observed about the overall population while I was running my trapline."

"Then the limits vary by year?"

"Theoretically, yes. But in the past few years the various populations have been stable, which means that the department has been doing its job right. Once in a while there's politicking involved. For example, fisher feed on turkeys and rabbits. The turkey and rabbit hunters lobby for a higher take of fisher, so that there will be more turkeys and rabbits left for them to hunt."

"Do they win?"

"No. At one point, in the early thirties, fisher were hunted nearly to extinction. The department is very protective of them now."

"But why the January deadline?"

"Because come February, the mating season begins. Trapping after that would be a double hazard to the population."

"Then you trap only three months a year?"

"I can take beaver through the end of March and coyote whenever I want. But the first I use mainly for bait, and the second don't interest me other than to keep them away from my traps. They'll eat the best of my catch if I let them. And they're smart, coyotes are. Trap a coyote in one place, and the rest don't go near that spot again."

Leah loved hearing him talk, not only for his low, husky voice, almost a murmur as they lay twined together, but for his knowledge, as well. "It must be an art—successful trapping."

"Part art, part science. It's hard work, even for those few short months."

"A little more complicated than sticking a spigot in a tree, hmm?"

He chuckled. "A little. The work starts well before

the trapping season opens. I have to get a license, plus written permission from any private landowners whose land I may be crossing. I have to prepare the traps— season new ones, repair and prime old ones. Once the season opens and I've set my traps, I have to run the line every morning."

"Every morning?"

"Early every morning."

"You don't mind that?"

"Nah. I like it." He never used to like getting up. When he'd worked in L.A., he'd hated early morning calls. More often than not he'd been partying late the night before, and particularly in the later years, he'd awoken hung over. There were no parties here, though, and no drinks. He had no trouble waking up. Indeed, he'd discovered that the post-dawn hours were peaceful and productive.

"Why early in the morning?"

"Because most of the furbearers are nocturnal, which means that they'll be out foraging, hence caught at night. I want to collect them as soon as possible after they step into the trap."

"Why?"

He laughed. It occurred to him that he'd laughed more in the past few hours than he had in weeks.

"What's so funny?"

He hugged her closer. "You. Your curiosity. It never quits."

"But it's interesting, what you do. Do you mind my questions?"

"No. I don't mind your questions." And he meant it, which surprised him almost as much as the sound of his own repeated laughter. The past four years of his life had been dominated by silence. He'd needed it at first, because he hadn't been fit to carry on any conversation, much less one with a woman. He'd spoken only when necessary, and then with locals who'd been blessedly laconic. Even the old man who'd taught him to trap had been a miser where words were concerned, and that had suited Garrick just fine. He welcomed words that held real meaning, rather than shallow platitudes. He'd had his fill of the latter—sweet talk meant to impress, crude talk meant to hurt, idle talk meant to pass the time, patronizing talk meant to buy or win.

He'd never had the kind of gentle, innocently genuine talk that he now shared with Leah, and he wasn't sure he'd ever get his fill. Unusual as it was to discuss trapping in the dark after lovemaking, he was enjoying it.

"Why do I want to collect my catch as soon as possible? Because if I wait, the fox may close in or the fur may be otherwise damaged. Once I've made the catch, I try to concentrate on the art of preparing the fur."

"There's an art to it?"

"Definitely. For example, when it comes to fleshing…" He hesitated. "You don't need to hear this."

"Okay," she said so quickly that he chuckled again, but she was immediately off on a related tangent. "So the trapping season is pretty short. What do you do during the rest of the year?"

"Read. Whittle. Go birding in the woods. Grow vegetables."

She popped up over him. "Vegetables? Where?"

"Out back."

"What's out back? There aren't any windows on that wall so I haven't been able to see."

He stroked her cheek with a lazy thumb. "There's a clearing. It's small, but it gets enough sun in the summer months to grow what I need."

"You eat it all?"

"Not all. You can only consume so much lettuce."

"Lettuce. What else?"

"Tomatoes, carrots, zucchini, peas, green beans. I freeze a lot of stuff for the winter months. Whatever is left over, I give away. Or trade. The maple syrup we had with the pancakes came that way."

"Not bad," she said. Her hands were splayed over his chest. Dipping her head, she dropped an impulsive kiss on the hollow of his throat. "Actually, I'm in awe. I have a brown thumb. Plants die on me right and left. I finally gave up trying to grow them, which I suppose is just as well. If I'd been attached to a plant and then had to give it away when I packed up to come here—"

"You could have brought it."

"It's a good thing I didn't. I mean, here I am with most of my stuff still in the car in the cold. Victoria's place is worthless, and I have no idea where I'll be going—"

Garrick cut off the flow of her words by flipping her onto her back and sealing her mouth with his. He didn't want her to talk about going anywhere. He didn't want her to *think* about going anywhere. He wanted her to love him again.

Leah needed little urging. The weight of his body covering her, pressing her to the mattress, branding her with blatant masculinity was enough to spark fires that she'd thought long since banked. They kissed again and again. They began to touch and explore with even greater boldness than before. Lines and curves that should have been familiar by now took on newness from different angles, heightening the fever that rose between them until, once again, they came together in the ultimate stroke of passion.

This time, when it was over and they'd fallen languidly into each other's arms, they lay quietly.

After a bit Leah whispered, "Garrick?"

"Hmm?"

"I've never done this before."

"Hmm?"

"Three times in one night. I never thought I had it in me. I never wanted to…more than once."

"Know something?" he returned in the same whisper. "Me, neither."

"Really?"

"Really." Strange, but he was proud to say it. How often he'd lied in the past, how many times he'd bragged about nonstop bouts of sex. He'd had an image to uphold, but it had been an empty one. If a woman had asked for more, he'd always had a ready answer; either she'd worn him out, or the woman the night before had worn him out, or he had an early call in the morning. The fact was that once his initial lust had been fed he'd lost interest.

But it wasn't lust he felt for Leah. Well, maybe a little, but there was love in it, too, and that made all the difference.

"How long have you been here, Garrick?"

"Four years."

"And you went places when you felt the need…the urge to…"

"I haven't felt it much, but there were women I could see."

"Were they nice?"

"They were okay."

"Do you still see any of them?"

"No. One-night stands were about all I could handle."

"Why?"

Again she'd given him an opening. He could easily explain that he'd been going through a rough time, finding himself, but then she'd ask more questions, and he didn't want to have to answer them. Not tonight. So he gave an answer that was honest, if simplified. "None of them made me want anything more."

"Oh."

"What does that mean—oh?"

"Are you gonna kick me out tomorrow?"

"I can't. Remember, the mud?"

She scraped the nail of her big toe against his shin. "If it weren't for the mud, would you kick me out?"

"We've already had more than a one-night stand."

"You're not answering my question."

"How can I kick you out? You have nowhere to go."

"Garrick…"

His elbow tightened around her neck. "No, Leah, I would not kick you out. I will not kick you out. I like having you here. You can stay as long as you want."

"Because I'm good in bed?"

"Yes."

"Garrick!"

"Because I like being *with* you. How's that?"

"Better."

"You want more?"

"Yes."

"Because you do things for my sweater that I never did."

"I thought you wanted it back."

"I want you to keep it. Wear it."

"Okay."

"And you can cook if you want."

"But you hate Chinese food."

"I didn't hate what you made tonight. I was just being

difficult." He paused, then ventured more cautiously. "Do you do anything besides Chinese?"

"I've taken courses in French cooking. And Indian. I doubt you have the ingredients for either of those."

"Do you always cook foreign for yourself in New York?"

"Oh, no."

"What do you normally eat?"

"When I'm not pigging out with Victoria?"

"Come to think of it, you do eat a lot. How do you stay so thin?"

"Lean Cuisines."

"Excuse me?"

"Lean Cuisines. They're frozen. I heat them in the microwave."

"You eat *frozen dinners?*"

"Sure. They're good. A little too much sodium, but otherwise they provide a balanced meal."

"Oh. If you say so."

She yawned. "I do."

"Tired?"

"A little. What time is it?"

"I don't know. I don't have a watch."

She held her wrist before his nose. "I don't have my glasses. What time does it say?"

"Twenty past a freckle."

"Oh." She dropped her hand to his chest. "I left my watch in the bathroom."

"That's okay. The fire's gone out, so I wouldn't have been able to read it anyway."

"It has a luminous dial."

"You come prepared."

"Usually." She burrowed closer, stifling another

yawn. "I don't want to go to sleep. I like talking with you."

"Me, too."

"Will we talk more in the morning, or are you going to go mute on me with the break of day?"

He chuckled. "We'll talk more."

"Promise?"

"Scout's honor."

"Were you a Scout?"

"Once upon a time."

"I WANT TO hear about it," she murmured, but she was fading fast.

"You will."

"Garrick?"

"Mmm?"

It was a while before she answered and then her words were slurred. "How old are you?"

"Forty." He waited for her to say something more. When she didn't, he whispered her name. She didn't answer. Smiling, he pressed a soft kiss to her rumpled bangs.

CHAPTER SIX

WHEN LEAH AWOKE the next morning, Garrick was beside her. He was sprawled on his stomach, his head facing away, but one of his ankles was hooked around hers in a warm reminder of the events of the night before. Heart swelling with happiness, she took a deep breath and stretched. Then she rolled against him, slipped a slender arm over his waist and sighed contentedly.

Weak slivers of light filtered through the shutters, dimly illuminating the room. It was still raining, she knew, but the patter on the roof had eased to a gentle tap, and anyway, she didn't care what the weather was. Garrick had said she could stay as long as she wanted. She wasn't going to think about leaving.

When the body against her shifted, she slid her hand forward, up over his middle to his chest. His own covered it, and then he was turning to look at her.

It was the very first time in his life that Garrick had awoken pleased to find a woman in his bed. He smiled. "Hi."

Oh, how she loved his voice, even that lone word, working like fine sandpaper to make her tingle. "Hi."

"How did you sleep?"

"Like a baby."

"You don't look like a baby." His gaze was roaming her face, taking in the luster of mussed hair on her forehead, the luminous gray of her eyes, the softness of lips that had been well kissed not so very long ago. "You look sexy."

She blushed. "So do you."

His eyes skimmed lower, over her neck to her breasts. "I've never seen you in daylight," he said softly.

"You have."

"Not nude." Very gently he eased back the covers, allowing himself a full view of her body. His gaze touched her waist, the visible line of her pelvis and the length of her legs before returning to linger on the shadowed apex of her thighs. "You're lovely."

Leah was trembling, but not only because of the way he was looking and the sensual sound of his voice. When he'd pulled back the covers he'd bared himself, as well, and what she saw was breathtaking. With his tapering torso, his lean hips and tightly muscled legs, he was a great subject for a sculptor. But it was his sex that held her spellbound, for it was perfectly formed, incredibly full and heavy.

"I do want you," he whispered. "I think I've been like this all night, dreaming of you."

"You don't have to dream," she breathed. "I'm here."

"So hard to believe…" Shifting so that he crouched over her, he let his hands drift over each part of her in turn. When he reached her belly, he sat back on his haunches, then watched his fingers lower to brush the dark tangle of curls. He stroked her lightly, but even that light touch spread heat like wildfire through her veins.

"Garrick…"

"Warm and beautiful."

"I need you…"

His eyes met hers, and there was an intensity in them that held more than one form of passion. "I want you, too. I want that more than anything."

When she reached for him, he lifted her and crushed her close. They held each other that way for a long time, bodies flush, limbs faintly quivering. Oddly, the desire to make love passed, replaced by the gratification of simply being together. At that moment it seemed much more precious than anything else in the world.

Garrick's arms were the first to slacken. "I need a shower," he said in a voice lingering with emotion. "Want to share?"

"I've never taken a shower with a man before."

"Never?"

"Never."

"Are you game?"

"If you are. It's a large shower."

"I'm a large man."

"Which means—"

"We'll be close."

"I'd like that."

"Me, too." Scooping her into his arms, he rolled to the edge of the bed. "Come on."

"I can walk."

"The floor's cold."

"You're walking."

"Would you rather switch places?"

"You're too heavy."

"Then hush."

When he reached the bathroom, he lowered her feet to the floor, turned to start the water, then knelt before her and very gently removed the bandage from her leg. She'd given up on gauze and adhesive the day before in favor of a Band-Aid, and the only discomfort she still felt was from the black-and-blue area surrounding the cut.

"Looks okay," he decided, then slid his gaze leisurely up her body. "I like the rest better, though."

She finger-combed his hair back from his forehead. "I'm glad."

After pressing a soft kiss on her navel, he stood and led her into the shower. They soaped themselves and then, for the hell of it, each other. And it *was* hell in some ways, because the glide of suds beneath palms over various bodily areas was erotic, but they didn't want to make love. Resisting the temptation was in part a game, in part a way of saying that there was more to their relationship than sex.

Touching was totally acceptable, and they did it constantly. It astounded Leah that two people who'd been alone for so long could adapt so easily to such closeness. Or maybe it was *because* they'd been alone that they were greedy. Either way, they never strayed far from each other. They watched each other dress—chipping in to help here and there with a button or a sock. Likewise, they chipped in making breakfast, then ate with their legs entwined under the table.

And they talked—constantly and about anything that came to mind.

"I love your hair," Garrick said. He'd settled her onto his lap when she'd come around to clear his plate. "Have you always worn it this way?"

"No. I had it cut the day my divorce became final."

"Celebrating?"

"Declaring my independence. When I was little I always wore my hair long. My mother loved combing it and curling it and tying it up with ribbons. Richard liked it long, too. It was part of the image. He thought long hair was alluring. Y'know," she drawled, "waving tresses sweeping over sequined shoulders." Her voice returned to its normal timbre. "Sometimes he'd have me wear it up, sometimes hitched back with a fancy comb. I used to have to spend hours getting it to look just right. I hated it."

"So you cut it."

"Yup."

He stroked the silky strands. "It's so pretty this way."

"It's easy."

"Then pretty *and* easy." He scalloped a gentle thumb through her bangs. "Did you like going out?"

"Where?"

"To parties, restaurants."

"With Richard? No. And I still don't like parties, but maybe that's because I feel awkward."

"Why would you feel awkward?" he asked in the same gravelly voice she found so soothing. It eased her over the embarrassment of expressing particular thoughts.

"I've never been a social butterfly. I was shy."

"Shy? Really?"

Smiling, she wrapped her arms around his neck and nuzzled his hair. "Really."

"Why shy?"

Sitting back, she shrugged. "I don't know. I was an English major, a bookworm, an…intellectual. I suppose one of the things that snowed me about Richard was that he was good with people in a way I wasn't. I could go places with him and be part of the crowd in a way I'd never been."

"Did you like that?"

"I thought I would, and I did at first. Then I realized that I wasn't really part of the crowd. *He* was, but I wasn't. I was just along for the ride, but the ride wasn't fun. The people were boring. I didn't have much to say to them. Richard was always after me to be more pleasant, and I could be charming when I tried, but under the circumstances, I hated it. The whole thing came to be uncomfortable."

He eased her to her feet and reached for the plates. "I can understand that."

Leah didn't have to ask him if he agreed, because she knew he did. If he liked crowds and parties and small talk, he'd never have chosen to live alone in the woods. As they began to load the dishwasher, it occurred to her to ask why he'd chosen to live this way. Instead she asked, "Why are you studying Latin?"

"Because it's interesting. So many of our words have Latin derivatives."

"You didn't study it as a kid?"

"Nope. I studied Spanish. My mom was a Spanish professor."

"No kidding!"

"No kidding." The way he said it—part drawl, part resignation—suggested more to the story. This particular chapter didn't threaten Leah.

"Oh-oh. It wasn't great?"

"She was very involved in her work. When she wasn't teaching, she was traveling to one Spanish-speaking area or another, and when she wasn't doing that, she was entertaining students at our house."

"You didn't like that?"

"I would have liked a little of her attention myself."

"What about your father? What did he do?"

"He was a gastroenterologist."

"And very busy."

"Uh-huh."

"You were alone a lot."

"Uh-huh."

"Do you have any brothers or sisters?"

He shook his head and handed her the pan he'd just washed. "How about you?"

"I was an only, too. But my parents doted on me. Isn't it strange that we should have had such different experiences? Perhaps if we'd been able to put our four parents in a barrel and shake them up, we'd each have had a little more of what we needed."

He chuckled, but it was a sad sound. "If only."

When they finished cleaning the kitchen, Garrick made a fire, then sat on the floor with his back against the sofa and pulled Leah between his legs. She nestled into the haven, crossing her arms over those stronger, more manly ones that wound around her middle.

"Have you always worn glasses?" he asked, his breath warm by her ear.

"From the time I was twelve. I wore contacts for Richard, but I never really liked them."

"Why not?"

"It was a pain—putting them in every morning, taking them out and cleaning them every night, enzyming them once a week. Besides, nearsightedness is *me*. On principle alone, I don't see why I should have to hide it."

"You look adorable with glasses."

Smiling, she offered a soft, "Thank you." Her smile lingered for a long time. "This is…so…nice," she whispered at last. "I feel so peaceful." She tipped her head back to see his face. "Is that what you feel living up here?"

"More so since you've come."

"But before. Is it the peace that appeals to you?"

"It's lots of things. Peace, yes. Lack of hassle. I work hard enough, but at my own speed."

Implicit was the suggestion that he'd known some-

thing very different four years before. Again she had
an opportunity to probe that past. Again she let it slide.
Returning her gaze to the fire, she asked, "Do you ever
get bored?"

"No. There's always something to do."

"When did you learn to whittle?"

"Soon after I came."

"Did the trapper teach you?"

"I taught myself. One good instruction book, and I
was on my way."

"What do you make?"

"Whatever strikes me. Mostly carvings of animals
I see in the woods."

"I don't see any here. Don't you keep them?"

"Some." They were out in the shed, which he'd come
to think of as a sort of studio-gallery. "I give some
away. I sell some."

"Do you?" she asked, grinning widely. "You must
be good."

"Yes to the first, I don't know to the second."

"If people buy them…" she said in a tone that made
her point. "Have you always been artistic?" Images of
the artists Richard employed crossed her mind. There
was a high burnout rate in the advertising world. Perhaps that was what had happened to Garrick.

But he was shaking his head, his chin ruffling her
hair. "Not particularly. It was only after I came here that
I found I liked working with my hands."

"You're very good with your hands," she teased, and
was rewarded with a tickle. "Anyway, I think it's great.
Do you have to use special kinds of wood when you
whittle?"

"Soft wood is best—like white pine. It has few

knots and very little grain. I use harder wood—birch or maple—when I carve chessmen."

"You make *chess* sets?"

He nodded. "Do you play?"

"No, but I've always admired beautiful sets in store windows. More than once, I thought of buying one just to use it for decoration on a coffee table, but somehow that seemed pretentious. I play checkers, though. Have you ever carved a checker set?"

"Not yet, but I can. God, I haven't played checkers since I was a kid!"

"It'd be fun," she mused. "What about knives?"

"I never played with them."

"Whittling. Do you have special knives? The thing you were using the other night looked like a regular old jackknife."

"It was."

Again she tipped back her head, this time looking up at him in surprise. "A regular old jackknife?"

"Carefully sharpened. It has three blades. I use the largest for rough cutting and the two smaller ones for close work."

She was staring at him, fascinated. "You have beautiful eyes. I don't think I've ever seen hazel shot with silver like that."

The suddenness of the comment took Garrick off guard. It was the type of observation he was used to from his past, yet now it was different. As it sank in, he felt a warming all over. He liked it when Leah complimented him, didn't even mind that she'd been distracted from what he'd been saying. Strange that she didn't recognize him...

"Do you ever watch television?" he asked.

"Rarely. Why?"

"I was just wondering…whether you missed it up here."

"No," she answered, turning her head forward, "and I don't miss a phone, either."

"Didn't use it much at home?"

"Yes."

"Then why don't you miss it now?"

"Because in New York it's a necessity. You have to call to find out whether the book you ordered arrived or to make a reservation at a restaurant. You have to call a friend in advance to make a date for lunch. Up here you don't."

"Did you leave many friends in New York?"

"A few. It's only since my divorce that I've been able to cultivate friendships. Richard wasn't interested in the people I liked."

"Why not?"

"He didn't think they were useful enough."

"Ahh, he's the user type."

"He didn't step on people. He simply avoided those with whom he couldn't clearly identify. He had to feel that there was a purpose in any and every social contact. Getting together with someone simply because you liked him or her didn't qualify as purposeful in Richard's mind."

Garrick was about to say something critical, when he caught himself. He'd been guilty of the same thing once, only it sounded as though Richard had weathered it better. So who was he to throw stones?

Shifting Leah so that she was cradled sideways on his lap, he asked softly, "What are your friends like?"

Arms looped loosely around his neck, she brushed her thumb against his beard. "Victoria you know. Then

there's Greta. We met at a cooking class. She has a phenomenal mathematical mind."

"What does she do?"

"She's an accountant."

"Do you see each other often?"

"Once every few weeks."

"What do you do together?"

"Shop."

"*Shop?* That's the last thing I'd expect an accountant to want to do."

"She doesn't want to. She *has* to. She's in a large
firm that makes certain demands, one of which is that
she look reasonably well put together. Poor Greta is the
first to admit she has no taste at all when it comes to
clothes. When we go shopping, I help her choose things,
soup to nuts." She grinned. "I'm great at spending other
people's money."

"That's naughty."

"Not when it's at their own request and for their
own good."

"Is Greta pleased with the results?"

"Definitely."

"Then I guess it's okay. Who are some of your other
friends?"

"There's Arlen."

"Is that a he or a she?"

"A she. I don't have any male friends. Except you."
She plopped a wet kiss on his cheek. "You're a nice
man."

"That's what you say now," he teased. "Wait till you
know me better." He'd been thinking about cabin fever,
about what could happen to two people, however compatible, when they were stuck with each other day after
day. He knew it wouldn't bother him; he was used to the

mountain, and he loved Leah. But suddenly he wasn't even thinking about whether Leah loved him back. He was thinking about all he hadn't told her about himself. What he'd said had to have been a Freudian slip.

"I am a nice man," he said seriously. "I wasn't always. But those days are done." He took a quick breath. "Tell me about Arlen."

Leah studied his face a minute longer, unaware of the fear in her eyes. *I wasn't always,* he'd said. What had he been before? Oh, Lord, she didn't want anything to pop her bubble of happiness. Not when she'd waited all her life to find it!

"Arlen." She cleared her throat. "Arlen and I met in the waiting room of the dentist's office. Three years ago, actually." They'd both been pregnant at the time. "We struck up a friendship and kept in touch, then started getting together after Richard and I split. She helped me through some rough times."

"The divorce?"

That, too. "Yes."

"Does she work?"

"Like a dog. She has five kids under the age of eight."

"Whew. She isn't a single mother, is she?"

"No, and her husband's as lovely as she is. They live in Port Washington. I've been to their home several times. She barbecues a mean hot dog."

He grinned. "You like hot dogs?"

"Yeah, but y'know which ones I like best?"

"No. Which ones?"

"You'll think I'm crazy."

"Which ones?"

"The ones you buy at the stands on the edge of Central Park. There's something about the atmosphere—"

"Diesel fumes, horse dung and pigeon shit."

She jabbed at his chest with a playful fist. "You're polluting the image! Think gorgeous spring day when the leaves are just coming into bloom, or hot summer day when the park is an oasis in the middle of the city. Brisk fall day when the leaves flutter to the ground. There's something about visiting the park on days like those and eating a hot dog that may very well kill you that's…that's sybaritic."

"Sybaritic?"

"Well, maybe not sybaritic. How about frivolous?"

"I can live with that." He could also come close to duplicating a sybaritic kind of atmosphere for her here on the mountain. "What else do you like about New York?"

"The anonymity. I feel threatened by large groups that know me and expect certain things that I may or may not be able to deliver. I don't like to have to conform to other people's standards."

He knew that what she was voicing related in part to the shyness she'd mentioned, but that it was a legacy of her marriage to Richard, as well. He was also stunned because the threat was one he himself felt.

"I'm a total unknown on the streets of New York," she went on. "I can pick and choose my friends and do my own thing without being censured. I think I'd die in a small suburban community. I don't want to have to keep up with the Joneses."

"If anyone's doing the keeping up, it should be the Joneses with you."

"God forbid. I don't want any *part* of people who compete their way through life."

"Amen," he said softly, then, "What else?"

"What else, what?"

"What else do you like about New York?"

She didn't have to think long. "The cultural opportunities. And the courses. I love taking courses, learning new things. Victoria said that there was an artists' community not far from here where I'd be able to learn to weave."

"I know just the one. You want to weave?"

"The process fascinates me. I'd like to be able to create my own patterns and make scarves and rugs and beautiful wall hangings." She lowered suddenly sheepish eyes to her fingers, which toyed idly with the cables on his sweater. "At least, I'd like to try."

"You'll do it." He'd build her a loom himself. The thought of seeing her working it, of listening to the rhythmic shift of harnesses, filled him with a mellowness that spelled home.

Home. Surprising. He hadn't spent much time thinking of having a home. What he'd known as a child had been far from ideal, and when he'd gone off to put his name up in lights, he hadn't had the time to think of it. His world had been the public eye. His interests had revolved around things that would make him more famous. A home didn't do those things. A home was personal, private. It was something for a man and his family.

"Garrick?" Leah whispered.

He blinked, only then realizing that his eyes had grown moist.

"What is it?" Her voice was laden with concern, her eyes with fear. During moments like these, when he looked so sad and faraway, she felt her bubble begin to quiver. He had a past, and for whatever his reasons, he wasn't telling her about it. She didn't have the courage to ask.

He forced a tremulous smile, then drew her in and

held her close. "I get to dreaming sometimes," he murmured into her hair. "It's scary."

"Can you share the dream?"

"Not yet."

"Maybe someday soon?"

"Maybe."

They sat that way for a while, holding each other quietly. When the fire gave a loud crack and hiss, they both looked around, startled.

"Is it trying to tell us something?" Leah whispered.

"Nah. It's just being insolent."

"Maybe we'd better feed it."

"I have a better idea. Why don't we get dressed and go out?"

Her eyes lit up. "Me, too?"

"You, too." He tipped his head. "Going stir-crazy being inside?"

"No. I just don't want you going out alone. I want to be with you."

"God, you have all the right answers," he breathed.

Her voice held a touch of sadness. "No. Not yet. Maybe soon."

So THEY WENT out in the rain, which, mercifully, was more like a drizzle. Garrick led her up the mountain, pointing out various signs of wildlife along the way. The going was sloppy, but in broad daylight and with as indulgent a guide as he was, Leah managed remarkably well. She wasn't quite sure how it happened, but the mountain that had seemed so hostile to her once was now, even in the wet mist, a place of fascination. Garrick belonged, and she was his welcome guest; it was almost as though the landscape had accepted her presence.

After they'd returned to the lower altitude, they trekked to Leah's car and came back carrying more of her things, which he enthusiastically made room for in the cabin and helped her stow.

Later in the day, they succumbed to their urges and made long, sweet love before the fire. In its aftermath, wrapped in each other and a quilt, Leah smiled. "I wonder if Victoria has ESP."

"If so, no doubt she's happy."

"Are you?"

"Very."

She tipped up her face and whispered, "I love you, Garrick."

His eyes went soft and moist. Taking a tremulous breath, he tightened his arms around her. "I love you, too. I've never said that to another living soul, but I do love you, Leah. God, do I love you!" His lips took hers with a fierceness that had never been there before, but Leah didn't mind, because she shared the feeling behind them. The love that flooded her was so powerful that it demanded no less ardent a release.

IN THE DAYS that followed, their love grew even stronger. They spent every minute together, and never once did they tire of each other's company. There was always something to say, usually in soft, intimate tones, but there were times when they were silent, communicating simply with a look, a touch or a smile.

Garrick showed her his shed and the whittled figures that sat on a long shelf. Not only did he carve them, she found, but many he painted in colors that were true to life. She particularly adored a pair of Canada geese and cajoled him into letting her take them back to the cabin.

He also showed her the toothpick models he built,

explaining how he'd started making them for his own amusement. But one of his fur buyers had mentioned them to a couple from Boston, who then wanted a model made of their own stately home. The commission had launched Garrick into a leisurely business.

Leah thought his models were exquisite, particularly those dramatic designs he'd made for himself, on which he'd let his imagination go wild. "You could be an architect," she said, awed by the scope of that imagination and the detail he'd achieved with as unlikely materials as toothpicks.

He was pleased with her comment, but said nothing. He couldn't be an architect. He didn't have the training, for one thing, and for another, to get either that training or employment, he'd have to return to the city. The city—any city—was a threat to him. He'd be recognized. He'd be approached. He'd be tempted.

But he didn't tell Leah that. The words wouldn't seem to come. She loved him for who and what he was right now. He didn't want to disillusion her. He didn't want her to know what a mess he'd made of his earlier life. He feared that she'd think less of him, and the thought of losing her respect or, worse, her love, was more terrifying than anything.

But it bothered him that he didn't tell her the truth. Oh, he'd never lied. He'd simply ignored those seventeen years of his life as though they'd never been. That Leah hadn't asked puzzled him in some ways. They shared so many other thoughts and feelings. He suspected that she knew he harbored a dark secret and that she was afraid to ask for the same reason he was afraid to reveal it.

Perhaps because of that, neither spoke of the future. They took life one day at a time, treating their love as a precious gift that neither of them had expected to receive.

With her dictionary and thesauruses, an atlas and a world almanac on hand, Leah began to work. The peaceful setting was conducive to production, even in spite of the spate of questions Garrick bombarded her with at first.

"Where do you start?"

"On a puzzle? Wherever I want. If it's a theme puzzle—"

"Define theme puzzle."

"One in which the longer entries have to do with a specific topic."

"Like phrases depicting madness—having bats in one's belfry, etc.?"

She grinned, remembering that particular inspiration as he did. "Or names of baseball teams, or automobile models, or parts of the body."

"Oh?"

"Nothing naughty, of course. Once I did a puzzle using phrases like 'keep an eye on the ball,' 'put one's best foot forward,' 'give a hand to a friend'—that type of thing would be part of a theme puzzle."

"So you start with the theme?"

"Uh-huh, and I work from there."

He sat for a few minutes, silently watching her add words to her puzzle before he spoke again. "Do you follow a special formula regarding numbers of black and white spaces?"

She shook her head. "It can vary. The same holds true for checked and unchecked letters."

"Checked and unchecked?"

"Checked letters are ones that contribute to both an across and a down word, unchecked to only one or the other. In the earliest puzzles every letter was checked. If you got all the across clues, you had the puzzle completed."

"Too easy."

"Right. Nowadays, as a general rule of thumb, only fifty-five to seventy-five percent of the letters should be checked."

He digested that, then a bit later asked, "How about clues? Do you spend a lot of time finding them and revising them?"

"You bet. Again times have changed. It used to be that primary definitions were used. For example, the clue for 'nest' would be 'a bird's home.' In recent years, I've seen clues ranging from 'a place to feather' to 'grackle shack.' Actually," she added sheepishly, "my editor is a wonder when it comes to clever clues. I have no problem with her revisions."

"Do you ever have problems with deadlines?" Garrick asked, somewhat sheepish himself now. "I'm not letting you get much work done."

"I don't mind," she said, and meant every word.

In truth, as the days passed, Leah wondered if she was dreaming. Garrick was everything she'd ever wanted in a man. He was patient when she was working, attentive when she wasn't. He was interesting, always ready to discuss whatever topic crossed either of their minds. Even in cases of disagreement, the discussion was intelligent and ended with smiles. He was perceptive, suggesting they go out or make dinner or play checkers with the set he'd carved, just when she needed a break. He was positively gorgeous, tall and rangy, rugged with his full head of hair and his trimmed beard, compelling with his hazel-and-silver eyes. And he was sexy. So sexy. He turned her on with a look, a

word, a move, and made love to her with passion, sometimes gently, sometimes fiercely, always with devotion.

The only thing to mar her happiness was the frown
that crossed his face at odd moments, moments that became more frequent as the days passed.

Five days became a week, then ten days, twelve, two
weeks. Garrick knew he had to tell her who he was.
His fear remained, but the need for confession grew
greater. He wanted her to know everything and to love
him anyway. He wanted her to respect him for the way
he'd rebuilt his life. He wanted—needed—to share past
pain and present fear, wanted her understanding and
support and strength.

Once, when the rain had stopped, he took her for
a walk, intending to bare his soul while they were on
the mountain. Then they caught sight of a doe and her
fawn, and he didn't have the heart to spoil the scene.

Another time he led her off the mountain and they
hitched a ride to town. He planned to confess all while
they were splurging on lunch at the small restaurant
there, but Leah was so enchanted by the charm of the
place that he lost his nerve.

And then she insisted on calling Victoria. "I told
her I'd give her a ring when I was settled. She may be
worrying."

"Yeah, about whether you'll speak to her again after
what she did."

"It didn't end up so terribly, did it?"

He grinned. "Nope. But maybe we ought to keep
Victoria in suspense."

That was exactly what Leah did. From a pay phone
inside the small general store, she dialed Victoria's number.

A very proper maid answered. "Lesser residence."

"This is Leah Gates. Is Mrs. Lesser in?"

"Please hold the phone."

Leah covered the mouthpiece and grinned at Garrick, who was practically on top of her, boxing her into the booth. "Can't you just picture Victoria? She's probably wearing an oversize work shirt and jeans, looking like a waif as she breezes round and about her elegant furnishings to reach the phone. I wonder what she's been doing. Playing the lute? Preparing sushi?" She removed her hand from the mouthpiece when Victoria's excited voice came on the other end.

"Where have you been?"

"Hi, Victoria."

"Leah Gates! I've been worried sick!"

Leah's eyes sparkled toward Garrick. "You shouldn't have worried. I told you I wouldn't have any problem. The cabin is wonderful. I can understand why Arthur loved it up here."

"Leah…"

"It's been a little rainy. That's why I didn't get around to calling sooner. My car is still mud-bound."

There was a pause. "Where are you calling from?"

"The general store."

Another pause. "How did you get there if your car is mud-bound?"

"Hitched a ride."

"Leah!"

Garrick stole the receiver from Leah's hand. "Victoria?"

There was another brief silence on the other end of the line, then a cautious, "Garrick?"

"You play dirty pool."

"Ahh." A sigh. "Thank God. She's with you."

"As you intended."

"Do you hate me?"

"Not now."

"But you did at first. Please, Garrick, I only wanted the best for you both. You were alone. She was alone. I'm sure my letter explained—"

"I haven't read your letter." His eyes held Leah's, while the arm around her waist held her close.

"Why not?"

"I didn't want to."

"You were that angry? I didn't tell her anything about you, Garrick," she rounded defensively, then paused and lowered her voice. "Have you?"

"Some."

"But not…that?"

"No."

"She is staying with you?"

"I couldn't very well turn her out into the rain with nowhere to go," he said, a wink for Leah softening his gruff tone. Of course, Victoria didn't see the wink.

"Oh, Garrick, I'm sorry. I thought for sure you two would get along. You're so *right* for each other."

Garrick covered the mouthpiece and whispered to Leah, "She says we're so right for each other."

"Wise busybody," Leah whispered back, then grabbed the phone. "I won't be sending any rent money, Victoria Lesser."

"But you called. You can't be totally angry."

"I have more of a conscience than you do," Leah said, but she was smiling and Victoria knew it.

"Should I ready the green room for you?"

"Not just yet."

"You'll be staying there awhile?"

Leah didn't bother to cover the phone this time when she spoke to Garrick. Her free hand was drawing lazy circles on the firm muscles of his back. "She wants to know if I'll be staying here for a while."

He took the phone. "She'll be staying. I've discovered that I like having a live-in maid."

"I am *not* his maid," Leah shouted toward the mouthpiece, while Victoria added her own comment.

"Garrick, you are not to use Leah—"

"And a cook," Garrick injected. "She makes super egg foo yong."

"I do not make egg foo yong!" Leah protested, snatching the phone. "He's pulling your leg, Victoria."

Garrick grinned. "Another body phrase. Write it down, Leah."

"Leah, what is he talking about?"

"He's making fun of my cooking and my crossword puzzles. The man is impossible! See what you got me into?"

"Let me speak with Garrick, Leah."

Rather smugly, Leah handed over the phone.

"Garrick?"

"Yes, Victoria."

"Are we alone?"

"Yes."

"I don't want her hurt, Garrick."

"I know that."

"She's been through a lot. It's fine for you both to rib me—I deserve it. But I want you to treat her well, and that means using your judgment. If you'd read my letter, you'd know that she's totally trustworthy—"

"I didn't have to read your letter to learn that."

"If the two of you don't get along, I want her back here."

"We get along."

"Get along well?" Victoria asked hopefully.

"Yes."

"Well enough for a future?"

"I…maybe."

"Then you'll have to tell her, you know."

"I know."

"Will you?"

"Yes."

"If you wait too long, she'll be hurt."

"I know that, Victoria," he said soberly.

"I trust you to do the right thing."

"Yes," he said, then added, "Here's Leah. She wants to say goodbye. Say goodbye, Leah," he teased as he handed her the phone, but inside he was dying.

The right thing. The right thing. He had to tell her. But when?

CHAPTER SEVEN

As IT HAPPENED, the truth spilled without any preplanning on Garrick's part, its disclosure as spontaneous as the rest of their relationship.

Leah had been with him for better than two weeks. On that particular morning they'd slogged through the mud to check on the progress of the beaver dam that had been growing steadily broader over a nearby stream. Later, returning to the cabin, they'd changed into clean, dry clothes and settled before the fire.

Garrick was reading one of the books Leah had brought with her from New York; they'd found they enjoyed discussing books they'd both read. Leah was close beside him on the sofa, her back braced against his arm, the soles of her feet flat against the armrest. She was listening to music, wearing the headset he'd salvaged from his nonfunctional CB and adapted for her cassette. On pure impulse, he set down his book and removed the earphones from her ears.

"Unplug it," he said over her forehead. "Let me hear."

She tipped back her head and met his gaze. "Ah, Garrick, you don't want to do that."

"Sure, I do."

"But you like the quiet."

"I want to hear your music. And besides, I don't like feeling cut off from you."

Turning, she came up on a knee and draped her arms

around his neck. "You're not cut off. I keep the music low. I'd be able to hear you if you spoke."

"I want to hear your music," he insisted, wrapping his arms around her hips. "If you like it, I might like it, too. We have similar tastes."

"You hated the new Ludlum book that I loved."

"But we both agreed that Le Carré's was great."

"You hated that curried chicken we had the other night."

"Because I added too much curry. And don't say you didn't find it hot, because I saw you gulping down water."

"You hated the roadrunner I folded for you."

"I didn't hate it. I just didn't know what it was." He closed his fingers on a handful of her bottom and gritted his teeth in a pretense of anger. "Leah, I want to listen to music. Will you unplug the headset and let me hear?"

"You're sure?"

"I'm *sure*."

Inwardly pleased, she removed the plug to the earphones. As the gentle sounds of guitar and vocalist filled the room, she sat back and watched Garrick's face.

He was smiling softly. "Cat Stevens. This is an old one."

"Seventy-four."

Sinking lower in the sofa, he stretched out his legs before him and listened quietly. He wore an increasingly pensive look, one that seemed to fade in and out, to travel great distances, return, then leave again. Leah knew the songs brought back memories, and when the tape was done, she would have been more than happy to put the machine away.

But he asked her to put on another tape. Again he recognized the song and its artists. "Simon and Garfunkel," he murmured shortly after the first bars had been sung.

"Do you like it?"

He listened a while longer before answering. "I like it. I've never paid much heed to the words before. I always associated songs like this with background music in restaurants."

"Where?" she asked, surprised at how easily the question came out.

"L.A.," he answered, surprised at the ease of his answer. It was time, he realized.

"Were you working there?"

"Yes."

"For long?"

"Seventeen years."

Leah said nothing more, but watched him steadily. When he swiveled his head to look at her, her heart began to thud. His eyes were dark, simultaneously sad, challenging and beseechful.

"I was an actor."

She was sure she'd heard him wrong. "Excuse me?"

"I was an actor."

She swallowed hard. "An actor."

"Yes." His eyes never left hers.

"Movies?" she asked in a small voice.

"Television."

"I...your name doesn't ring a bell."

"I used a stage name."

An actor? Garrick, the man she loved for his private life-style, an *actor?* Surely just occasionally. Perhaps as an extra. "Were you on often?"

"Every week for nine years. Less often before and after."

She swallowed again and twined her arms around

her middle as though to catch her plummeting heart. "You had a major part."

He nodded.

"What's your name?"

"You know it. It's the one I was christened with."

"Your stage name."

"Greg Reynolds."

Leah paled. There wasn't a sound in the cabin; she felt more than heard her bubble of happiness pop. She'd never been a television fan, but she did have eyes. Even had she not had an excellent memory, she'd have been hard-pressed not to recall the name. It had often been splashed across the headlines of tabloids and magazines, glaring up from the stand at the grocery store checkout counter, impossible to miss even in passing.

"It can't be," she said, shaking her head.

"It is."

"I don't recognize you."

"You said you didn't watch television."

"I saw headlines. There must have been pictures."

"I look different now."

She tried to analyze his features, but they seemed to waver. There was the Garrick she knew and…and then the other man. A stranger. Known to the rest of the world, not to her. She loved Garrick. Or was he… "You should have told me sooner."

"I couldn't."

"But…Greg Reynolds?" she cried in horror. "You're a star!"

"Was, Leah. Was a star."

She lowered her head and rubbed her forehead, trying to think, finding it difficult. "The show was…"

"*Pagen's Law.* Cops and robbers. Macho stuff—"

"That millions of people watched every week." She

withered back into her corner of the sofa and murmured dumbly, "An actor. A successful actor."

Garrick was before her in an instant, prying her hands from her waist and enveloping them in his. "I *was* an actor, but that's all over. Now I'm Garrick Rodenhiser—trapper, Latin student, whittler, model maker—the man you love."

She raised stricken eyes to his. "I can't love an actor. I can't survive in the limelight."

He tightened his hold on her hands. "Neither can I, Leah. Greg Reynolds is dead. He doesn't exist anymore. That's why I'm here. Me. Garrick. This is my life—what you see, what you've seen since you've been here."

If anything, she sank deeper into herself. She said nothing, looked blankly to the floor.

"No!" he ordered, lifting her chin with one hand. "I won't let you retreat back into that shell of yours. Talk to me, Leah. Tell me what you're thinking and feeling."

"You were a phenomenal success," she breathed brokenly. "A superstar."

"*Was*. It's over!"

"It can't be!" she cried. "You can't stay away from it forever. They won't *let* you!"

"They don't want me, and even if they did, they don't have any say. It's my choice."

"But you'll *want* to go back—"

"No! It's over, Leah! I will not go back!"

The force of his words startled her, breaking into the momentum of her argument. Her eyes were large gray orbs of anguish behind the lenses of her glasses, but they held an inkling of uncertainty.

"I won't go back," Garrick said more quietly. His hand gentled on her chin, stroking it lightly. "I blew it, Leah. I can't go back."

The anguish wasn't hers alone. She saw in his eyes the pain she'd glimpsed before. It reached out to her, as it had always done, only now she had to ask, "What happened?"

For Garrick, this was the hard part. It was one thing telling her he'd been a success, another telling her how he'd taken success, twisted it, spoiled it, lost it. But he'd come this far. He owed it to Leah—and to himself—to tell it all.

Backing away from her, he stood and crossed stiffly to the window. The sun was shining, but the bleakness inside him blotted out any cheer that might have offered. Tucking his hands into the back of his waistband, he began to speak.

"I went out to the coast soon after I graduated from high school. It seemed the most obvious thing to do at the time. The one thing I wanted more than anything was to be noticed. I think you know why," he added more softly, but refrained from going into further self-analysis. "I had the goods. I was tall and attractive. I had the smarts that some others out there didn't have, and the determination. I just hung around for a while, getting a feel for the place, watching everything, learning who held the power and how to go about tapping it. Then I went to work. First, I talked a top agent into taking me on, then I willingly did whatever he asked me to do. Most of it was garbage—bit parts—but I did them well, and I made sure I was seen by the right people.

"By the time I'd been there three years, I was consistently landing reasonable secondary roles. But I wanted top billing. So I worked harder. I learned pretty quick that it wasn't only how you looked or acted that counted. Politics counted, too. Dirty politics. And I played the game better than the next guy. I kissed ass when I had to, slept around when I had to. I rationalized it all by saying that it was a means to an end, and I suppose it was.

"Five years after I arrived, I was picked to play Pagen." He lifted one shoulder in a negligent shrug. "Don't ask me why the show took off the way it did. Looking back on it, I can't see that it was spectacular. But it hit a vein with the public, and that meant money for the sponsors, the network, the producers, the directors and me. So we kept going and going, and in time I believed my own press. I convinced myself that the show was phenomenal and that it was phenomenal because of me."

He hung his head and took a shuddering breath. "That was my first mistake. No, I take that back. My first mistake was in ever going to Hollywood, because it wasn't my kind of place at all. Oh, I told myself it was, and that was my second mistake. My third mistake was in believing that I'd earned and deserved the success. After that the mistakes piled up, one after another, until I was so mired I didn't know which side was up."

He paused for a minute and risked a glance over his shoulder. Leah was in the corner of the sofa, her knees drawn up, her arms hugging her body. Her face seemed frozen in a stricken expression. He wanted to go down on his knees before her and beg forgiveness for who he'd been, but he knew that there was more he had to say first.

He turned to face her fully, but he didn't move from the window. "The show ran for nine years, and during that time I flared progressively out of control. I grew more and more arrogant, more difficult to deal with." His tone grew derisive. "I was the star, better than any of the others. I was the hottest thing to hit Hollywood in decades. What I touched turned to gold. My name alone could make the show—any show—a success.

"And there were other shows. After five years in the top ten with *Pagen,* I started making movies during the series' filming break. I fought it at first. I didn't know why at the time. Now I realize that something inside me was telling me that it was too much, that I needed a break from the rat race for a couple of months a year. That I needed to touch base for a short time with who I really was. But then I got greedy. I wanted to be more famous, and *more* famous. I wanted to become an indelible fixture in the entertainment world. I wanted to be a legend."

He sighed and bent his head, rubbing his neck with harsh fingers in an anger directed at himself. "I was running scared. That's really what it was all about. I was terrified that if I didn't grab it all while I had the chance, someone would come along and take it from me. But I wasn't all that good. Oh, I was Pagen, all right. I could play that part because it didn't take a hell of a lot of acting. Some of the other stuff—the movies—did, and I couldn't cut the mustard. None of them were box office hits, and that made me more nervous. Only instead of being sensible, taking stock and plotting a viable future for myself, I fought it. I berated the critics in public. I announced that the taste of the average moviegoer sucked. I got worse and worse on the set."

He looked at her then. "I was paranoid. I became convinced that everyone was waiting for me to fail, that they were stalking me, waiting to pounce and pick the flesh from my bones. I was miserable, so I began to drink. When that didn't help, I snorted coke, took whatever drugs I could get my hands on—anything that would blot out the unhappiness. All I succeeded in blotting out was reality, and in the entertainment world, reality means extraordinary highs and excruciating lows."

Taking a shuddering breath, he sighed. "*Pagen's Law* was canceled after a nine-year run, mostly because I'd become so erratic. The producers couldn't find directors willing to deal with me. They even had trouble gathering crews, because I was so impatient and demanding and critical that it just wasn't worth it. More often than not I'd show up on the set drunk or hung over, or I'd be so high on something else that I couldn't focus on the script. When that happened, I'd blame everyone in sight."

Very slowly he began to walk toward the sofa. His hands hung by his sides and his broad shoulders were slumped, but the desolation he felt was such that he simply needed to be near Leah. "It was downhill all the way from there. There were small parts after the series ended, but they came fewer and farther between. No one wanted to work with me, and I can't blame them. New shows took over where *Pagen* left off. New stars. The king was dead. Long live the king."

Very carefully he lowered himself to the sofa. His hands fell open, palms up in defeat, perhaps supplication, on his thighs. "In the end, I had no friends, no work. I was a pariah, and I had no one to blame but myself." He looked down at his hands and pushed his lips out. "I'd gotten so obsessed with the idea of being a star that I couldn't see any future if I didn't have that. So one day when I was totally stoned, I took my Ferrari and drove madly through the hills. I lost control on a turn and went over an embankment. The last thing I remember thinking was thank God it's over."

Leah's sharp intake of breath brought his gaze to hers. Her hands were pressed to her lips and her eyes were brimming with tears. He started to reach out, then drew back his hand. He needed to touch her, but he didn't know if he had the right. He was feeling as low, as worthless, as he'd felt when he'd awoken in that hospital after the accident.

"But it wasn't over," he said brokenly. "For some reason, I was spared. The doctors said that if I hadn't been so out of it, I'd have been more seriously hurt. I was loose as a goose when I was thrown from the car and ended up with only contusions and a couple of broken bones." His expression grew tight. "Someone had sent me a message, Leah. Someone was telling me that I hadn't spent thirty-six years of my life preparing for suicide, that there was more to me than that. I didn't hear it at first, because I was so wrapped up in self-pity that I couldn't think beyond it. But I had plenty of time. Weeks lying in that hospital bed. And eventually I came to accept what that someone was saying."

His voice lowered and his gaze softened on hers. "As soon as I could drive, I left L.A. I didn't know where I was going, only that I needed to get as far away from that world as possible. I kept driving, knowing that when I hit a comfortable place, I'd feel it. By the time I hit New Hampshire, I'd just about reached the end of the line.

"Then I saw this place. Victoria's husband had owned it—he used it for hunting parties—and Victoria kept it for a while after his death. Shortly before I came, she put it on the market through a local broker. From the first it appealed to me, so I bought it." He looked away. "It's odd how ignorant you can be of your own actions sometimes. Through all those years of success—of excess—the one thing I did right was to hire a financial adviser. He managed to invest the money I didn't squander, and he invested it wisely. I can live more than comfortably on the income from those investments without ever having to touch the capital."

He reached the end of his story, at least as far as the past was concerned. "I've made a life for myself here, Leah. I've been clean for four years. I don't touch alcohol or drugs, and I've sworn off indiscriminate sex." He looked at his hands, rubbed one set of long fingers with the other. "That other life wasn't me. If it had been, I wouldn't have botched it so badly. This is the kind of life I feel comfortable with. I can't—I won't—go back to the other."

Hesitantly his eyes met hers. "You're right. I should have told you all this sooner. But I couldn't. I was afraid. I still am."

Leah's cheeks were wet with tears, and her hands remained pressed to her lips. "So am I," she whispered against them.

Garrick did touch her then, almost timidly cupping her head. "You don't have to be afraid. Not of me. You know me better than any other person ever has."

"But that other man—"

"Doesn't exist. He never really did. He was a phony, an image, like everything else in Hollywood. An image with no foundation, so it was inevitable that it collapse. I don't want that kind of life anymore. You have to believe that, Leah. The only life I want is what I have here, what we've had here for the past two weeks. It's real. It's totally fulfilling—"

"But what about the need for public recognition? Doesn't that get in your blood?"

"It got in mine and nearly killed me. It was like a disease. And the cure was almost lethal, but it worked." He took a quick breath. "Don't let the mistakes I've made in the past turn you off. I've learned from them. Dear God, I've learned."

Leah wanted to believe everything he said. She wanted to believe it so badly that she began to shake, and her hands shot out to clutch his shoulders. "Greg Reynolds wouldn't be attracted to me—"

"Garrick Rodenhiser is."

"I'd be nothing in Greg Reynolds' world."

"You're everything in mine."

"I couldn't play games like that. I couldn't even play them for Richard."

"I don't want games. I want life. This life. And you."

Unable to remain apart from her a minute longer, he captured her mouth in a kiss that went beyond words in expressing his need. It was possessive and desperate and demanding, but Leah's was no less so.

"Don't ever be that other man," she begged against his mouth. "I think I'd want to die if you were."

"I won't, I won't," he murmured, then, while his hands held her head, took her mouth again and devoured it with a passion born of the love he felt. His lips opened wide, slanted and sucked, and he was breathing hard when he released her. "Let me love you," he whispered hoarsely, fingers working on the buttons of her shirt. "Let me give you everything I have…everything I've saved for you…everything that's come alive since you came into my life." Her shirt was open and his hands were greedily covering her breasts. "You're so good. All I've ever wanted."

Leah gave an urgent little cry and began to tug at his sweater. This was the Garrick she knew, the one who turned her on as no man ever had, the one who thought her beautiful and smart, the one who loved her. She felt as though she'd traveled from one end of the galaxy to the other since Garrick had begun his story. On a distant planet was the actor, but on progressively nearer ones was the man who'd suffered fear, then disillusionment, then pain. Even closer was the man who'd hit rock bottom and had begun to build himself up again. And here, with her, was the one who'd made it.

"I love you so," she whispered as his sweater went over his head. He brought her to his chest and held her there, rotating her breasts against the light matting of hair, then wrapping his arms around her and crushing her even closer.

He sighed into her hair, but that wasn't enough, so he kissed her again and again, then eased her back on the sofa and began to tug at her jeans. When her body was bare, he worshiped it with his mouth, dragging his tongue over her breasts and her navel, taking love bites from her thighs, burying his lips in the heart of her.

Leah's knuckles were white around the worn upholstery, her eyes closed tight against the sweet torment of his tongue against that ultrasensitive part of her. The world began to spin—this galaxy, another one, she didn't know—and her thighs tensed on either side of his head.

"Garrick!" she cried.

"Let it come, love," he whispered, his warm breath as erotic as his thrusting tongue.

Wave after wave of electrical sensation shook her, and she was still in the throes of glory when he opened the fly of his cords, stretched over her and thrust forward. She cried out again. Her knees came up higher. And it was like nothing she'd ever dreamed possible. Her climax went on and on—a second, then a third— while Garrick pumped deeply, reaching and achieving his own spectacular release.

He didn't leave her, but brought her up from the sofa until she was straddling his lap. And he began again, stroking more slowly this time, kissing her, dipping his head to lave her taut nipples with his tongue, using his hands to add extra sensation to the similarly taut nub between her legs, until it happened again and again and again.

Only when they were dripping with sweat and their bodies were totally drained did they surrender to the quiet after-storm where emotions raged. Leah cried. Damp-eyed himself, Garrick rocked her gently. Then, when she'd quieted, he pressed his lips to her cheek.

"I want to marry you, Leah, but I won't ask you now. Too much has happened today. It wouldn't be fair. But I'll be thinking it constantly, because it's the one thing that I want in life that I don't have right now."

Leah nodded against him, but she didn't breathe a word. She was sated, exhausted and happy. Yes, too much had happened today. But there was something else, something that went hand in hand with marriage that she hadn't told him. She had her secrets, too, and the burden of disclosure was now hers.

BUT THE BURDENS had a way of falling from shoulders when one least expected them to. Such had been the case with Garrick's soul baring. Such was the case with Leah's.

A month had passed since she'd arrived at the cabin, one day blending into the next in a continual span of happiness. With the ebbing of mud season, Garrick's Cherokee was functional again. They drove into town for supplies, drove to the artists' colony, where Leah inquired about weaving lessons, drove to Victoria's cabin and freed the Golf, which Leah drove back to Garrick's and parked behind the cabin. They took long walks in the woods, often at daybreak when Garrick checked the few traps he'd set for coyotes, and picnicked in groves surrounded by the sweet smell of spring's rebirth.

Then, one morning, Leah awoke feeling distinctly muzzy. The muzziness passed, and she pushed it from mind, but the next morning it was back, this time accompanied by sharp pangs of nausea. When Garrick, who'd been fixing breakfast, saw her dash for the bathroom, he grew concerned. He followed her and found her hanging over the commode.

"What is it, sweetheart?" he asked, pressing a cool cloth to her beaded forehead.

"Garrick…oh…"

He supported her while she lost the contents of her stomach, then, very gently, closed the commode and eased her down. "What is it?" he repeated as he bathed her face. Her skin was ashen. His own hands shook.

"I didn't think it would happen…could happen…"

"What, love?"

She looked bewildered. "And I was never sick like this…"

"Leah?"

"Oh, God." She covered her face with her hands, then removed them to collapse against Garrick. "Hold me," she whispered tremulously. "Just hold me."

His arms were around her in an instant. "You're frightening me, Leah."

"I know…I'm sorry.… I think I'm going to have a baby."

For a minute he went very still. Then he began to tremble. Framing her face with his hands, he held her away from him and searched her eyes. "I thought," he began, "I guess I assumed that you...I shouldn't have... are you sure?"

"No."

"But you think so?"

"The nausea. I felt a little yesterday, too. And I haven't had a period." She was as bewildered as ever. "I didn't think...it was never like this."

"You weren't using birth control...an IUD?"

Her eyes were brimming with tears. "I've never had to worry about it. I always had trouble conceiving."

"Not now," Garrick said, pride and excitement surging within him. But something about what she'd said, and her expression, tempered his joy. "Have you conceived before?"

She nodded, then dissolved into tears.

Pressing her face into the warmth of his shoulder, he soothingly stroked her back. "What happened?" he whispered.

It was a while before she could answer, and when she did it was in a voice rife with pain. "Stillborn. I carried for nine months, but the babies were born dead."

"Babies?"

"Two. Two separate pregnancies. Both babies stillborn."

"Ahhhh, Leah," he moaned, holding her closer. "I'm sorry."

She was crying freely, but her words somehow found exit through her sobs. "I wanted...them so badly...and Richard did. He blamed me...even when the doctors said...I did nothing wrong."

"Of course you didn't do anything wrong. What did the doctors say caused it?"

"That was the...worst of it. They didn't know!"

"Shhhh. It's okay. Everything's going to be okay."

As he held her and rocked her, a slow smile formed on his lips. A baby. Leah was going to have a baby. His baby. "Our baby," he whispered.

"I don't...know for sure."

"Well, we'll just have to find the nearest doctor and have him tell us for sure."

"It may be too early."

"He'll know."

"Oh, Garrick," she wailed, and started crying all over again. "I'm...so...frightened!"

He held her back and dipped his head so that they were on eye level with each other. His thumbs were braced high on her cheekbones, catching her tears. "There's nothing to be frightened of. I'm here. We'll be together through it all."

"You don't understand! I want your b-baby. I *want* your baby, and if something happens to it I don't know wh-what I'll do!"

"Nothing's going to happen. I won't let it."

"You can't *stop* it. No one could last time, or the time before that."

"Then this time will be different," he said with conviction. Scooping her into his arms, he carried her from the bathroom and set her gently back on the bed. "I want you to rest now. Later today we're going out to get a marriage license."

"No, Garrick."

"What do you mean, no?"

"I can't marry you yet."

"Because you're not sure if you're pregnant? I want to marry you anyway. You love me, don't you?"

"Yes."

"And I love you. So if you're pregnant, that'll be the frosting on the cake."

"But I don't want to get married yet."

"Why not?"

"Because I don't know if I can give birth to a living child. And if I can't, I'll always worry that you married me too soon and are stuck with me."

"That's the craziest thing I've ever heard. I *love* you, Leah. I told you two weeks ago that I wanted to marry you, and that was before there was any *mention* of a child."

"Don't you want children?"

"Yes, but I've never counted on them. Up until a month ago, I'd pretty much reconciled myself to the idea of living out my life alone. Then you came along and changed all that. Don't you see? Baby or no baby, having you with me is so much more than I've ever dreamed of—"

"Please," she begged. "Please, wait. For me." She pressed a fist to her heart. "*I* need to wait to get married. I need to know what's going to happen. If…if something goes wrong with the baby and you still want me, then I'll marry you. But I wouldn't be comfortable doing it now. If I am pregnant, the next eight-plus months are going to be difficult enough for me. If, on top of that, I have to worry about having my marriage destroyed…" Her voice dropped to an aching whisper. "I don't think I could take that again."

Garrick closed his eyes against the pain of sudden understanding. He dropped his head back, inhaled through flaring nostrils, then righted his head and very slowly opened his eyes. "That's what happened with Richard."

"Yes," she whispered.

"You mentioned other things—"

"There were. And maybe the marriage would have

fallen apart anyway. But the baby—the babies—they were the final straw. Richard expected me to bear him fine children. They were part of the image—the wife, the home, the kids. The first time it happened we called it a fluke. But the second time, after all the waiting and praying and worrying—well, there was no hope left for us as a couple."

"Then he was a bastard," Garrick growled. "You could have adopted— No, forget I said that. If you'd done it, you'd probably still be married to him and then I wouldn't have you. I want you, Leah. If the babies come, I'll love it. If they don't and we decide we want children, we'll adopt. But we can't adopt a child unless we're married."

Leah closed her eyes. She was feeling exhausted, more so emotionally than physically. "I hadn't planned on getting pregnant."

"Some of the best things happen that way."

"I would rather have waited and had a chance to enjoy you more."

"You'll have that chance. Marry me, Leah."

Opening her eyes, Leah reached for his hand and slowly carried it to her lips. She kissed each one of his fingers in turn, then pressed them to her cheek. "I love you so much it hurts, Garrick, but I want to wait. Please. If you love me, bear with me. A piece of paper doesn't mean anything to me, as long as I know you're here. But that same piece of paper will put more pressure on me, and if I am pregnant, added pressure is the last thing I'll need."

Garrick didn't agree with her. He didn't see where their marrying would cause her stress, not given what he'd told her about his feelings. But he knew that she believed what she said, and since that was what counted, he had no choice but to accede.

"My offer still stands. If you're not pregnant, will you consider it?"

Feeling a wave of relief, she nodded.

"And if you are pregnant, if at any time over the next few months you change your mind, will you tell me?"

Again she nodded.

"If you are pregnant, I want to take a marriage license out before you're due to deliver. When that baby comes screaming and squalling into the world, it's going to have to wait for its first dinner until a judge pronounces us man and wife."

"In a hospital room?" Leah asked with a wobbly smile.

"Yes, ma'am."

She moved forward into his arms and coiled her own tightly around his neck. She loved the thought of that—a new husband, a healthy baby. She didn't dare put much stock in it, because she'd been let down on the baby part twice before, but it was a lovely thought. A very lovely thought.

CHAPTER EIGHT

LOVELY THOUGHTS HAD a way of falling by the wayside when other thoughts took precedence. That was what happened to Leah once the local doctor confirmed that she was pregnant. Her initial reaction was excitement, and it was shared with, even magnified by, Garrick's. Then the fear set in—and the concern, and the practical matter of how to deal with a new pregnancy after two had gone so awry.

"I'd like to speak to my doctor in New York," she said one night while she and Garrick were sitting thigh to thigh on the cabin steps. It had been a beautiful May day, marred only by Leah's preoccupation.

"No problem," Garrick said easily. "We can drive into town tomorrow to make the call. In fact, I've been thinking I'd like to have a phone installed here." It was something he'd never dreamed of doing before, but now that Leah was pregnant, concerns lurked behind his optimistic front. Having a phone would mean that help could be summoned in case of emergency.

Timidly she looked up at him. "I'd like to go back to New York." When he eyed her in alarm, she hurried on. "Just to see John Reiner."

"Weren't you comfortable with the doctor you saw here?"

"It's not that. It's just that John knows my medical history. If anyone can shed some light on what happened before and how to prevent it from happening again, it's him."

"Couldn't we just have Henderson call him?"

"I'd rather see John in person."

Garrick felt a compression around his heart, but it wasn't a totally new feeling. He'd been aware of it a lot lately, particularly when Leah's eyes clouded and she grew silent. "You're not thinking of having the baby in New York, are you?" he asked quietly.

"Oh, no," she answered quickly. "But for my peace of mind, I'd like to see John. Just for an initial checkup. He may be able to suggest something that I can do— diet, exercise, rest, vitamins—anything that will enhance the baby's chances."

Put that way, Garrick could hardly refuse. He wanted the baby as much as Leah did—more, perhaps, because he knew how much it meant to her. Still, he didn't like the idea of her leaving him, even for a few days. He didn't like the idea of her traveling to New York.

And he couldn't go with her.

"I don't want you driving down," he said. "You can take a plane from Concord. I'll have Victoria meet you at LaGuardia."

"You won't come?" she asked very softly. She had a feeling he wouldn't. Garrick didn't seem to dislike the city as much as he feared it. Even here she would have preferred seeing a doctor at a hospital, but that would have meant entering a city, and Garrick shunned even the New Hampshire variety. He'd insisted that she see a local man, though the closest one was a forty-minute drive from the cabin. He hadn't even wanted to stop for dinner until they'd reached the perimeter of the small area in which he felt safe.

His eyes focused on the landscape, but his expression was one of torment. "No," he finally said. "I can't come."

Nodding, she looked down at her lap. "Can't" was something she'd have to work on. It was a condition in Garrick's mind and represented a fear that she could understand but not agree with. On the other hand, who was she to argue? Hadn't she been firm in putting off marriage? Hadn't Garrick disagreed, but understood and conceded?

"I'll have to call to make an appointment, but I'm sure he'll see me within the next week or so. I can make it a day trip."

That Garrick wouldn't concede to. "That's not wise, Leah. Lord only knows I don't want you gone overnight, but for you to rush would defeat the purpose. I don't want anything happening. If you have the pressure of flights and appointments, you'll be running all day. You'll end up tense and exhausted."

"Then I'll sleep when I get back," she protested. She didn't want to be away from Garrick any longer than was necessary. "The baby is fine at this stage. Even the fact that I've been sick is a good sign. Dr. Henderson said so. I didn't have any morning sickness with the other two."

But he was insistent. "Spend the night with Victoria. At least that way I won't worry quite as much."

So the following week she flew to New York, saw John Reiner, then spent the night at Victoria's. It should have been a happy reunion, and in many ways it was. Victoria was overjoyed that Leah and Garrick were in love, and she was beside herself when, promptly upon landing and in part to explain her doctor's appointment, Leah told her about the baby.

But some of the things that the doctor said put a damper on Leah's own excitement. She was feeling a distinct sense of dread when Garrick met her plane back in Concord the next afternoon.

"How do you feel?" he asked, leading her to the car. He'd called Victoria's on his newly installed phone the night before and knew that the doctor had pronounced Leah well, and definitely pregnant.

"Tired. You were right. It was a hassle. Hard to believe I used to live in that…and like it."

He had a firm arm around her shoulder. "Come on. Let's get you home."

She was quiet during most of the drive. With her head back and her eyes closed, she was trying to decide the best way to say what she had to. She didn't find an answer that night, because when they arrived back at the cabin, Garrick presented her with a small table loom and several instruction books on how to weave belts and other simple strips of cloth. She was so touched by his thoughtfulness that she didn't want to do anything to spoil the moment. Then, later, he made very careful, very sweet love to her, and she could think of nothing but him.

The next morning, though, she knew she had to talk. It didn't matter that she was dying inside. What mattered was that their baby, hers and Garrick's, be born alive.

"Tell me, love," Garrick said softly.

Startled, she caught in her breath. She'd been lying on her back in bed, but at the sound of his voice her head flew around and her eyes met his.

He came up on an elbow. "You've been awake for an hour. I've been lying here watching you. Something's wrong."

She moistened her lips, then bent up an arm and shaped her fingers to his jaw. His beard was a brush-soft cushion; she took warmth from it and strength from the jaw beneath.

"John made a suggestion that I'm not sure you'll like."

"Oh-oh. He doesn't want us making love."

She gave a sad little grin and tugged at his beard. "Not that."

"Then what?"

She took a deep breath. "He thought that it would be better if I stay close to a hospital from the middle of my pregnancy on."

"'Stay close.' What does that mean?"

"It means live in the city. He gave me the name of a colleague of his, a man who left New York several years ago to head the obstetrics department at a hospital in Concord. John has total faith in him. He wants him to be in charge of the case."

"I see," Garrick said. He sank quietly back to the pillow and trained his gaze on the rafters. "How do you feel about it?"

Withdrawing her displaced hand, yet missing the contact, Leah said, "I want what's best for the baby."

"Do you want to move to the city?"

"Personally? No."

"Then don't."

"It's not as simple as that. My personal feelings come second to what's best for this baby's chances."

"What, exactly, did your doctor think that his man in Concord would be able to do?"

"Perform certain tests, more sophisticated ones than a local doctor is equipped to do. Closely monitor the condition of the baby. Detect any potential problem before it proves fatal."

Garrick had to admit, albeit begrudgingly, that that made sense. It was his baby, too. He didn't want anything to go wrong. "Didn't they do all that before?"

"Not as well as they can now. Nearly three years have passed. Medical science has advanced in that time."

"Well," he said, sighing, "we don't have to make a decision on it now, do we?"

"Not right away, I suppose. But John suggested that I see his man soon. They'll be in touch on the phone, and John will forward any records he thinks may be of help. Usually…" She hesitated, then pushed on. "Usually there'd be monthly appointments at this stage, but John wants me to be checked every two weeks."

Garrick shut his eyes tight. "That means tackling Concord every two weeks."

"Concord isn't so bad."

He said nothing.

"And besides, we're getting into good weather. It's not such a long drive." But she knew that it wasn't the drive, or the weather, or any conflicting time demand that was the problem. "Will you drive me down twice a month?" she asked. She could easily drive herself, but she desperately wanted Garrick to be with her.

He didn't answer at first. In fact, he didn't answer at all. Instead he rolled toward her and took her into his arms. She felt the pulsing steel of his strength, smelled the musky, wood scent that was his and his alone, and when their lips met, she tasted his fear and worry… and love.

GARRICK DID DRIVE her to Concord twice a month, but he was tense the whole way, and the instant each appointment was done, he quickly tucked her into the car and drove her home. Only on familiar turf was he fully at ease, but even that ease ebbed somewhat as late spring became early summer.

Outwardly life was wonderful. They shed sweaters and long pants for T-shirts and shorts, and more often than not, when he worked in the clearing around the cabin, Garrick was bare chested. Leah could have spent entire days just watching him. Sweat poured freely from his body. The muscles of his upper back and arms rippled with the thrust of a shovel or the swing of an ax. His skin turned a rugged bronze, while the sandy hue of his hair lightened. He was positively gorgeous and she told him so, which, to her surprise and delight, brought a deeper shade of red to his cheeks.

He put in his garden and spent long hours cultivating it. During those times Leah sat near him, either watching, weaving, basking in the sun or working on puzzles. She was regularly shipping parcels off to New York, and the fact that there was now a phone at the cabin facilitated communications with her editor. The queasiness and fatigue that had initially slowed her down had passed by the end of June; come July, she was feeling fine and beginning to show.

They were as deeply in love as ever. Leah made a point of protesting when Garrick doted on her, but she drank in his attention and affection. In turn, she did whatever she could to make his days special, but she had a selfish motive, as well. The busier she was, the more dedicated to his happiness, the less she thought about the child growing inside her.

She didn't want to think about it. She was frightened to pin hopes and dreams on something that might never be. In mid-July she underwent amniocentesis,

and though she was relieved to learn that, at that point
at least, the baby was healthy, she didn't want to know
its sex.

Neither did Garrick. There were times when he was
working the soil or whittling or listening to Leah's
music when his mind would wander. At those odd moments he had mixed feelings about the baby. Oh, he
wanted it; but he resented it, too, for in his gut he knew
Leah was going to leave. She didn't say so. They deliberately avoided discussion of what was to come in
August, when she reached the midway point of her pregnancy. But he knew what she was thinking when her
eyes lowered and her brow furrowed, and he dreaded
the day when she'd finally broach the subject.

More than anything he would have liked to stop time.
He'd have Leah. He'd have the baby thriving inside her.
He'd have the bright summer sunshine, the good, rich
earth, the endless bounty of the mountain. He didn't
want things to change; he liked them as they were. He
felt safe and secure, productive and well loved.

But he couldn't stop time. The heat of each day
turned to the chill of evening. The sun set; darkness
fell. The baby inside Leah grew until her abdomen was
as round as the cabbage he'd planted in the garden. And
when Leah approached him in the middle of August, he
knew that his time of total satisfaction was over.

"We have to talk," she said, sitting down beside him
on the porch swing he'd hung. She'd gone inside for a
sweater to ward off the cool night air; it was draped
over the T-shirt—Garrick's T-shirt—that covered the
gentle bubble of her stomach.

"I know."

"Dr. Walsh wants me closer to the hospital."

He nodded.

"Will you come?"

Looking off toward the woods, Garrick took a deep breath. When he spoke, his voice was gritty. "I can't."

"You can if you want."

"I can't."

"Why not?"

"Because this is my home. I can't live in the city again."

"You can if you want."

"No."

"I'm not asking you to move there for good. It would be for four months at most. Dr. Walsh is planning to take the baby by section in the middle of December."

Garrick swallowed. "I'll be with you then."

"But I want you with me now."

He looked at her sharply. "I can't, Leah. I just can't."

Leah was trying to be understanding, but she had little to work with. "Please. Tell me why."

He bolted up from the swing, and in a single stride was leaning against the porch railing with his back to her. "There's too much to do here. Fall is my busy time. Trapping season opens at the end of October. There's a whole lot to do before then."

"You could live with me part-time in Concord. It'd be better than nothing."

"I don't see why you have to live in Concord. I drive. The Cherokee is dependable. If there's a problem, I could have you at the hospital in no time."

"Garrick, it takes *two hours* to get there. Both times before, things went wrong after I'd gone into labor. Those two hours could be critical."

"We have a phone. We could call an ambulance… or…or call for a police escort if there's a need."

"Ambulance attendants don't have the know-how to handle problem deliveries. Neither do police."

"Okay," he said, turning to face her. "Then we can go to Concord in November. Why September?"

"Dr. Walsh wanted August, but I put him off."

"Put him off for another few months."

Tugging the sweater closer around her, Leah studied the planked floor of the porch. "Do you want this baby, Garrick?"

"That's a foolish question. You know I do."

"Do you love me?"

"Of course!"

She looked up. "Then why can't you do this for me— for the baby—for all three of us?"

With a low growl of frustration, he turned away again. "You don't understand."

"I think I do," she cried, pushing off from the swing and coming up to where he stood. "I think you're frightened—of people, of the city, of being recognized. But that's ridiculous, Garrick! You've made a good life for yourself. You have *nothing* to be ashamed of."

"Wrong. I spent seventeen years of my life behaving like a jackass."

"But you paid the price, and you've rebuilt your life. So what if someone recognizes you? Are you ashamed of who you are now?"

The pale light of the moon glittered off the flaring silver flecks in his eyes. "No!"

"Why can't you go out there and hold your head high?"

"It's got nothing to do with pride. What I have now is much finer than anything I had then. *You're* much finer than any woman I knew then."

"What is it, then? What is it that makes you nervous

each and every time we approach civilization? I've seen it, Garrick. Your shoulders get tense. You keep your head down. You avoid making eye contact with strangers. You refuse to go into restaurants. You want to get out of wherever we are as quickly as possible."

"It bothers you not going out on the town?"

"Of course not! What bothers me is that you're uncomfortable. I love you. I'm proud of you. It hurts me to see you slinking around corners as though there's—" she faltered, searching for an analogy "—as though there's a trap set around the next one."

"I know all about traps. Sometimes you don't see them until you're good and caught."

"Then there's the case of the coyote, who won't be caught in the same place twice."

"The coyote's an animal. I'm human."

"That's right. You're smart and fine and strong—"

"Strong? Not quite." He turned to face her. The faint glow spilling from inside the cabin side-lit his features, adding to the harshness of his expression. "What I had for seventeen years was a disease, Leah. It was an addiction. And the one thing a former addict doesn't do is let the forbidden be waved before his nose. I won't go into restaurants with bars because I'd have to walk by all those bottles to get to a seat. I won't look people in the eye because if they were to recognize me I'd see their star lust. I don't watch television. I don't go to movies. And the last thing I wanted when you came here was heavy sex." He snorted. "Guess I blew it on that one."

"You don't trust yourself," she said, at last comprehending the extent of his fear.

"Damn right, I don't. When you first showed up, I thought you were a reporter. I wanted to get rid of you as soon as possible, and you want to know why? If a reporter—especially a pretty one—were to interview me, I'd feel pretty important. And then I'd get to thinking that I'd done my penance for screwing up once, and maybe I should try for the big time again."

"But you don't *want* that anymore."

"When I'm here I don't. When I'm thinking rationally, I don't. But I spent a good many years thinking irrationally. Who's to say that I wouldn't start doing it again?"

"You wouldn't. Not after all you've been through."

"That's what I tell myself," he said in a weary tone, "but it's not a hundred percent convincing." He thrust a handful of fingers through his hair, which fell back to his forehead anyway. "I don't know how I'd react face to face with temptation."

She slipped her hand under the sleeve of his T-shirt to his shoulder. "Don't you think it's time you tried? You can't go through the rest of your life living under a shadow." She gave him a little shake. "You've been happy here. You feel good about your life. Wouldn't it be nice to prove to yourself, once and for all, that you have the strength that *I* know you have?"

"You love me. You see me through rose-coloured glasses."

Leah's hand fell away as she tamped down a spurt of anger. "My glasses are untinted, thank you, and even if they weren't, that's a lousy thing to say. Yes, I love you. But I've been through love once before, and I'm a realist. I entered this relationship with my eyes wide open—"

"You're nearsighted."

"Not where feelings and emotions are concerned. Oh, I can see your faults. We all have them, Garrick. That's what being human is about. But you took on your weaknesses once before and came out a winner. Why can't you take on this last one?"

"Because I might fail, damn it! I might face temptation and succumb, and where would that leave me, or you, or the baby?"

"It won't happen," she declared quietly.

"Is that an ironclad guarantee?"

"Life doesn't come with guarantees."

"Right."

"But you have so much more going for you now than you had before," she argued. "You have the life you've made, and it's one you love. And you have me. I wouldn't sit idly back and watch you fall into a pattern of self-destruction. I don't want that other life any more than you do. And I don't want you hurt. I *love* you, Garrick. Doesn't that mean anything?"

He bowed his head and, in the shadows, groped blindly for her hand. "It means more than you could ever imagine," he said hoarsely, weaving his fingers through hers, holding them tightly.

"Come with me," she pleaded. "I know it's asking a lot, because it cuts into the trapping season, but you don't need the money. You said so yourself. And these are extenuating circumstances. It won't happen every year. It may never happen again."

"God, Leah…"

"I need you."

"Maybe you need something I don't have to give."

"But you're a survivor. Look at what you've been through. It isn't every man who can land in a canyon, half-broken in body and more than that in spirit, and rise again to be the kind of person who can—" again she floundered for words "—can take in a bedraggled mess of mud from your doorstep half suspecting that she was planning to stab you in the back with a poison pen story."

He made a noise that, in other circumstances and with a stretch of the imagination, might have been a laugh. "You were a little pathetic."

"The point is," she went on, "that your heart's in the right place. You want the best—for you, for me, for the baby. You can do anything you set your mind to. You can *give* anything you want."

Closing his eyes, Garrick put a hand to the tense muscles at the back of his neck. He dropped his head to the side, then slowly eased it back and around. "Ahhh, Leah. You make it sound so simple. Perhaps I could do it if I had you by my side every minute, whispering in my ear like a Jiminy Cricket. But I can't do that. I won't. I need to stand on my own two feet. Here I can do it."

"You asked me to marry you. Are you saying that we'd never take a vacation, never go somewhere different?"

"If it bores you to be here—"

"It doesn't, and you know it! But everyone needs a change of scenery sometimes. Suppose, just suppose this baby lives—"

"It *will* live," he barked.

"See, you can be optimistic, because you haven't been through the hell I have once, let alone twice. But I'm willing to try again—"

"It happened. We didn't plan it."

"I could have had an abortion."

"You're not that kind of person."

"Just as you're not the kind of person who gave up on life when you came to in that hospital. You could have, y'know. You could have gone right back to drinking and taking whatever else you were taking, but you didn't. You were willing to make a stab at a new life. Some people wouldn't have the courage to do that, but you did. All I'm asking now is that you take it one step further." She gave a frustrated shake of her head. "But that wasn't what I wanted to say. I wanted to say that if the baby lives, and grows and gets more active and demanding, there may be times when I'll want to go off with my husband somewhere, alone, just the two of us. Maybe to somewhere warm in winter, or somewhere cool in summer. Or maybe I'll want to go somewhere adventurous—like Madrid or Peking or Cairo. It would have nothing to do with being bored here, or not loving our child, but simply a desire to learn about other things and places. Would you refuse?"

He was silent for a minute. "I haven't thought that far."

"Maybe you should."

He eyed her levelly. "Before I mention marriage again?"

"That's right."

"Are you issuing an ultimatum, Leah?"

She turned her head aside in disgust. "An ultimatum? Me? I've used the word dozens of times in puzzles, but I wouldn't know how to apply it in real life if I had to." Removing her glasses, she rubbed the bridge of her nose. "No ultimatum," she murmured. "Just something to think about, I guess."

When she didn't raise her head, Garrick did it for her. The tears that had gathered in her eyes wrenched his insides, but he said what he had to say. "I love you, Leah. That won't change, whether you're here or in Concord. But I can't go with you. Not now. Not yet. There are still too many things I have to work out in my mind. I want to marry you, and that won't change, either, but maybe it would be good if we were separated for a time. If you're in Concord, under Walsh's eye, I'll know you're well cared for. While you're there, you'll be able to think about whether I *am* the kind of man you want. Except for two days, we've been together constantly for nearly five months. If it were fifty months or years, I'd still feel the same about you. But you have to accept me for what I am. Baby or no baby, you have a right to happiness. If my shortcomings are going to prevent that down the road, then…maybe you should do some rethinking."

Leah didn't know what to say, which was just as well, because her throat was so clogged she wouldn't have been able to utter a word. There were things she wanted to say, but she'd already said them, and they hadn't done much toward changing Garrick's mind. She'd never been one to nag or harp, and she refused to resort to that now. So she simply closed her eyes and let herself be enfolded in his arms, where she etched everything she loved about him into memory for the lonely period ahead.

SHE LEFT THE next day while Garrick was out on the mountain. It didn't take her long to pack, since she had a limited supply of maternity clothes. The things she wanted most were her resource books, her music and her loom, and these she carried to the car in separate trips. She worked as quickly as she could, pausing at the end to leave a short note.

"Dear Garrick," she wrote, "We all have our moments of cowardice, and I guess this is mine. I'm on my way to Concord. I'll call you tonight to let you know where I'll be staying. Please don't be angry. It's not that I'm choosing the baby over you, but that I want you both. You've said that you'll love me no matter where I am, and I'm counting on that, because I feel the same. But I want a chance to love a child of ours, and I want you to have that chance, too. That's why I have to go." She signed it simply, "Leah."

THOUGH SHE DIDN'T have an appointment set up for that particular day, Gregory Walsh saw her shortly after she arrived.

"Aren't you feeling well?" he asked as soon as she was seated.

She forced a small smile. "I'm feeling fine, but I... need a little help. I've just driven in. All my things are still in the car. I'm...afraid I haven't planned for this very well. It seems—" she grimaced "—that I don't have a place to stay. You're familiar with the area around the hospital. I was hoping you could suggest an apartment or a duplex, something furnished that I could rent."

Walsh was quiet for several minutes, his kindly eyes gentle, putting her at ease as they had from the start. "You're alone," he said at last, softly and without condemnation.

Her gaze fell to her twisting thumbs. "Yes."

"Where's Garrick?"

"Back at the cabin."

"Is there a problem?"

"Not really. He just didn't feel that he could...be here for such a long stretch."

"How do you feel about that?"

"Okay."

"Really?"

"I guess."

Again the doctor was silent, this time steepling his

fingers beneath his chin and pursing his lips. His eyes remained on her bowed head. When he spoke at last, his voice was exquisitely gentle. "People often assume that my job is purely physical, examining one pregnant lady after another, prescribing vitamins, delivering babies. There's much more to it than that, Leah. Pregnancy is a time of change, and it brings with it a wide range of emotional issues. It's my job—and wish— to deal with some of those issues. From a medical standpoint, a more relaxed mother-to-be is a healthier one, and her baby is healthier." He lowered his hands. "Given your medical history, you have had more than your share of worries. Having you close by the hospital gives me a medical edge, but I was also hoping that it would serve to ease your fears."

She raised her head. "It will. That's why I'm here."

"But you've always been with Garrick before. It'd take a blind man not to see how close you two are. It'd take an insensitive one not to guess that it bothers you he's not with you now. I'd like to think I'm neither blind nor insensitive. I'd also like to think that you feel comfortable enough with me to tell me, honestly, what you're feeling."

"I do," she said softly. She didn't know how one could *not* feel comfortable with a man like Gregory Walsh. In his early fifties, he was pleasant to look at and talk with. He seemed to have a sensor fine-tuned to his patients' needs; he knew when to speak and when to listen. She'd never once sensed any condescension on his part, quite a feat given his position.

"Then tell me what you really feel about Garrick's staying behind at the cabin."

She thought for a minute, and when she spoke, her voice was unsteady. "I feel...lots of things."

"Tell me one."

"Sadness. I miss him. It's only been a few hours, but I miss him. Not only that, but I picture him alone back at the cabin and I hurt for him. I know it's stupid. It was his choice to stay there, and besides, he's a big boy. He lived there alone for a long time before I arrived. He's more than capable of taking care of himself. Still, I... it bothers me."

"Because you love him."

"Yes."

He nodded in encouragement. "What else are you feeling?"

She grew pensive and frowned. "Dismay. I've lived alone, too. I've taken care of myself. Yet here I am, all but crying on your doorstep, not knowing where I'm going to spend the night. I feel...handicapped."

"You're pregnant. That has to make any woman feel a little more vulnerable than usual."

"That's it. Vulnerable. I do feel that."

"What else?"

She lifted one shoulder and tipped her head to the side, her eyes dropping back to her hands. "Anger. Resentment. Garrick has his reasons for doing what he is, and I'm trying to understand them, but right about now it's hard."

"Because you're feeling alone?"

"Yes."

"And a little betrayed?"

"Maybe. But I don't have a right to feel that. Garrick never said he'd come. In all the time I've known him, he's never promised anything he hasn't delivered."

"You can still feel betrayed, Leah. It's normal."

"He was the one who wanted to get married."

"Has he changed his mind?"

"No. But even if we were married, I doubt he'd be here. He has a certain…hang-up. I can't explain it."

"You can, but you won't, because that would be betraying him," Walsh suggested with an insight that drew her grateful gaze to his. "I respect you for that, Leah. And anyway, I don't pretend to be a psychiatrist. All I want to do is help you out where I can. Will you be in touch with Garrick while you're here?"

"I told him I'd call tonight. He'll worry otherwise."

"Will he be down to visit?"

"I don't know. He said he'd be here when the baby's due."

"Well, then, that's something to look forward to. The anger, the resentment, the sense of betrayal—those are things you and Garrick will have to work out. All I can say is that you shouldn't deny them or feel guilty for feeling them." He held up a hand. "I'm not criticizing Garrick, mind you. I haven't heard his side of the story, and I wouldn't deign to imagine what's going on in his mind."

"He probably feels betrayed himself, because I chose to come here instead of staying with him. I do feel guilty about that, but I had no choice!"

"You did what you felt you had to do. That's your justification, Leah. It doesn't mean that you have to like the situation. But if you were to drive back to him right now you'd probably show up on my doorstep again tomorrow. In your heart, you feel that what you're doing is best for the baby. Am I right?"

She answered in a whisper. "Yes."

"So. I want you to keep telling yourself that." He grinned unexpectedly. "As for feeling alone and having nowhere to stay, I think I have a perfect solution. My place."

"Dr. Walsh!"

He laughed. "I love it when gorgeous young women take me the wrong way. Let me explain. My wife and I moved up here when the last of our boys—we have four—graduated from college. They were all out doing their own thing, and we felt it was time we did ours. We liked New York, but progressively it was getting more difficult for Susan—that's my wife—to handle. She has crippling arthritis and is confined to a wheelchair."

Leah gasped. "I'm sorry."

"So am I. But, God bless her, she's a good sport about it. She never complained in New York, but I knew that she'd love to be in a place where she could go in and out more freely. When the offer came from this hospital, I grabbed it. We bought a house about ten minutes from here." He chuckled. "In New York that would still be city. Here it's a quiet, tree-shaded acre. One of the things we loved about the house was that there was an apartment in what used to be a garage. Separate from the house. Set kind of back in the trees. We thought it would be ideal for when the boys came to visit. And they do come, but never for more than a night here or there, and then they usually sleep on the living room couch." He sat forward. "So, the apartment's yours if you want it. You'd be close to the hospital but away from the traffic. And Susan would love the company."

Leah was dumbfounded. "I couldn't impose—"

"You wouldn't be imposing. You'd be in your own self-contained unit, and I'd know you were comfortable."

"Is it wise for a doctor to be doing this for a patient?"

"Wise? Let me tell you, Leah. There's another reason I left New York, and that was because I was tired of the internal politics at a large city hospital. Here I do what I want. I decide what's wise. And yes, I think my offer is wise, just as I think you'd be wise to take me up on it."

"I'd want to pay rent," she said, then winced. "The last time I said that, I got to where I was going and found it demolished."

"This place isn't demolished, and you can pay rent if it will make you feel better."

"It will," she said, smiling. "Thank you, Dr. Walsh."

"Thank *you*. You've just made my day." At her questioning look, he explained. "When I can make a patient smile, particularly one who walked in here looking as sober as you did, I know I've done something right."

"You have." Her smile grew even wider. "Oh, you have."

CHAPTER NINE

THE APARTMENT WAS as perfect as Gregory Walsh had said it would be. With walls dividing the space into living room, bedroom and kitchenette, it seemed smaller than the cabin, but it was cozy. The furnishings were of rattan, and where appropriate, there were cushions in pale blue and white, with draperies to match, giving a cheerful, yet soothing effect. Leah had free access to the yard, which was lush in the wild sort of way that reminded her of the woods by the cabin and made her feel more at home.

Susan Walsh was an inspiration. "Good sport" was a mild expression to describe her attitude toward life; her disposition was so sunny that Leah couldn't help but smile whenever they were together, and that was often.

But there were lonely times, times when Leah lay in bed at night feeling empty despite the growing life in her belly. Or times when she sat in the backyard, trying to work and being unable to concentrate because her mind was on Garrick. He called every few days, but the conversation was stilted, and more often than not she'd hang up the phone feeling worse than ever.

The desolation she felt stunned her. She'd never minded when, during each of her previous pregnancies, Richard had gone off on business trips. She tried to tell herself that her separation from Garrick was a sort of business trip, but it didn't help. Garrick wasn't

Richard. Garrick had found a place in her heart and life that Richard had never glimpsed. She missed Garrick with a passion that six months before she wouldn't have believed possible.

Physically, she did well. She saw Gregory at the hospital for biweekly appointments. His examinations grew more thorough and were often accompanied by one test or another. She didn't mind them, for the results were reassuring, as was the fact that the hospital was close should she feel any pang or pressure that hinted at something amiss. She didn't feel anything like that, only the sporadic movements of the baby, movements that became stronger and more frequent as one week merged into the next.

She wanted Garrick to feel those sweet little kicks and nudges. She wanted him to hear the baby's heartbeat, as she had. But she knew she couldn't have it all. In her way, she had made a choice. The problem was learning to live with it.

Then shortly before dawn one morning, after she'd been in Concord for nearly a month, she awoke to an eerie sensation. Without opening her eyes, she pressed a hand to her stomach. Her pulse had automatically begun to race, but she couldn't feel anything wrong. No aches or pains. No premature contractions. She was barely breathing, waiting to identify what it was that had awoken her, when light fingers touched her face.

Eyes flying wide, she bolted back and screamed.

"Shhhhh." Gentle hands clasped her shoulders. "It's just me."

All Leah could make out was a blurred form in the pale predawn light. "Garrick?" she whispered as she clutched frantically at the wrists by her shoulders. He felt strong like Garrick. He smelled good like Garrick.

"I'm sorry I frightened you," said the gravelly voice that was very definitely Garrick's.

She threw her arms around his neck and held him for a minute, then, unable to believe he was really squatting by her bedside, pushed back and peered at him. She needed neither her glasses nor a light to distinguish each of the features she'd missed so in the past weeks.

"Frightened? You *terrified* me," she exclaimed in a hoarse whisper. "What are...why are you...at this hour?"

He shrugged and gave a sheepish smile. "It took me longer than I thought to get everything packed."

"Packed?" Her fingers clenched the muscles at the back of his neck. "Are you—"

"Moving in with you? Yes. I figured you owed me."

Softly crying his name, she launched herself at him again. This time she hung on so relentlessly that he had to climb into bed with her to keep from being choked to death.

He didn't mind. Any of it. "I've been in agony, Leah," he confessed in a ragged whisper. "You've ruined the cabin for me. I'm miserable there without you. And those phone calls suck."

She couldn't restrain an emotional laugh. "Ditto for me. To all of it."

"You weren't at the cabin. You don't know how empty it was."

"I know how empty *I've* been." Her mouth was against his throat. "But what about...you were so adamant about not coming..."

"You said the word in the note you left. Cowardice. It nagged at me and nagged at me until I couldn't take it anymore. I don't know what's going to happen to me here, but I have to take the chance. I don't have any other choice. Being with you means too much."

With a soft moan of heavenly thanks, she began to kiss him—his neck, his beard, his cheekbones, eyes and nose. By the time she'd reached his mouth, she was bunching up his jersey, dragging it from the waistband of his jeans. Her progress was impeded briefly by his hands, which were all over her body, then homing in on those places that had altered most during their separation.

"I want you badly," he groaned. "Can we?"

"Yes, but—"

"Let me make love to you."

"You already have by coming here," she whispered, her breath hot against his skin. She was kissing his chest, moving from one muscled swell to the next, one tight nipple to the other. "Now it's my turn."

Garrick couldn't stop touching her, but he closed his eyes and lay back. He raised his hips when she unzipped his jeans and kicked his legs free after she'd peeled them down.

Leah loved him as she'd never done before. Her appetite was voracious, and the small sounds of pleasure that came from his throat made her all the more bold. His hands were restless in her hair, on her shoulders and back, and while she touched him everywhere, kissed him everywhere, he squeezed his eyes shut against the agony of ecstasy. When she took him into her mouth, he bucked, but her hands were firm on his hips, holding him steady for the milking of lips and tongue. The release he found that way was so intense, so shattering for them both, that the first rays of the sun were poking through the drapes before either of them could speak.

"You make me feel so loved," he whispered against her forehead.

"You are," she returned as softly. "I hadn't realized how much of my time at the cabin was spent showing you that—until I got here and didn't know what to do with myself."

He moved over her then, fingers splayed on either side of her head, eyes wide and brilliant. "You...have... no idea how much I love you."

"I think I do," she said with a soft smile. "You're here, aren't you?"

"Yes. And I intend to make it. For you."

"No, for *you*."

"And for you."

"Okay, for me."

"And for baby," he said, lowering a hand to properly greet his child.

LEAH LET GARRICK find his own pace in Concord. She would have been happy if he just sat with her in the yard or the apartment and accompanied her to the hospital for her appointments. But he did more than that. Within days of his arrival, he signed up to take several courses at the local university. She knew that the first few trips he made there were taxing for him, because he returned to her pale and tired. But he stuck with it, and in time he felt less threatened.

Likewise, he insisted on taking her for walks each day. Gregory had recommended the exercise, and though they began with simple neighborhood trips, Leah's eagerness and Garrick's growing confidence soon had them covering greater distances. Often Garrick wheeled Susan in her chair while Leah held lightly to his elbow; other times Leah and Garrick went alone.

"How do you feel?" Leah asked on one of those private outings.

"Not bad."

"Nervous?"

"Not really. No one seems to recognize me. No one's looking twice." He snorted. "If I had any brains, I suppose I'd be offended."

"It's because you do have brains that you're not. How about at school? Have there been any double takes there?"

"No." He didn't tell her about the anxiety he'd felt when, during one of those very tense first days of class, he'd stood for five minutes outside a local tavern, aching for a drink, just one to calm him down. Nor did he tell her of the flyers he'd seen posted around the university, advertising dramatic productions in the works; he'd stared at those, too, for a very long time.

But he was with her, and he was doing all right, and *she* was doing all right, which was what really mattered.

MID-OCTOBER BROUGHT THE turning of the leaves. Garrick would have liked to show Leah the brilliance of the autumnal spectacle from the cabin, but he didn't dare make even a day trip back to the mountain. The baby was growing bigger and Leah's body more unwieldy; in terms of both comfort and safety, he knew that she was better off staying in Concord.

November brought a marked downshift in the temperature, as well as Garrick's insistence that he and Leah file for a marriage license. It also brought orders from Gregory soon after, that Leah was to stay in bed. She wasn't thrilled with the prospect, for it meant an end to her outings with Garrick. And that she'd have more time on her hands to worry about the baby.

She'd had every test imaginable. Gregory had made detailed comparisons between the results of those tests and the information gleaned from less frequent and less detailed tests done during her last pregnancy in New York. All signs were good, he declared. The baby appeared to be larger, the heartbeat stronger than ever.

"I think you've planted a monster in me," she complained to Garrick one afternoon when she felt particularly uncomfortable.

"Like father, like son," he teased.

"Ah, but we don't know that. What if we get an amazon of a daughter?"

"She can be a Cyclops, for all I care, as long as she's healthy."

Which was the password. Healthy. Boy or girl, they didn't care, as long as the child was born alive.

Increasingly, though she warned herself not to, Leah did think about the child—what sex it was, what they would name it, whether it would have Garrick's eyes or her hair, whether it would like to read. And the more she daydreamed, the more nervous she became, for the critical time was fast approaching.

Garrick, too, was growing nervous, and only part of it had to do with the coming delivery. When he was on campus, he found himself drawn more and more often to the building that housed the small theater. Any number of times he simply stood outside and stared at it. Then one day, with his hands balled into fists in the pocket of his high-collared jacket, he ventured inside.

The theater was dim, with rows and rows of vacant seats, one of which he slipped into while he trained his eyes on the lit stage. Though he'd never acted in a classic himself, he knew Chekov when he saw it. The set was distinct, as were the lines. Slouching lower, he propped his chin on a fist and watched the fledgling actors and actresses do their thing.

They were impressive, he decided after a time. Not quite there yet, but on their way. They were interrupted from time to time by the director, a woman whose voice he could hear, though he couldn't see her. The students were attentive, listening quietly to her criticism, then attempting to follow her suggestions. Sometimes they succeeded; sometimes they didn't. But they tried.

Garrick wondered what would have happened if *he'd* tried the way they did. He wondered whether, if he'd listened to directors, perhaps taken formal acting instruction, he would have been able to evolve into a truly good actor. He'd never really given it a shot. *Pagen* had come along and made him a star, so he hadn't had to.

Watching the young performers, he wondered if any of them dreamed of being stars. More aptly, he wondered if any of them *didn't*. He focused on one young man whose voice wasn't quite forceful enough but whose interpretation was a bit more compelling than that of the others. What would he do after college? Go to New York? Work off-Broadway for a while? Make it to Broadway itself? Or think beyond all that and hightail it to the coast, as he'd done?

His eyes skimmed the stage again, this time alighting on a girl, blond haired and petite of build. As she moved the faint bobbing of her breasts was visible beneath an oversize sweatshirt that tucked snugly under her bottom. He wondered whether she was having an affair with one of the boys—perhaps the good-looking one standing off by the wings? If so, it probably wouldn't last. If her career surpassed his, she'd leave him behind and move on. To what? Male leads? Directors? Producers?

He wondered what she'd think if she knew that Greg Reynolds was sitting at the back of the theater, watching her. Then he snorted softly. She was too young. She probably didn't know who in the hell Greg Reynolds was! And besides, he reminded himself, it wasn't Greg Reynolds who sat unnoticed. It was Garrick Rodenhiser, and unnoticed was precisely what he wanted to be.

Shoving himself up from his chair, he strode quickly out of the theater.

But he was back several days later, sitting in the same seat, watching a rehearsal that had benefited from those several days' practice and become more refined. The best of the performers were clearly emerging—the strong ones distinguishing themselves from the weak as the director focused her coaching more and more on the latter. He watched for a while longer, not quite sure why he stayed, knowing that he didn't need the knot in his belly, that there were other things he'd rather be doing, but unable to move. At last he did move, and when he reached the fresh air, he felt a distinct sense of relief. Theaters were confining things, he decided.

Yet he went back again. A week later this time, and still not quite knowing why. But he was there. And this time he stayed in his seat until the rehearsal had ended and the performers, one by one, filed past him. The director was the last to leave, but while the others hadn't given him a glance as they'd passed, she stopped.

She was a pretty woman, Garrick noticed, viewing her up close for the first time. Tall and willowy, she had long brown hair that was pulled into a high clasp at her crown, only to tumble smoothly down from there. She wore jeans and a heavy jacket and was clutching an armload of papers to her chest. She was younger than he'd expected, perhaps in her mid-twenties; he

guessed her to be either a teaching assistant or a graduate student.

"I've seen you here before," she said, cocking her
head.

Garrick remained sprawled in his seat. "I've stopped
by a few times."

"We'll be doing the show next weekend. I'd think
you'd rather see it then."

"Rehearsals are more interesting. They allow you to
see what really goes into the production."

"Are you a student of the theater?"

He took in a breath and pushed himself straighter.
"Not exactly."

"A connoisseur?"

He shrugged, then hoisted himself to his feet. He
didn't miss the slight widening of the woman's eyes at
his height. "Not exactly. What about you?"

"A grad student. We often direct undergraduate productions." When she turned and started walking toward
the door, he followed. His heart was pounding in protest, but his legs seemed not to hear.

"Doing Chekov is an ambitious endeavor," he remarked.

"Isn't that what learning is about—challenge?"

He didn't answer that. He'd never associated the acting he'd done with learning, and his major challenge had
been in topping the Nielsens for the week. "Do you get
much of a crowd at your shows?" he asked.

"Sometimes yes, sometimes no. This one probably
won't be as well attended, since it's more serious and
heavy. We'll get some of the university types, but the
local crowd is drawn to lighter things." They'd passed
through the lobby and reached the door, which Garrick

held open with a rigid hand. As she stepped into the daylight, she looked up at him. "Do you live locally?"

"For now."

"Are you affiliated with the university?"

"I'm taking a few courses."

They'd stopped at the top of the stone steps. She was staring at him. "Studying anything special?"

"Latin."

She laughed. "That's an odd one." But her laughter died quickly. Her eyes were fixed on his. She frowned for an instant.

"Is something wrong?"

"Uh, no. You look vaguely familiar. I, uh, I don't think I know any Latin students."

He didn't know if it was a come-on. Yes, he thought her attractive, but it was an objective judgment. She didn't turn him on in any way, shape or fashion. Still, he didn't leave.

"Is this your first year here?" she asked as she continued to study him closely.

"Yes." Feeling inexplicably bold despite the damp palms he pressed to the insides of his pockets, he returned her gaze unwaveringly.

"Are you a professional student?"

"Nope."

"What did you do before you came here?"

"Work."

"Doing…?"

"I work up north."

Again she frowned. Her gaze fell to his beard, then returned to his eyes. "I'm really sorry, but you do look familiar."

"Maybe I just look like someone else," he suggested with an outer calm that was far from matched inside.

She started to shake her head, but paused. "That may be it." Her eyes sharpened; Garrick noticed that they were brown, rather nondescript, nowhere near as warm or interesting as Leah's gray ones. Then she grinned. "That *is* it. Has anyone ever told you that you look like Pagen?"

"Pagen?"

"You know, the guy on television a few years back? Actually, his name was Greg Reynolds. I was a teenager when Pagen was in his heyday. He was one beautiful man." She blushed, then frowned again. "He disappeared from the scene pretty quickly after the series ended. I wonder what happened to him."

"Maybe he left the business and went to live in the woods," Garrick heard himself say.

"Maybe," she mused, then her look grew skeptical. "Are you sure you're not him?"

Of course I'm not, Garrick could have said, or *Are you kidding?* or *No way!* Instead, and for reasons unknown to him, he shrugged.

"You are," she said, an inkling of excitement in her voice. "You are Greg Reynolds. I can see it now. Your hair's a little different and you have a beard, but the eyes are the same…and the mouth." She was looking at the last in a way that made him press it closed.

"You're not talking," she announced with a sage nod, then held up one hand. "And your secret's safe with me. I promise." Then, suddenly, all pretense of maturity crumbled. "I don't believe it's you," she singsonged, eyes aglitter. "What was it like in Hollywood? It must have been so exciting doing the series! I thought you were wonderful! I'd like to be there for one day—one week—one month! You really *made* it. What have you done since then? Have you ever considered doing something here? You can't have retired from acting completely, not after…all that!"

"I've retired," he said quietly, but the statement was ineffective in staunching her enthusiasm.

"I had no idea we had a celebrity in our midst. No one else did, either, or word would have spread. My students would *love* to meet you. You'd be an inspiration!"

He shook his head. "I think not." He took a step to leave, but she put a hand on his sleeve.

"Maybe you'd speak before the theater group. I know the other grad students and the professors would be as excited as I am—"

"Thank you, but I really can't."

When he started off, she fell into step beside him. "Just me, then. Would you let me take you to lunch some day? You have no idea how much I'd like to hear about your experiences. God, they'd make a fantastic book. Have you ever thought of writing about your years as Pagen?"

"No," he said, and quickened his step.

"How about it? Just lunch, or…or dinner? I know a fantastic little place that's dark and quiet. No one would have to know we were there—"

"I'm really not free." He strode on.

The young woman stopped, but she couldn't resist calling after him. "Mr. Reynolds?"

He didn't answer. He wasn't Mr. Reynolds. Not anymore.

THAT NIGHT, WHILE he and Leah were finishing off the last of the stew he'd made, Garrick told her what had happened.

"You told her who you were?" Leah asked in astonishment. It was the last thing she'd have expected him to do.

"She guessed, and I didn't deny it." He was reclining in his chair, one arm hooked over its back, the other fiddling absently with the spoon he hadn't used. He looked nearly as confused as Leah. "It was strange. I think I wanted her to know, but for the life of me I can't understand why. You know how I feel about my anonymity." He looked up, those wonderful hazel-and-silver eyes clouded. "Why did I do that, Leah?"

"I'm not sure," she answered quietly. "Did you feel anything…sitting there in the theater?"

"It was interesting. The kids were pretty good. But did I feel envious? No."

"Did you get the urge to jump up there?"

"God, no."

"You didn't miss being on center stage?"

"I didn't miss being on stage period. I was very happy to be sitting in the dark."

She breathed a tiny sigh of relief.

"I heard that," Garrick chided, narrowing one eye. "You were worried."

"I don't want you to miss anything about that life," she said a little evasively, then added, "What about the woman?"

"What about her?"

"Do you think that somehow, maybe subconsciously, you wanted to impress her?"

He shook his head. "No. She was pretty and all, but not like you."

"But she's a thespian."

"Good word, but it has no relevance."

"Sure it does. She's involved in the same kind of life you came from. A person like that might not go gaga over trapping, but she would about acting, particularly big-time acting."

"What I used to do was small time compared to the people who do Chekov or Williams or—even more so—Shakespeare. No, I wasn't trying to impress her."

"Maybe you just got tired of the waiting."

"What do you mean?"

Leah searched for an example to illustrate her point. The only one was the most obvious, and since it filled so much of her thoughts, she went with it. "There are times," she began quietly, "when I just want this baby to be born—one way or the other. It's the waiting and worrying and not knowing that's so bad. Even if the worst happens, at least I'll know, so I can go on with my life."

"Leah…"

"I'm sorry, but it's the only thing I can think of, and it makes my point. I would assume that for you, it must be nearly as bad wandering around Concord, waiting for someone to recognize you, worrying about what will happen when someone does. Maybe you wanted to get it over with. Maybe one part of you wanted that woman to know who you were."

He opened his mouth to protest, then clamped it shut and was silent for a minute. "Maybe."

"How did you feel when the truth came out?"

His tawny brows knit as he tried to verbalize his thoughts. "Weird. A little proud, but a little like an imposter, too. I felt distanced…like she was talking about someone else entirely when she started bombarding me with questions. I felt like I was playing a game, letting her *believe* I was Greg Reynolds, superstar, when I knew that I wasn't."

"Did she bring back memories of how the fans used to be?"

"Yes and no. She went all wide-eyed and high-voiced like a typical fan, but I didn't like it the way I used to. To tell you the truth, it was disgusting. Up to that point, she'd seemed dignified." He gave a lopsided grin. "I have to admit that I felt damn good walking away from her."

"Do you think she was offended?"

"Lord, I hope so," he answered without remorse. "With luck, she'll dismiss me as a fraud. If she starts blabbing about who I am, things might get a little hairy."

"She doesn't know your real name."

He scowled. "No, but she knows I'm studying Latin. It wouldn't be hard for her to track me down. Maybe I'll cut the next class or two and stay here with you."

"Chicken."

"Nuh-uh." He covered her hand with his and began a gentle massage. "I do want to be here with you. It's getting close."

"Three weeks."

"How do you feel?"

"Tired."

"Emotionally?"

"Tired. I meant what I said before. The waiting's getting to me."

"Everything's been fine so far."

"It was the other two times, too."

"You've never had a cesarean section before. It'll minimize stress on the baby during delivery."

"I hope."

He squeezed her hand. "It will. Things will work out fine, love. You'll see. A month from now, we'll have a squirming little thing on our hands."

"That's just what I told myself eight months into two other pregnancies."

"But this time is different. That's *my* baby you're carrying."

She sighed, then smiled sadly. "Which is precisely why I want it so badly."

THE NEXT WEEK was an uneventful one for Leah, but, then, she'd known it would be. Aside from when she was eating or using the bathroom, she remained in bed. She didn't do much reading because she couldn't seem to concentrate. She didn't do much weaving because, with the bulk of the loom and that of her stomach, she couldn't get comfortable. She listened to music, which was fine for a time, particularly since Garrick kept her supplied with new tapes that they both enjoyed. Susan came to visit often, usually—and deliberately, Leah suspected, to keep an eye on her—while Garrick was in school.

She didn't do much work of the official puzzle-making variety because she'd declared herself on a temporary leave of absence. But she found herself working on that private puzzle, the one involving words that related to what she'd fondly come to think of as the life and times of Garrick and Leah. It was a whimsical endeavor and it helped keep her occupied.

Garrick's week wasn't quite as uneventful. He went back to school without missing a class, and though he was edgy during the first two days, he saw no sign of the young woman from the theater. On the third day, just when he was beginning to relax again, she accosted him as he was leaving his class.

"I have to talk to you for a minute, Mr. Reynolds," she said quickly and a little nervously as she fell into step beside him. "I was serious about what I said the other day. It would mean the world to all of us if you would agree to speak."

He kept walking at the same even pace. "I have nothing to say."

"But you do. You've had experiences we've only dreamed of having."

"I'm not who you think I am."

"You are. After we talked the other day, I went to the library and pored through the microfilms. The last anyone heard from or saw of Greg Reynolds was shortly before an automobile accident. The accident was reported in the papers. Greg Reynolds survived it, then disappeared. With your face and body, it would be too much of a coincidence to think that you're not him."

He sliced her a glance, but she went on, clearly proud of herself.

"I researched further. Greg Reynolds's real name is Garrick Rodenhiser. That's the name you've enrolled under here."

Garrick stopped then. "I'm a private citizen, Miss—"

"Schumacher. Liza Schumacher."

"I don't give talks, Miss Schumacher—"

"Liza. We could keep it to a small group, if that's what you'd prefer."

"I'd prefer," he said quietly, almost beseechingly, "to have my privacy respected."

"We'd pay you—"

"No, thanks." He started off again.

"An hour. A *half*-hour. That's all we'd ask—"

But he simply shook his head and kept going. Fortunately she didn't follow.

Again he told Leah about the encounter. Again she explored his feelings about it. "Are you sure you don't want to do it?"

"Speak? Are you kidding?"

"She's right, in a way. You have had the kind of experience that many of them want. It's not unusual for representatives of different careers to talk to groups of students."

"Whose side are you on, Leah?"

"Yours. You know that."

Thrusting his legs from the bed, he landed on his feet and stalked off to the window. "Well, I don't want to speak—before students or any other group. For one thing, I don't think much of the kind of experience I had. For another, I don't relish the idea of confessing my sins to an audience."

"There was a positive side to what you did."

"Mmm. Somewhere. I can't seem to see it, though. I suppose I could make up a good story...."

"Garrick..."

He continued to stare out the window.

"Why—really—won't you speak?"

He was silent for several more minutes, but he knew that Leah suspected the truth. It remained to be seen whether he had the courage to confirm it.

"Ah, hell," he muttered at last. "The truth of it is that deep down inside, I'm afraid I'll like the feeling of power that comes when you've got an audience in your thrall—the rapt faces, the adulation, the applause. If I do it once, I may want to do it again, and if I do it a second time, a third could follow, and by that time I could be hooked on how wonderful I am."

"You are wonderful."

He bent his head and smiled, then turned and retraced his steps to the bed. Stretching out on his stomach before Leah, he grabbed her hand and pressed it to her lips. "You're the only one I want to hear saying that, because you're the only one who knows the real me. I've never talked to anyone the way I have to you. You're better than an analyst any day."

Leah wasn't sure if she liked the idea of being an analyst, because knowing another person's thoughts meant knowing his fears, and Garrick still had many. She thought he'd made progress since he'd been in Concord, and perhaps, to some extent, he had—but he still didn't trust himself. And that frightened her. She knew that she'd need his strength in the coming weeks and she didn't want anything to dilute it.

"I'll settle for being your soul mate," she said, and offered her lips for a kiss.

THE SUDDEN SNOWSTORM that hit during the first week of December did nothing for Leah's peace of mind. True, Garrick's classes were canceled, so he stayed home with her. But she had visions of going into premature labor while they were snowbound, in which case everything they'd gone through might have been in vain.

They weren't truly snowbound, as it happened. Nor did she go into premature labor. Day by day, though, she felt the baby move lower, and though Gregory had made arrangements to do the section on the fifteenth of December, she wondered if Garrick's monster would wait that long.

It was harder to see Garrick off to class now. She was physically uncomfortable and emotionally strung out. Only when he was with her could she begin to relax, knowing that he'd take over if something happened. But she did send him off. She felt he needed it, in more respects than the obvious one of taking his mind off the baby and her.

On the eleventh of December she wished she'd been more selfish.

CHAPTER TEN

GARRICK LEFT CLASS and walked to his car, but he'd barely reached for the door, when a loud call echoed across the parking lot.

"Mr. Reynolds!"

His grip tightened on the handle. Only one person would call him that, and the last thing he wanted to do was to talk with her now. He wanted to be home with Leah.

"Mr. Reynolds! Wait! Please!"

He opened the door and fleetingly contemplated jumping inside, slamming down the locks and wheeling off. But he wasn't a coward. Not anymore.

Propping one arm above the window, he turned his head toward the young woman approaching. "Yes, Miss Schumacher?"

Breathing hard from the run, she skidded to a halt by his side. "Thank you for waiting…I wanted to get here earlier…my class ran late."

"I'm running late myself. Was there something you wanted?" His breath was a white cloud in the cold air, though not quite large enough for him to vanish into as he wished he could do.

"Since you didn't feel comfortable speaking, I had another idea." She darted a quick glance behind her. To Garrick's dismay, a young man was trotting up to join them. "Darryl's with the town newspaper. I thought—

we thought—that it would be super to have an article...."

Garrick frowned. "I thought you said this would be our secret."

"I did. But then I started thinking." She was slowly catching her breath. "It didn't seem fair to be selfish—"

"About what?"

"About knowing who you are. It seemed unfair that I should keep everything to myself—"

"Unfair to *you?*"

"No, no. To the people around here who would find your story interesting."

Garrick studied her steadily. "What about me? What about what's fair and unfair where *I'm* concerned?"

If anything, she grew bolder. "You're a star, Mr. Reynolds. Doesn't that bring with it certain responsibilities?"

"I'm not a star anymore," he stated unequivocably and with an odd kind of pride. "I'm a private citizen. I have many responsibilities, but as far as I can see, none of them have to do with you, or your fellow students, or your professors, or your friends." He cocked his head toward the reporter. "Is he your boyfriend?"

She exchanged an awkward look with Darryl. "We've gone out a few times, but that doesn't have anything—"

"Are you lovers?"

"That's not—"

"Is she good?" Garrick asked Darryl.

Liza went red in the face. "That's none of your business. I don't see what my private life has to do with—"

"*My* private life?" Garrick finished. "Nothing, Miss Schumacher. My questions are as much an invasion of your privacy as anything you— or Darryl—would ask *me*. I've already told you that I'm not interested in appearing publicly. That goes for big talks, small talks, newspaper articles and whatever *else* you come up with."

While he'd been speaking, Liza's expression had gone from embarrassment to dismay. In the silent minute that followed, it moved to anger. "The papers I read were right," she decided, abandoning all pretense of deference. "You are arrogant."

"Not really," Garrick said, surprised by the feeling of peace that was settling over him. "I'm simply trying to explain my feelings." And not only to her. Suddenly things were falling into place. His vision of who he was and what he wanted in life was becoming crystal clear.

Liza drew herself straighter. "I think you're a has-been. You disappeared from the acting scene. I think it was because you couldn't land any good parts after *Pagen*. I think you're afraid to stand before a group, knowing that."

She was tall, but Garrick was taller. Setting his shoulders back, he took a deep breath. "You know something, Miss Schumacher? I don't care what you think. The fact of the matter is that I'm not afraid to stand before anyone. I'm simply…not…interested. I chose to give up acting because it did nothing good for my life. You could offer me top billing in your next production and I'd refuse. You could offer to let me direct and I'd refuse. You could offer me headlines in the paper and I'd refuse. I live quietly now. I have a life that is much richer than anything I've known before. If you'd like to do an article, I'd be happy to tell you about trapping, or studying Latin, or whittling chess sets. As for acting, it's not *me* anymore. I've been away from it for nearly five years now, and I don't miss it."

"I find that hard to believe," Liza said.

"I'm sorry."

"You're satisfied being a…a trapper?"

"That's only one of the things I do, but, yes, I'm satisfied. Very satisfied."

"But the publicity—"

"Means nothing to me. I don't need it, and I don't want it." His tone was a mellow one, but it held undisputable conviction, just as the glance he sent Darryl held more sympathy than apology. "I'm sorry you won't get your story, but I really have nothing more to say."

"Mr. Rodenhiser? Mr. Rodenhiser!"

His head shot up in response to the alarmed cry, eyes flying in the direction of the voice. It came from a woman he recognized as being a secretary in the language department. She was clutching a coat around her with one hand, waving a small piece of paper in the other as she speed-walked toward the car.

"Thank goodness you haven't left," she panted.

The sense of peace Garrick had experienced earlier was gone. His blood ran cold.

"You just received a call from a Susan Walsh. She said that you were to meet Leah at the hospital."

"Oh, God," he whispered hoarsely, but the words hadn't left his mouth before he was in the car, leaving Liza Schumacher to jump out of the way of the slamming door. She and her boyfriend, the secretary, the school, the newspaper—all were forgotten. The only things he could think of were Leah and their baby. *What had happened?*

Over and over he asked the question, sometimes silently, sometimes aloud. He drove as fast as he could, swerving after what seemed an eternity into a space outside the hospital's emergency entrance. After being directed from one desk to the next, he finally connected with Gregory, who quickly put a reassuring arm around his shoulder.

"Her water broke. We're prepping her now. Come on. We'll both scrub up."

"How is she?"

"Terrified."

"And the baby?"

"So far, so good. I want to take it as quickly as possible."

Garrick didn't ask any more questions. He was too busy praying. Besides, he knew that Gregory didn't have the answer to the one question he most wanted to ask. Only time would give that, and time was precious. He matched his step to the doctor's as they hurried down the hall.

Leah's eyes were on the door when Garrick entered the delivery room. She held out a shaking hand and clutched his fingers fiercely. "They said you were on your way. Thank God you're here."

"What happened?"

"My water broke. I was lying in bed and it just broke. I hadn't moved, I hadn't done anything—"

"Shhhh." He was bending over her, pressing his mouth to her matted bangs. "You've done everything right, Leah. You've followed doctor's orders to the letter. Tell me, how did you get here?"

"I called Susan. Wasn't that stupid? I should have called Gregory directly, but I remember thinking that Susan was closer and that I was glad we had a phone so I wouldn't have to walk from the apartment to the house."

"It was smart of you to call Susan. She's cool under fire."

"She called Gregory, and Gregory called the ambulance while I just sat there, *trembling*."

"It's okay, honey." He had a hand in her hair but was looking around the room in bewilderment, trying to interpret every nuance of the bustling activity. "Everything's going to be okay." A cloth barrier was being lifted into place to shield the operation from their view. He knew that it was standard procedure for a cesarean section, but then it struck him that, since her water had broken, she had to be in labor. His eyes shot to hers. "Are you in pain?"

She gave a rapid little shake of her head. "I felt a few contractions before, but the spinal's taken effect. I don't feel a thing." Her eyes widened and her fingers tightened around his. "I don't feel anything, Garrick. Maybe something's happened—"

Gregory came up at that moment. "The baby's fine, Leah. We're monitoring the heartbeat, and it's fine." His gaze swung from her face to Garrick's, then back. "All set to go?"

Their nods were identically jerky. Gregory moved off. The anesthetist came to sit by Leah's head, while a nurse slid a stool beneath Garrick.

"Please, let it live," Leah whispered to no one in the room.

"It will," Garrick whispered back, but his eyes were worried as they sought out Gregory.

"We're all thinking positive," was Gregory's response. He wasn't making promises, but he appeared fully confident, which was as much as Leah could have asked.

"Garrick?" she murmured.

"Yes, love?"

"How did everything go at school today?"

He was momentarily startled. His thoughts weren't on school. It was an unlikely subject to discuss given the time, place and circumstance. But he quickly understood what Leah was doing, so he forced himself to shift gears. "Not bad. I aced the exam."

"No kidding?"

His smile was wobbly. "Would I kid at a time like this? I got a ninety-seven."

"They say that older students do better."

"And I aced something else today."

"What?"

"Liza Schumacher."

They were talking in hushed tones, eyes locked into each other's with an urgency that acknowledged something momentous was taking place.

"What happened with Liza Schumacher?" Leah asked.

"She approached me with a local journalist in tow."

"Journalist!"

"They wanted an interview."

"Oh, no." Her fingers tightened around Garrick's, but it didn't have to do with the interview as much as the quiet talk coming from beyond the cloth barrier. She wanted to ask what was happening but didn't dare.

Garrick seemed in a similar quandary. He darted frantic eyes toward Gregory, who was concentrating on his work, his lower face covered by a mask. Garrick quickly calmed his expression when he looked down at Leah again.

"I said that I wasn't interested and it struck me that I wasn't. I really wasn't."

"Temptation—"

"Isn't temptation. I don't want what's being offered. There's nothing to threaten me."

"But if she'd already told one reporter who you are—"

"It doesn't matter. She can tell ten reporters, and it still won't matter."

"And if this one reporter writes something—"

"That's fine. He can write about how I've found a better life. It's not the kind of story that will sell papers, so one installment will be enough. He'll lose interest. Other reporters will, too. And it won't bother me at all."

"I'm glad," she whispered, then added quickly, "What are they doing?"

"Baby's doing well, Leah," came Gregory's call. "You two keep talking. It sounds like a fascinating discussion."

"I want the baby, Garrick," she whimpered.

"Me, too, love. Me, too. Are you feeling anything?"

"No."

"Any pain?"

"No."

All too aware of the emotional pain she was undergoing, he sent a panicky glance toward the anesthesiologist. "Maybe you should have knocked her out."

"No!" Leah cried. "I want to know."

"We're getting there, Leah," came Gregory's utterly calm voice.

It settled Leah momentarily. Tipping her head farther toward Garrick, she pressed their twined hands to her warm cheek. "When...when are finals?" she asked in the same small whisper she'd used before.

"Another week. I may skip them."

"Oh, no—after all the work you've done?"

"I'm only taking the courses for fun."

"Then take the exams for fun."

"Exams aren't fun."

"I'll help you study."

"That might be fun. But then you might be—"

A tiny cry cut off his words. His heart began to slam against his ribs, and he jerked up his head.

Leah's breath was catching in her throat. "Garrick?" She raised her voice. "Gregory?"

Another stronger cry echoed through the room, followed by Gregory's satisfied, "Ahhh, she's a lusty one."

"She," Leah breathed, tear-filled eyes clinging to Garrick's face.

He was rising from the stool, tearing his gaze from Leah to focus on the small bundle Gregory held. A tiny arm flailed the air. Grinning through unchecked tears, he returned to Leah.

"She waved."

"She's moving?"

"See for yourself," said Gregory as he held the baby high.

Leah saw. Arms and legs batted the air to the tune of a sturdy pair of lungs. Leah started to cry, too. "She's... alive...beautiful...Garrick...do you...see?"

He had an arm curved around Leah's head. "I see," he managed to croak, then pressed his wet cheek to her forehead.

"Show's over," came the decree from the pediatric specialist who'd been assisting in the proceedings. He gently took the infant from Gregory. "Sorry, folks. She's mine for a few minutes."

It was just as well. Leah's arms were around Garrick's neck, and they were burying their faces against each other, muffling soft sobs of gratitude and joy.

"AMANDA BETH. IT's as beautiful as she is." Leah was lying flat in bed, per doctor's orders, but Garrick was sitting by her side, so she didn't mind the temporary restriction.

Garrick's face was alight with pride. "The pediatrician can't find a thing wrong with her. They'll keep a close watch on her for a few days, but they don't foresee any problem."

"Seven pounds, five ounces."

"Not bad for an early baby."

"Oh, Garrick, I'm so happy!" She was smiling broadly, as was Garrick, neither of them able—or caring—to stop.

"We did it. *You* did it. Thank you, Leah. Thank you for giving me a beautiful daughter, and for giving me self-confidence, and for loving me."

Grabbing his ear, she tugged him down for a kiss. "Thank *you.* I feel so complete."

"That's good," he said, raising his head a trifle. "Because we're expecting visitors in a few minutes, and I want you at your best."

"Victoria?" she asked in excitement.

"Nope. She'll be here later in the week. Insists on helping you out when we take baby home."

Her smile grew dreamy. "Take baby home. I never thought we'd be saying those words." For the first time her smile faltered. Her eyes went wide behind her glasses. "Garrick! Clothes, diapers, a crib—we haven't got *anything!*" After two pregnancies when she'd been fully equipped, only to find herself without a baby, she'd been superstitious.

Garrick was unfazed. "No sweat. I'll pick up a crib— I think maybe a cradle—tomorrow. Victoria's buying the rest."

"Victoria? But she can't—"

He arched a brow. "Victoria?"

"Well, she can, but we can't let her!"

"I'm afraid we can't stop her. She was in a rush to

get off the phone so that she could get to the stores before they closed."

Leah was smiling again. "That does sound like Victoria."

"She feels responsible for the baby," he said, eyes
twinkling.

"Maybe we should let her think she is. We couldn't
very well make her interrupt her shopping to research
the facts of life, could we?"

He kissed her nose. "Certainly not."

"Garrick?"

But it wasn't Garrick who answered. "Hello, hello"
came Susan's singsong voice from the door. Gregory
was wheeling her in, followed closely by a man Leah
had never seen before.

"Ah. Our visitors." Garrick stood up quickly, kissing Susan, shaking hands with Gregory, then with the
other man, whom he brought forward. "Leah, say hello
to Judge Hopkins. He's agreed to marry us."

"Marry us?" Leah cried. "But…but I can't get married now!"

"Why not?"

"I…because I look a mess! My hair's tangled and
I'm sweaty—"

"But you are wearing white," Garrick pointed out in
a mischievous tone.

"A hospital gown," Leah returned in dismay. "They
won't even let me sit up to change."

"No problem," said Susan as she tugged a box from
where it had been stowed between her hip and the chair.
She turned to the men as a group. "Out." Then to her
husband. "Be a sweet and send a nurse in here to give
us a hand." Then to the judge. "We'll only be a min-

ute, Andrew." Then to Garrick. "Think you can control yourself that long?"

None of them answered, because Gregory was busy pushing them toward the door.

LEAH WAS MARRIED in the gown and matching robe that Susan had somehow known to buy in pale pink. Garrick, wearing the same sweater and cords he'd worn to school that day, stood by her bedside, holding her hand, while the judge conducted the brief ceremony. When, at its conclusion, Gregory produced a bottle of champagne, Leah threw an apprehensive look at Garrick, who leaned low and spoke for her ears alone.

"You can't have any for another few hours, but then we'll share a little. Just a sip in token celebration. I don't need any more of a high than the one I'm on now. I don't think I ever will."

Five days later, Garrick and Leah brought Amanda Beth back to the small garage apartment. Leah was healing well, and the baby was as strong and healthy as they'd prayed she would be.

Victoria, who was staying in the Walsh's main house, was in her element. Declaring that Amanda was more interesting than the Maori any day, she fought Garrick for the honor of bathing, diapering and dressing her.

Since Leah was nursing, the feeding chores were hers alone. She loved those times when Amanda was suckling and the rest of the world became a warm, fuzzy periphery. Even more, though, she loved the times at night when Garrick would stretch out beside her and watch.

"What does it feel like?"

"When she nurses?"

"Mmm. Does it hurt?"

"Oh, no! It's a delightful kind of gentle tugging."

"Like when I kiss you there?" He drew a light fore-finger across the upper swell of her breast.

"A little. There's a sense of depth. I feel like there are strings inside me that she's pulling on. Sometimes I feel contractions. But it's different, too."

"How?"

"When she does it, it's satisfying in and of itself. When you do it, it makes me want more." She blushed. "Different kinds of sensations."

Garrick moaned and shifted his legs, making no attempt to hide his problem. The light in the eyes he raised to hers wasn't one of uncontrollable desire, though, as much as love. "I can't conceive of life without you, Leah. You…Amanda…when I think of the sterile existence I had before…"

"Don't look back," she urged in a whisper as she bent forward and brushed his lips with hers. "We've conquered the past. We have a wonderful present. Let's look forward to the future for a change."

They did just that. After long discussions with Leah, Garrick decided that he rather liked the idea of working toward the college degree he'd never earned. Baby and all, he managed to study for and do well in his finals, paving the way for his acceptance at Dartmouth, which had an excellent Latin department.

"You'll love Hanover," he told Leah. "It's got charm."

"I know I'll love it, but what about you? Don't you miss the cabin?"

"To tell you the truth, no." He seemed as surprised as she that the answer came so quickly. "I love it up there, but my life now is so full that I rarely think of it. I'd like to get a house in Hanover and use the cabin as a vacation retreat."

That was exactly what they did. With Amanda

strapped into a carrier against Garrick's chest, they looked at every possible home in Hanover, finally falling in love with and buying a small Victorian within walking distance of Garrick's classes. During school vacations, weather permitting, they returned to the cabin. Come June, shortly before they were to retreat there for the summer, Garrick approached Leah with a proposal.

"How about a trip to New York?"

Her eyes lit up. "New York?"

"Yeah. I know you hated it last time you went—"

"I was pregnant and tired and worried, and you weren't with me." Her voice lowered. "Will you go this time?"

"I won't let you and Amanda go alone, and Victoria has been begging us for months to visit."

She wrapped an arm around his waist. "I'd love to go, Garrick, but only if you're sure."

"I'm sure." He winked down at her. "We may even be able to get some time to ourselves."

Their visit to New York was enlightening in several respects. Garrick found that he was relaxed and at ease. Leah found that though they had a wonderful time, she was ready to leave again when the time came.

Equally as gratifying was Victoria's news. She'd heard through the grapevine that Richard and his wife had had a second baby—this one stillborn. And while Leah's heart went out to them, she couldn't help but close her eyes in relief. It seemed that Richard's wife, not about to take the tragedy sitting down, had done some research. Richard had been adopted at birth, but she'd managed to work through the courts to determine his biological parents—and had discovered that infant mortality had been documented over two generations on his father's side.

"All our worrying was for nothing," Leah breathed, but Garrick was quick to disagree.

"No, love. The worry may have been unnecessary, but it served a purpose. If you hadn't been worried, you'd never have left me and moved to Concord. And if you hadn't done that, I would have stayed at the cabin, where I would be to this day. Think of all we'd have missed."

She knew that he was right. His self-confidence had been fully restored, and his self-respect had taken on new dimensions. He'd survived the auto accident and found a fresh basis for life, but only since Leah had come had he begun to really grow.

Which was what she wanted to do...again. "This means we can have another baby—"

"Without worry."

"But not just yet."

"Maybe when Amanda's two."

"We'll go for a boy this time."

"How're we gonna arrange that?"

"There are ways. I was reading an article recently that said—"

"Since when do you read articles about planning a baby's sex?"

"Since the world has opened up to me and I've begun to dream again."

THROUGH THE YEARS to come, Leah and Garrick both did their share of dreaming, each time setting out to make those dreams come true. But during that first summer at the cabin with Amanda, they were too content to do much dreaming. The sun was warm, the air fresh, the forest as magnificent and lush as they'd ever seen it. Garrick worked in his garden, often with Amanda babbling in sweet baby talk beside him. Leah was always nearby, often constructing puzzles to send off to her editor. The crossword from which she took the most pleasure, though, was the one that chronicled the life and times of Leah and Garrick. Now there was Amanda to fit into the grid, but doing so was simple.

"Aha," Garrick teased. "So *that's* why you wanted to name her Amanda. Three *A*'s. You need them."

"I named her Amanda because I love the name and you love the name and because, obviously, *she* loves the name."

"She'd love *any* name, as long as there's banana ice cream after we call her."

"I love banana ice cream."

"So do I. But I love you and Amanda more. Hey—" he studied her puzzle "—have you got it here?"

"What?"

"Love."

"Sure. It's all over the place—in every noun, every adjective, every—"

"Four letters. L-O-V-E."

"It's there."

"I can't find it."

"Look closer."

"I can't find it."

"Look higher."

"I can't find it."

"To the right."

"I can't—I can. Ahhhh. There it is. Twelve across. L-O-V-E. Very simple and straight to the point. Now that's my kind of word."

* * * * *

THREATS AND PROMISES

PROLOGUE

THE DARK OF night lay thick in the garden of the lavish Hollywood Hills estate where two shadowed figures conversed in low tones. Both were men. One was tall, broad and physical; the other was smooth, arrogant and cerebral.

"Are you sure? Absolutely sure?" the smooth one demanded, sounding less smooth than usual as his eyes pierced the darkness to bead mercilessly at his companion.

"She wasn't in that car," the tall one insisted quietly.

"You said she was. I buried her."

"You buried ashes of what we thought was her. We were wrong."

The smooth one's nostrils flared, but he kept his voice low. "And how can you be sure it wasn't her?"

"One of our men heard talk around the coroner's office. There was no evidence of a body, charred or otherwise. A burned purse and shoes, but no body. Unofficially, of course. Officially, at least as far as the heat's concerned, she's dead."

The arrogant one cursed under his breath. He pulled a pack of cigarettes from his pocket and barely had time to raise one to his mouth when the underling snapped a match with his thumbnail and lit it.

"No body," he muttered, squaring his shoulders. "So she got away."

The physical one had enough sense to keep still. He knew what was to come, knew he had his work cut out for him.

"I want her found," the smooth one growled. "I want her found *now*."

Still the physical one remained silent.

"She didn't have any family, at least none she ever told me about. She wasn't in touch with anyone else, and her friends were mine." A long drag on the cigarette momentarily brightened its glowing red tip. "She must have had help." Smoke curled out with the words and dissipated into the air. "New identity, new location, money.... Damn it," he gritted out as the wheels of his mind turned, "she sold the jewels. There wasn't any burglary. The bitch took the jewels herself and sold them!"

"I'll find her."

"Damn right you will. Half a million in diamonds and rubies, not to mention another hundred thou in furs—no woman can steal like that from me!"

"Do you want me to bring her back?"

The tall man's boss pondered that as he stroked the closely shaved skin above his lip. When he spoke, his voice was low once more and as dark as the night. "She's a thief. And a traitor. I've given her a funeral fit for a queen. I won't suffer the embarrassment of having her materialize from the grave." He paused for a moment before continuing smoothly, arrogantly, cerebrally, in his own perverted way. "She's dead. That's how I want her. Make her squirm first. Let her know that I know what she's done. Get the jewels and whatever else you can from her. Then see that she's buried, this time with an unmarked stone."

Tossing the cigarette to the grass, he ground it out

beneath the sole of his imported leather shoe. Then he straightened his silk evening jacket, thrust out his chin and walked calmly, coolly, back toward the house.

CHAPTER ONE

LAUREN STEVENSON LOOKED at herself in the mirror. And looked. And looked. "It doesn't matter how long I stand here," she said breathlessly. "I still can't believe it's me!"

Richard Bowen grinned at her reflection. "It's you, and if I do say so myself, it's smashing."

She slanted him a shy glance. In the weeks during which she'd come to know this man, she'd grown perfectly comfortable with him as her doctor. But she couldn't ignore the fact that he was attractive; hence his compliment was that much more weighty. "I'll bet you say that to all the women you've worked on."

"Not necessarily. Some only look good. Some only look better than they did before. For that matter," he added with a wink, "some looked better before the surgery."

"You don't tell them that, do you?" she chided.

"Are you kidding? If it's vanity that's brought them down here, I'm not about to make an enemy for life. But it wasn't vanity that brought you here, Lauren Stevenson, was it?"

She shook her head. "It was sheer necessity." Once again she eyed herself in the mirror. "I'm amazed, though. I knew there'd be an improvement..." She faltered. Narcissism was foreign to her nature. Her cheeks grew red, her voice humble. "I didn't expect half this."

Richard's laugh was filled with intense satisfaction.

"Cases like yours are the most gratifying. You had the makings of a real beauty when you walked in here. All it took was a little rearranging."

Very lightly, she ran her fingertips down her straight nose, then along her newly reformed jawline. "More than a little." Her hand fell to graze her hip as she turned back to Richard. "And I've put on ten pounds in as many weeks. Funny, but I would have thought that having my jaws banded together and drinking through a straw would make me lose weight."

"You couldn't afford to have that happen, which was why I put you on a high-calorie liquid diet. And now that you can take in solids, I want you to follow the regimen I gave you to the letter. You could still use another five pounds on that slender frame of yours, which means you'll have to work at eating. Remember, you'll be able to chew just a little at a time until the muscles of your jaws regain their strength. How's it been since we removed the bands?"

"A little sore, but okay."

"It's only been three days. The soreness will ease off. You're talking well. In some cases we have to bring in a speech therapist, but I don't think you have to worry about that." He rose from where he'd been perched on the corner of his desk. A soft breeze wafted from the open window behind him, bringing with it the gentle rustle of palms and the fragile essence of frangipani blossoms. "So what do you think? Are you ready to go home?"

Her sigh was a teasing one, and her eyes twinkled. "I don't know. Ten weeks in the Bahamas…body wraps, massages, manicures…sun and sand and sipping all kinds of goodies through straws…. It's not a bad life."

"But the best is ahead. When does your plane leave?"

"In two hours."

"Nervous?"

"About my debut?" She sent him a helpless look of apology. "A little."

"Will someone be meeting you when you land in Boston?"

"Uh-huh. Beth."

He squinted and raised a finger, trying to keep names straight. "Your business partner, right?"

Lauren smiled. "Right. She's dying to show me everything she's done since I've been gone. She rented the spot we wanted in the Marketplace, and from what she writes, the renovations are nearly done. We've got prints and frames on order and have been in close contact with the artists we'll be representing, so it's just a question of getting everything framed and on display."

"For what it's worth, Lauren, you strike me as a patient but determined woman. I'm sure you'll be successful." He threw a gentle arm over her shoulders as she started for the door. "You'll drop me a line and let me know how things are going?"

"Uh-huh."

"And you've got the name I gave you of the specialist in Boston in case you have a problem?"

"Uh-huh."

"And you'll be sure to eat—and eat well?"

"I'll try."

Releasing her shoulder, he turned to study her face a final time. His gaze took in the symmetry of her nose, the graceful line of her jaw and the now-perfect alignment of her chin before coming to rest with warmth on her pale gray eyes. "Smashing, Lauren. I'm telling you, you look smashing."

"Thank you. Thank you for everything, Richard."

"My pleasure, sweet lady." He gave her hand a tight go-get-'em squeeze, then turned back to his office. The last thing Lauren heard him say was a smug but thoroughly endearing "Good work, Richard. You done us proud this time."

Laughing softly, she retrieved her suitcase from the reception area and headed for the airport.

"YOU...LOOK...*SMASHING!*" was the first thing Beth Lavin could manage to say through her astonishment when, after Lauren had grinned at her for a full minute, she finally realized that it was indeed Lauren Stevenson who stood before her.

The two women hugged each other, and Lauren laughed. "You sound like my doctor."

"Well, he's right!" Beth's eyes were wide. Hands on Lauren's shoulders, she shifted her friend first to one side, then the next. "I don't believe it! Your profile is gorgeous, and you've filled out, and your eyes look huge and wide-set, and you had your hair cut...."

In a self-conscious gesture, one of pure habit, Lauren threaded her fingers into the hair above her ear to draw the thick chestnut fall forward. Then she caught herself. With a concerted effort, she completed the backward swing, letting her hair swirl gently around her ears so that her face was free of the cover she'd hid behind for years. "I really look okay?" There was honest anxiety in her voice.

"You have to ask?"

Lauren gave an awkward half shrug. "I look at myself in the mirror and see a new person, but in my mind I'm the way I've always been."

"I'm no psychologist, but I'd say that's normal." Beth's expression brimmed with excitement and the touch of mischief Lauren knew so well. "A different person—think of the possibilities! What if you were to bump into someone you'd known before, someone like Rafe Johnson—"

"Macho Rafe?"

"Macho Rafe, who would never have thought to look at either of us, but all of a sudden he sees this gorgeous woman and makes his play. You could string him along, then reveal your true identity and cut him off dead. Ah, the satisfaction!"

"You're awful, Beth."

But Beth was staring at her again, this time with a touch of awe. "Maybe.... God, you look marvelous," she said, moments before her face twisted in mock horror. "And *I'm* going to look positively plain next to you!"

"Fat chance, Beth Lavin." Lauren hooked her elbow through her friend's and started them both toward the baggage pickup. She knew that Beth was attractive; she also knew that Beth had worn her dark brown hair in the same long, straight hairstyle for fifteen years and that her clothes—the round-collared blouse, wraparound skirt and flat leather sandals she wore now being a case in point—were as down-country as Lauren's own had always been. "Neither one of us is going to look plain by the time we're ready to open that shop. I learned a lot down there, Beth. There were seminars on hairstyling and makeup and dressing for success. I took tons of notes—"

"You would."

"So would you, so don't give me that," Lauren teased gently. "Tell me, what's the latest with the shop?"

Beth took a deep breath. "I finally got the ad to look the way I wanted it. It'll appear in the next issue of *Boston*. The workmen should be done in another day or two—which is good, because the prints have started arriving. Not to mention the order forms, sales slips and stationery. And the frames and hooks, wire and labels. I've got everything stashed in my apartment."

"How *is* the apartment?"

"I like it. It's compact and within easy walking distance of the shop. Beacon Hill is exciting." Beth paused to ogle her friend again. "I can't believe you!"

"In another minute I'm going to put a bag over my head."

"Don't you dare. I'm thoroughly enjoying riding on your coattails. For that matter, I still wish you'd let me take a bigger apartment so we could room together."

"Rooming together *and* working together, we'd get on each other's nerves in no time. Besides, you want the city, while I want the country. Lots of room, wide-open spaces, trees, peace and quiet."

"You're thinking of that farmhouse."

"Uh-huh."

"You'll be isolated!"

"In Lincoln?" Lauren crinkled her nose. "Nah. I'll only have three acres. When the trees are bare, I'll be able to see neighbors on either side. And the commute will be little more than half an hour."

"But that farmhouse is a wreck!"

"It's simply in need of loving."

"Tell me you've already put in an offer."

Lauren grinned. "I've already put in an offer." At Beth's moan, Lauren delivered an affectionate nudge to her ribs. "When I couldn't get the place out of my mind, I called the realtor. The purchase agreement is ready and waiting to be signed."

"Lauren, Lauren, Lauren, what am I going to do with you?"

Lauren's eyes twinkled. "You're going to put me up at your place tonight. Then, tomorrow morning, you're going to take me on a grand tour of our pride and joy. After that we are both going shopping on Newbury Street."

"Oh?"

"Uh-huh."

"Could be expensive."

"That's right," Lauren agreed remorselessly.

Beth hunched up her shoulders and gave a naughty chuckle. "I love it, I love it." Then she abruptly narrowed her eyes and flattened her voice to a newspaper-headline drone. "Country bumpkins take city by storm. Effect transformation reminiscent of Clark Kent."

"Clark Kent?" was Lauren's wincing echo.

"Or Wonder Woman, or whomever. Of course, you know we're both a little crazy, don't you?"

"We're twenty-nine. We deserve it."

"I'll tell that to the creditors when they come calling."

Lauren Stevenson wasn't worried about the creditors. She wasn't a spendthrift, but she'd finally come to the realization that life was too short to be lived in a cocoon of timidity. Thanks to her saving prudently and the legacy she'd received when her brother had died nearly a year ago, Lauren had enough money to buy and renovate the farmhouse, pay what little wasn't covered by insurance for the corrective surgery she'd had, get a wardrobe befitting the new Lauren and establish the business.

"Here we go," she said as her luggage appeared on the revolving carousel. "Did you drive over or take a cab?"

"I drove. Your poor car was so glad to see me, I swear it got all choked up."

Lauren grunted. "Must need an oil change. On second thought, it needs to get out of the city. See, *it* wants to live in the country, too."

They left the enclosure of the terminal and headed for the parking lot. "Will you be driving north this weekend?" Beth ventured.

"To see my parents? I guess I'd better."

"I'd think you'd be excited—the new you and all."

Lauren grimaced. "You know my parents. For ultraliberals, they're as narrow as a pair of shoelaces. They didn't see the need for facial reconstruction. They thought I was just fine before."

"But medically, you were suffering!"

"I know that and you know that, and one part of them must know it, too. They're both brilliant, albeit locked in their ivory towers. I think they associate plastic surgery with vanity alone, and vanity isn't high on their list of admired traits. They said they loved me the way I was, and I'm sure they did, because that's what being a parent is all about. But let me tell you, I feel so much better now, even aside from the medical issue, I'm not sure they'd understand."

"Of course they would."

Lauren didn't argue further. Her trepidation about seeing her parents went far beyond the reconstructive surgery she'd had. She was starting a new life, and much of that life was being underwritten by her brother's bequest. Her parents resented that. Brad had been estranged from the family for eleven years preceding his death. Colin and Nadine Stevenson had neither forgotten nor forgiven what they'd considered to be their only son's abdication from the throne of the literati.

Lauren sighed. "Well, whatever the case may be, I'll see them this weekend. It may be the last time I'll be able to in a while." Lips toying with a smile, she darted a knowing glance at Beth. "I have a feeling that the next few weeks are going to be hectic."

"Hectic" was putting it mildly, though the pace was interlaced with such excitement that Lauren wouldn't have dreamed of complaining. With the completion of the redecoration of the shop, she and Beth began transferring things from Beth's apartment. Prints were framed and hung on the walls. Large art folders, filled with a myriad of additional prints and silk screens, were set in open cases on the floor for easy browsing. Vees of mat board in an endless assortment of colors were placed on Plexiglas stands atop the large butcher-block checkout counter, behind which were systematically arranged frame-corner samples, each attached to the wall with Velcro to facilitate their removal and replacement. Bolts of hand-screened fabric were attractively displayed beside bins containing unstained-wood frame kits; matching pillows were suspended from the ceiling like bananas from a tree.

Lauren signed the agreement on the farmhouse in Lincoln and, since it was already vacant, moved in a short week later. Her enthusiasm wasn't the slightest bit dampened when she saw at firsthand the amount of renovation the place would need. She had only to stand on her front porch and look across the lush yard to the forested growth surrounding her, or to smell the roses that climbed the porch-side trellis, or to listen to the birds as they whistled their spring mating ritual, to know that she'd made the right decision.

And, more than anything, she had only to look in the mirror to realize that she'd truly begun a new life.

In keeping with that new life, she and Beth did go shopping. They bought chic slacks, skirts, bright summer sweaters and lightweight dresses. They bought shoes and costume jewelry to coordinate with the outfits, all the while feeling slightly irresponsible yet enjoying every minute of it. Neither of them had been irresponsible before in their lives, but now they had earned the luxury.

Three weeks after Lauren returned from the Bahamas, the print-and-frame shop opened. It was the second week of June, and the fair-weather influx of visitors to the Marketplace kept a steady stream of shoppers circulating. With sales brisk, Lauren and Beth were ecstatic, so much so that on the first Friday night after closing, they took themselves to nearby Houlihan's to celebrate.

"If business continues this way, we'll have to hire someone to help," Lauren suggested. They were sitting at the crowded bar nursing cool drinks while they waited for their table.

"Tell me about it," Beth complained, but in delight. "There isn't enough time during the day to do bookkeeping, so I've been taking care of it at night. And you're going to need time to work with printmakers and the framer."

"I'll call the museum. Maybe they'll know of someone who'd be interested. If not, we can advertise in the newspaper."

In slow amazement, Beth shook her head. "I can't believe how good things were this week. We really lucked out with the location. There are people all over the place."

"Summer's always a busy season, what with tourists in the city. The Fanueil Hall is one of *the* spots to see."

"Wintertime's supposedly as good. At least, that's what Tom next door—you know, at the sports shop—told me."

Lauren's lips twitched mischievously. "So you've befriended Tom, have you? See what a new hairdo and clothes can do?"

Raking a hand through wavy black hair that had newly been cut to shoulder length, Beth wiggled her brows. "Look who's talking. That guy over there hasn't taken his eyes off you since we walked in."

"He's probably in a drunken stupor and I just happened into his line of vision."

"That's a crazy thing to say. You don't believe how good you look!"

Beth was right. Lauren had been accustomed to being practically invisible where men were concerned, and old habits die hard. Now she dared a quick glance in the mirror behind the bar to remind herself of the woman she'd become. Even her smart cotton sundress of crimson and cream was an eye-catcher.

With a conspiratorial glimmer in her eyes, she turned again to Beth. "Tell me about him. I don't want to be obvious and stare."

Beth had no such qualms, but she spoke in little more than a whisper. "He's of medium height and build and is wearing a brown suit. His hair's dark, a little too short. He's got aviator-style glasses—must be an affectation, since they don't go with the rest of him." Her voice suddenly frosted. "Oops, there's a wedding band." She instantly swiveled in her seat and stared straight ahead. "Forget him. He'd only be trouble."

Lauren grinned. "Forgotten."

"Doesn't it bother you? I mean, I'm sure he'd make a play for you if you flirted a little, and the bum's married."

Shrugging with her eyebrows alone, Lauren took a sip of her drink. "I think you're making too much of it. I was probably right the first time. He's probably in a fog."

Beth grew more thoughtful. "We're going to have to do something about this situation."

"What situation?"

"Our love lives."

"What love lives?"

"That's the point. They're nonexistent. We have to meet guys."

"We have. There's Tom from the sports shop, and Anthony from the music store across the way, and Peter, who sells those super hand-painted sweatshirts, and your neighbors, those three bachelors... We could always reconsider and go to one of their parties."

Beth snorted. "We'd probably get high just walking into the room. I'm sure they're on something. Whenever I run into them, they seem off the wall. I'm telling you, we were smart to chicken out last time. We're so naive that the place could be raided and everyone would run out through the back and leave us holding the bag."

"Hmm. Maybe we'd meet a cute cop."

"I don't know, Lauren. I still think you should have gone out with that guy who came in on Wednesday."

"He was a total stranger, just browsing around."

"He was nice enough. And he did ask you out for drinks. For that matter, the fellow who came in this morning was even nicer and better-looking."

"He was a pest—trying to be so nonchalant about asking where I come from and where I live and, by the way, what my astrological sign is. I don't know what my astrological sign is. I've never been into that."

"You're scared."

Lauren hesitated for only a minute. "Yup."

"But why? You've dated before."

"That was different."

"You're right. This is supposed to be a new life you're leading!"

"On the outside it is. On the inside, well, I guess it'll take me a little longer to catch up. I don't know, Beth. Those guys seemed so…fast. So slick and sophisticated."

"You look slick and sophisticated."

"*Look*, not *am*. You know me as well as anyone does. I've lived a pretty sedate life. What dates I had were with quiet men, more serious, bookish types."

"Bo-ring."

"Maybe. But I'm not a swinger."

"Maybe you're gonna have to learn."

The hostess called their table then, but Beth picked up the conversation the instant they were seated in the glass-domed room just below street level. "Maybe we should try a singles bar, or a dating service."

"If we didn't have the guts to go to your neighbors' party, we'd never have the guts to go to a singles bar. And blind dates give me the willies."

"Blind dates gave the 'old' you the willies. The 'new' you doesn't have anything to worry about. Besides, it's not really a blind date if you go through a dating service. You get to express your preferences and pick through the possibilities."

"Just like they get to pick through us. Uh-uh, Beth. I don't really think I'm up for that."

"Well, we have to do something. Here we are, two

wonderful women who are bright and available, and we should be having dinner with two equally as captivating men."

"Maybe we should put an ad in the paper," Lauren joked, then promptly scowled. "Only problem is that we're cowards. All talk, no action." Her eyes grew dreamy. "They say that good things come to those who wait. I'm more than willing to wait if one day some gorgeous guy who is bright and available and gentle and easygoing will walk up to me and introduce himself."

"According to women's lib," Beth offered tongue-in-cheek, "we shouldn't have to sit back and wait. We can take the bull by the horns."

Lauren glanced over Beth's shoulder toward the table at which a lone man sat, just finishing his dinner. He wasn't gorgeous, but he was certainly pleasant-looking. When he looked up and caught her eye, he smiled. Curious, Beth turned also; he shared his smile with her.

"There's your chance," Lauren coaxed in a stage whisper filled with good-humored challenge. "I don't want him, so he's all yours. Go ahead. Take the bull by the horns."

Turning back to their own table, Beth opened her menu and concentrated on its contents. Lauren followed suit. Neither woman noticed when the lone man took his check from the waitress and headed for the cash register.

CHAPTER TWO

THE SECOND WEEK of the shop's existence was as promising as the first had been. Just as Lauren was wondering how she and Beth would be able to cope with the continued pace on their own, a freelance photographer came in, peddling his wares. He was a young man—Lauren guessed him to be no more than twenty-five—and his pictures were good. He was also looking for part-time work to pay for the increasing costs of his materials and equipment. She hired him instantly, and neither she nor Beth regretted the decision. Now they could take an hour off here or there—albeit separately—to do paperwork, go out for lunch or shop through downtown Boston.

On one such occasion, a week after Jamie had signed on, Lauren returned to the shop with a new sweater in a bag under her arm and a faint pallor on her face. Beth quickly joined her in the back room. "Are you okay?"

Setting the bag on the desk, Lauren sank into a chair. "I think so. You wouldn't believe what just happened to me, Beth. I'd bought this sweater and was walking back along Newbury Street when a car lost control and veered onto the sidewalk. I was daydreaming, feeling on top of the world, looking at my reflection as I passed store windows. I mean, I was so caught up in being happy that I wasn't paying attention to what was going on around me. If it hadn't been for some stranger who grabbed me out of the way in the nick of time, God only knows what would have happened!"

"Don't think about that. You're safe, and that's all that matters. Was the driver drunk?"

"Who knows? He regained control of the car and went on his merry way again. Didn't even bother to stop and make sure no one was hurt."

"Bastard."

"Mmm."

"The stranger who saved you...was he cute?"

"He was a she," Lauren snapped, but her annoyance was contrived. "And what kind of question is that to ask at a time like this?"

"Have to restore a little humor here. Just think how romantic it would have been if you'd been snatched from the hands of death by a tall, dark and handsome stranger. You could have fainted away in his arms, and he'd have lifted you, holding you ever so gently against his rock-hard chest while he gazed, smitten, upon your lovely face."

Lauren rolled her eyes. "Oh, God."

Beth wagged a finger at her. "Someday it might happen. Miracles are like that, y'know."

"Is this the same woman who was putting in a plug for women's lib not so long ago?" Lauren asked the calendar on the wall, looking back at Beth only when she felt a hand on her arm.

"Are you okay now?" The question was soft and filled with concern. "Want a cold drink or something?"

Taking a deep breath, Lauren shook her head. "I'm fine. It was after the fact, while I was walking, that the shakes set in. But I'm better now. I'd really like to get back to work. That'll keep my mind occupied."

It did, and by the time Lauren arrived in Lincoln that

evening, she'd pretty much forgotten the incident. By the next day, it was lost amid more important and immediate activities relating to the shop.

That night she went home, changed into a T-shirt and jeans and made herself dinner, dutifully following the guidelines Richard Bowen had given her. It was an effort at times, since she seemed to be eating so much, but she'd gained three of the five pounds Richard had prescribed, and she had to agree that they looked good on her.

What with the time demands that the shop had made since her return from the Bahamas, she'd had precious little opportunity to organize her thoughts with regard to renovating the farmhouse. Now, pen and paper in hand, she walked from room to room, making lists of what she wanted to have done. The realtor who'd sold her the house had given her the names of a local contractor, a carpenter, an electrician and a plumber. Though she wasn't about to hire any one of them without checking them out further, she wanted to have her thoughts together before arranging preliminary meetings.

After more than an hour of taking detailed notes, she put down the pen and paper and went out to the front porch. The night was clear, the moon a silver crescent in the star-studded sky. On an impulse, she wandered across the yard and stopped at its center, then tipped her head back and singled out a star to wish on.

But what did one wish for when life was already so good? She was totally healthy for the first time in many years. She had a new look, which she adored. She had a new business, and it was well on its way to becoming a success. She had a home of her own, with potential enough to keep her happy for a long, long time.

What did one wish for? Perhaps a man. Perhaps children. In time.

Lowering her head, she started slowly back toward the house. A sound caught her ear. She stopped and frowned. It was a sound of nature, yet odd. It had been distinctly unfriendly.

When it came again, she whirled around. A low growl. She cocked her head toward the nearby trees, then narrowed her eyes on the creature that slowly advanced on her. A dog. She breathed a sigh of relief. Probably one of the neighbors' pets.

Pressing a hand to her racing heart, she spoke aloud. "You frightened me, dog. Is that any way to greet a new neighbor?" As she took a step forward to befriend the animal, it bared its teeth and issued another growl, this one clearly in warning. Lauren held her hands out, palms up, and said softly, "I won't hurt you, boy." She lowered one hand. "Here. Sniff."

Rather than approaching her, the dog growled again, accompanying the hostile sound with a crouch that suggested an imminent attack.

"Hey, don't get upset—" She barely had time to manage the tremulous words when the dog was on her, knocking her to the ground, snarling viciously. Struggling to fend off the beast, she put her arms up to protect herself and kicked out. But as quickly as it had lunged, the dog retreated, galloping toward the trees and disappearing into the dense growth.

Trembling wildly, Lauren pushed herself up to a seated position. Then, not willing to take a chance that the dog might return, she stumbled to her feet and made a frantic beeline for the house.

Once inside, she leaned back against the firmly shut door, closed her eyes and dragged in a shaky breath.

When the worst of the shock had subsided, anger set in. Had it not been so late at night, she would have called the Youngs, her neighbors on the side from which the dog had come. Then again, she realized, perhaps it was lucky it was too late to make a call. Furious as she was that anyone would let such a savage animal loose in even as rural an area as this, she was apt to say something she might later regret. She'd met Carol Young only once. She didn't want to alienate the woman, or her husband, or one of their teenaged boys. Better to let herself calm down. She'd call tomorrow.

Hence, from work the next morning, she dialed the Youngs' number and was relieved to hear Carol herself answer the phone. "Carol, this is Lauren Stevenson. We met several weeks ago when I moved in next door."

"Sure, Lauren. It's good to hear from you. How's it going?"

"Really well.... I hope I'm not dragging you away from anything."

"Don't be silly. One of the luxuries of working at a computer terminal out of my house is that I can take a break whenever I want. The boys have gone to visit their grandparents in Maryland for a week, so I've got more than enough time for a phone call or two. How's the house?"

"Pretty raw still. I've been so busy here at the shop that I haven't had much of a chance to look into hiring workers to fix things up. But that's not why I called." Lauren chose her words carefully, striving to be as diplomatic as possible. "I had an awful scare last night. I was walking out in the yard sometime around eleven when I was attacked by a dog."

"*Attacked?* Are you all right?"

"I'm fine. The dog jumped me, bared its teeth and made ugly noises, but it ran off before it did any harm."

"My God! I didn't think there were any wild dogs around here!"

"Then…it's not yours?"

"God, no. Is that what you thought?"

"It came from the trees on your side…. I'm sorry, I just assumed…"

"You should have called us last night. We might have been able to help you track it down. What did it look like?"

"It was big and dark. Short-haired. Maybe a Doberman, but it was too dark out for me to see the dog's exact coloration, and besides, I was too terrified to notice much of anything."

"You poor girl. I'd have been terrified, too." Carol paused, thinking. "To my knowledge, no one in the neighborhood has a dog like that, certainly not one that would attack a person. Sometimes strange animals do wander into the area, though. Maybe you should call the local police."

Lauren was lukewarm to that idea. As a new resident, she hated to make a stir. "I—I don't think that's necessary. As long as I know the dog wasn't from the immediate vicinity, I feel better. It's probably a watchdog that escaped and got lost. And it didn't hurt me, much as it looked like it could have."

"Listen, we'll keep an eye out for it, and I'll mention it to some of the other neighbors. But if you catch sight of it again, you really should file a complaint. There's no reason why you should be frightened to walk on your own property."

Lauren sighed. "I'll be on guard in the future. Thanks, Carol. You've been a help."

"I wish I could do more. Let me know if something comes up, okay?"

"Okay."

As Lauren hung up the phone, Beth straightened up from where she'd been leaning unnoticed against the door. "A dog? First a car, now a dog. Lord, the new you is attracting some pretty weird elements."

"Go ahead," Lauren teased, "have a good laugh at my expense."

"I'm not laughing." Beth rubbed her hands together in anticipation of high drama. "Maybe someone's out to get you…someone who lived in that old farmhouse a century ago and whose ghost will never be laid to rest until the rightful owner of the place returns."

"Beth…"

Beth held up a hand. "No, listen. Suppose, just suppose, the ghost is determined to run you out of town, so it plots all kinds of little 'accidents' designed to scare you to death—"

"Beth!"

"And then some gorgeous hunk arrives and just happens to have a secret weapon that can zap even a ghost and reduce it to—to a shredded sheet…."

Lauren sat back in her chair, helpless to contain the beginnings of a grin. "Are you done?"

"Oh, no. The best part comes after the ghost is shredded and you and the gorgeous hunk fall madly in love and live happily ever after."

"Why aren't you working?"

"Because Jamie's working."

"I think *you* should be working." Lauren pushed herself out of her seat. "I think *I* should be working." With a fond squeeze to Beth's arm as she passed, she returned to the front of the shop.

SEVERAL DAYS LATER, Lauren knew that she had to do something about starting the renovation work on her house. The garage door had unexpectedly slammed to the ground when she'd been within mere inches of it. Ironically, if the garage had been nearly as old as the farmhouse itself, its doors would have swung open from the center to the sides, and she would never have been in danger of a skull fracture. But the garage had been added twenty-five years before. Apparently, she mused in frustration, it had been as neglected by recent owners as the house.

She made several calls, setting up appointments to discuss repairs with the men whose names she'd been given. None of them had impressed her on the phone, though she reasoned that there was no harm in meeting with them before she sought out additional contacts. She wanted her home to be perfect, and she was willing to pay to make it so.

With that settled in her mind, she sat down on the living room floor, using the low coffee table as a desk, to write up orders for the framer. But she was distracted. Repeatedly her pen grew still and her gaze wandered to the window. It was dark as pitch outside. She was alone. Anyone could see in, watch her, study her.

Cursing both Beth for her fanciful imaginings and herself for her own surprising susceptibility, she returned to her work. But that night, to her chagrin, she fell asleep wondering if one-hundred-year-old ghosts were capable of sabotaging twenty-five-year-old garage doors.

SHORTLY AFTER NOON on the following day, Lauren saw him for the first time. She was working in the front window of the shop, replacing a framed picture that had been bought that morning, when she happened to glance toward the bench just outside. He was sitting there, quietly and intently. And he was staring at her.

With a tight smile, she looked quickly away, finished hanging the new print, then took refuge in the inner sanctum of the shop.

Fifteen minutes later, during a brief lull in business, she glanced out to find that he hadn't moved. One arm slung over the back of the bench, one knee crossed casually over the other, he appeared to be innocently people-watching—until his gaze penetrated the front window once more.

Again Lauren looked away, this time wondering why she had. There was nothing unusual about a man sitting on a bench in the Marketplace; people did it all the time. And this man, wearing a short-sleeved plaid shirt, jeans and sneakers, looked like a typical passerby. Though he wasn't munching on fried dough or licking an ice cream cone, as so many of the others did, she assumed he was enjoying the pleasant atmosphere. Or waiting for someone. Or simply resting his legs. The fact that he kept looking into the shop was understandable, since it was smack in front of him.

A telephone call came through from one of the print-makers she'd been trying to reach; then customers occupied her time for the next hour and a half. She'd nearly forgotten about the man outside until she left the shop to buy stamps, and even then she was perplexed that she should think of him at all.

He was nowhere to be seen.

AT HOME THAT NIGHT, Lauren was strangely on edge. She didn't know why, and for lack of anything better, she blamed it on the two cups of coffee she'd had that afternoon.

With a critical eye, she looked around the kitchen as she waited for the bouillabaisse she'd bought at a gourmet take-out shop to heat. She intended to do this room in white—white cabinets with white ash trim, white stove and refrigerator, white ceramic tile on the floor. The accent would be pale blue, as in enamel cookware, patterned wallpaper, prints on the wall. Perhaps she'd order a pale blue pleated miniblind—not that she'd originally planned to put anything on the windows, but it occurred to her that she might like the option of privacy for moments like these when the night seemed mysterious.

She was edgy. Too much coffee. That was all.

THE FOLLOWING MORNING, the man was back. Wearing a crisp white polo shirt with his jeans, he was sitting on the bench again, this time with his legs sprawled before him.

"Remarkable, isn't he?" Beth quipped, coming up beside Lauren.

"Who?"

"That guy you're looking at. Have you ever seen such gorgeous hair?" It was light brown with a sunstreaked sheen and was neatly brushed, but thick and on the long side.

"No."

"Or such long legs?"

"No."

"Wonder who he is."

"I don't know."

"Probably just another tourist. Why is it the good ones are here today, gone tomorrow?"

"This one was here yesterday."

"What?"

Lauren blinked once, dragging her gaze from the man to her friend. Absently she wiped damp palms on her slim-cut green linen skirt. "I saw him here yesterday."

Beth's eyes widened. "You're kidding! Do you think he's waiting for...us?"

"Come on, Beth. Why in the world would he be waiting for us?"

"Maybe he heard about these two terrific ladies who own the print-and-frame shop, and he's come to investigate."

"If he had any guts, he'd come in."

"If we had any guts, we'd go out."

"Well, we don't, and apparently he doesn't, either, so that's that." As the two watched, the man got to his feet and ambled off. "That's that," Lauren repeated, not quite sure whether to be relieved or disappointed. There had been something fascinating about the man, not only his legs and his hair but also a certain sturdiness. She wondered if he'd ever owned a black dog that snarled. Then she promptly pushed that thought from her mind, along with all other thoughts of the man—until she caught sight of him again that afternoon.

At first he walked slowly past the shop without sparing it a glance. A few minutes later he returned from the opposite direction, this time pausing near the door before heading for the bench. When Lauren saw him sink onto it, leaning forward with his knees spread and his hands clasped between them, she couldn't help but grow apprehensive. There was something definitely suspicious about the way he glanced toward the shop, then away, then back again.

"Who *is* that man?" she whispered to Beth, who promptly looked up from the VISA charge form she was filling out to follow Lauren's worried gaze.

"So he's back, is he?" Beth resumed writing but spoke under her breath. "He's a little too rugged for my tastes. You can have him."

"I don't want him," Lauren grumbled from the corner of her mouth, "but I would like to know why he's been loitering around here for two days straight."

"Why don't you go and ask him?" Beth murmured, then, smiling, handed the charge slip and a pen to her customer. "If you'll just sign this and put your address and phone number at the bottom…"

Lauren whispered back in a miffed tone of voice. "I can't just walk out there and *ask* him! He's probably got a very good reason for being there, and I'd feel like a fool."

"Then stop worrying. I'm sure he's harmless."

Lauren wasn't so sure. The man was too intent in his scrutiny of the shop, and she felt the touch of his gaze too strongly to forget him.

When a customer approached her to buy a piece of fabric and have it stretched onto a frame, Lauren welcomed the diversion. When another customer selected a print and needed advice on its framing, she was more than happy to oblige. When a third customer entered the shop in search of several prints to coordinate with swatches of fabric and wallpaper, she immersed herself in the project.

By the time the closing hour drew near, Lauren was tired. She was in the back room, dutifully updating inventory cards and looking forward to a leisurely drive home, a quiet dinner and what was left of the evening with a good book.

"Lauren?" The low urgency in Beth's voice brought Lauren's head up quickly. "He's here, asking for *you*."

"Who—"

"Him." Beth's eyes darted back over her shoulder. "The guy from the bench."

Lauren put down the cards. "He's asking for *me*?"

"By name."

"How did he…he must have…where is he?"

"Right here," Beth mouthed in a way that would have been comical had Lauren been feeling particularly confident.

But she wasn't. This man was different. Not boring-looking. Not slick and sophisticated-looking. Very… different.

Beth made an urgent gesture with her hand.

"I'm coming. I'm coming," Lauren murmured unsteadily. She stood up, smoothing the hip-length ivory cotton sweater over her skirt and squared her shoulders. Then, praying that she looked more composed than she felt, she slowly and reluctantly left her refuge.

CHAPTER THREE

HE WAS MUCH taller close up than he'd appeared through the shop window. And broader in the shoulders. And more tanned. What was most surprising, though, was that he seemed just a little unsure of himself.

"Lauren Stevenson?" he asked cautiously.

She'd come to a stop several feet away and rested her hand on the butcher-block table. "Yes?"

As he studied her more closely, his puzzlement grew. "It's really strange. You're not at all as I expected you to be."

Lauren held her breath for a minute, then asked with a caution of her own, "What had you expected?"

"Someone...well, someone different."

If he had some connection to her past, she realized, not only was his puzzlement understandable but his tact was commendable. Still, she couldn't deny her wariness. The man had been staking her out for two days. "Do you know me? Should I know you?"

For the first time, he smiled. It was a self-conscious smile, endearing in its way. "My name's Matthew Kruger. Matt." He hestitated for a split second. "I was a friend of your brother's."

Lauren wasn't sure what *she* had expected, but it hadn't been this. "Brad's friend?" She was unable to hide either her surprise or her skepticism.

"That's right. I was with him just after the accident. I'm…sorry about his death."

"I am, too," she returned honestly, her brow lightly furrowed as she studied Matthew Kruger. He didn't quite fit into the mold she'd constructed of Brad and his friends. Strange that she'd never heard of him. Then again, perhaps not so strange. She hadn't been any closer to Brad before his death than her parents had been. "But…it's been a year since he died." Silently she asked herself why this so-called friend of Brad's had waited this long to contact her.

"I know you weren't close, but Brad did mention you to me several times, and since I had to come east on business, I thought I'd look you up."

"What kind of business are you in?"

Another split second's hesitation. "I'm a builder. The development firm I work for has just contracted to do some work in western Massachusetts. I'm here to set things up—to get the ball rolling, so to speak."

She nodded. A builder. Given the pale crow's feet at the corners of his eyes, he was not a builder who directed things from his desk. He was a builder who got his hands dirty. And whose body was well-toned through hard physical labor. *That* she could associate with the image she'd formed of her brother's new life and friends, though if her parents' opinion had been valid, she would have expected someone far coarser. On the surface, at least, Matthew Kruger didn't appear to be coarse. "Clean and all-American" was a more apt description. Could the surface appearance be deceptive?

"I see," she said. Then, feeling uncomfortable, she averted her gaze. In truth, she'd known little about her brother and his way of life…and then there was the matter of this man's physical presence. He intimidated her. "Have you, uh, have you been in Boston very long?"

"A week."

She nodded.

"I'm staying at the Long Wharf Marriott."

"If your work is in the western part of the state, wouldn't it be easier to stay out there?"

"I have been, but our investors are here and there's some paperwork to do, so I decided to take a few days to sightsee." When he suddenly looked beyond her, Lauren swung her head around.

"I'm going to lock up," Beth whispered, darting a curious glance at Matt as she started to pass.

Lauren reached out and caught her arm. "Uh, Beth, this is Matthew Kruger. He is—was—a friend of Brad's." Lauren still had her doubts about that, but saying it simplified the introduction. "Matt, Beth Lavin."

Beth had known Brad Stevenson before he'd struck out on his own, and since she wasn't a member of his immediate family, she'd been more objective about his departure. Hands clasped tightly before her, she smiled shyly at Matt. "I'm pleased to meet you."

"The pleasure's mine," Matt said, returning her smile. His gaze quickly grew apologetic when it sought Lauren's again. "I don't want to hold you up if there's something you should be doing now."

Lauren opened her mouth to say that she really did have work to finish, but Beth spoke first. "Oh, you're not holding her up. We were pretty much done for the day when you came in. I finished the inventory cards, Lauren. Why don't you and Matt take off? I'll close up."

The last thing Lauren wanted to do was to take off with Matt. She wasn't convinced he was who he said he was, and even if it was so, they were on opposite sides of a rift. Besides, he hadn't asked her to "take off" with him.

As though on cue, he did. "How about it, Lauren?" He paused, then took a quick breath. "I heard there was a sunset cruise around the harbor. If we hurry, we can make it."

"Uh, I really shouldn't...."

"Go on, Lauren," Beth coaxed. Subtlety had never been her forte. "You haven't been out much. It's a beautiful night. The fresh air will do you good."

"I'd really like the company," Matt urged softly.

His last words trapped Lauren. If he'd come on strong, she might have easily refused. But he sounded sincere, and she caught a drift of the same unsureness she'd seen when she'd first faced him. Though large and rugged-looking, he had an odd gentleness to him. His eyes were brown, warm and soft. At that moment they hinted at vulnerability; above all, Lauren Stevenson was a sucker for vulnerability.

Releasing the breath she'd subconsciously been holding, Lauren acknowledged an internal truce. "I'll get my things," she whispered.

Soon after, she and Matt were walking side by side toward the waterfront. He was as quiet as she, casting intermittent glances her way, and she wondered if he felt as strange as she did.

In an attempt to break the silence, she asked the first thing that came to mind. "How did you know I was in Boston?"

"Your parents told me."

"My *parents!*"

He sent her a sidelong glance. "Shouldn't they have?"

"No—yes—I mean, I'm just surprised. That's all."

They walked a little farther before he spoke again.

"You're thinking that they wouldn't have willingly given your address to any friend of Brad's."

"I...guess that says it."

A muscle in his jaw flexed. "At least you're honest."

She shrugged. "How much do you know about Brad's reasons for leaving?"

"Only what Brad told me—that your parents couldn't accept his wanting to work with his hands rather than with his mind, that they flipped out when he left college and pretty much washed their hands of him."

Perhaps Matt had known Brad after all. "Spoken that way, it sounds cruel."

"It was, in a way. Brad was badly hurt by the split."

"So were my parents, yet none of the three tried to mend it."

"And you, Lauren? Did you do anything?"

Her gaze shot sharply to his, then softened and fell. "No," she admitted quietly. "I think I might have in time. Then time ran out."

"You regretted the distance?"

"Brad was my only brother. We had no other siblings. He was four years older than I, and his interests were always different. We weren't close as kids, but I like to think that we might have found common ground as we'd gotten older."

They had reached Atlantic Avenue. Matt put a light hand on her elbow as they trotted across to avoid an onrushing car. He dropped it when they reached the median strip, where they waited for a minute before finishing the crossing.

"Then you were seventeen when Brad left."

Lauren blew out a breath. "You really *do* know about Brad, don't you?"

"He told me he was twenty-one when he dropped

out. If you were four years his junior…" Matt's voice trailed off and his features tensed. "Did you think I was lying about being his friend?"

"No. Well, maybe. I have to take your word for it that you knew him, since he can't verify it, can he?"

"Are you always distrustful?"

She looked him in the eye. "Only when I see someone lurking outside my shop for two days before coming in."

"Oh. You saw me."

"Yes." Was that a sudden rush of color to his cheeks? She wondered if it was guilt, or embarrassment. In case it was the latter, she softened her tone. "I assume you weren't trying to hide."

"Actually," he confessed, "I was trying to get up the nerve to come in."

That was a new one in her experience. "Why ever would you have to get up the nerve to approach *me?*"

"Several reasons. First, I knew there were hard feelings where Brad was concerned and I wasn't sure how I'd be received. Second, I wasn't sure if it was really you." His gaze slid from one to another of her features. Again that puzzled look crossed his face. "You look so different. Very…very pretty."

Lauren clutched the shoulder strap of her bag more tightly. "Brad had a picture."

"An old one. You were sixteen at the time."

For reasons she wasn't about to analyze, she didn't want to go into the matter of her reconstructive surgery. "It was a long time ago," she said quietly. "People change."

"I'll say," Matt drawled. "Still, it's amazing…" He seemed about to go on, and for an instant Lauren wondered just how much Brad had told him about her. She was saved when he looked up and announced tentatively, "I think this is it."

She followed his gaze toward where the wharf and its cruise boats loomed. "Looks like it. This is really the blind leading the blind. I went to college in Boston, but that was a while ago. I haven't been back for very long."

"Are you living here in the city?"

The glance she sent him held subtle accusation, but there was a whisper of amusement underlying her words. "What did my parents tell you?"

Reading her loud and clear, he fought back a grin. "Just the name of the shop. I assume they wanted to keep things on a strictly business level."

"I'm sure they did."

"And you?"

"And me what?"

He was suddenly serious. "Would you put me down because I don't have a Ph.D. in some esoteric subject?"

"I don't have a Ph.D. in *any* subject."

"You have a master's degree in art. I never went to college."

"But you're successful in what you do. At least, if you're traveling across the country, the firm you work for must be doing well…you must be valued." Having doubted his story such a short time ago, she amazed herself by coming to his defense. Suckers for vulnerability weren't always the most prudent. She took a deep breath. "No, Matt. I'm not like my parents. Brad wasn't the only one who had differences with them. It's just taken me a little longer to act on those differences."

Their conversation was cut short when they arrived at the ticket booth. Matt paid their fare, and they boarded the boat. Wending their way through the other groups that had gathered, they climbed to the top deck and found an empty place by the rail to look back at the city skyline.

"I love Boston," Lauren mused after several minutes of silent appreciation.

"Explain."

"It's bigger than Bennington and that much more exciting, yet smaller than New York and that much more manageable. You can understand it, get to know it. It's livable."

"You have an apartment?"

"A farmhouse."

"In the *city?*"

"In Lincoln—" She caught herself and scowled at him. "That was sneaky. You took advantage of me when my defenses were down."

He grinned amiably. "Sorry about that. Do you really own a farmhouse?"

Somehow further prevarication seemed silly. "Uh-huh. It's old and needs a whole load of work before its potential can be realized, but it's on a great piece of land and has charm, real charm."

"Old places are like that. History adds character. That's one of the reasons *I* like Boston. Wandering around, seeing where the Boston Massacre took place or where the Declaration of Independence was first read—it gives you goose bumps." He paused, staring at Lauren. "Why are you grinning?"

"You and goose bumps. You're so big and solid. It seems a contradiction."

"No," he said gently. "The goose bumps I'm talking about have an emotional cause. Big and solid don't necessarily mean unfeeling."

"I didn't mean—"

"I know." His point made, he left it at that.

They lapsed into silence, watching as the gangplank was drawn up and the boat inched away from the dock. Soon the engines growled louder. The boat made a laborious turn, then picked up speed and entered the main body of the harbor, moving at a steady, if chugging, pace.

"Would you like a drink?" Matt asked.

Lauren drew herself back from her immersion in the scenery. "No—uh, make that yes. A wine spritzer, if they can handle it, or lemonade. Something cool."

With a nod, he made his way back across the deck and disappeared down the stairs leading to the lower level. Following his progress, Lauren had to admit that he was as attractive as any other man in sight. It wasn't that he was beautiful in the classic sense; his chin was too square, his nose a shade crooked, his skin too weathered. But he exuded good health and strength and competence. He'd crossed the shimmying deck without faltering.

The wind whipped through her hair as she turned to face the sea once more. She concentrated on the sights—the Aquarium, the Harbor Towers, the piers with their assortment of fishing boats and tankers, the waterfront restaurants. Only when Matt returned and she smiled did she realize how much nicer the setting seemed with him by her side.

"Two lemonades." He handed her one. "The spritzer was beyond the bartender, and the other drinks were heavier. There were some hot dogs down there, but they looked pretty sad." He took a bag of potato chips from under his arm, opened it and held it out. She munched one, then washed it down with a drink.

"Tell me about Brad," she surprised herself by saying.

Somber-eyed, he studied her expression. "I'm not sure you really want to know."

She attributed his hesitancy to her own obvious ambivalence. "You may be right. But…I guess I really am curious. I've never met anyone who knew him after he left. I'm not sure I should pass the opportunity by."

Matt tossed several chips into his mouth. "What do you want to know?" he asked between stilted bites.

"Did he work for your company?"

"No."

"Had he always been in San Francisco?" She knew that was where he'd died.

"He started out in Sacramento."

"As a carpenter."

"That's right. By the time he came to San Francisco, though, he was doing a lot of designing."

"Designing what?"

Matt hesitated for an instant. "Houses, mostly. Some office parks. As an architect, he was a natural."

"Is that how he was viewed—as an architect?"

"No. He didn't have the credentials. He was like a ghost-writer, presenting rough sketches to the company's architect, who then embellished and formalized the sketches."

"Were you familiar with his company?"

"We were competitors."

The words were simple and straightforward, yet something about the way they'd been offered gave Lauren the impression that Matt hadn't particularly cared for Brad's outfit. "But still, you were friends. How did that work?"

Matt seemed to relax somewhat. "Very comfortably. Our respective superiors held the patent on rivalry. Brad and I rather enjoyed fraternizing with the enemy."

"How did you meet?"

"In a bowling league."

Her expression grew distant. "Funny, I can't picture Brad bowling. But then, I can't picture him sweating on the roof of a house, either." She tore herself from her musings. "What else did you do together?"

"Ate out. Sometimes double-dated. We vacationed together—there were six of us, actually. We rafted down the Colorado, went on horseback through parts of Montana. It was fun."

"Very macho," she teased and was rewarded by a sheepish grin from Matt.

"I suppose."

Her smile lingered for a minute before fading. "Brad never married." She'd learned that when she'd been informed by the lawyer that she was the sole beneficiary of her brother's estate. "I wonder why."

"Maybe he never met the right girl, one who could accept him as he was."

"Have you ever married?" she asked on impulse. Matt stared at her for a minute, then shook his head.

"Why not?"

"Same reason."

She pondered his answer quietly. "I can understand it in Brad's case. He grew up in an atmosphere in which intellectual excellence was the only valid goal. He struggled to keep up for a while, then simply threw in the towel. Neither my parents nor their circle of friends could accept his behavior. Long before he left, he was labeled a misfit. I'm sure he was sensitive about it."

"We all have our sensitivities."

"What are yours, Matt? Why would a woman have trouble accepting you as you are?"

He chomped several more potato chips and would

have seemed perfectly nonchalant had it not been for the ominous darkening of his eyes. "I'm blue-collar all the way. I don't have a pedigree, or a series of fancy qualifying initials to put after my name. Over the years I've done well in my work, but that doesn't mean I aspire to own my own company, or that one day I won't decide to chuck it all and go back to building log cabins. If a woman thinks she's getting a future real-estate tycoon in me, she'd better think again."

Lauren couldn't miss the bitterness in his words. "You've been burned."

"Several times." He looked out over the water and his tone gentled, growing apologetic enough to defy arrogance. "I've always attracted women pretty easily. But physical attraction isn't enough. Not by a long shot."

"The grass is always greener..." she said softly. "There are those of us who'd *love* to have looks that would attract."

Matt eyed her as if she were crazy. "But you *do!* I can't believe there isn't a line of men waiting to take you out!"

It took Lauren a minute to realize what she'd said and why Matt had answered as forcefully as he had. She'd forgotten. That happened a lot. A slow warmth crept up her neck. Compliments were still new to her, and from as physically superb a man as Matthew Kruger... "I don't know about a line," she said simply.

"Then there's one man?"

She shook her head.

"You're a beautiful woman, Lauren. Surely you've had offers."

Again she shook her head, this time with a self-conscious half smile.

"Why not?"

At his bluntness, she burst out laughing. "You're almost as undiplomatic as Beth."

"I'm sorry. I was just curious." He held up a large, well-formed hand. "Not that I'm saying you should be married. You're only, what, twenty-nine, and you're obviously building a career for yourself." A new thought hit him, and he frowned. "You said you haven't been in Boston for very long. Then the shop is a recent thing?"

"We've been open barely a month."

"And before that?"

"I worked in a museum back home."

He rubbed his forefinger along the rim of his paper cup. "Back home. That could explain it. Brad told me about back home."

"What did he say?"

"That it was stifling. One-dimensional. You were either an artist or an academician affiliated with the college."

"He was being unfair. Bennington's a beautiful place. Some fascinating people chose to live there. Brad just didn't."

"Nor did you, apparently. Why did you leave, Lauren?"

"Because I wanted to open the shop."

"But you could have opened a shop in Bennington."

She shook her head. "Too small a market."

"So you're going for the big time."

"I want the shop to be a success, yes," she said on a defensive note. "I may not aspire to put out one profound treatise after another the way Mom and Dad have, but that doesn't mean I can't aim to do what I do well."

There was a wistfulness to Matt's smile. "Now you *do* sound like Brad. He was so determined...." A flicker of uncertainty crossed his brow.

"So determined...?"

It was a while before Matt finished his sentence, and then it was with care. "To be successful. Recognized. I'm not sure he realized it, or realized what was driving him, but as often as he claimed that he was doing his own thing and didn't care what his family thought, I think he was kidding himself."

"Was he happy, Matt?"

Matt had to consider that. "In a way, yes."

Peering down at the bits of lemon pulp clinging to the sides of her cup, Lauren spoke more slowly. "All we were told about the accident was that he was supervising some blasting and got caught in the mess. Was there...anything more to it?"

"That was it."

He'd answered quickly and with finality. Not knowing why, Lauren was taken aback. "You saw him right after?"

"At the hospital." His tone was clipped. As he went on, its harshness eased. "Brad was lucid for a time, but between the internal injuries and everything else—well, maybe it was for the best. If he'd lived—and the chances of that were slim from the start—he would have been a quadraplegic. I don't think he would have been able to bear that."

"No," she whispered, and when she looked up, her eyes were moist. "I feel guilty about it sometimes."

"Guilty?"

"Everything I have now—the shop, the farmhouse, this—" she gestured broadly toward herself "—has come from the money he left me. Did you know that?"

Matt put his hand on her shoulder and massaged it gently. His voice was much, much softer, his focus shifted. "That was Brad's wish. I was the one who passed it on to the lawyer. Given the circumstances, Brad gained a measure of peace from it."

Lauren nodded, then somehow couldn't stop the overflow of words. "If it hadn't been for Brad, I'd probably still be back in Bennington. Even aside from the money, his death was a turning point for me. For the first time in my life, I stopped to think of my own mortality, of what I'd have to my credit when the time came, of what I'd be leaving behind. That was when I decided to move to Boston and open the shop. I only wish Brad could know how much better I feel about myself now."

"It's enough that you know, Lauren. If Brad were here to see you, I'm sure he'd be proud."

She looked timidly at Matt, then away, and took a long, shuddering breath. "It's too bad we can't have it both ways—too bad I can't have what I do and have Brad alive to see it."

Slipping his arm across her back, Matt drew her to his side. His warmth was the comfort she needed. "Life is cruel that way, filled with choice and compromise. Even those who reach the heights make sacrifices along the way. The best we can do is to decide exactly how much we're prepared to give up and move on from there."

As she raised her gaze to his, her cheek brushed his shoulder. It seemed a perfectly natural gesture. "But that's a negative view."

"It's realistic."

"Maybe I'm more of a romantic, then. I want to focus on the goals and face the hurdles as I come to them."

He shrugged. "And I want to be prepared for the hurdles. It's just a different approach. Who's to say which one is better?"

She didn't answer. Her gaze was suddenly locked

with his, lost in his, and she struggled to cope with the intensity. He was a virtual stranger, yet she'd told him things she'd never told another soul. Was it the fact that he was a link to her brother, or that he was a good listener, or that he'd shared his own thoughts with her? She'd been wary of him at first; she still was, in some respects. And yet...and yet she was drawn to him....

The sudden blast of the boat's horn made them both jump. They looked around to find the bulk of the passengers crowded on the other side of the deck, waving to a passing tall ship. Without releasing her, Matt moved to join them.

"Impressive," he breathed, taking in the towering masts and ancient fittings of the proud vessel. "Too bad she's not under sail."

"Mmm. It's almost disillusioning. There weren't any motors in the old days."

"Or Sony Walkmans." He pointed to the sailor perched on the rigging, headset firmly in place. Lauren smiled at the sight, then shifted her gaze to the airport.

"If I had a downtown office with a view of all this, I doubt I'd ever get any work done. I could sit for hours watching the planes take off and land."

"Not me. Even watching gives me the willies. I'm a white-knuckle flier."

Lauren stared at him in disbelief. "A big guy like you?"

"Big guys crash harder."

She suppressed a smile. "I suppose you've got a point. But you do fly."

His expression was priceless, a blend of revulsion and resignation. "When necessary."

"Which is far too often for your tastes."

"You got it."

Her eyes took on an extra glow. "I don't think I could ever fly too often for my tastes. Not that I've flown that much, but I've always been so excited about getting where I'm going that I just sit back and relax. That's about all you can do, y'know. Once you're in the air, you're in fate's hands. It's not as if you have control over anything that might happen to the plane."

His grunt was eloquent. "That's what bothers me. I *like* to be in control. Just like measuring hurdles...."

Lauren narrowed her eyes playfully. "I'll bet you're the type who checks over every blessed inch of a new car before you venture to slide behind the wheel."

"I also sample the whipped cream, then the nuts, then the hot fudge, then the ice cream before I take a complete spoonful of a sundae."

"But where's the surprise, then?"

"The surprise is in the perfect blend of ingredients. The way I do it, y'see, I minimize the chance of disappointment. If something's not quite right, I can get it fixed, and if I can't do that, at least I'm prepared, so my expectations are on a par with reality."

"You're a man of caution."

"Quite."

"Another reason why you sat outside my shop for two days." She tipped her head. "Tell me, what would have happened if I'd looked exactly like that picture you'd seen?"

"I'd have come in the first day."

Lauren had wondered if he would ever have come in. "I don't understand. My looks made you *cautious?*"

"That's right."

"But...I look better than I did in the picture, don't I?"

"You look gorgeous."

"Then?" Mired in confusion, she made no protest

when he turned her into him and crossed his wrists on the small of her back.

"Gorgeous women intimidate me. I've been burned, remember?"

His smile didn't ease her this time. Her eyes widened. "Do you think I'm after your *body?*"

He winced and shot an embarrassed glance to either side. "Shh."

She grasped his arms to push him away. When he held her steady, she whispered, but vehemently, "Is that what you think? Well, let me tell you, *I* didn't ask you to walk into my shop. I didn't ask you to take me on a cruise. I don't want any part of your body! And even if I did, that wouldn't be all I'd want. Before I ever got around to your body, I'd make sure that I wanted the rest." She snorted in disgust and turned her face away. "Of all the self-centered, arrogant—"

"That wasn't what I meant, Lauren. You're jumping to conclusions. Has it ever occurred to you that you can intimidate a man?"

"Me?"

"Yes, you. I'd expected to find a quiet—" he hesitated, then cleared his throat "—rather thin and plain-looking young woman living an equally quiet life in the country. At least, that was what Brad had implied. If he could only see you now! You own your own shop—in the city, no less. You're beautiful. You dress smartly. You're bright as all get-out. And you're sure as hell not falling at *my* feet." He took a begrudging breath. "Yes, I'm intimidated."

Lauren had felt suspended during his short speech. Now she realized how absurd her own attack must have sounded. "Funny," she managed to say in a small voice, "you don't look intimidated."

He squeezed his eyes together. Even before they relaxed and opened, a smile had begun to form on his lips. "I guess I'm not now, at least not as much as I was before. For someone who is beautiful and chic and super-intelligent, you're really pretty normal."

She smiled self-consciously, averting her gaze. "I think we're missing the sunset."

"I think you're right."

They returned to their own side of the boat, then switched when the vessel made a slow turn and headed back to the docks. Neither of them said very much. Lauren, for one, was lost in her own thoughts.

In spite of Matt's explanation, she still felt stunned that her looks had put him off. Initially her pride had been hurt. The thought that she'd drastically improved her appearance only to find that it kept men away was unsettling; hence she'd lashed out.

Or had she simply been searching for a wedge to put between Matt and her?

He was too attractive, too easy to be with, too firmly aligned with Brad and a way of life that she'd been indoctrinated to frown on. No, she wasn't exactly frowning now, but neither could she turn her back on the disappointment of Brad's long-ago desertion. And then came the guilt. She'd acceded to her parents' view of Brad as a failure, yet she'd accepted his money—lots of it. Did an architect masquerading as a carpenter earn that much money? Had he banked every spare cent for some eleven years?

She realized that there were many more questions she wanted to ask Matt about Brad. In hindsight, she wondered if he'd been evasive when talking about her brother's work. His answers had been short, his expression solemn. He'd opened up more about Brad's personal life, yet she couldn't help but wonder if there were some things he hadn't said.

The boat pulled alongside the dock, its lines were secured, and the gangplank was lowered.

"You must be starving," Matt said. "Want to catch a bite at my hotel?" The Marriott was only a short distance from where they stood, but Lauren quickly shook her head.

"I'd better be getting home. It's been a long day."

"Are you sure?"

This time she steeled herself against the cocoa softness of his gaze. She needed time to acclimate herself to his appearance in her life. He was a figure from Brad's past, yet the immediacy of him unbalanced her. What she craved was the solid footing of her own home.

"I'm sure," she said with a gentle smile. "But...thank you, Matt. This has been lovely."

"At least let me walk you to your car. It's pretty dark."

"And the path to my car is well lighted all the way. Really, I'll be fine."

Matt straightened his shoulders and nodded. "Well, take care, then."

She started off, half turning as she walked. "Good luck with your work. I hope it goes well."

He nodded again and waved, then turned and headed for his hotel. Lauren didn't look back until she'd crossed Atlantic Avenue, and by then he was gone.

THE LATE-AFTERNOON SUN glanced brilliantly over the Hollywood Hills, but the shades in the study were drawn as its proprietor entered, strode across the tiled floor to the desk and picked up the telephone.

"Yes?"

"We're on our way."

"It's about time. I'd assumed I would have heard from you sooner."

"She's a clever girl. Covered her tracks like a pro— almost. I still don't know who helped her out of L.A., but you were right about the Bahamas. She went back to the same clinic she visited when the two of you were vacationing on the islands last fall. That was her only slipup."

"Then you've found her?"

"She had plastic surgery, just like you thought she would. Not much. Subtle changes. There was a phony 'before' shot stuck into the doctor's files and a bunch of misleading medical reports, but the 'after' shot had just enough similarity to the real thing to give her away. Her hair's different now, darker and shorter. And she's taken a different name."

"We knew she would. Where is she?"

"Boston. She just opened a little print-and-frame shop."

"With the money from the gifts *I* gave her. A print-and-frame shop. That's priceless."

"You'd be amazed if you saw her. She's the image of innocence. Dresses just so—stylish but understated, nothing flashy like before. Drives a Saab she must have picked up secondhand. Has this woman working with her who looks nearly as snowy-pure as she does, and a young guy who's probably eating out of—"

"What about the jewels? Have you located the fence?"

"No. No sign of the jewels at all. She may have started with the furs. They'd be easy to sell and nearly impossible to trace."

"Have you made contact with her?"

"Got a good man on it. She's already had a couple of little 'accidents'—nothing to hurt her actually, just set her to wondering."

"Is she?"

"Yeah. She's looking nervously around her front yard each time she leaves the house."

"The house?"

"An old farmhouse she picked up outside the city."

"With my money!"

"It'll all come back to you. Between the shop and the house, she's made investments that'll come back with interest."

"I want you to find the jewels."

"We're looking. She doesn't have them at home. I went through the place myself today."

"Ransacked it?"

"Nothing that obvious. Just moved little things here and there. She'll suspect someone's been snooping, but she won't be sure enough to call the cops."

"She wouldn't *dare* call the cops. She knows how long my arm is, and she wouldn't do anything to risk blowing her cover. So where do we go from here?"

"I've got a few more mishaps up my sleeve. You want her to squirm. I want her to squirm. She's gonna squirm."

"You're having fun, aren't you?"

"You could say that. I feel like I let you down before, and it was her fault. This is my revenge."

"It's *my* revenge, and don't you forget it."

"No way, boss. No way."

CHAPTER FOUR

BETH WAS LYING in wait for Lauren when she arrived at work the next morning. "Well? How did it go? What happened? Your parents would *die* if they knew you were dating him, but I think it's great! A sunset cruise... I've never heard of anything so romantic in my life. He may be rugged, but he's got style. Was he nice? Did you invite him back to Lincoln after the cruise? I almost called you, but I didn't dare. *Tell* me, Lauren. Tell me *everything!*"

Closely shadowed by her friend, Lauren continued through to the back room and plunked her purse in the bottom drawer of the file cabinet. "How can I tell you anything if I can't get a word in edgewise?"

"Okay. I'll shush. Give."

Lauren only wished she could. She'd spent a good part of the night thinking about Matthew Kruger, and she still didn't know what to make of him. "Yes, he was nice. Yes, the cruise was nice. Romantic? Well, I don't know about that. And no, I did not invite him back to Lincoln."

"Why not?"

"Because it wasn't called for. And we weren't on a *date*. He was my brother's friend. That's all. We talked a little about Brad and a little about other things. Period."

"Did he explain why he'd been hanging around outside for so long?"

For the first time that morning, Lauren smiled. Dryly. "If you can believe it, he was trying to get up his nerve to come in. Brad had shown him a picture of me. I wasn't quite what he'd expected."

"That's marvelous!" Beth's eyes grew rounder. "The handsome prince was so taken with your beauty that he was actually awestruck. I love it!"

Lauren screwed up her face and carefully enunciated her words. "Handsome prince? Taken with my beauty? Awestruck? What *have* you been reading, Beth?"

"Come on. I think this is great. Are you seeing him again?"

"I don't know."

"What do you mean, you don't know?"

"Just that. He didn't say anything about seeing me again, and I wasn't about to put him on the spot." Lauren reached for a can and began to spoon fresh coffee into a filter.

"'Put him on the spot.'" Beth snorted. "Straight from the mouth of the old you. The new you is sought-after. You'd be doing him a favor to *consider* seeing him again.... Well?"

"Well, what?"

"Are you?"

"What?" Lauren measured out water and poured it into the top of the coffee maker.

Beth sighed in frustration. "Considering seeing him again."

"I don't know."

As coffee began to trickle slowly into the carafe, Beth rolled her eyes and muttered, "This is absurd. We're going in circles. Do you or do you not want to see the man again?"

Lauren turned toward her friend. "I don't know!

Damn it, Beth, how can I give you a better answer if I don't have one myself? Yes, I liked him, and under normal circumstances I'd be glad to see him again. But these aren't exactly normal circumstances. In the first place, the man lives on the West Coast. He's only here doing business, most of which keeps him in the western part of the state. He'll be going back to San Francisco and he hates to fly. I don't exactly have the time to zip out to see him every weekend—not to mention the money, when there are so many other things I have it earmarked for." She sucked in a breath. "And in the second place, he was Brad's friend. You're right. My parents would go bonkers."

"You're an adult. They didn't want you to go to the Bahamas, but you did it. They didn't want you to leave Bennington or open this shop, but you did both. You don't need their permission. You can do whatever you want and see whomever you want."

Lauren sighed loudly. "I know that, Beth. I'm not asking their permission for anything. I have qualms of my own about seeing Matt again. He was a friend of Brad's. He sees me and my parents through Brad's eyes. And he's a confirmed bachelor who loves taking off with the guys and shooting the rapids for a week. So what's the point?"

"The point," Beth murmured, wiggling her brows, "is that he's single and gorgeous."

"I thought he was too rugged for you."

"For me, yes. For you, no. The two of you looked great walking out of here together last night. I'm telling you, see where it leads."

"You have a one-track mind," Lauren grumbled, brushing a wisp of hair from her low-belted, apricot jersey dress.

"And you're in a lousy mood. Where's your sense of humor? Hey, I'll bet Matthew Kruger would be the *perfect* one to ward off the ghost that's hanging out at your farm."

"Humph. I'm beginning to think I need something. That ghost was at work again."

Beth blinked once, then again. The coffee continued to trickle in the background, its rich aroma wafting from the carafe and spreading through the small room. "Excuse me?"

"That ghost. I swear it went through my things yesterday."

"Wait a minute, Lauren. There are no such things as ghosts."

"You're the one who's been touting them."

"I was teasing."

"Then I guess you've teased once too often. I'm almost becoming a believer."

"You're not serious!"

"Well, maybe not. But still…it was weird." She made a face accordingly. "I could have sworn I'd put certain things in certain places at home, and they were still there, just…shifted somehow."

Beth leaned back against the desk and crossed her arms over her chest. She might have been a psychiatrist for the indulgent tone of her voice. "I think you're going to have to be more specific. In what ways were they 'shifted'?"

"Small ways. A bottle of perfume turned around so that the sculpted bird faced the wall. A pair of shoes neatly set in the closet, with the right shoe on the left and the left one on the right. A pair of underpants perfectly folded, but inside out. I always turn them the right way before I fold them. *Underpants.*" She shuddered, then whispered in dismay, "Can you believe it?"

"Maybe you should call the police."

"I thought about that, but I feel like a fool! I mean, it's not as if anything were taken. The locks on the doors were intact, and as far as I could tell, none of the windows had been jimmied open. Ruling out a breaking and entering, I'd say someone might have just walked in, except that I'm the only one with a key."

"How about the realtor who sold you the place?"

"I had the locks changed right after I moved in." Lauren gave a guttural laugh. "That's about all I've done, but it does preclude a human visitor." She took a deep breath. "So either it *was* a ghost, or I'm simply not as meticulous about things as I used to be. Maybe that's it. I mean, I suppose I have been preoccupied with the shop. It's very possible that I wasn't paying attention when I put the perfume bottle back or took the shoes off or folded the laundry." She looked beseechingly at Beth. "So what are the police going to say?"

"Mmm. I see your point. Maybe you should get a dog."

"One encounter with a dog on my property was enough."

"Then a burglar alarm system."

"A burglar alarm isn't going to stop a ghost. And it sure isn't going to improve my own absentmindedness, if that's what it was." She reached for a clean mug and poured herself some coffee. When she looked up to find a smug smile spreading over Beth's face, she scowled. "Now what are you thinking?"

"That I was right all along. Matthew Kruger may be just the one to protect you. All you have to do is to coax him along. Before you know it, he'll be thinking of that farmhouse as his second home."

"Matt is going back to San Francisco. How many times must I tell you that? And even if he wasn't, I can't use the man that way."

"Seems to me he'd get something out of the arrangement."

"Humph. When—and if—I take a live-in lover, it'll be because I truly adore whoever he is, not because I need him as a bodyguard."

"You could truly adore your bodyguard."

Lauren sank into a chair and raised her mug. She spoke slowly and distinctly, as though her friend might not understand her otherwise. "I am going to drink my coffee now and gather my thoughts. Then I am going to face this new day with a bright smile and a free mind." She closed her eyes, brought the mug to her lips, sipped the coffee, then sighed.

Somewhere between the sip and sigh, Beth gave up on her and left the room.

THE SHOP GREW BUSIER as the noon hour approached, and Jamie's arrival at one was a relief. Beth ran out to pick up sandwiches, returning shortly thereafter with news far more interesting than that the rye bread had caraway seeds.

"Have you looked outside lately?" she murmured excitedly to Lauren as she passed on her way to the back room.

Lauren had been helping a customer decide which of two silk-screen prints to buy. She glanced toward the front window.

Matt. Sitting on the bench she was coming to think of as his. Reading a book.

Reading a book? That was a novel approach! Not
that she doubted he was a reader; he looked more than
comfortable with the paperback in his hand. But reading a book in the middle of the bustling Marketplace
and on that particular bench? What was he thinking?
What did he want?

She returned her attention to her customer, pleased
that in the minute she'd been distracted he'd decided on
the print she'd originally recommended. Decisions on
its framing proved to be more difficult, what with so
many different mat boards and frames to choose from,
but Lauren didn't mind. This was the part of the job
she really enjoyed, and the shop made far more money
on matting and framing than on the sale of the prints
themselves.

It was only after she'd written up the customer's
order, taken a deposit and let her gaze follow him to
the door that she glanced again at the bench outside.

Matt was still reading.

Beth, who'd finished her lunch and come to relieve
Lauren, was perplexed. "What's he doing out there?"

"Reading, obviously."

"But what's he *really* doing?"

"Beats me."

"Aren't you curious?"

"Sure."

"Aren't you going to satisfy your curiosity?"

"I'm going to have lunch. I'm famished."

"You're hopeless, is what you are," Beth declared.
Lauren merely shrugged as she headed for the back
room.

"Hopeless" wasn't exactly the word for it. She was
flattered. Matt couldn't have chosen that bench by

chance. But she was also puzzled. If he wanted to see her, wouldn't he simply come into the shop?

Did she want to see him? She still wasn't sure. There was something intimidating about him, and she couldn't quite pinpoint its cause.

Unwrapping her sandwich, she ate it slowly, sipping occasionally from a can of Coke. By the time she was finished, her curiosity had risen right along with her energy level. She *did* want to know what Matthew Kruger was up to. What right did he have to monopolize that bench? What right did he have to distract her? What right did he have to make her feel *guilty* for not acknowledging his presence?

Without further thought, she crossed through the shop, breezed out the door and approached the bench. Matt didn't look up. She stood there for a minute, then quietly eased herself down on the bench several feet away from him, far enough to preclude any implication of intimacy.

While he continued to read, she studied him closely. Other than his eyes, which moved rhythmically from one line to the next, his features were at rest. His lean cheeks were freshly shaved. His tawny hair was clean and vaguely windblown, haphazardly brushing his forehead and collar. He wore his usual jeans and sneakers, but today he'd put on a pink oxford cloth shirt. If she'd ever thought pink was feminine, she quickly revised that opinion. With his sleeves rolled to just beneath the elbow, and with the bronzed hue of his forearms, neck and chin contrasting handsomely with the shirt, he looked thoroughly male. Almost rawly so.

Reaching out, Lauren removed the book from his hands. She caught a brief glimpse of his startled expression before she turned the book over, carefully holding his place with her fingers, and examined the cover.

"A Savage Place," she read aloud. "It's a good one. But some of Parker's other books are set more in Boston. His descriptions of the city are priceless. You really should read them."

"I have," Matt answered. His liquid brown eyes caught hers when she lifted her head. "I've been a Parker fan for years."

Any indignance Lauren might have felt when she'd marched out of the shop had vanished. For that matter, she couldn't remember what doubts she'd had about Matt yesterday, last night, this morning. She couldn't seem to think of anything except the fact that his eyes were the warmest she'd ever seen and that his smile did something strange to her insides.

With a determined effort, she refocused on the book. "Like mystery and a little bit of violence, do you? Or is it Spenser's machismo that intrigues you?" The softness of her tone kept any sting from her words.

"Actually, it's Parker's writing style I enjoy. It's clean and crisp. Fast-paced. Filled with wit and dry humor."

She nodded. So it hadn't been an act, Matt's immersion in the book. He obviously knew his Parker and appreciated him.

"Why this bench?" Lauren asked suddenly. Her eyes had narrowed and were teasing in their way.

Matt stared at her, opened his mouth, then promptly shut it again. As she watched, his expression grew sheepish, filled with a boyish guilt that tugged at her heartstrings. When he finally did explain, she knew she was lost.

"I like this bench because it's close to your shop. I guess I was hoping you'd come out. What I was

really hoping was that you'd take off with me for the afternoon and we'd rent a sailboat and join the others on
the Charles. I got a view of the Basin from the thirty-
second floor this morning. It looked so inviting." His
voice fell, along with the expression on his face. "But
you have to work. I know. It's not fair for me to come
along and expect you to drop everything you're doing.
You have responsibilities. I accept that, and respect it."

Lauren didn't know whether to hug him in consola-
tion or hit him over the head with his book. "How can
you *do* this to me, Matt? It's not fair!" That he should
be a lovable little boy in a virile man's body. That he
should be a stranger, yet so very familiar. That he should
offer excitement in such a gentle and undemanding way.
None of it was fair.

"Then you'll come sailing with me?"

"You were right the first time. I can't."

"But you would if you could."

"Yes."

He smiled and relaxed against the bench. "I guess
I can live with that." Almost as soon as he'd sat back,
he came forward again. "How about tonight? There's a
Boston Pops concert on the Esplanade. We could pick
up something to take out and eat while we listen."

Lauren knew that an hour later, or two or three, she'd
find all kinds of reasons why she shouldn't go. At the
moment, however, she couldn't think of one. "That'd
be fun. I'd like it."

"Great! What time can you get off?"

"What time does the concert start?"

Matt's eyes widened. "I hadn't thought that far." He
jumped up, staying her with his hand. "Don't move.
I'll be right back."

She watched him sprint toward Bostix, the ticket

and information booth adjacent to Fanueil Hall, where
he managed to wedge himself through the crowd at the
window. Within minutes, he had trotted back to her.

"Eight o'clock. They suggested we get there early for
the best spots on the grass, but the music carries pretty
far, so if you can't get away from the shop until later—"

"I think I can convince Jamie to give Beth a hand
until the shop closes. If we want to allow time to walk
over the hill… How about your coming by at, say,
seven? I'll call in an order for dinner—"

"Let me take care of that. I'm on a quasi vacation,
remember? My work is done for the day, while you've
still got more to do."

With a shy smile, she stood up. "Okay, then. I'll see
you later?"

"Sure thing."

She nodded and had started for the shop when Matt
called out to stop her. "Uh, Lauren?" Brows raised in
question, she looked back. His gaze dropped from hers
to the book she still held in her hand. She blushed, hurried back and gave it to him.

"Sorry. I'd forgotten I was holding it."

"I hadn't. If I can't go sailing this afternoon, I'll
have to keep myself occupied somehow. Even aside
from Parker's style, I suppose there is something to be
said for mystery and a little bit of violence. And as for
machismo—"

"Don't say it," she interrupted with a teasing glint in
her eyes. "I don't think I want to hear it. A girl can take
only so much, y'know." She'd pretty much reached her
limit already. Another minute or two, and she'd chuck
the shop and run off to the Charles with Matt. And that
she would certainly regret. The shop was lasting. Matt
wasn't. She'd have to remember that.

It was hard for her to remember much of anything that afternoon—other than the fact that Matt would be coming by for her at seven, of course. Beth teased her mercilessly when she rang something up wrong on the cash register, then again when she began to stretch fabric on a frame backside-to.

She thought seven o'clock would never arrive, but it did, bringing Matt, a blanket "compliments of the Marriott" and a large brown bag filled with all kinds of promising goodies. They walked over Beacon Hill, past the State House, the Common and the Public Garden, then across to Storrow Drive and the Hatch Shell.

They weren't the first to arrive, but they found a patch of grass within easy viewing of the raised stage. In truth, Lauren could have sat half a mile off under a tree by the water. The fact of the concert was secondary to that of the pleasure she felt being with Matt. She didn't analyze it, didn't stop to wonder why she was letting herself get so carried away about a man who'd be gone before she knew it. She simply wanted to enjoy, and enjoy she did.

Matt doubled up the blanket and spread it on the grass; then, after they had both sat down, he pulled out one container of food after another. He'd brought spinach turnovers, chicken salad with grapes and walnuts, Brie and crackers, fruit and a tumbler of frothy raspberry cooler. Lauren wondered where they'd ever put such a feast and told him so. He merely laughed, then laughed again when they'd eaten nearly everything. The concert was well under way by that time. He stuffed the remains of their picnic back into the bag, then sat close to Lauren with one arm propped straight on the grass behind him.

The assembled crowd was far from quiet; esplanade

concerts were that way, informal evenings geared toward lighthearted company and relaxation. Families with children, young couples, middle-aged couples, elderly couples, mixed groups—all shared the pleasure of an evening along the Charles with the sweet smell of the outdoors, the gentle breeze, the exquisite blend of strings, horns and percussion.

As the evening progressed, Lauren and Matt sat closer and closer together. Lauren couldn't remember ever having felt so replete, and the dinner was only partly responsible. Matt was with *her*. Not with the pretty blonde to their right or the adorable redhead to their left. He was with *her*. She had only to drop her eyes from the stage to see his strong legs stretching endlessly before him. He'd changed into a white shirt and a pair of tan slacks that were more tailored than the jeans but no less sexy. His thighs were solid beneath the lightweight cloth, his hips proportionally lean. She felt the warmth of his shoulder as it gently supported her back; felt the goodness of its fit and its strength. His arm cut a diagonal swath to her hip, beside which his hand was flattened. His hand...long, tanned fingers, fine golden hairs, a well-formed wrist...

One song ended on a round of enthusiastic applause. When another began, the applause never quite stopped, for this song was a popular one with a heady beat, and the temptation to clap along was too great to resist. Too great, at least, for everyone but Lauren and Matt. They grinned along with the others, but neither seemed to want to disturb the physical closeness they'd captured. It seemed natural, and right, and very, very special.

Bidden by a silent call, Lauren turned her head to look up at Matt, and what she saw made her breath catch. His eyes were dark, drawing hers with a magnetic warmth, and his expression was one of gentle but insistent hunger. She might have been frightened by it, had her own body not been as insistently hungry. A glowing sun seemed to have risen inside her, radiating sparkles that speeded up the beat of her heart and her pulse and gave the faintest quiver to her limbs.

Lowering his head just the fraction that was necessary, he shadow-kissed her, openmouthed, not quite touching her lips. He drew back for an instant, dazed, then tipped his head and kissed her the same way, but from a different angle. The first kiss had been tantalizing enough for Lauren, but the second one was devastating. Acting purely on instinct, driven by the ache of desire, she opened her mouth in the invitation he'd been waiting for.

When he lowered his head this time, there was nothing shadowy about his kiss. It was full and binding, caressing her with a passion she'd never have believed mere lips to be capable of. She smelled the faint musk of his skin, tasted the fresh, fruity tang of his mouth, felt the sensual abrasion of his tongue as it swept through the moist recesses she offered.

She was about to turn into him, wrap her arms around his neck and draw him closer, when he dragged his mouth from hers and pressed it to her forehead. Though he didn't speak, the harsh rasp of his breath was eloquent and comforting, since Lauren was working equally hard to suck in the air she needed. Eyes closed, she gradually regained control.

Matt shifted and drew her back against his chest, fully this time, with her head resting on his opposite shoulder and his arms wrapped tightly around her waist. They stayed very much that way until the last encore was over. Then, with reluctance, they got up, gathered their things together and let the leisurely movement of the crowd carry them back the way they'd come.

Matt held the folded blanket under one arm. His other arm was draped over Lauren's shoulder. She held tightly to the hand that dangled by her collarbone.

They were nearly at the State House before he spoke. "I've got to be heading back to Leominster."

"When?"

"Tomorrow morning. Early. I have a nine o'clock appointment and probably should have driven out tonight, but I wanted to be with you."

She nodded, not knowing what else to say.

"I'll have to be there through Sunday. I'm sorry. It would have been nice to do something together on the weekend."

"That's okay. The shop's open seven days a week. I've forgotten what a weekend is."

"You have to have *some* time off each week."

"I will, once things get more settled. We weren't sure how soon we'd be able to hire extra help, but business has been going so well that we're trying to convince Jamie to work full-time so Beth and I can stagger days off for ourselves."

"That'd be nice. There must be things you need to do."

"At least a million. Sundays are a help—we're only open from one till six—but I'd really like a day off in the middle of the week once in a while. If I don't start hiring people to fix up my farmhouse, it's apt to give a final groan and crumble at my feet."

"Maybe I could help with that."

"With the farmhouse? But you're leaving."

"I've got some good contacts, and while I'm in

Leominster I can check around for more. What do you need?"

"You name it. Plumber, electrician, roofer, carpenter. Actually, I was exaggerating before. The structure of the house is sound. I had that checked out before I bought the place. But I want to do extensive modernizing inside, and I need good people I can trust, since I won't be able to stand around and supervise."

He gave her hand a squeeze. "Got it. I'll see what I can do."

They walked on in silence for a time. Lauren felt simultaneously content and unsettled, if that were possible. Finally she couldn't help but ask, "When will you be flying back to San Francisco?"

"Not for another week or two. I'll be here in the city early next week, then back in Leominster.... Where are you parked?"

She pointed in the direction of the garage. "You don't need to—"

"I insist."

"But it's out of your way."

"What else do I have to do?" he teased.

"Sleep. You'll have to be on the road very early to get to Leominster by nine."

"It's okay. I'll sleep tomorrow night."

All too soon, they had reached the garage, climbed to the third level and found her car. Reluctantly, she unlocked the door and opened it, only then turning to Matt. "Can I give you a lift back to the hotel?"

He shook his head. "It's out of your way."

"But this was out of yours."

"I'm on foot. It's ten times harder by car, what with one-way streets and all."

"I don't mind. Really—"

Any further words she might have said were stopped at her lips by the single finger he placed there. The dim light of the garage couldn't disguise the way his eyes slowly covered her face. They were hypnotic, those mellow brown eyes, and they conspired with the unmistakable vibrations from his body to suspend Lauren's thought processes once more.

His finger slid to her chin, where it collaborated with his thumb to tip her face up. He kissed her once, then again, then brushed his lips over her cheeks, eyes and nose. Lauren was entranced. Her own lips parted, then waited, waited until he'd completed the erotic journey and returned home.

But if she'd thought what he'd already done was erotic, she was in for an awakening. The tip of his tongue flicked out to paint her lips in the rosy hue of passion, and if she hadn't been clutching the top of the car door, she might have collapsed. She'd never experienced anything as electric, and the hardest part to believe was that the only points where their bodies touched were his tongue and her lips.

When he severed that connection, she stood still, eyes closed, mesmerized by the lingering flicker of a sweet, sweet longing. With regret, she finally opened her eyes.

"Can I come out to see you when I get back to town?" he asked. There was a trace of hoarseness in his voice.

Clearly implied was that he wanted to see her in Lincoln. Without a second thought, she nodded. "I'd like that."

He smiled, then cocked his head toward the car. "Get in. I might not let you leave if you wait much longer."

"Is that a threat or a promise?" she quipped softly, but she was already sliding behind the wheel. One part of her was tempted to wait much, much longer. The other part knew that things were happening quickly and that there were too many considerations to be made before she dared Matt to follow through.

After he had shut the door, she locked it, then started the car and backed out of the space. Matt stood to the side, watching. He gave a short wave as she began the slow, twisting descent. Soon he was lost to her view.

Lauren smiled all the way down Cambridge Street. She was still smiling when she curved into Storrow Drive and was ebullient enough to ignore the harsh beam of headlights from a car following too close on her tail. When she crossed the Eliot Bridge onto Route 2 and the same car remained behind her, she indulgently assured herself that if she was patient, the car would turn off soon.

It didn't.

She passed through Fresh Pond, circled the far rotary and moved into the right lane of what was now a comfortable superhighway. The car stayed with her. She tossed frequent glances in the rearview mirror and frowned. The traffic wasn't heavy. Surely whoever it was could move to the left and pass her, rather than tail her at forty-five miles per hour.

The highway was well lighted. She could see that the car was a late-model compact and that the driver was alone. Some kid having fun? There was no weaving to suggest he was drunk. Neither was there any hint that he was trying to tell her something, such as that her car had a flat tire or was on fire. He was simply following her and succeeding in making her extremely nervous.

Lauren pressed her foot on the gas pedal, pulled into the middle lane and held steady. The other car accelerated, pulled into the middle lane and held steady. She moved back into the right lane. The compact followed suit. She pumped her brakes lightly in an attempt to signal the driver to pass her, but he only slowed accordingly, then resumed speed when she did. In a last-ditch attempt to free herself of the tail, she flicked on the signal lights, moved into the breakdown lane and came to a cautious stop, prepared to floor the gas pedal if the other car stopped.

It swung to the left and passed her.

Breathing a shaky sigh of relief, Lauren sat for several minutes to recompose herself. Since she'd realized she was actively being followed, her imagination had taken her to frightening places. Too many little things had happened to her lately—the near accident on Newbury Street, the vicious dog in her yard, the garage door's fall, the subtle suggestion that someone had been in her home—for her to dismiss summarily this instance as a prank.

Yet as she entered the driving lane once more, that was exactly what she forced herself to do. A prank. A dangerous prank.

Then she crested a hill and saw taillights in the breakdown lane. She passed them by, instinctively speeding up, but within minutes the same car was behind her once more.

She swore softly, but that did no good. The car remained in pursuit. Five minutes went by. She searched the road for a sign of a police cruiser she might hail, but there was none. Another five minutes elapsed, and her knuckles were white on the steering wheel.

She approached her exit and held her breath, praying that when she turned off, the driver of the compact car would consider the game not worth any further effort.

He exited directly behind her and proceeded to follow her along the suddenly darker, narrower road.

Praying now that her car wouldn't break down and leave her at the mercy of the nameless, faceless lunatic, she drove along the road as fast as she dared, heading directly for the center of town.

For the first time she blessed every chase movie she'd suffered through in which the dumb innocent was pursued up and down hills, around corners and through dark alleys without grasping at the simplest solution. Lauren Stevenson was no dummy. She had no intention of heading off into a side street, much less leading someone to her farmhouse, where she would be totally unprotected.

She headed for the police station.

What she hadn't expected when she pulled up in front was that the car that had been on her tail all the way home would swing smoothly—with no qualms or hesitation—into a space in the parking lot. Between two police cruisers.

Lauren quickly shifted into drive and headed home.

She was mortified. Apparently she'd imagined the worst for nothing. Yes, she was angry. For an officer of the law, plainclothes or otherwise, to have behaved in such an irresponsible fashion was inexcusable!

But what could she do? If she marched into the police station and complained, she'd be making a certain enemy. Policemen protected their own, and if what she'd read so often in the newspapers was correct, they weren't beyond administering their own subtle forms of punishment. Someday she might need them, really need them. Could she risk turning them off to her now?

Moreover, what could she say? That she'd been terrified because so many strange things had happened to her of late? They'd think she was nuts. A wild dog. A garage door that went bump. A ghost in her underwear. Maybe she *was* nuts.

No one was following her now, but then, she hadn't expected that anyone would be. Some cop had been playing his own perverse game, perhaps simply practicing up on the technique of the chase. It must be boring being a cop in as peaceful a town as Lincoln. No doubt he'd enjoyed the excitement of his little escapade. At that moment he was probably sitting in the back room with his police buddies, having a good laugh.

Lauren put the car in the garage, then all but ran for the side door of the farmhouse. No doubt about it, she was spooked. She'd left her pursuer at the police station. She'd reasoned away all of her other little near-mishaps. Still, she was spooked.

Coincidence and imagination were a combustible combination.

Turning on every available light, she walked from room to room before satisfying herself that everything was the same as when she'd left that morning. That morning seemed so very far away. And that evening had been so very special, but somehow tarnished by the terrifying experience she'd just been through.

After leaving a single bright light on downstairs, she went up to bed, thinking about the outside floodlights she would have put in when she finally found an electrician. Perhaps she *should* consider a burglar alarm. God, she hated that thought. One of the reasons she'd bought a home in the country was to avoid the stereotypical city fears.

She was making something out of nothing, she reminded herself for the umpteenth time as she lay in the dark of her bedroom, afraid to move. She was letting

Beth's wild imagination get to her. She was letting her own wild imagination get to her. Maybe Beth was right. Maybe she did need a bodyguard. The thought of Matt Kruger—strong, capable of protecting her, capable of thrilling her with a kiss—brought some measure of relaxation, so that at last she was able to fall asleep.

THAT WEEKEND, WORKING around the hours when the shop was open, Lauren met with three different general contractors to discuss what she wanted to do with the farmhouse. None of the three impressed her.

The first was too traditional in his orientation. What she wanted wasn't exactly restoration, she tried to explain. Yes, she wanted the outside of the farmhouse to look much the way it always had. But she wanted the inside to be a modern surprise of sorts.

Unfortunately, number one didn't have much imagination when it came to modern surprises.

Number two was both patronizing and condescending. "I know exactly what you want," he informed her, then proceeded to tell her what he'd do to the farmhouse. It was exactly what she didn't want.

Number three was not only late for the appointment, but both he and his truck were filthy. That said a lot in her book. She could just picture hiring the man and having him show up for work when the mood suited him. He'd probably leave a mess behind every day for her to trip over, and then she'd have to hire a team of workers to clean up after him.

She'd gone to the contractors first in the hope of finding someone who would then issue subcontracts for things like plumbing and electricity. Now, having struck out, she debated calling the plumbers and electricians herself. Lord only knew she desperately needed to get the job done.

She decided to wait for Matt to return. He'd help her. And she trusted him. She'd never seen his work, but she somehow knew that any recommendations he made would be solid.

By Sunday night, she was thinking of Matt more and more, wondering when he'd be returning and what would happen then. She liked him—very, very much. She wanted to believe that his finest qualities—his gentleness, honesty and spontaneity—were indicative of the way Brad had been, too. She still wondered about Brad, still had questions for Matt to answer. But when she was with Matt she wasn't thinking brotherly thoughts. Matt intrigued her. He excited her. He seemed to take the best of both worlds—brain and brawn—and emerge superior. He wasn't quite like anyone she'd ever known before.

Nor did he kiss like anyone she'd ever known before. Not that she was anywhere near to being an expert on kissing. But she'd dreamed of feeling things in a kiss, and Matt had taken her far, far beyond those dreams— so much so that the restlessness she felt was no mystery.

Knowledge of the cause of a problem was not, however, a solution in itself. And since the solution was for the present out of reach, Lauren did the next best thing. Leaving a light burning in the living room, which had become a habit, she headed upstairs to treat herself to a long, soothing shower.

"Treat" was the operative word. As with most everything else pertaining to the farmhouse, the hot-water heater was small and outmoded. Even with its thermostat set on high, the "hot" was negligible. She'd quickly learned that she couldn't take a shower and then expect there to be enough hot water for the laundry. But she wasn't doing laundry that night, and she fully intended to indulge herself until the water ran cold.

Tossing her clothes into the hamper, she took a fresh nightgown from her drawer and went into the bathroom. The shower was little more than a head rigged high in the bathtub, but it served the purpose. She turned on the water, drew the curtain, waited until steam rose above it, then stepped inside.

Heaven. Just what the doctor ordered. Eyes closed, she tipped back her head and let the warmth flow over her hair, shoulders, back and legs. Soap in hand, she lathered her body, then turned, inch by inch, to rinse off. Relaxation seeped through her. She rocked slowly to the pulse of the water.

Then she heard a noise. Her head shot up and her eyes flew open. The slam of a door? Or was it her imagination? She lingered beneath the spray, listening closely. She thought she felt vibrations.

Without pausing to decide whether the vibrations were footsteps or her own thudding heart, she reached back and quickly turned off the water. Then she grabbed her towel and, with jerky movements, began to dry off. Under the circumstances, she did a commendable job, though her nightgown didn't realize that. It stuck so perversely to the damp spots she'd left that she was all but screaming in frustration by the time she finally managed to get it on properly.

Holding her breath, she peered around the bathroom door into the bedroom. When she didn't see anyone there, she dashed out to her closet and grabbed the first weapon she could find. The heavy, workhorse of a Nikon camera, which she hadn't used in years, would certainly serve as a makeshift club, particularly when heaved from its strap.

She tiptoed to the wall by the open bedroom door, flattened herself against it and listened. And listened. Nothing.

She took a deep breath, then yelled as forcefully as she could, "I've already connected with the police department and they're on their way! Better get out while you can!"

Silence.

Of course, she hadn't connected with the police department. They'd think she was a fool. Old houses made noises all the time, and she wasn't sure she'd lived long enough in this one to be able to identify all its characteristic moans and groans. No, she wasn't convinced there was an intruder.

On the other hand, she wasn't convinced there wasn't one, either.

Figuring that she'd need every precious moment if someone should storm in, she reached for the light switch and threw the room into a darkness that was broken only by a faint glow from the bathroom. Then, moving as silently as she could, given that she was more than a little unsteady on her feet, she wedged herself behind the bedroom door and peered through the crack, waiting for someone to creep up the stairs or emerge from one of the other two bedrooms.

No one did.

Noiselessly, Lauren sank to the floor, her gaze never once leaving the narrow slit of a peephole. She waited and watched and listened, growing stiff with tension but not daring to move. Five minutes passed, and there was nothing. Ten minutes passed, and she continued to wait, her temple now pressed wearily to the wall. By the time fifteen minutes had elapsed, she had to admit that she'd very possibly jumped to conclusions.

She wasn't convinced enough to leave herself unprotected, though. To that measure, she carefully closed the bedroom door, carried over a chair and propped it beneath the knob. Then, with the strap of the camera still wound around her hand, she climbed into bed and lay stiffly, listening, waiting. The only thing she was sure about as the hours crept by was that she very definitely would have a burglar alarm system installed when the house was sufficiently readied for it. Nights like this she didn't need.

Unless, of course, she had that bodyguard.

CHAPTER FIVE

WHEN THE PHONE rang early the next morning, Lauren jumped. She was in the kitchen, trying to force down a breakfast she didn't really want, and the unexpected sound jarred her already taut nerves. Snatching up the receiver after the first ring, she gasped a breathless "Hello?"

"Lauren? It's Matt."

Hand over her heart, she let out a sigh of relief. It wasn't that she'd actually expected someone menacing to be on the other end of the line but, rather, that the sound of Matt's voice was an instant and incredible comfort. "Matt," she murmured. "I'm so glad...."

There was a slight pause. "Is something wrong?"

"No, no. Just me and my imagination." She put her hand on the top of her head and found herself spilling it all. "I had the worst time last night. I was in the shower and thought I heard a noise. It turned out to be nothing, but the weirdest things have been happening lately, Matt. You wouldn't believe it. After I left you the night of the concert, some car tailed me all the way home. Well, not all the way, but almost. And before that the garage door had missed me by inches, and the dog had attacked me, and the car had swerved into the sidewalk—"

"Whoa, sweetheart. Slow up a bit. It doesn't sound like it's all been your imagination."

"No, but my imagination has been connecting all these little things that have nothing to do with one another and could really have happened to anyone—"

"But they happened to you." His voice was low and distinctly grim. "When did this all start?"

"I don't know…maybe a week and a half ago. It's like every few days something happens. I never thought I was accident-prone, but I'm beginning to wonder. Beth thought it was a ghost—"

"A ghost? Come on!"

"I know, I know, but if someone's trying to scare me out of this farmhouse, he's doing one hell of a job."

Matt was silent for several long seconds. "Listen, I'm still in Leominster, but I'll be driving back later this afternoon. Why don't I meet you at home? If I get there before you do, I can take a look around."

Lauren was without pride at that moment, and self-sufficiency was a luxury she couldn't afford. "Would you? I'd be so grateful, Matt! I've never been one to be spooked, but I'm as spooked as they come right about now. I don't think I slept more than two or three hours last night, and that was with a chair propped against the bedroom door and a camera nearby."

"You were going to take pictures?" he asked in meek disbelief.

"I was going to hit whoever it was over the head! My camera was the closest thing to a weapon I had. And then this morning I crept around the house looking for signs of an intruder. Crept around my own house in broad daylight—I must be getting paranoid!"

"Shh. Don't say things like that, Lauren. I'm sure there are perfectly logical explanations for everything that's happened."

"That's what I've been telling myself, but it's getting harder to believe. I mean, I can't deny that a car nearly ran me down, or that a dog attacked me, or that the garage door fell…but someone going through my lingerie?"

Matt cleared his throat. "Someone going through your lingerie?"

"See? You think I'm crazy, too!"

"I do not think you're crazy. Never that. You strike me as one of the most together women I've ever known."

"But you don't know me. Not really."

"Well, we'll have to do something about that, then. Tonight?"

"Promise you'll come?"

"I promise."

Lauren gave him directions; then, for the first time that morning, she smiled. "Thanks, Matt. I feel better already."

"So do I, sweetheart. See ya later."

LAUREN ARRIVED HOME from work that night to find a car in the drive. It was a brown Topaz and had local license plates. She assumed it was Matt's rental, but, seeing no sign of him, she felt a momentary tension. The car that had tailed her the Thursday before had been of a similar size, and though she'd had only glimpses of it when it passed beneath lights, she'd guessed it was either maroon or brown.

Staying where she was, safely locked inside her car with the motor running just in case, she leaned heavily on the horn. Then she waited. She seemed to be doing a lot of that lately.

This time she didn't have long to wait. Within a minute, Matt opened the front door of the house and loped out to greet her. The relief and sheer pleasure she felt upon seeing him eclipsed the fact that he'd somehow entered her house without a key.

Killing the motor, she scrambled from the car and threw herself into his arms. It seemed the most natural thing to do and, given the way Matt's arms wound tightly around her, he appeared to have no objections.

When at last he set her down, they exchanged silly grins.

"You look wonderful," he said. "A little tired, maybe, but a sight for sore eyes."

"I could say the same." Her hands were looped around his neck, her lower body flush with his. He looked positively gorgeous, sun-baked skin, slightly crooked nose, too-square chin and all. "Thanks for coming, Matt. I really needed you here. Did you have any trouble finding the place?"

"Nope. Your directions were perfect. I got here a couple of hours ago. It's a nice place, Lauren. I can see why you bought it. It does have charm."

"But does it have ghosts? That's what I *really* need to know."

Taking her hand, he started with her toward the house. "No ghosts. Just lots of things that need repairing." He cleared his throat. "For starters, the lock on one of the back windows is broken. I had no trouble climbing inside."

So that was how he'd done it. Simple enough. "But I tested all the locks. I was sure they worked!"

"Oh, this one works, all right. Until you raise the window. The wood around the screws has rotted. The entire lock simply slides up with the window. Close the window and the lock is in place again." He paused. "Which means that there's good news and bad news."

"Mmm." She dropped her purse on the chair just inside the front door. "The good news is that there's no ghost. The bad news is that the moving around of things inside the house was caused by a human intruder."

"Right. Hey, don't look so down. Every other lock in the house is solid, so it's just a matter of fixing this one. I've already been to the hardware store and picked up larger screws and packing. That'll hold the lock until the wood can be replaced."

"Oh, Matt, you didn't have to."

"I did it for my own peace of mind, if nothing else. Besides, fixing things is my speciality." He eyed her apologetically as they entered the kitchen. "I'm not sure I did as well with dinner. I picked up some things in town, but I'm afraid I'm not all that good a cook."

"I could have taken care of that."

"You'll still have to. I made a salad and husked some sweet corn, but I didn't know what in the hell to do with the chicken. At home I douse it in barbecue sauce and throw it on the grill, but you don't have a grill, and for the life of me I couldn't figure out how the broiler in that stove of yours works." His eyes shot daggers at the appliance in question.

She laughed. "It doesn't. The stove has to be replaced along with the refrigerator, the hot-water heater, the furnace—I could go on and on."

"So what do we do with the chicken?" Opening the refrigerator, he removed the plastic-wrapped package.

"We bake it. And I've got a super sauce. You'll think you're eating the best of barbecue." She looked toward the single cabinet on the wall beside the sink, then down at her sleeveless beige jumpsuit. "I'd better change first. By the way, was that a bottle of wine I saw in the refrigerator?"

He nodded. "California's finest, already chilled. I'll pour while you change. Then we can talk."

Talk. For a minute she'd forgotten what they needed to discuss. She felt so good, so safe, with Matt that the last thing on her mind had been her series of recent misadventures. But she wanted to tell him. Matt was levelheaded and straightforward. She trusted that he'd be honest with her and let her know if she was making a mountain out of a molehill.

She trotted upstairs to her bedroom, changed into a pair of jeans and an oversize gray shirt that she knotted at the waist, then returned to the kitchen in record time.

Matt stood at the kitchen window, looking out at the field beyond. He spun around in surprise when she breezed into the room, then stared at her and swallowed hard.

"I…is something wrong?" She glanced down at herself.

"No. Not at all. It's just that I've never seen you in play clothes."

Lauren could have kicked herself for not having taken the time to touch up her makeup and brush out her hair. In the past those things had never mattered. She'd looked as good—or as bad—with or without the primping. She'd forgotten that she had something to work with now. But it was too late.

Self-consciously, she reached up to finger-comb her hair toward her cheek, but Matt crossed the room in two long strides and stayed her hand. "Don't. Don't do that." Releasing her hand, he used his own fingers as a comb to smooth the hair back. "You look so pretty. I want to see your face."

You look so pretty. I want to see your face. So hard

to believe. So…strange. "I look tired. I should have done something."

"You look beautiful—and with only two or three hours' sleep." Dipping his head, he brushed a kiss on her cheek, another closer to her mouth, then another closer still. His hand was curved around her jaw by the time he reached her lips, though Lauren wouldn't have pulled away even if he hadn't held her. His nearness was drugging, his kiss intoxicating. His breath mingled with hers, seeming to bring her to life as she'd never lived it before. She forgot all else but the sweet sensation of closeness, of awareness, of longing that the caress of his mouth inspired.

"Ahh," he breathed against her lips at last, "your kiss takes me…"

"You have it…the wrong way around."

"Then it's reciprocal, which is why it happens to begin with."

"This is getting confusing."

"Mmm." He smacked his mouth to hers, then set her back and put his wineglass in her hand. She sipped the wine, perfectly content to drink from his glass while he laid claim to the second he'd poured. "Now, let me watch you make this super sauce of yours. I want to see what you put in it."

She grinned. "Cautious Matthew. Hungry but cautious."

"Quite" was all he said, but the grin he gave her stole her breath almost as completely as his kiss had. Fearing for the state of her health, she quickly set to work mixing the ingredients of her super sauce, then indulged Matt by offering him the spoon for a taste.

"Mmm." He licked his lips. "Not bad. Not bad at all."

"Don't give me 'not bad.' It's *super*. At least," she

added in a demure undertone, "that's what it was called in the cookbook I took it from."

"Ah, a cookbook reader." He glanced around. "But I don't see any cookbooks."

She flipped open the cabinet and pointed.

"Two cookbooks? That's all? A cookbook reader is supposed to have a huge collection."

"I'm, uh, I'm a little new at it." She unwrapped the chicken and rinsed it under the faucet.

"You didn't used to cook?"

"I didn't used to eat."

Matt chuckled and scratched his forehead. "That picture. I'd forgotten. You were pretty skinny back then—no offense intended."

"None taken. You're right, I was pretty skinny. It's just recently that I've been forcing myself to eat. I don't dare tell that to many people, mind you," she added, patting the chicken dry with a paper towel. "Most of them get annoyed."

"Jealousy, plain and simple."

She sent him a mischievous grin, then knelt down to remove a baking dish from the lone lower cabinet. That took some doing on her part. Pots were piled on top of pots, which were piled on top of pans, which were piled on top of the baking dish. "Top priority in this kitchen," she announced, rising at last, "is new cabinets, and plenty of them."

"Cabinets—easily done. What else?"

As Lauren dipped the pieces of chicken, one by one, into the sauce and placed them in the baking dish, she outlined her concept of the perfect kitchen, only to find that Matt's suggestions and additions made her plans more perfect than before.

"Why didn't *I* think of a center island?" she asked as she shoved the baking dish into the oven.

"Because you're not a builder."

"And you do this kind of thing?"

His shrug was one of modesty. "The development we're planning in Leominster is a cluster-home type of complex, a planned-community thing. Modern and elegant but also practical. Island counters in the kitchens are an option. They can be used for storage underneath and eating above, or for a sink and a stovetop. Lord only knows, this kitchen's big enough to handle an island."

"And you know people who can do this for me?"

He patted the breast pocket of his shirt. "Names and numbers, already checked out."

With exaggerated greed, she put out her hand. "Gimme. I'll make the calls tomorrow." She proceeded to tell him of the contractors she'd interviewed herself; well before she had finished, he'd closed her fingers around his list. She promptly secured the piece of paper with a decorative magnet on the refrigerator door, then reached for the foil-wrapped loaf of French bread Matt had brought.

He clasped her wrist. "Set the timer for twenty-five minutes. That'll be plenty early to put the bread in the oven." While she did so and then put a pot of water on to heat for the corn, he refilled their wineglasses. "Come on. Let's go out back. I want to hear more about your…escapades."

With vague reluctance, since she'd enjoyed talking with Matt about lighter subjects, Lauren led the way through the back door to the yard. A weathered bench under the canopy of an apple tree provided them with seats. Sunset approached; shards of orange and gold sliced through the trees and threw elongated shadows on the grass.

"Okay," he said. "Start from the top. I want to hear about each thing as it happened."

Encouraged that at least he was taking her seriously, she turned her thoughts to the days that had passed. "The first incident took place more than a week and a half ago, I guess." She related the Newbury Street story. "I don't know if the driver was drunk. I don't even know if it was a man or a woman."

"How about the car? Size? Color?"

She shook her head. "It came from behind. I don't think it was red or yellow. Nothing bright—that would have stuck with me. It must have been some nondescript color. As for the size, God only knows."

"Did you go to the police?"

"What could the police do? The car was gone."

"Maybe there was a witness who caught the license number."

"If there was one, he or she certainly didn't come forward. I just assumed I'd had a close call with a freak accident and left it at that."

He nodded. "Okay. What next?"

"Next was the dog. My run-in with him was…I don't know, maybe two days after the incident with the car." She described what had happened. "As soon as I was down on the ground and thoroughly frightened, he took off. Like he'd simply lost interest."

"You said it was a Doberman?"

"I said it *might* have been a Doberman. It's the same with the car. You're so stunned when it happens that the details slip by you. And anyway, it was dark."

"Was the dog wearing a collar?"

"That's the last detail I'd have noticed."

"Not if your hand had hit something when you tried to push him away."

"My hands were busy protecting my face. I kicked out with my legs—pretty ineffectively, I'd guess. If that dog hadn't wanted to leave, he wouldn't have."

Matt seemed about to say something, then stopped and took a breath. "Did you call the police?"

Lauren shook her head. "The dog was gone. It hasn't been back since."

Even in the fading light, the tension on Matt's face was marked. "Then what?"

She took a drink of wine for fortification. On the one hand, Matt's grim concern was reassuring. On the other, it seemed to make the situation all the more real and, therefore, ominous. "Then the garage door crashed down. It's an old garage, an old door. I'd simply assumed it would hold."

"I checked it out. There's no apparent reason why it didn't. The chains are strong. So are the coils."

"Then what could explain it?"

He looked off toward the shadowed trees and didn't speak for several minutes. "There are ways to rig a door like that."

"But it worked perfectly the next day, and every day since!"

"There's rigging—and unrigging."

Apprehension made her gray eyes larger. "You're suggesting that whoever might have tampered with it before it crashed down went back and fixed it again? But why would anyone *do* that?"

"What happened next?"

Lauren stared at him. He hadn't attempted to answer her question. Not that he ought to have an answer when she didn't, but at least he could have tried to soothe her.

Brows lowered, she looked away. What had happened next? "I'm not sure about the next thing. It wasn't as obvious as the others…I mean, it could have been me."

"What was it, Lauren?"

She took a short breath. "After we'd gone on the cruise that night, I came home and noticed that some things were out of place in my bedroom. At least, they seemed out of place to me, but it might have been my own carelessness." When his silence demanded further explanation, she told him about the perfume, the shoes and the underwear.

"Nothing was taken? Money? Jewelry?"

"I don't have much of either lying around, but no, nothing was taken."

"And it was only the bedroom that was touched?"

"As far as I could tell."

"Did you go through the other rooms?"

"Of course I did! And nothing was touched—*as far as I could tell*. Honestly, Matt! I mean, it's possible that the spoons in the kitchen drawer were rearranged, but I don't set them up in any special pattern, so how would I know?"

He held up a hand. "Okay, okay. Take it easy."

Even the softening of his tone did little to calm her. "How can I take it easy? I feel like I'm at an inquisition, and the implication is that you think I've been irresponsible. Well, I haven't! Taken separately, not one of these incidents is particularly unusual. People on the streets have close calls with cars all the time. Wild dogs get loose; they attack innocent victims. Garage doors malfunction. And as for my personal effects, that could just as well have been my own fault. I'm not perfect! I might have been distracted! And *don't* ask me if I called the police, because I didn't!"

"I didn't ask," he said. His words were gently spoken; his gaze was solicitous. "And I'm sorry if I sounded critical. It's just that I'm concerned...and I'm a stickler for details. I like to know exactly what I'm facing." He slanted her a lopsided smile. "You were supposed to know that already."

Immediately ashamed of her outburst, Lauren sent him a look of apology. "I forgot."

"Well, don't," Matt went on in the same soft voice. "I'm looking for any possible detail that would give us some clue to whether the things that have happened are unrelated or not."

She shivered at the latter thought. "I know. And I appreciate your listening to all this. But I don't know in which direction to turn at this point."

"Which is why you should tell me everything." He paused. "All set?" When she nodded, he released a breath. "Okay. Some things were amiss in your bedroom. Possibly your own fault. What was the next thing that happened?"

"The car followed me home."

"Did you see where it picked you up?"

She shook her head. "It could have been anywhere. I was on Storrow Drive when I first noticed the headlights in my rearview mirror."

"Make of the car?"

She shrugged and shook her head.

"Color?"

"Dark. At the time I thought it was maroon or brown, but it was hard to tell." Her eyes widened. "Do you think it could have been the same car that nearly hit me on Newbury Street?"

"I don't know. There are a hell of a lot of maroon

and brown cars on the road. Without a make and model, we're clutching at straws."

"I'm sorry," she murmured. "Cars aren't my thing. I'm no good at identifying them."

"That's okay, Lauren. Do you remember when it finally dropped away?"

"It didn't, in a sense." She explained how she'd headed straight for the police station, where the car had nonchalantly pulled into a parking space. When Matt remained silent, she feared that he would chide her for not entering the station and complaining; she still wondered if she should have done that. "Well?"

"It's odd," he said at last. "Could have been a policeman having a little fun on his way to work, but all the way from Boston? And he stopped, then picked you up again."

"But he had to be harmless if he was a policeman."

"If, and that's a big if."

"Matt, he pulled into that space as if he knew just where he was going!"

"He may have pulled out just as smoothly once you drove on."

"And if I'd gone in to file a complaint?"

"He could have driven off anyway. You would have led the officer on duty to the parking lot, only to find that there wasn't any car there."

"Mmm. And the officer would have thought I'd dreamed the whole thing up."

"Possibly. Okay, the only thing left, then, is the matter of strange noises last night. Tell me exactly what you heard."

She did. "By the time I came out of the shower, there was nothing. Maybe I imagined it all."

"Maybe."

Then again, maybe not. "If someone had gotten *in* the house, wouldn't he have had to get *out?* I was so spooked that even the tiniest creak in the floorboards would have sounded like thunder to me. But there was nothing. I'm sure of it."

"And when you got up in the morning, there was no sign of an intruder?"

"Nothing."

"No window partway open? No dirt tracked onto the floor?"

"Nothing."

"And is that it? No other suspicious incidents in the past few weeks? Anything that, with a twist of the imagination, might seem odd?"

She thought about it, going back over the days with a fine-tooth comb. Eventually she shook her head. "Nothing."

Matt sat back on the bench, deep in thought. Sandy brows shaded his eyes. His mouth was drawn into a tight line. Lauren studied him, waiting to hear what he had to say. When he stood up abruptly and began to walk back toward the house, she was mystified.

"Matt?" She bolted to her feet, jogging to catch up. He looked at her almost in surprise, and she wondered where his thoughts had been.

"Oh. Sorry. I thought I'd put the bread in the oven now."

"But the timer—"

"We wouldn't have heard it." Sure enough, as they mounted the back steps they caught the insistent buzz.

Biding her time with some effort, she watched him open the oven door, flip over each piece of chicken, then slip the prebuttered loaf onto the lower shelf. Without missing a beat, he carefully dropped the husked ears of corn into the now-boiling water.

Finally she couldn't wait any longer. "Well? What do you think?"

"Mmm. Chicken smells good."

"Not the chicken. My *predicament. Is* someone after me?"

Straightening, he leaned back against the chipped counter and studied her. "Is there a *reason* that someone should be after you?"

She couldn't believe the question. "Of course not! I haven't done anything. I haven't hurt anyone. To my knowledge, I don't have any enemies. I'm amazed you'd even ask that!"

"Just ruling it out. It's as good a place as any to start."

"Well, we've started. A more probable possibility is that these incidents have something to do with the farmhouse. Everything began after I moved in."

"When, exactly, did you move in?"

"The first week in June."

"And the car incident took place, what, at the end of the month?" He thrust out his jaw. "The delay doesn't make sense. If someone legitimately didn't want you living here, the incidents would have started while you were first looking over the place, or certainly as soon as you'd moved in. Besides, not all of the things have happened here. Nah, I don't think they have anything to do with the farmhouse."

"That'd be the most plausible explanation," she pointed out. "And it'd be the easiest one to follow up. I've considered the possibility that one of the neighbors doesn't want me here, but the few I've met have been pleasant enough, and I can't think of any reason that my presence would be objectionable. I know nothing about the former owners, though. I could speak with the Realtor and go through the records of who has lived here in the past. If necessary, I could call in a private investigator, or even the police—"

"Don't do that," Matt interrupted, then quickly gentled his voice. "Not yet, at least."

Though Lauren herself hadn't been anxious to call the police, she was surprised by his vehemence. It occurred to her that he might be indulging her in her fancy while not quite taking it to heart. "What do you suggest?" she asked more cautiously.

"Let's consider the possibilities." He squinted with one eye. "Are you sure you can't think of someone who might get his jollies by scaring you?"

"Like who?"

He shrugged. "An old boyfriend?"

"An old boyfriend who'd come all the way from Bennington in search of a little mischief?"

"Then maybe someone you might have met since you've been here. Someone who asked you out. Or followed you around. Or just…looked at you for hours on end."

"You're the only one who's done that," she replied with a smirk. "Maybe you've got a Jekyll and Hyde thing going."

The twitch of his nose told her what he thought of that idea.

"Well," she went on, thinking aloud, "it could always be a random lunatic."

He shook his head. "Too persistent. Your average random lunatic may hit once, even twice, but not six times. Your average random lunatic wouldn't have access to a trained attack dog—"

Horrified, Lauren interrupted him. "Trained? Do you think that dog was trained?"

Matt gnawed on his lower lip, as though regretting what he'd said, but the damage had been done. "It's possible. If it was trained to respond to a high-pitched whistle that our ears can't detect, that would explain why it retreated so abruptly."

"Just enough to frighten me...not enough to harm me. What kind of insanity are we dealing with?" Her voice had reached its own high pitch.

He gave her shoulder a reassuring squeeze. "We don't know anything for sure, except that so far you haven't been hurt."

"But I *could* have been. If I'd been a little slower in leaving my garage that night...if there'd been no Good Samaritan near me on Newbury Street that day..."

Responding to the sudden pallor of her skin, Matt drew her against him and slowly rubbed her back. "Don't think about what might have been," he murmured. "Nothing's happened, and if I have any say in the matter, nothing will."

With her head pressed to his heart, Lauren believed every word he said. She didn't stop to ask him how he intended to protect her. She didn't stop to ask herself why she, who valued her independence highly, welcomed the protection. She only knew that Matthew Kruger filled a spot that, at this particular point in her life, was open and waiting for him.

He drew back from her to ask, "Think that chicken's almost ready?"

"The chicken!" Pushing herself away from him, Lauren flung open the oven door, reached for a pair of mitts and pulled out first the chicken, then the bread. "Thank goodness it's not burned! I'd forgotten all about it!" She teased him with a punishing glance. "And it's *your* fault."

"My fault?" He was the image of innocence. "You said *you* were the cook around here."

"But you've kept me preoccupied. I haven't even set the table!" The item in question was of the card-table variety, albeit inlaid with cane, and there were folding chairs to match. She'd picked them up to use until she bought regular furniture.

"Then you do that while I toss the salad," Matt suggested. He was already draining the sweet corn. "I picked up a creamy cucumber dressing—unless you've got a super dressing of your own."

The twinkle in his eye brought fresh color to her cheeks and a momentary curl of warmth to the pit of her stomach. "Creamy cucumber's fine. Super sauce I can handle; super dressing is still a way down the road." As she reached for the dishes, she said, "It's amazing…"

"What is?" Matt asked, removing the salad from the refrigerator.

"That you can take my mind off things. Not only dinner, but everything else. One minute I can be worried sick about what's been happening; the next, I forget all about it."

"Maybe you've been worrying for nothing," he ventured quietly. "Maybe all that's happened really *is* a coincidence."

"Maybe…but it's crazy. Everything's been so wonderful. I left Bennington. I have a new job, new home, new look—" The last had slipped out. She rushed on. "Maybe it's all too good to be true."

Matt poured dressing on the salad and began to toss it. "I'm sure that whatever's been going on can be taken care of."

"But how can it be taken care of if I don't know what it is?"

"In time, Lauren. In time. Let's get back to the random-lunatic theory. Lunatic, perhaps. Random, unlikely." He held the salad tongs in the air for a minute before resuming his tossing. "Are you absolutely sure you can't think of anyone who might be behind it?"

Lauren set the silverware on the table with far greater force than necessary. "Yes, I'm sure. I've told you that, Matt. I don't know anyone who'd be capable of doing what has been done. Why do you keep harping on it?"

He hesitated. "Because the only other possibility is that we're facing someone who is neither lunatic nor random, but who has a very specific ax to grind. Maybe someone who has a grudge against your family."

Her jaw fell open, then snapped back into place. "If you knew my parents, you'd never even suggest that. They are utterly harmless. They live in an insulated little world. There may be competition within the academic community, but my parents have been so well accepted for so long that I can't begin to imagine anyone's acting out of jealousy, much less trying to seek revenge. And if someone did, he or she sure as hell wouldn't do it through me. I've declared my independence in ways that have my parents climbing those ivy-covered walls of theirs—" Her voice broke abruptly, and for a minute she wished she could retract what she'd said. Then she realized that there was no point in being coy. Matt, more than anyone, would understand.

He brooded for a minute as he placed the salad on the table, then reached for the wine. "What do you mean?"

Lauren opened the foil-wrapped bread with care. It was hot. "What I'm doing with my life isn't exactly what my parents had wanted me to do."

"In what sense?"

"Oh," she began, juggling the steaming loaf into a bread basket, "they would have preferred that I stay in Bennington and work at the museum. I'd be surrounded by culture, attend plays and lectures, take part in a weekly reading-and-discussion group. Then I'd marry some nice, pale-faced fellow whose interests lay in Babylonian astronomy or medieval art or comparative linguistics. I'd go on to have sweet little children who would take up the cello at age four, read Dostoyevsky at age eight, write a novel at age twelve and beg for college admittance at age fourteen."

"And you? What would you prefer?"

"Me?" She set the bread basket on the table and looked up at him pleadingly. "I want to be happy. I want to do well at whatever I choose to do. I want to feel good about myself."

"And a husband and children?"

Shrugging, she brought the plates to the stove. "I haven't thought that far yet."

"Sure you have. Every woman dreams."

"Every man does, too," she countered.

"But I asked you first. What do you want in a husband? What do you want for your children?"

She put two pieces of chicken on Matt's plate, a single piece on her own. "The same thing I want for myself, I suppose. If a person is happy, and feels good about himself, everything else falls into place." She added an ear of corn to each plate before bringing both to the table.

"How can your parents argue with that?"

"They believe that certain things make a person happy. We just disagree on what those things are."

Matt was standing with one hand on his hip as he

watched her. Straightening suddenly, he tilted a chair out and gestured for her to sit. "Brad's philosophy was similar. It's amazing how alike you are in so many ways. Then again, there are differences."

"Tell me more about him, Matt. Did he really feel the same way I do?"

Matt slowly seated himself and didn't speak until he'd pulled his chair in and spread a napkin on his lap. His expression was pensive. "He felt that what your parents wanted was different from what he wanted. But you already know that. I think he would have been surprised that you agree with him. He saw himself as the black sheep of the family."

"So much so that, regardless of what he did, it didn't seem to measure up?" she asked.

Matt frowned, then shifted in his seat. He drew the salad bowl toward him and prodded the lettuce with the tongs. In a sudden spurt of movement, he began to pile salad on Lauren's plate. "Is that the way *you* feel? That nothing you do can measure up?"

"Hey." She put her hand on his and pushed the tongs toward his own plate. "That's enough."

He served himself. "Do you feel that way, Lauren?"

"No. I'm pleased with what I'm doing. Brad tried to meet my parents' expectations, failed, then took off. I went along with their wishes and was fairly successful at it before realizing that it wasn't what I wanted. I left because I chose to. Brad left because he had to. I could have gone on forever up there, I suppose. Brad couldn't have survived." She took a breath. Her fork dangled over the chicken. "It wasn't that he didn't have the brains for it, but his temperament was totally different. He was more impulsive, more restless. Hyperactive, my parents always said, but I think they were wrong. He just wanted to use his brains for things other than scholarly pursuits."

"He did that," Matt drawled under his breath, but there was no humor in his expression. When he saw Lauren staring at him, puzzled, he spoke quickly. "Designing houses, interesting houses, takes brains, although it's not considered a scholarly occupation. It's too bad your parents couldn't have seen some of the work Brad did."

"They never even knew about it" was her sad reply. "They didn't know who he worked for or what he did. They were shocked at the amount of money that came to me when he died." She rolled her eyes. "For that matter, so was I."

Matt's hesitation was a weighty one. "They didn't begrudge it to you, did they?"

"No." She snorted. "The only thing they begrudged was what I *did* with it." Spearing a tomato wedge, she waved it for an instant. "Family interrelationships are weird things. Expectations are often so unrealistic. It's as if we have blinkers on. I suppose I'm not that much more understanding of my parents than they are of me, but it's a shame. I'm an adult now. They're adults. Wouldn't it be nice if we *liked* one another?"

"It's not that simple. You're right. Unrealistic expectations can stand in the way. Or ego needs. It must be difficult in a situation like yours, where it would be impossible for you to rise above what your parents have done. They've been so successful in their fields. Maybe that's why both you and Brad felt the need to strike out on your own."

"Maybe. I hadn't thought about it that way." Lauren mulled over the prospect for several minutes, but what lingered with her was how insightful Matt was. "What about you? Are you close to your family?"

"Very."

"Are they in San Francisco, too?"

He shook his head. "L.A. I guess I needed a little distance, just as you do. The pressure coming from my parents was a more traditional one. They're retired now, but for years they both worked in a factory. They wanted my sister and me to rise higher, to advance socially. Unfortunately, there wasn't much money for college. I suppose I could have tried for a scholarship, but I wanted to work. Once I got going, I discovered that I could get the education I needed on the job. I've taken business courses here and there, and I've advanced, so I can't complain."

"How about your sister?"

Matt warmed Lauren with a grin. "Maggie's a speech therapist. She *did* go for a scholarship, won it and wowed 'em all at UCLA. I'm really proud of her. We all are."

"I can see that," Lauren said. His grin was contagious, or was it the way his cheeks bunched up and his eyes crinkled? Whatever, she was grinning back at him, wondering how a man could be so gentle and giving, yet so wickedly attractive. "Tell me more," she urged. "About when you were a kid, what you were like, what you did."

He made a face and tilted his head to the side. "It's really not all that exciting."

"Tell me anyway." She perched her chin in her palm and waited expectantly.

"Only if you eat while I talk. You haven't had more than a bite, and the chicken is fantastic."

Listening to Matt and watching him drove all thought

of food from her mind. But if eating was his precondition, well…

He talked and she ate. She made observations and asked questions while he ate, then resumed her own meal when he talked more. By the time they'd had seconds of just about everything, including wine, she'd learned that, though a mischievous Matt had received his share of spankings as a boy, he'd grown up in a house filled with love. She'd also learned, but between the lines, that what Matt craved most was his own house filled with love.

When he offered to help her clean up, she accepted. It wasn't that she needed the help or that she was liberated enough to demand it. She'd thoroughly enjoyed the way they'd worked together getting the dinner ready, and she wanted to draw out the evening as long as possible.

Apparently Matt had the same idea. When the kitchen was as spotless as one that age could be, he suggested they relax for a few minutes before he left. They settled in the living room, which, aside from Lauren's bedroom, was the only room with furnishings. There was one sofa and two side chairs. They shared the sofa.

Lauren felt peaceful and happy and tremendously drawn to the man beside her. His arm was slung across the back of the sofa, his fingers tangling in her hair. The clean, manly scent that clung to his skin heightened her senses, while his warmth bridged the small space between them with its invisible touch.

"This has been nice," she told him, slanting a shy glance his way. "I'm glad you came."

His voice was like a velvet mist. "So am I." Sliding his arm around her shoulders, he drew her closer even as he met her halfway. His lips touched one corner of her mouth, then the other, then her cupid's bow, then her lower lip. He'd opened his mouth to kiss her fully when, unable to help herself, she laughed.

He drew back and stared at her for a minute, then cried in mock dismay, "Lauren! What kind of behavior is that? Didn't anyone ever tell you not to laugh in a man's face when he's about to kiss you?"

"I'm sorry… It's just that…you were tasting me one little bit at a time…. You really *are* cautious!"

His eyes danced mischievously. "Caution's gone" was all he said before he covered her mouth with his and proceeded to deliver the most thorough kiss she'd ever received. No part of her mouth was left untouched by any part of his, and by the time he buried his face in her hair, she felt totally devoured. She might have told him so had she been able to speak, but her breath was caught somewhere between her lungs and her throat, for his hand was sliding over her waist, over and up, ever higher, and anticipation had become as tangible as those long, bronzed fingers. When at last they reached her breast, she let out a soft moan and succumbed to the exquisite sensations shooting through her.

Lauren had never been touched this way, yet there was nothing demure in her response. Both mind and body said that what she was experiencing was right and natural; instinct, goaded by desire, set her fingers to combing through his thick hair, running over his broad shoulders, splaying eagerly across his sinewed back.

"Lauren." His voice was hoarse. "Lauren…I have to…we have to stop…."

"No," she whispered. She held his head with one hand, pressing it to her neck. Her other hand covered his at her breast. "Don't stop."

A groan came from deep in his chest. "Do you know what you're saying, sweetheart? What it does to me?"

His voice was thicker now, foreign to her ears yet exciting. She held her breath when he transferred her hand to his own chest and slowly slid it lower.

Lauren could feel the strength beneath her palm, the tautness of his stomach, then the stunning rigidity beneath the fly of his jeans. She wanted to hold him, explore him, let him satisfy the ache that had taken hold deep in her belly, but the newness of it all brought a measure of sanity. With a shuddering breath, she sagged against him.

"Yes. Do stop," she whispered. She was shocked by her own abandon, not quite sure what to make of it. "Everything...everything's happened so fast...and there's still the other matter." Of her own accord, she retreated from him, taking refuge in her corner of the sofa and clasping her hands tightly in her lap. The aura of arousal, a telltale quiver, lingered in her body, but thought of that "other matter" gradually put it to rest.

Matt, too, retreated to his corner of the sofa. He shifted in an attempt to get comfortable, finally hunching forward with his elbows on his knees. His fingers were interlaced, not quite at ease. He cleared his throat. "Yes...that other matter."

"We didn't reach any conclusions."

A pause. "No."

"What do you think?"

Another pause. "I don't know."

"Should I call the police?"

"No." Emphatically.

"Why not?"

He didn't answer, but studied his hands and frowned. "I have to ask you this, Lauren. I know it may sound terrible...but you did mention that your parents were against your coming here—"

"My parents? You think my *parents* could have been behind what's happened?" Vehemently she shook her head. "No. Absolutely not. They may disagree with me, but they'd never try to harm me."

"Maybe just scare you into going back—"

"No." She was still shaking her head. "Not possible! They wouldn't be capable of conceiving of violence."

"Maybe not violence, but if they've already lost one of their children—"

"Forget it, Matt. It's simply not possible.... I think I should call the police."

"No."

"You've been very firm about that. Why, Matt?"

He offered the longest pause yet. "Maybe it's...premature."

"Premature? Then you don't think there's a connection between the things that have happened?"

"I didn't say that. I just think we ought to give it a little time. Let me see what I can do."

"What can you possibly do? Neither of us knows where to begin!"

He didn't argue with her; neither did he agree. Instead, he scowled at his hands.

"Matt, I'm frightened." As much by the strangeness of his response as by everything else, she told herself. "I haven't been hurt so far, but maybe I've just been lucky. What if the next time—"

"You won't be hurt," he gritted out, raising his dark brown eyes to hers. She tried to read his feelings, but they were shuttered. "I'll stay here. If something happens, I can take care of it."

Lauren stared at him. "You can't stay here! My bed's the only one—and—and anyway, you can't be with me every single minute of the day. You have to work.

So do I. How can you anticipate when something will happen?"

"*If* something happens."

She bolted from the sofa and began to prowl the room. She was confused and upset. "You think I'm paranoid. I know you do. You think I'm making something out of nothing." Whirling to face him, she stuck her fists on her hips and glared. "The little lady with the rampant imagination. The fanciful little woman to be indulged—that's the macho attitude, isn't it? That's where *you're* coming from!"

Matt's face paled. He sat up straight, then rose and began to walk stiffly toward the front door. His voice was flat. "I think I'd better leave. If that's the way you feel…"

Lauren watched him open the door, then close it behind him. What had she said? Had *she* put that look of hurt in his eyes? Had she been responsible for draining the emotion from his voice, that very same voice that had always been so wonderfully expressive?

Her gaze flew to the window. It was dark outside. Once Matt left, she'd be alone. Unable to take back the ugly words she'd said. Open prey to her own impulsiveness and…

The growl of his engine hit her ears as she wrenched open the front door. "Wait!" she cried, arms waving as she tore down the walk. "Matt, wait!" The car was halfway down the drive. Thinking only that she needed him with her, she flew in pursuit. "Don't go, Matt! I'm sorry! Please…don't…go!"

The taillights went on at the end of the drive, and the car slowed, about to turn onto the street. Lauren's steps faltered. She came to a tapering halt. She'd lost him. He was gone.

The car began to turn, then stopped.

She held her breath, then started running again. "Matt! Please! Wait!"

His tall figure emerged from the car but didn't move farther. Again she faltered and stopped. But the hesitation was only momentary. She knew what she wanted, knew what she needed. With a tiny cry of thanks that she'd been given a second chance, she raced forward.

CHAPTER SIX

FLINGING HER ARMS around him, Lauren hung on for dear life. "I'm sorry—so sorry, Matt!" She pressed her cheek to the warm column of his neck. "I didn't mean what I said. I was nervous and frustrated. I took it out on you." Slowly she eased her grip on him and met his gaze. Her voice grew softer. "Don't go. Please?"

"I don't disbelieve you, Lauren," he stated quietly.

"I know that. I accused you unfairly. I expected you to have answers where I didn't. It was wrong of me."

"Nothing's changed. I still don't have answers."

"I know that."

"And you still have only one bed." His hands came to rest lightly on her hips, fingers splayed. "If I were a saint, I'd offer to sleep on the couch, but I'm not a saint."

His words and the look in his eyes sent ripples of excitement through her. "I know that," she whispered.

"Then you know what I want?" he asked as softly.

Unable to speak, she nodded.

His gaze held hers captive for a minute longer; then he grabbed her hand. "Get into the car."

"What—?"

He was urging her into the driver's seat, his hands on her shoulders. "Slide in. Over a little. That's it." He was mere inches behind her, then flush to her side. "I'm not taking the chance that you'll change your mind." Tucking her arm through his, he put the car in reverse and sped backward up the drive. Then he all but swung her from the car, fitted one strong arm over her shoulder and half ran to the house.

"Matt?" She was laughing, breathless.

"Shhh."

Once inside, he continued up the stairs, straight to her bedroom. The light was off. He made no attempt to alter the darkness, and Lauren was relieved. She knew that she wanted what was about to happen. She also knew that the darkness added to its dreamlike quality. That a man like Matt wanted *her* was mind-boggling. Surely if he turned on the light, he'd have second thoughts; she'd have second thoughts....

He took her in his arms and kissed her until the only thoughts she had were how wonderful he was, how unbelievably desirable he made her feel, how lucky she was to have found him. She gave herself up to his kiss, to his hands as they unbuttoned her shirt and unclasped her bra, to his fingers as they charted her flesh, branding her woman with fire and grace.

A soft moan came from deep in her throat, and she arched her back to offer herself more fully. Acceding to her wordless plea, he stroked her with gentle expertise. His fingers made firm swells of her breasts; his thumbs, tight buds of her nipples. And all the while his tongue correspondingly familiarized itself with every nook and cranny of her mouth.

His hands left her only to free himself of his shirt, and then he was back, crushing her close. His chest was warm and lightly furred. Its texture exhilarated her, though she wondered if it was simply the closeness, male to female, that pleased her so. There was something very, very right about what she felt. There was something very, very right about Matt. At that moment she didn't know how she'd ever doubted him.

While he held her lips captive, he reached for the snap of her jeans, released it, lowered the zipper. She gasped for breath when he knelt and eased the denim from her legs, then did the same with her panties. She clutched his shoulders for support and shivered, though her blood was hot, her body aching for completion. Modesty was nonexistent; she wanted him too badly.

"Please," she whispered shakily, "I need you, Matt."

For an instant, he buried his face in her stomach while he caressed the backs of her legs and her bottom. His breath was ragged, his hair damp against her hot flesh. She drove her fingers into the thick, sun-streaked pelt and held him closer, then urged him upward.

He didn't need much urging. Standing, he shed the rest of his clothes, then came to her naked, pressing her to him, graphically showing her that the need wasn't hers alone. She thrilled to the knowledge, unable to be afraid when Matt was all she'd ever wanted, all she'd ever dreamed about. The fact that she could arouse him to the state he was in was as heady as the state of arousal he'd himself brought her to.

He moved from her only to tug back the spread before lowering her gently to the sheets. "Lauren…God, Lauren…" he murmured, then kissed her again. He caressed and teased with his hands, his lips, his tongue, but the play took its toll. His body seemed on fire, trembling under the strain of the heat, finally unable to withstand it. Threading his fingers through hers, he anchored them by her shoulders and positioned himself between her thighs. With one powerful thrust, he surged forward.

Lauren arched her back against the sudden invasion,

and a tiny cry escaped her lips. When he stiffened, she wrapped her arms around him to draw him close to her. He resisted.

"Lauren?" His voice was little more than a throaty whisper.

"It's okay...don't stop...don't stop."

His breathing grew all the more labored and he pressed his forehead to her shoulder. "I couldn't if...I wanted to," he finally managed, "but I can be more... gentle."

"Don't be!" she cried, for the instant of pain was gone, leaving only that swelling knot of need low in her belly.

But he was gentle and caring, moving slowly at first, letting her body adjust to his presence before he adopted the rhythm designed to drive her insane. What he didn't realize was that even his initial, cautious movements were delicious. His fullness inside her gave Lauren an incredible sense of satisfaction; the idea of receiving a man, of receiving Matt in this way, was the sweetest delight.

By the time he moved faster, Lauren was right with him. She adored the way his thighs brushed hers, the way their stomachs rubbed. When he bent his head, she strained higher. His mouth closed over her breast and began a sucking that pulled at her womb from one direction while the smooth stroking of his manhood pulled at it from another. Her hands roamed over and around his firm body, but even had she not touched him, she would have been intimately aware of every hard plane and sinewed swell he possessed. Their bodies were that close, working in tandem.

He murmured soft words of encouragement and

praise. "That's it, sweetheart…ahhh…your legs…yes, there…so good…"

They moved as one then, each complementing and completing the other. Lauren experienced a beauty she'd never imagined. She was drawn beyond herself into Matt, sharing, collaborating, merging with him into a greater being for those precious moments of emotional and physical bliss.

After the climax had passed, it was a long time before either of them could speak. They gasped for air, alternately panting and moaning, laughing from time to time at their inability to do anything more. At last Matt slid slowly to her side, leaving one leg and an arm over her in a statement of possession she had no wish to deny. His head was beside hers on the pillow, his cheek cushioned in her hair.

"How do you feel?" he asked in a thick whisper.

"Stunned," she whispered back. "I never imagined…"

"*You* never imagined…"

She forced her lids open and looked at him. "Then… it was okay?"

"It was more than okay," he teased in throaty chiding, "but you had to know that."

"No. I didn't."

His grin faded, replaced by a look of tender concern. He brought a shaky hand up to smooth damp strands of hair from her brow. "I'm sorry if I hurt you, Lauren. If I'd known, I might have been able to make it easier."

"It couldn't have been easier. I've never felt so wonderful in my life."

"Even at the start?" His arched brow dared her to deny the moment of pain she'd felt.

"Even then. If I hadn't felt a thing, something would

have been lost. I wanted the pain. Does that make any sense?"

He didn't answer. Instead, he traced her eyebrow with his finger. "Why didn't you tell me, sweetheart?"

"I didn't think it mattered." She paused, experiencing a frisson of apprehension. "Did it? I mean, we're both adults. I knew what I was doing."

"Did you?"

"Yes!" She didn't understand what he was getting at.

"Lauren, I didn't do anything to protect you. It's possible I've just made you pregnant."

Her jaw slackened only slightly. Then, unable to control herself, she burst into a smile. "What an exciting thought!"

Matt closed his eyes for a minute. "You're supposed to be worried, sweetheart." He propped himself up on an elbow and looked down at her. "You're supposed to be thinking about this new life you have, the shop, your independence."

"But a baby!" Her eyes were wide. "I could adjust to that. It would be marvelous!"

"I didn't know you wanted a baby so badly."

"Neither did I." She scrunched up her nose. "But it probably won't happen. Just once, Matt. And it's the wrong time of the month." She brushed the strands of hair from his forehead and left her fingers to tangle in the wet thatch. "Are *you* worried?"

"Of course I'm worried. Babies should be planned, the logistics worked out. Everything should be clear from the start."

"There you go again. So cautious." She tugged playfully at his hair. "If I were to become pregnant, I'd manage. One way or another I would, because I'd want the baby enough to make everything fall into place."

"Such a romantic," Matt murmured, but there was a sadness in his eyes.

Her smile faded. "You're thinking that you'll be leaving soon."

"Sooner or later I will."

"It's okay, Matt. There are no strings attached to what happened tonight. I won't ask any more of you than you want to give."

He snorted and flopped back on the pillow. "That's cavalier of you."

"Would you rather I demand marriage?" she asked, confused. "Times have changed. Just because we made love doesn't mean you have to make an 'honest woman' of me. I don't feel dishonest. I feel...lucky."

He turned his head on the pillow so that he faced her again. "Explain."

"I never expected what happened tonight. What I felt, what I experienced, were so much more than I've ever dared to dream."

"Why not? That's what I don't understand. I don't understand why you were a virgin. You're beautiful, charming and intelligent. And you're right. Times have changed. Women your age are rarely inexperienced."

"Would you have had me throw myself at just any old man for the sake of experience?"

At the sound of hurt in her voice, he rolled over to cover her body. With his large hands cupping her face, he spoke gently. "No, sweetheart. Of course not. I'm the one who's been lucky tonight. To know that you've given me what you've given no other man...that was one of the reasons I couldn't stop when I realized what was happening."

"One of the reasons?"

Even in the dark she caught his sheepish grin. "The

others are right here." He dropped a hand to her knee and lifted his body only enough to permit that hand a slow rise. He touched each and every erogenous zone before tapping his finger against her temple. "All of you—mind, body, soul. You turn me on, Lauren."

"Oh, God" was all she could whisper, because his tactile answer had set her body to aching again, and she hadn't believed it could be possible. She didn't know whether to be pleased or embarrassed, but that was her mind talking. Of its own accord, her body shifted beneath his with a story of its own.

As she'd already learned, Matthew Kruger was a good reader.

When the last page of this second chapter had been turned, she fell asleep. Her body was exhausted yet replete, her mind at peace. She was totally unaware that Matt lay awake beside her for long hours before curving his body protectively around hers and at last allowing himself the luxury of escape.

LAUREN AWOKE THE next morning to a strange sensation of heat running the entire length of the back of her body. Her lids flew open and she held her breath. Only her eyeballs moved, questioning, seeking, finally alighting on the large, tanned hand flattened on the sheet by her stomach.

Matt.

Shifting her head, she followed a line from that hand, up a lean but powerful arm to an even stronger shoulder.

Matt.

Quietly, almost stealthily, she turned until she faced him, and her heart melted. He was sound asleep, tawny lashes resting above his cheekbones, his mouth slightly parted, lips relaxed. Unable to help herself, she let her gaze fall along his body. Last night she'd savored him with her hands; this morning it was her eyes' turn to feast.

He was magnificent. Soft hair swirled over his chest, tapering toward his navel, below which the sheet was casually bunched. His hips were lean, as she'd known they'd be; the sheet was nearly as erotic a covering as the air alone might have been.

A self-satisfied smile spread over her face. She felt good. Complete. All woman. Giving in to temptation, she leaned forward and kissed his chest. He smelled of man, earthy but wonderful. Eyes closed, she drank in that essence as she continued to press the lightest of kisses into the warmest of skin.

When a hand suddenly tightened around her waist, her head flew up. Matt's eyes were still closed, but he wore the roguish shadow of a beard on his cheeks and a faint smile on his lips. "Am I dreaming?" he whispered.

In answer, Lauren shimmied higher, slid her arms around his neck and kissed his smile wider. She was further rewarded when he rolled onto his back and hauled her over him. Only then did he open his eyes.

For long minutes, they simply looked at each other. She wasn't sure what her own eyes were saying, but Matt's quite clearly spoke of pleasure. And affection. They made her feel special.

"Hi," he whispered at last.

She swallowed the lump of emotion in her throat. "Hi."

"How'd you sleep?"

"Fine."

"No ghosts?"

She shook her head.

"No strange noises?"

She shook her head. "Beth was right. She said I needed a bodyguard."

He closed his hands around her bottom and gave her a punishing squeeze. "So that's why you did it? Because you wanted a bodyguard?"

"You know better than that." She sucked in a breath when his hands pressed her intimately closer. "Matt?"

He was grinning. "It's your fault. You started it. In case you didn't know, a man's at his peak in the morning."

"I thought a man was at his peak in his twenties, and you're a mite beyond. You're shocking me."

"You're the one with the bag of surprises. A virgin is supposed to be shy and demure."

She grinned. "I'm not a virgin anymore, so my behavior is excusable."

Rolling over, he set her on her back, then held himself up so that he could look at her. Just as hers had done moments earlier, his eyes touched her body as only his hands had done the night before. "You are beautiful, Lauren. God, I can't believe it." He met her gaze. "No regrets?"

Still basking in his approval, which both stunned and thrilled her, she shook her head. "How about you?"

One long forefinger drew a bisecting line from the hollow of her throat to the apex of her thighs. "No," he answered, but gruffly. "Not about this. About not having the answer to your problem, yes, I have regrets."

"Don't think about that," she whispered, feeling a strange urgency not to let anything intrude on this precious time with Matt. "Not now."

His grin was lopsided, slightly forced, and his eyes lingered on the soft curves of her body. "I think I'd better. It's either that or ravish you again, and I imagine you're going to be a little sore."

"Me? Sore?"

"Yes. You, sore."

"Oh."

With a deep growl, he gathered her into his arms and held her tightly. When his grip loosened, it was with reluctance. "I could use a shower and some breakfast. It's a workday, or had you forgotten?"

"Oh, my God!" She twisted toward the clock on the dresser, then pushed herself from his arms and bolted out of bed. "I'll take the shower first," she called over her shoulder. Remembering her sadly deficient water heater, she added, "Real quick."

Lauren was true to her word, but by the time she had returned to the bedroom, Matt was nowhere in sight. For a split second she panicked. Then she caught sight of his clothes on the floor. "Matt?" Wrapped in her towel, she headed for the stairs. "Matt?"

The aroma of fresh coffee filled the air, but he didn't answer. She was halfway down the staircase when the front door opened and Matt strode through, carrying a large leather suitcase. He was stark naked.

"Matthew Kruger! Where is your sense of decency? If one of my neighbors saw you—"

He'd taken the stairs by twos, and the smack of his lips on hers cut off her teasing tirade. He continued upward. "The trees were my cover. It's a gorgeous day outside."

Lauren couldn't think to argue. He was spectacular. Tall and straight. Broad back, narrow hips, tight buttocks. If it hadn't been for the time, she'd have followed him into the shower just to touch him again. The mere sight of him took her breath away.

But time was of the essence. She blow-dried her hair and put on makeup while Matt showered and shaved; then she dressed quickly and hurried to the kitchen. They were seated side by side, finishing off the last of the scrambled eggs and toast, when Matt laid out his plans for the day.

"I've got meetings set for ten and two. We can take my car into Boston, meet for lunch, then grab something on the way home tonight. Sound okay?"

His words were offered gently, not at all imperiously, yet they brought back to Lauren the crux of Matt's present mission. He intended to protect her as he'd promised, which meant that he was going to stick as close to her side as possible. On one level, she was thrilled with that prospect. On another...

"About my problem, Matt. Are we just going to... wait?"

"Pretty much. It'll be interesting to see if my presence here makes any difference."

"But if nothing happens, we won't know if you've scared someone off for good or simply put him off for a while. And you can't stay here forever."

"I know." He looked away. "I'm going to make some calls today."

"What kind of calls? To whom?"

"People who may have more insight than we do." There was an edge to his voice, but his gaze was soft when he glanced back at her. "Let me do the worrying for now, Lauren. You've done your share."

"But it's my problem! I can't just dump it on your shoulders and wipe my hands of it. That's not fair to you. You don't owe me anything."

For a minute he looked as if he would argue. He gnawed on the inside of his cheek, then lifted his mug and drained the last of his coffee. "Let's just say I owe it to Brad, then. He was my friend and you're his sister. The least I can do is to help you out when you need it."

That wasn't quite the answer she wanted, but she knew she'd have to settle for it.

"Anyway," he added with an endearing grin, "I've got broad shoulders. I can handle it. Maybe it's the Spenser in me coming out, after all."

"Better you than Robert Urich. But are you sure?"

"Very sure. Hey, as far as work on the house goes, are you going to call those names I gave you or would you like me to do it?"

She winced. "Got a cold shower, did you?"

"Well…"

"I'll do it. You're doing enough. I'd love it if you were here when I meet with them, though. I have a feeling some of those guys show more respect when a man's around." The last had been offered on a dry note. She paused, then asked cautiously, "How long will you be here?" She envisioned two or three days, and the thought left her feeling empty.

He rubbed the back of his neck. "I was thinking about that last night. I have to be in Leominster on Thursday and Friday, but I could almost commute from here." He took a fast breath. "Unless you'd rather have the house to yourself again. I'll understand, Lauren. It's okay, really it is— Hey, crumpled napkins in the face I can do without first thing in the morning!"

"Then don't give me that little-boy pout," she chided as she carried their plates to the sink. But when she returned to the table, she gave him a hug from behind. "Of course I want you here," she murmured with her cheek pressed to his. "For as long as you can stay. Besides, you *do* owe it to me."

His hands clasped hers at the open collar of his shirt. "I do?"

"Uh-huh. You've awakened me to some of the finer points in life. Seems to me there's got to be an awful lot I still don't know."

"Then you *are* after my body! I knew it all along!"

"Could be," she answered with a grin. "Could be."

DURING THE NEXT few days, Lauren and Matt spent every possible minute with each other. They drove to and from Boston together. They met for lunch each day. When Matt wasn't working but Lauren was, he was parked so frequently on the bench outside the shop that Beth suggested they charge him rent.

"Either that, or hire him part-time."

Lauren wrinkled her nose. "After all we went through to convince Jamie to start full-time next week? No way. Besides, what does Matt know about art?"

"What does he know about *other* things?" Beth drawled suggestively. "That's what *I* want to know."

"Oh, quite a bit" was all Lauren would admit. She knew Beth was fishing. She hadn't made a secret of the fact that Matt was staying with her in Lincoln. But some things were sacred, not to be discussed with even the closest of friends, and for more than the obvious reasons. Lauren felt she was living a fairy tale. By her own admission, Beth was envious. The last thing Lauren wanted to do was to rub it in.

"Well," Beth said with a sigh, "at least he's managed to keep you safe."

"That he has."

Since Matt had been with her, there'd been no accidents, no close calls, no questionable occurrences.

Indeed, Lauren felt safe enough almost to forget there was a problem.

Almost, but not quite.

Tuesday evening she asked Matt if he'd made any calls to those "people who may have more insight than we do." He said he had and that the ball was rolling. His tone was light. She hadn't dared ask more.

Wednesday evening, though, she couldn't help herself. As gently as she could, she inquired about it again.

"Have you heard anything yet?"

"No. It takes time."

"Time to do what? I don't understand."

"Questions can be asked, people consulted. Trust me, Lauren. Please?" Put that way, with an eruption of tension dissolving abruptly into beseechfulness, she'd surrendered.

But much as she tried, she couldn't shake the conviction that the things she'd experienced were linked and that, despite Matt's protective shield, they were bound to resume at some point. And she was frightened.

THURSDAY MORNING MATT crawled out of bed at dawn, showered, shaved and dressed, then woke Lauren to say goodbye. She was groggy. It had been another late night of sweet, prolonged loving. Only the realization that Matt was leaving brought her from her self-satisfied stupor.

"You should have wakened me sooner," she whispered, reaching up to touch his freshly shaved cheek. "I'd have made you breakfast."

"No time. They'll have coffee and doughnuts there."

"I wish you didn't have to go."

"I'll be back tonight."

"I know, but I've been spoiled. Leominster seems so far away."

He sighed. "I agree." He pressed his lips together, then forced a smile. "You take care of yourself, sweetheart, you hear? Drive carefully, and be sure to lock the doors."

"I will."

Lifting her in his arms, he hugged her before setting her back with a kiss on the tip of her nose. She knew not to ask for more. Where temptation was concerned, they were both decidedly weak.

"Good luck, Matt. I hope everything goes well."

He waved as he left the room. Climbing from the bed, she crossed to the window and watched him slide into his car, start the engine and drive off. In an attempt to parry the unease that settled over her, she took a shower and dressed, then forced herself to make breakfast for one and eat every last bit.

Only when she'd finished did she permit herself to sit back and think. She missed Matt. Already. After only two full days together, she'd gotten used to his presence. More than used to it. Addicted to it. Breakfast wasn't the same without him. Neither would lunch be. For that matter, she'd miss being able to look up at odd times and find him on the bench outside the shop.

She wished he could stay forever, but that was an unrealistically romantic thought if ever there was one. Today he was off to Leominster. Next week, or soon after, he'd be back in California. What then? Would they talk on the phone? Visit each other from time to time?

She knew it wouldn't be enough for her. She wanted him in Lincoln with her. Whatever initial reservations she'd had about his background, his occupation or his character were nonexistent now. His background was blue-collar and strong, his occupation solid, his character sterling. She'd never once glimpsed anything coarse in him. Rather, he'd proved to be unfailingly gentle and giving. Even his reticence about discussing Brad had ceased to matter. He was simply protective, skirting around what he knew to be a sensitive subject.

And he'd brought out a new side of her. Since she'd met him, she'd matured as a woman. He made her believe in both her looks and her sexuality. Whereas her confidence had come from looking in the mirror when she'd first returned from the Bahamas, now it came from the reflection of admiration in Matt's eyes. She didn't care what anyone else thought of her. Only Matt mattered.

So where was she to go from here? Sighing, she rose from the table. She'd clean up the kitchen, go to work and come home. Soon after that, Matt would return. She wasn't even going to think about tomorrow.

One day at a time. All she could do was take one day at a time.

Cleaning up the kitchen was no problem at all. Going to work was another matter. When she tried to start her car, the engine refused to turn over. Not one to beat a dead horse, she returned to the house, called AAA, then sat waiting for half an hour until the tow truck arrived.

"Battery's dead" was the mechanic's laconic diagnosis.

"But that's impossible. This battery's barely four months old!"

"It's dead."

"How can a four-month-old battery die?"

Taking jumper cables from his truck, the man set to work recharging the battery. "Maybe you left the headlights on."

"I never do that."

"Anyone else drive this car? A kid? Maybe he forgot and left 'em on."

"There's no kid, and I'm the only one who drives the car. It's been sitting in the garage since Tuesday morning—" that was when Matt, in fact, had put it away, but he wouldn't have left the lights on "—but it's sat for longer than that without any trouble."

"No sweat, lady. The battery looks okay otherwise. I'll have it working in no time."

He did, and Lauren was only fifteen minutes late for work, but she was bothered by the incident. It occurred to her that the same person who'd sabotaged her garage door might have entered the garage during those days when the car was idle, switched the lights on for a good, long time, then switched them off without her being any the wiser. She decided to discuss it with Matt that night, but the sense of solace in that resolution wasn't enough to prevent a certain nervousness when she returned to the car after work. She found herself glancing around the large parking garage and into the back seat of the car before she dared climb into the front.

She held her breath. The car started. She drove to Lincoln without any trouble.

Matt wasn't due back until nine at the earliest, so she took the time to stop for groceries before arriving at the farmhouse. It was still light out, and she was grateful. She imagined herself being watched and knew that, had it been dark, she would have been terrified.

Relief came in small measure after she was locked safely inside the house. Focusing determinedly on Matt's return, she stowed the groceries, prepared all the fixings for dinner, then poured herself a glass of wine and took refuge in the living room. While lights were burning in the rest of the house, she chose to sit in the dark. Hiding. Brooding. Wondering. Worrying. She knew that her imagination was getting the best of her, but that didn't stop it from happening.

Minutes seemed to stretch into an eternity, though it was barely after nine when finally she heard a car whip up the drive. Hurrying to the window, she peered cautiously out. Her relief was immediate and considerable when Matt climbed from the car. Even before he'd stepped over the threshold, her arms were around his neck.

"Matt, it's wonderful to have you back!"

He had one hand at the back of her head, the other arm around her waist. "Mmm. You're good for my ego. Such a welcome, and I haven't even been gone fourteen hours."

"Close. Thirteen and a half." She lifted her face for a kiss that was instantly comforting and thoroughly satisfying. "How did it go?"

"Very well. I think we've finally worked out the last of the bugs with the locals, so we can get the permit we need, which is great, since we've got everyone else lined up and ready to go."

"Good deal!"

"And I spoke with Thomas." Thomas Gehling was the general contractor whom Lauren had called on Tuesday. "He's looking forward to meeting with us Sunday morning."

"But if he's going to be involved with your project, will he have time to do mine?"

Matt threw an arm around her shoulder and drew her into the house with him. "You have to understand construction lingo. When I say that everyone is lined up and ready to go, it means that if we're lucky, we'll have broken ground within six weeks. And then there's the heavy work that has to be done first—blasting, digging, pouring foundations. The plumbers and electricians and carpenters you'll need won't be required at our site for three months minimum. Thomas will have more than enough time to oversee work here—that is, if you find that you like him and what he has to say. You're under no obligation to use him. There are other names on that list."

"Of the ones I spoke with, I liked him the best. Call it instinct, or whatever, but something meshed even on the phone." She was well aware of the fact that Matt's using Thomas Gehling for his own work might have slanted her view. She trusted Matt's judgment. But she had liked Thomas. He spoke intelligently and seemed perfectly comfortable dealing with a woman.

"I think you'll be impressed when you meet him." Having reached the kitchen, Matt went directly to the sink, turned on the water and squirted a liberal amount of liquid soap on his hands. "So how was your day, sweetheart?"

"Fine—I mean, okay. God, I can't believe it happened again."

"What?"

"I've been a nervous wreck all day, counting the minutes until you got back so I could tell you what happened. Then you walk in here, bringing a sense of security, and I forget all about it."

He stared at her over his shoulder. "What happened?"

"My car wouldn't start this morning. The battery was dead. I had to get a truck here to jump-start it."

"The battery was dead? Didn't you say you'd gotten a new one just before you left Bennington?"

"I did. That's what's so weird. The man from the

garage suggested that I'd left my lights on by mistake. I'm sure I'd never do that."

A thick cloud of suds coated Matt's hands, but he paid it little heed. His brows knitted low over his eyes. "I was the last one to drive your car. I put it in the garage Tuesday morning before we left for Boston in mine. I'm sure the lights were off. There'd have been no reason for me to turn them on to begin with, and the car started perfectly, so they couldn't have been left on the night before."

"That's what I figured." She was standing close by the sink. "The only logical explanation is that someone's been tampering in the garage again."

He shot her a sharp glance. "Was anything else wrong with the car?"

"No, and it started perfectly when I left work tonight."

Bending over the sink, Matt splashed soapy water on his face. Lauren reached into a drawer and had a clean towel waiting by the time he'd rinsed and straightened up. No amount of wiping, though, could remove the concern from his features.

"It may have been a fluke," he suggested quietly.

"Do you believe that?"

He hesitated. "No."

"Matt, don't you think it's time we called the police? I mean, when it was only a couple of incidents, they might have thought I was crazy, but at this stage the situation has to be considered suspicious. At least if the police were aware of the possibilities, they could patrol the area more closely."

Matt's expression grew more troubled than ever. "The police might scare him off, and then he'd only wait for things to die down before starting again. What we need to do is to catch him."

"Come on, Matt," she chided, "I was only kidding about playing Spenser."

"It wouldn't be too hard to rig up some booby traps." His eyes were growing animated; he was obviously warming up to the idea. "I think I could manage it, with a little help from a friend."

"From what friend?"

"One of the guys I met in Leominster. He works at a nearby lumberyard." Matt gave a mock grimace and scratched the back of his head. "Seems to me that he mentioned something about having done time."

"A convict? You're going to enlist a *convict* to save me?"

"An ex-convict. And he's been straight for ten years."

"Matt, what *is* this?"

"His specialty was breaking and entering, and he was a genius at it."

Lauren narrowed her eyes. "How long did you spend with this guy?"

"Not long. Can I help it if he's proud of what he's done?"

"Not only after, but before." She grunted, then muttered under her breath, "I can't believe I'm standing here listening when I should be on the phone talking to the police."

Matt put his hands on her arms and stroked her coaxingly. "Come on, Lauren. It's worth a try. You know how the police are—"

"I don't know how the police are. I've never had dealings with them before, contrary to *some* of your friends."

He kissed her forehead. "The police ask millions of

questions and then get their minds set on an answer that isn't the one you've given or the one you want to hear. These local departments just aren't geared to taking the offensive, and they sure as hell wouldn't call in the state police or the FBI in a situation like this." His voice softened, taking on a hint of teasing that was reflected in his eyes. "If you were worried about contractors being chauvinists, just wait until you've met the police. They'll treat you like a sweet little thing who's slightly soft in the head." He cupped said item in his hand and gently massaged her scalp. "And even if they decided that you just might be on to something, there's the matter of red tape. They could step up their patrols, but that'd be all. They'd have trouble getting authorization for much else. More than anything, they'd be reluctant to do something that might backfire in court."

Lauren was having trouble fighting him when he was so close and touching her so gently. "You're not reluctant," she stated, but the accusation she'd intended came out sounding more like admiration.

"Not one bit." His thumbs traced the delicate curves of her ears. "I want whoever's been harassing you to be caught. I have to believe that once we find out who it is, we'll find a motive as well."

"You're seducing me," she breathed.

"Me?"

"Don't look so innocent. You're seducing me."

"I am not. I'm simply trying to convince you to let me have a go at it."

"At what? That's the issue." Her voice was whisper-soft, not seductive in itself, simply…taken. "Do you want a go at playing cops and robbers, or at making love with me?"

"I'll make you forget, Lauren," he murmured, lowering his head until his lips feathered hers. "I'll make you forget everything else."

She caught her breath when he nipped at her lower lip. He was already making her forget, damn him— bless him. At this moment, she wanted to forget.

"I'll make you forget everything else," he repeated hotly against her neck. "And that's a promise. Word of honor."

MATT MADE GOOD on his promise. Right there, propping Lauren against the kitchen counter, he made love to her with such daring that she forgot everything else but what she felt for him, with him.

He also made good on the promise to call his friend, the breaking-and-entering expert, who showed up at the farmhouse bright and early the very next morning with a carload full of booby-trap makings the likes of which Lauren had never imagined. She had to leave for work before the last of the snares were set, and remarked only half in jest that she'd never make it back into the house alive.

Matt called her from Leominster in the middle of the afternoon to say that he was going to have to attend a dinner meeting and that he wouldn't be back until late. Disappointed but fully appreciative of the demands of his work, she decided to stay in the city after the shop closed to have dinner with Beth and then see a movie.

"Nervous about going home?" Beth teased.

Lauren chuckled—yes, nervously. "It'll be dark, and they've hooked up so many gadgets that it's very possible I'll be the first one caught. You wouldn't believe it, Beth. There's a gizmo on the garage door that has to be deactivated, or else a huge black net descends on an intruder. And once the net falls, *it* sets off a god-awful clanging. The doors to the house have hidden latches that are attached to electrical devices that deliver a shock powerful enough to stun, and the shock in turn sets off an alarm."

"You're right in the middle of a spy novel. I love it!"

"You wouldn't if you had to negotiate everything yourself. There are even hidden snares along the edge of the woods. You'd think we were trapping mink."

"I'm telling you, you've got all the makings of a bestseller. Just think, when this is over, you can write it up. Before you know it, you'll be signing autographs and doing the talk-show circuit."

"Thank you, Beth. I'll settle for catching one man and turning him over to the police."

"But what if it isn't *one* man?" Beth tossed out with imaginative anticipation. "What if there's a whole syndicate that's got some kind of grudge against you? What if you catch one man and another takes over where the first leaves off, so you catch the second? Meanwhile, the first dies mysteriously in jail, so the second decides to sing, and before you know it, there's enough evidence to convict the *entire* syndicate. You'll be a hero!"

"Heroine," Lauren correct dryly. "And I don't believe we're dealing with any syndicate. What would a syndicate have against me?"

"Maybe it was using your vacant farmhouse as its headquarters, and then you came along and, boom, moved in lickety-split, and there's still some very valuable and potentially condemning material stored in the cellar—"

Lauren scowled at her. "What happened to your theory about the ghost of inhabitants past?"

"Too passé. I think I like the syndicate idea better."

"I don't like *either* of them, and if we're going to have

dinner together, you'll have to swear you won't go on like this. You're making me nervous."

"I thought you were already nervous."

"You're making me *more* nervous."

Beth patted her arm, then squeezed it. "I'm just teasing, Lauren. You know that. Just teasing."

THAT WAS WHAT Lauren told herself when, later that night, after the movie had let out and she and Beth had gone their separate ways on the streets of Boston, she had the uncanny sensation of being followed.

CHAPTER SEVEN

THE SENSATION WAS vague at first, and Lauren wondered if her imagination was simply working overtime. She glanced over her shoulder, then faced forward again. There were people around—she wished there were even more—but none appeared to be suspicious. At least, no one had ducked into a doorway when she'd looked back.

She had walked a bit farther and turned a corner when the sensation intensified. A prickling arose at the back of her neck, accompanied by a frisson of fear. Instinctively she quickened her step, mentally charting the course she'd have to take to reach the garage. It consisted of main streets for the most part, with a single alleyway at the end.

She darted another glance behind her and saw the same outwardly innocuous people—several couples, a handful of singles, all staggered at intervals. If someone grabbed her, she'd yell. There were plenty of bodies to help.

She walked on. Fewer people were ahead of her now; some had turned off toward the subway stop. She assumed the same was true for those behind her, and the thought added to her unease.

She turned another corner. There was no one ahead of her now, and she didn't dare look back. Unbidden, she recalled her childhood. There'd been a dog in the neighborhood, a large German shepherd of which she'd been terrified. Her mother had always instructed her to walk calmly past it on the theory that dogs could smell fear. Could people smell fear? Lauren wondered now. She was sure she reeked of it.

Imagination. That was all it was. Imagination getting a little out of hand. The sounds she heard not far behind weren't footsteps. They were the knocking of the air-conditioning unit in the building she passed... or the creaking of heat as it escaped from the engine of a newly parked car alongside the curb...or...

Eyes wide, she shot a frightened glance over her shoulder and gasped. There was a man. He was very tall, large-set, dressed in black, and he was not twenty feet behind and gaining steadily on her.

Uncaring if she was jumping to conclusions, she began to run. She turned another corner and ran even faster. Her heels beat a rapid tattoo on the pavement, merging with the thundering of her heart to drown out all other night sounds of the city.

She passed another long—agonizingly long—building, then reached the alley, in actuality a single-lane driveway. At its end stood her salvation, a guard booth.

She was breathless and shaking, terrified of looking back and losing time, tripping or slamming into the wall. She cursed her side, which ached; cursed the shoes she wore and the heat that seemed to buffet her and slow her progress. By the time she reached the booth, she felt as though she'd run a marathon.

"Thank God," she whispered, panting as she sagged against the thick plastic enclosure. Then, with a burst of energy, she scrambled to the booth's opening. The guard, a young man with a punk hairstyle at odds with his uniform, sat balanced on the back legs of his chair. A dog-eared magazine lay open on his lap. The heavy beat of rock music thrummed from the stereo box by his side. He was chewing gum; the vigorous action of his jaw only enhanced the indolence of his stare.

"Someone was following me," Lauren gasped and darted a frantic glance toward the alley through which she'd run.

Looking thoroughly bored, the guard followed her gaze. There was no one in sight.

"He must have turned away when he saw me heading toward you," she explained, trying to calm herself enough to think clearly. "Listen, I need a big favor."

The young man blew a bubble, popped it and licked the gum back into his mouth. "Depends what it is."

"Could you walk me to my car?"

He gave a one-shouldered shrug. "I'm on duty."

"I know, but there aren't many cars leaving the garage now. With the gate down, they'll wait. It won't take you long—two, maybe three minutes. Just until I lock myself in."

He fingered his earlobe, which sported a crescent of multiple studs. "I'm not supposed to leave this booth."

"But I'm in danger!"

Slowly, his head nodding in time with the music, he looked back toward the street. "Don't see anyone."

"He may have taken the stairs. Please! I need your help!"

After what seemed forever, the front legs of the chair hit the floor. "So. Chivalry calls." The guard stood up, yawned, then pushed his shoulders back.

The show was wasted on Lauren, who saw right through it to the scrawniness of his physique. Not much to protect her with. But he wore a uniform. There was safety in a uniform.

"I'm the new guy on the block," he drawled. "I was given specific instructions—"

She felt sweat trickling down her back. "Look, I'll argue on your behalf if you get into trouble. It seems to me your boss would reward you for helping a regular tenant."

"You're a regular tenant?" His gaze drifted down her body.

"Yes." She sighed in exasperation, feeling suddenly tired. Instinctively she knew she was safe standing at the booth with even as unlikely a guard as this, but there was still the threat of the inner garage to overcome. She wanted nothing more than to be locked in her car and on the road, headed for home. "Please. Just walk me upstairs. You could have been up and back in the time you've spent talking with me."

He grinned. "Yeah, but talking with you beats sitting here by myself." He cocked his head to one side. "Sure. I'll walk you upstairs."

Lauren jerked her eyes toward the thick pipes overhead. "Thank you," she breathed. By the time she looked down, the guard had let himself out of his cage and was swaggering toward her.

She glanced worriedly back toward the exit, but it remained empty.

"Come on, love. Up we go." He took her elbow and she jumped, wondering for an instant if she'd leaped from the frying pan into the fire. Unfortunately, she was the proverbial beggar who couldn't be choosy. So she clamped her mouth shut and let her cocky gallant lead the way to the stairs.

He dropped her elbow to open the door. Her apprehensive gaze examined every nook of the stairwell as they started up.

"Floor?"

"Third." Had the stairwell always been this narrow? He chewed away at his gum. "Work around here?"

"Yes." Had the stairwell always been this confining?

"Kind of late leaving, aren't you?"

"Yes." He wouldn't try anything. He wouldn't dare. She knew where and for whom he worked.

"Hot date?"

"Yes…he'll be waiting for me on the corner as soon as I leave here."

They climbed the last set of stairs in silence. Though Lauren didn't look, she could feel the smirk on her companion's face. He hadn't believed her. She'd hesitated too long, then spoken too quickly. Damn, but she wasn't good at this.

He swung open the door, then stood aside to let her through. "Always park on the third floor?"

She was looking nervously from side to side, trying to see into corners where a tall, large, dark form might be lurking. "It depends," she offered distractedly. With no assailant in sight, she blindly fumbled in her bag for the keys.

"Where's your car?"

She pointed. They reached it half a minute later.

"There," he announced as she unlocked the door, checked the back seat, then all but threw herself behind the wheel. "Safe and sound."

She locked the door and rolled her window down, just enough to murmur a heartfelt "Thank you. I do appreciate what you've done."

"How about a ride down?"

"Uh…" Dumbly, she looked at the passenger seat, then leaned over and tugged up the button on the opposite door. Already striding around the front of the car, the guard let himself in.

She had her window up tight and the car started before he'd closed the door, and she took the ramps at breakneck speed. Her passenger didn't seem to mind. She suspected he enjoyed the daring ride.

She brought the car to an abrupt halt by the booth, let the guard out and quickly relocked the door. By the time she'd straightened up, he was at her window and making a rolling gesture with his hand. Again she lowered the window several inches.

"Your card?" he asked with an impudent grin.

"Oh." She rummaged in her purse, drew out the card and handed it over. While he studied it, her gaze alternated between the rearview mirror and the windows on either side.

"Looks okay…Lauren." Chomping briskly on his gum, he returned the card, then winked. "Drive carefully now." The last word was muted through her reclosed window. He twisted backward in a move she was sure he practiced regularly on the dance floor, pressed a button and released the gate.

Without another word, Lauren stepped on the gas. She held her breath and didn't expel it until she'd reached the relative safety of Government Center.

With great effort, she forced her rigid fingers to relax on the steering wheel. She took long, deep breaths, feeling safer with each block she put between herself and the parking garage. No one appeared to be following her. To double-check, she swung from one lane to the other, then, a block later to the first lane. She annoyed several drivers, but she didn't care. All that mattered was that the headlights in her rearview mirror were ever varied.

During the drive home, her emotions ran the gamut from fear to confusion to anger. It was the latter that was dominant by the time she pulled up in front of her own garage. She left the engine running and the headlights on; she had a death grip on the wheel again, and her teeth were clenched. She barely had time to debate whether she should sit this way until Matt returned—she didn't expect him for a while yet—when a pair of headlights pierced the darkness behind her.

She sucked in a breath. It was *him!* He'd followed her after all! Frantic, she struggled to decide on the best course of action. The other car neared. She had to think quickly. She could make a mad dash for the safety of the house, but it would take time for her to work around the booby traps.

Too late.

She could run from the car and head for the woods in an attempt to make it to a neighbor's before being overtaken, but the woods, too, were booby-trapped, and that man had been large and ominously physical-looking.

Too risky.

She could lean on the horn in the hope that the noise would either scare him off or arouse someone's attention.

That seemed her only option.

Her hand was on the horn, about to exert force, when the car behind her sounded its own horn in short, repetitive blasts. Her fear-filled gaze snapped to the rearview mirror.

Matt! It was *Matt!*

Lauren had never felt so relieved, or so foolish, or so furious in her entire life. Storming from her car, she met him halfway between the two. "I cannot *take* any more of this!" she screamed, hands clenched by her sides.

"Lauren, what—"

"It's gone on too long! Why *me?* What have *I* ever done to deserve this—this torture?"

"Take it easy, sweetheart—"

"I've *had* it, Matt!" She took a step back, eluding the hands he would have put on her shoulders. "This isn't fair! I'm a nervous wreck. I'm getting a permanent crick in my neck from looking over my shoulder. Someone's following me. Someone isn't. Someone's been in the house. Someone hasn't. Someone's sicced a dog on me. Someone hasn't. I don't know who to trust and who not to. For all I know, *you* were the one who stalked me in Boston!"

"*Me?* I just this minute got back from Leominster!"

"But how do I know that?" she fired at him. She was visibly shaking; the emotional strain was taking its toll. "How do I know *anything?* It's always in the dark. *I'm* always in the dark. I'm afraid to pull into my garage for fear I'll become a sitting duck in a big black net. I'm afraid to go into my house for fear I'll be electrocuted at the front door." Her voice grew as wobbly as her knees. "I can't live this way." She ducked her head and withered into herself, whispering, "Damn it, I can't live this way."

She didn't have the strength to elude Matt this time. He put his arms around her and held her while she cried softly.

"It's okay, sweetheart," he murmured. "Let it out. You'll feel better, and then we'll talk."

"I won't feel...better...."

His arms tightened, hands gently kneading her back. "Sure you will. You're upset now. Sounds like you had a bad day."

"Bad night...."

"Come on. Let's go inside."

A short time later, Lauren was huddled in a corner of the living room sofa, holding the glass of brandy Matt had pressed into her hand. He drew one of the side chairs close and propped his elbows on his knees. "Okay. From the top. What happened tonight?"

"It's not just what happened tonight. It's *everything.*"

"But tell me about tonight. I need to know, Lauren."

She studied the rim of the brandy snifter and shrugged. "I panicked." Painstakingly, she explained how she'd walked back to the garage. "Then there was that awful last stretch when only one man was behind me."

"Did you see what he looked like?"

She tipped the snifter until the brandy came perilously close to its rim. "Not really. I glanced back once and got the impression of someone big and tall and dark. Then I started running and didn't look back again."

"He didn't follow you once you ran?"

"I don't know. I didn't look. By the time I reached the garage, I couldn't see him. I conned the guard into walking me up to my car."

"Smart girl."

She snorted. "Fine for you to say. You didn't see the guard."

"It was still smart. A paid guard wouldn't try anything. He'd never get away with it."

"That was what I figured, not that I had much choice at the time."

"But you made it to your car safely. Did you see anyone when you were driving away from the garage?"

"I wasn't looking." She paused to take a healthy swallow of brandy, made a face, recovered, then went on. "I just locked the doors and drove. No one followed me home, at least no one I could see. I was checking for that." Her voice rose. "But when I got here, I didn't know what to do. Everything was dark, and I was sure that if I tried to get into the house, I'd get caught in one of your snares. Then you drove up, and I thought it was *him*—but I really don't know if there *was* a him. The man I saw could have been after me. Then again, he could have been minding his own business."

Matt closed his hand over hers and urged the snifter to her lips again. The brandy was doing its thing; at least she'd stopped shaking.

"I'm sorry I frightened you," he said.

"I thought you'd be later."

"I left Leominster as soon as I could. I was worried."

The eyes Lauren raised brimmed with discouragement. "What am I going to do, Matt?" she whispered. "I can't go on this way."

"I know, sweetheart. I know." His expression was grim. "Do you think someone's keeping tabs on you during the day?"

"While I'm at work, you mean?"

He nodded. "Have you ever gotten the feeling that you're being followed in broad daylight?"

She thought for a minute. "No."

"Ever remember seeing anyone who might fit the description of the man you saw tonight?"

Again she pondered his question, then shrugged in frustration. "There have to be dozens of tall, large-set men who wander through the Marketplace each day. I've never noticed anyone special...other than you." When he glowered at her, she added a sad "That was a compliment," and his glower promptly faded.

"Oh. Thank you."

"What *am* I going to do?"

"I'm thinking. I'm thinking." It was a while before he spoke again, and then it was almost to himself. "You haven't gotten any strange phone calls, heavy-breathing type of thing? And there hasn't been any direct contact, like a note or anything?"

She shook her head, but Matt's attention was on the floor. His brows were knitted together, his lips clamped into a thin line.

"I think," he said at last, "that you should finish your brandy and get to bed. You've had a frightening—"

"Finish my brandy and get to bed? That won't solve anything!"

"There's nothing to be solved tonight. You're safely locked in, and I'm here."

"But tomorrow! I have to go to work tomorrow! You can't be with me every minute, and I don't even want that. I've never been helpless or clinging before, but it seems that lately I'm throwing myself at you the instant you get here."

"I don't mind," he volunteered with a half grin, only to be cut off.

"Well, I do! I don't like what I've become, Matt. I can't continue living this way. I won't!"

What had existed of a grin was wiped clean from his face. "I agree, Lauren. Something has to be done. It's simply a matter of deciding what. Just…just let me sleep on it, okay?"

"I know what should be done. The police should be called in."

He took her hand. "Do you trust me?"

"Of course I trust you. I just think that—"

"Do you *trust* me?"

She knew he was testing her. There was nothing

of the little boy about him now. He was all man. Eyes locked with his, she nodded.

"Then let me sleep on it. Give me until morning to figure out what the next step should be."

At that moment, Lauren came out of herself enough to see the lines of fatigue that shadowed Matt's face. He was tired. And worried. "But it's not your responsibility—"

"Till morning?"

She clamped her lower lip between her teeth, then let it slide out. Her nod was slower in coming this time, but when it did, it conveyed the trust he sought.

MORNING ARRIVED, AND Lauren awoke to find that Matt was no longer in bed. Tossing her robe on, she hurried off in search of him. He was just replacing the telephone receiver when she entered the kitchen.

"Matt?" She halted abruptly and stood suspended on the threshold. There was something about the tired slump of his shoulders that filled her with dread.

He covered the distance between them and took her in his arms. His words came out in a rush. "I have to go back to California for a couple of days, Lauren. I've just spoken with the airline and made a reservation."

For a minute she couldn't say anything. She'd known that sooner or later he'd be leaving, but... "Now?" she whispered through a tight throat. "Why *now?*"

"It's important. You know I wouldn't leave if it weren't."

"But...what should I do?" The instant she said the words, she hated them, hated herself, hated the situation.

"I think you should consider visiting your parents."

"No."

"What about Beth? You could sleep over at her place."

"No."

"Then take a room at a hotel. Maybe the Bostonian, or the Marriott. Something close to work."

"No!" She freed herself from his grasp and wrapped her arms around her waist. "I'm not running away. I won't be forced out of my own home!"

Matt ran a hand through his hair, which looked as if he'd done that more than once. For that matter, between the creases on his brow and the weary look in his eyes, she wondered if he'd slept at all. He seemed to be exerting a taut control over himself, but then, so was she. She refused to fall apart, to be reduced to a simpering weakling. No strings, she'd told Matt, and no strings there would be.

"It's very important that I go, Lauren."

Her chin was firm. "It's all right. You can go."

"I don't want to."

"But it's all right. I'll be fine." Hadn't she always been before?

"It's just for two or three days."

"I understand."

"No, you don't. You think I'm running out on you."

"I think just what you told me, that it's important for you to fly back." She was feeling distinctly numb. "When does your plane leave?"

He glanced at his watch. "In two hours."

"I can drop you at the airport on my way—"

"You'll be late. I'll drive myself and leave the car at the airport."

She nodded. Without another word, she turned and retraced her steps to the bedroom. She thought of nothing but getting ready for a regular day's work.

Matt showered while she dressed. They said little to each other during breakfast. Only when she had swung her pocketbook to her shoulder did she look at him. Even her self-imposed anesthetization couldn't fully immunize her against the swell of emotion that hit her.

"Have a safe flight," she whispered.

He walked her to the door. "You know how to work the latch for this thing?"

"Yes." He'd reviewed the process in detail when they'd entered the house last night.

"Be sure to reset it once you've let yourself in or out."

"I will."

They passed through and headed for the garage. "And this one?"

"Yes. I've got it now."

"Lauren, I really wish—"

"Shh. Please, Matt. You have to do your thing, and I have to do mine." She pressed the hidden switch that allowed her access to the garage without mishap, but before she could enter the car, Matt stopped her. He put both hands on her shoulders and looked her straight in the eye.

"I know you're angry, Lauren, and hurt. Believe me, I'd never be leaving if I didn't think it was absolutely necessary."

She stared up at him, saying nothing because there was nothing she would permit herself to say. Only when he tugged her close and wrapped his arms tightly around her did she allow herself a moment's softening. Closing her eyes, she leaned into his strength. By the time he'd released her, though, she was on her own again.

"Be cautious, Lauren," he said. His voice was thick, his gaze clouded. "When in doubt, go with your instincts. They're good. Trust them."

For a split second, she wavered. Her instincts told her that Matt shouldn't go, that she needed him here, that whatever it was that drew him back to California wasn't as important as what was happening between them in Massachusetts. Her instincts told her that his trip would bring no good where they were concerned.

But reason ruled. Matt's home and job were in San Francisco. She had no claim on either. She was right in what she'd told him; he had to do his thing and she had to do hers. And hers was to carry on with her life, just as it had been before Matthew Kruger had entered it.

"Take care," she whispered, then slipped into her car. She didn't look back to see Matt by the garage door after she'd backed out and around, or to see him still standing there when she drove down the drive and turned into the street. If she was aware that she'd left part of herself with him, she put that particular ache down to the general upheaval her life had gone through in the past few weeks. Doggedly she kept her sights ahead.

As THE DAY PASSED, Lauren had less control over her emotional state than she might have liked. Much as she tried not to, she thought of Matt. *He's arriving at the airport now. His plane is taking off now. He's over Pennsylvania, Illinois, Kansas, Utah.* Out of the blue, she'd feel tears in her eyes, and though she cursed her preoccupation, she knew that it was diverting her mind from other thoughts.

Beth, who'd been quick to sense something amiss, tried to get her to talk, but all Lauren would say was that Matt had been called back to his home office for a few days.

"But I thought he was here for another week at least."

"Things come up."

"And he didn't elaborate?" There was an undercurrent of accusation in Beth's words.

Lauren, who was carelessly flipping through the morning's mail, ignored it. "Other than to say it was important that he go." She frowned. "I don't believe it. Another letter for Susan Miles."

"Who's Susan Miles?"

"Beats me. But it's addressed to her, care of this shop. There was one yesterday, too."

"Mark it 'return to sender, addressee unknown' and stick it back in the mail."

"I would if I could, but I can't. There's no return address."

"Postmark?"

"Boston. If whoever sent it doesn't get an answer, he'll just have to show up here to see what's wrong."

"He? How do you know it's a he?"

Lauren held out the letter. "Look at the handwriting. It's heavy. And messy. Has to be a he."

Beth donned her imagination-at-work look. "A he. Hmm, I smell possibilities in this one. You've already got a guy, so forget you. Let's concentrate on me. Suppose, just suppose, some fellow was given the name of a girl he was told worked here. A blind-date kind of thing. Only either he got the girl's name screwed up or the friend who set him up was playing a joke."

"Why would a guy *write* to set up a blind date?"

"Maybe he's too shy to call. Or he's simply taking a new approach. A new approach—that's it." She eyed Lauren through a playful squint. "Not all that different from sitting on a bench for two days, or sitting on it for hours a third day just reading."

"Point taken," Lauren admitted dryly. "I suppose this guy's gorgeous and witty and bright."

"Naturally."

"Then why does his handwriting look like a thug's?"

"It's not like a thug's. It's...creative."

"Ahh. Then whatever is inside this envelope," Lauren said, waving it, "must be equally as creative."

"I'm sure it is." Beth's voice dropped conspiratorially. "Let's open it."

"We can't do that, Beth. It's not addressed to us."

"It's addressed to our shop."

"And what if your gorgeous guy comes in to collect the letters he's incorrectly addressed? He'll be mortified."

"He'll be so taken with me that he won't have time to be mortified. Besides, we can say we threw the letters out. So what harm is there in opening them first? Do you have the other one?"

"Yes, but, Beth, I don't think this is a great idea."

"Don't think." Snatching the gray envelope from Lauren's hand, Beth quickly opened it. She removed a sheet of matching stationery, unfolded it, then turned it over, puzzled. "Blank. There's nothing on it."

Lauren, too, stared at the blank sheet. "Maybe he lost his nerve the second time around."

"Where's the first?"

Lauren fished the envelope from a drawer in the desk and, her own curiosity piqued, opened it. "The same. The paper is blank. What's going on here, Beth?"

"Who knows?" Beth continued the game, but her enthusiasm was waning. "Maybe his tactic is to be mysterious for a while."

"So we have to wait for the next installment to find out who the mad letter writer is?"

Beth shrugged. "Looks that way." She headed for the front of the store, leaving Lauren to dispose of the blank love letters as she saw fit. For some reason Lauren herself didn't understand, she folded both sheets back into their envelopes and tucked the envelopes into the drawer.

This activity had provided only a temporary respite for Lauren, as did most of work that day. Unfortunately, by the time she knew that Matt had landed and been swallowed up in his own life again, she could no longer free herself of those other, more ominous thoughts.

"How'd you like a roommate for a night or two?" she asked Beth when they were getting ready to close the shop. She'd tried to sound nonchalant, but the gesture was lost on Beth, who knew better.

"I'd love it, Lauren. You know that. You're welcome to stay at my place whenever you want."

"I know you have a date—"

"No, I don't."

"Listen, it's okay. I just don't feel like driving back to Lincoln. You can go out. I'll make myself at home—"

"I don't have a date, Lauren."

"But that fellow Joe—"

"Asked me out and I refused. He wanted to go camping. Overnight. I didn't have equipment, and I'm not keen on camping, and I'm even less keen on Joe."

"How do you know? You've just met the guy."

"Exactly. Have you ever heard of camping overnight for a first date?"

Lauren shrugged. "Might have been interesting."

"Maybe for you and Matt. No, chalk that." Beth grunted. "Matt might have left you stranded in the woods while he raced off to scale some nearby peak. How could he simply abandon you this way, Lauren? I still can't believe it."

Lauren kept her voice calm. "He has his own life."

"But he's barged his way into yours—"

"He didn't barge his way in anywhere."

"Okay, then he wormed his way in. He's made himself nearly indispensable—"

"He has *not*. I can do just fine without him."

"Mmm. That's why you can't bear the thought of going home."

Lauren's gaze lowered to the scrap of fabric she was fraying. "It's not that. But after last night I feel…uncomfortable." She'd told Beth earlier about the episode near the garage. "It's still too fresh in my mind."

"Matt wasn't around then, either. Why do men do this, Lauren? Why aren't they around when you need them?"

"It's not a question of need," Lauren rationalized. "I'm independent. I can take care of myself."

"You should go to the police. I think what you're facing is more than even Matt can handle. Why is he so vehement against it?"

"He has good reasons. He may be right."

"Maybe his reasons aren't so noble."

Lauren tensed. "What do you mean?"

"It's occurred to me that much of what's happened to you has been since Matt showed up."

"That's not true! Three of those incidents happened before he ever got here!"

"No," Beth returned, determined to make her point. "If my memory's correct, three of those incidents happened within mere days of his first introducing himself to you. He said he was here in Boston on business. For all you know, he was here in the city that very first time, when the car just missed you on Newbury Street."

"I'm not sure I like what you're implying."

"I'm not sure I do, either, but it may be worth considering."

"Absolutely not! What could Matt possibly have to do with those incidents? What reason could he have to wish me harm?"

"Maybe something to do with Brad?"

"That's impossible. Don't even think it, Beth. It's out of the question."

No more was said about it, but Beth had accomplished her objective. Lauren fought it. She told herself that Beth was either playing the game she played so well or simply jealous. Lauren closed her mind to it while she and Beth walked over Beacon Hill to Beth's apartment, where they shared a congenial dinner and evening. Later that night, though, while Lauren lay quietly on the sofa bed trying to fall asleep, unwanted thoughts flitted in fragments through her mind.

Ironically, Matt's phone call didn't help. It came at two in the morning, shortly after Lauren had fallen into a restless sleep. The phone was on the table by her head. She nearly jumped out of her skin when it rang.

"Hello?"

"Lauren! I've been worried sick! When there was no answer at the farmhouse, I started calling hotels. You said you *weren't* going to Beth's!" He sounded angry. That was all Lauren needed.

"Why, Matt, how good of you to call in the middle of the night. I'm fine, thank you. How are you?"

"Lauren, you said you weren't going anywhere!"

"I changed my mind."

"Damn it, you could have let me know. I was sure something had happened!"

"How could I have let you know? I don't know where you are, much less at what phone number."

"I'm at home, and I'm the only Matthew Kruger in the San Francisco book!"

"How did I know you'd be trying me? You didn't say anything about calling."

She heard a deep sigh at the other end of the line. "Right. I'm sorry. It was my fault. Are you okay?"

"I'm tired, Matt." *And confused. Very confused.* The sound of Matt's voice, imperious, then gentle, only added to her confusion.

"I'm sorry to be calling so late. I started trying the house an hour and a half ago. When there was no answer, I figured maybe you'd gone to another movie or something, but when you didn't return, I started imagining things and it all began to spiral. You are okay?"

"Yes, I'm okay."

"Nothing happened today?"

"No, nothing happened."

"Thank goodness."

His voice clearly held relief. For that matter, Lauren mused, everything about his voice was clear. He could just as well be calling her from around the corner....

"Well," he went on, less sure of himself now, "I just wanted to hear your voice. And to tell you that I'm going to try to catch an afternoon flight out of here tomorrow. By the time I get into Logan and on the road, it's apt to be pretty late. It may be easier if I go to a hotel—"

"No!" she interrupted. She could hear the fatigue in his voice, and it pulled a string somewhere deep inside her. This was Matt, the man she missed, the man she wanted to see, to be with. "No. Meet me in Lincoln. I'll be there."

"But you may be sleeping. I'll frighten you."

"Just give a honk like you did the other night and I'll know it's you."

394   THREATS AND PROMISES

"Are you sure?"

"I'm sure."

"Okay, sweetheart." His voice lowered. "I miss you."

"Me, too, Matt."

"See you tomorrow night, then?"

"Uh-huh."

"Take care, sweetheart."

"You, too. Bye-bye, Matt."

She replaced the receiver and sank back to the bed, only then realizing that she hadn't even asked how he was doing. Maybe she hadn't wanted to. Maybe she'd been afraid he'd give her an evasive answer. He hadn't spelled out the reason for his abrupt return to San Francisco—if indeed he was there. Was his business on the West Coast shrouded in mystery, or was her imagination at work again?

After tossing and turning for better than an hour, she finally fell back to sleep. When she awoke on Sunday morning, she felt weary and tense. Even Beth's lighthearted chatter didn't lighten her mood; irrationally, perhaps, she blamed Beth for having planted the seeds of doubt in her mind.

Driving to Lincoln in broad daylight was accomplished comfortably. Lauren arrived there moments before Thomas Gehling pulled up. She liked him instantly, finding him easygoing, intelligent and polite. As they walked through the house, they discussed a wide range of possibilities. She hired him on the spot.

That was the high point of her day. The tension, the confusion, the worry, were back in full swing by the time she'd returned to Boston. Work at the shop was a blessing, but a short-lived one. All too soon she was headed back to Lincoln. This time around, she was a bundle of raw nerves.

A confrontation was imminent. She felt it in every fiber of her being. By nature she was a peaceful, accommodating sort, but the events of the past few weeks had upset her equilibrium. It was one thing to suspect that an unknown lunatic was after her, yet quite another to suspect that it was Matt. He was either with her or against her. She had to know one way or the other.

Arriving home at dusk, she was assailed by every one of the fears she'd been free of that morning. Glancing anxiously from side to side, she inched her way up the drive. Her first thought was to leave the car outside, but she knew that its protection, and hence her own, came from the trap that was set inside. Dashing quickly from the car to the garage, she fumbled to disengage the alarm and raise the door. That done, she quickly brought the car inside, lowered the door and reengaged the snare, then tackled the front door of the house. Beads of sweat were dotting her upper lip by the time she'd finally closed the door behind her and reset the alarm.

Then she made dinner, ate practically none of it and waited. She picked up a book, turned page after page without absorbing a word and waited. She dozed on the living room sofa, awakening with a jolt at the slightest sound—though most were in her dreams—and waited.

Midnight came and went. Then one o'clock. It was nearly one-thirty when she finally heard a car approach. This time she didn't rush to the window. She didn't so much as shift on the sofa. She sat quietly in the dark, waiting.

CHAPTER EIGHT

LAUREN HELD HER breath when she identified the click and scrape at the front door as the disengagement of the makeshift electrical alarm. Her eyes pierced the darkness, never once leaving the broad oak expanse as, with an aged creak, the door slowly opened. The man who came quietly through was tall, very tall, and large-set. Though he could have doubled for the man she'd seen behind her in Boston on the previous Friday night, there was no doubt in her mind that this time it was Matt.

"You didn't honk," she accused in a voice that shook.

His head twisted. "Lauren!" Setting his suitcase on the floor, he groped for the light switch. The weak glow that subsequently filtered into the living room from the hall was enough to reveal her position on the sofa. "What are you doing up, sweetheart? I thought for sure you'd be in bed."

"You didn't honk."

He paused, turning his head slightly. "The thought of it seemed jarring at this hour. I really didn't want to wake you up." He stood backlighted in the archway of the living room, his face in shadows. "But you weren't sleeping, were you?" Crossing the room, he hunkered down and curled his fingers lightly around her arms. Her skin was cold. "Why aren't you in bed?" he asked softly.

"We have to talk."

"You sound strange. What's wrong?"

She didn't move. "I'm not sure. That's one of the things we have to discuss."

He frowned at his hands, dropped them to the sofa on either side of her hips, then met her gaze. "What is it, Lauren?"

"I've been sitting here thinking. I've spent most of the day thinking. And last night, too."

He sank back on his heels, hands falling to his sides. "About what?"

"You. I want the truth, Matt." It was a struggle to keep her voice steady when so much was at stake, but she managed commendably. "I want all of it. No evasion. No seduction. I want to ask questions and have them answered."

"I don't understand. I've always given you answers—"

"They were never enough, but that may be my fault. Maybe I haven't *asked* enough."

"I don't know what you're getting at."

She tucked her legs more tightly beneath her. "Three weeks ago I was happy. My life was shaping up so beautifully that I had to pinch myself to make sure it was real. Then certain things started happening, and I'm suddenly stuck in the middle of a nightmare. Someone is after me. I don't know who or why."

"What's this got to do with *me?*"

"You showed up right after it all began, Matt. By some coincidence, you appeared out of nowhere. You claim to be a friend of my brother's, but my brother has been dead for a year, so I can't ask him about it. You have biographical facts about Brad, any of which you could have picked up by reading a standard job résumé. You have insight into his character, most of which you could have gained in one night of heavy drinking with him, even if he'd been a total stranger up until then."

"I don't believe this," Matt muttered, but Lauren was just beginning.

"That first night when you introduced yourself to me, you said you'd been in Boston for a week. It was during that very week that I was nearly run down by a car on Newbury Street. Nothing about the car registered with me. It could very easily have been a nondescript rental, just like the one you've been driving."

"Lauren—"

"Then a dog attacked me. You were the one who suggested it might have been trained to pull away when a special whistle was blown. That thought wouldn't even have occurred to me, yet it did to you. Why?"

"It's common knowledge—"

"And then my garage door crashed down." Despite the warmth of the night, her hands were freezing. She tucked them more deeply in the folds of her shirt. "You're a builder. You seemed familiar enough with the workings of that door to be able to rig, and unrig, a malfunction."

"This is absurd, Lauren! Do you know what you're saying?"

"I'm not done," she declared. "Let me finish."

He was on his feet, prowling the room. "I can't wait to hear the rest."

She ignored his sarcasm, knowing only that the time for silence had passed. "There was the matter of an intruder in my house. You found the problem immediately. A lock on one of the windows was broken. In fact, you used that very window to get into the house, supposedly to scout around. How can I be sure it was the first time you'd entered the house that way?" When

Matt took a sharp breath to defend himself, she rushed on. "The car that followed me all the way home from Boston was compatible in both size and shade to your rental. And the timing was perfect. You could have left me at my garage, picked up your own car—even on another floor of the same garage—and tailed me out. Then there was the night when I heard strange noises. You said you were in Leominster. It was a convenient alibi, but I have no proof, do I?"

"I'll give you names and numbers—"

"My car battery went dead; you were the last one to drive the car. Someone followed me late at night in Boston; you conveniently arrived here within minutes after I did."

"I was in *Leominster*—but I told you that once before, didn't I? I thought we agreed on it."

"That was what you wanted, for me to agree on it."

"I wanted you to trust me."

"So you told me. Many times. And I've been completely taken in, because I thought you were one of the most sincere, straightforward men I've ever met. Maybe I was wrong, Matt. Maybe I've been playing into your hands all along."

He stood before her then, hands on his hips, his face a mask of steel. The oblique light from the hall did nothing to blunt his obvious irritation. "What brought all this on? That's what I'd like to know. You did trust me. At least, I thought you did. Where did I go wrong?"

Lauren's composure was beginning to slip. If Matt was innocent—and his reaction was far from conclusive on that score—she was going to hate herself for the accusations she'd made. On the other hand, if he was guilty as charged, she was in a lot of trouble.

"You went wrong," she began with a shaky breath,

"when you took off for California on Saturday morning."

"You *were* angry."

"No. But I was puzzled and maybe a little hurt, because the trip was so sudden and you were so tight-lipped about it. And that got me to thinking, and suddenly there were more questions than ever. I'm an intelligent person, Matt. 'Together,' to quote you. You could have told me anything and I'd have understood. Okay, what happens with your work is your business. But you've shared other things with me, which I realize in hindsight you've been very selective about. Why discuss some things and not others? Unless you're hiding something. Unless there's something you don't want me to know."

He threw a hand in the air. "It's Beth. You've been listening to Beth. This sounds like one of her hare-brained plots."

Lauren stared him out. "Days ago I wanted to go to the police. Any person in his right mind would do that in a situation like mine. But I didn't go to the police, because you told me not to. You've been adamant about it! *Why?*"

"You want to know why?" Matt raged suddenly. His eyes were narrowed, his head thrust forward. "I'll tell you why! Because your brother, Brad, was up to no good during the last few years of his life, and if I'd gone to the police when I suspected that Brad's boss was behind what was happening to you, it would have all come out. *You'd* have been hurt. I was trying to protect *you!*"

Lauren sat in stunned silence as the warm summer night crowded in on her. One minute she felt smothered, the next chilled. In the third, she was stifling again and began to sweat. Dropping her gaze to the floor, she pressed a finger to her moist upper lip, frowned, then looked back at Matt. "What did you say about Brad?' she asked in a timid whisper.

Matt stood with his feet braced apart, one hand massaging the taut muscles at the back of his neck. At her question, he lowered his head, put two fingers to his forehead and rubbed. "Brad was in trouble." His voice held a blend of sadness and defeat. Lauren knew he'd have to be a consummate actor to produce such a heart-wrenching tone on cue.

"What kind of trouble?" Her stomach had begun to jump. She pressed a hand to it.

"Please. Lauren, you don't want—"

"What kind of trouble?" When he didn't answer, she repeated the question a third time. *"What kind of trouble?"*

Matt sighed in resignation. "He'd been padding invoices and expense vouchers, then pocketing the difference."

"I don't believe you."

"Maybe that's just as well. Brad's dead. Nothing will ever be proved one way or another. Just rumors. Lousy rumors."

"You believe them."

"I knew Brad." He took a quick breath. "Please, don't misunderstand me. Brad and I were close. He was a loyal friend. I respected him in many, many ways."

"But?"

"But all along I knew there was one part of him that was unsettled. It was as if he was looking for an opening, and his boss unwittingly gave him one. Chester Hawkins was a crook. We both knew it. We discussed it many times. Bribes, kickbacks—you name it, Hawkins did it."

"But padding expense vouchers—that's small-time stuff. What could Brad have hoped to gain?"

"It's not small-time when it's done over and over again."

"For how long?"

"Two years, maybe three. It adds up."

"But *why?* Why would he have done it?"

Matt dropped into a side chair. "Maybe he felt it was poetic justice, stealing from a thief. More likely he felt that an accumulation of wealth was the only way he could prove his worth."

Lauren moaned softly. Her head fell back against the sofa and she closed her eyes. When she spoke, her voice was wobbly. "I knew there was too much money. It didn't make sense. Right from the start I wondered, but I took it. I took it and I used it."

"Which was exactly what you *should* have done!" Matt sat forward and spoke with renewed force. "Brad earned every cent of that money. He was overworked and underpaid for years. What he did might have been punishable in a court of law, but there was still a certain justice to it. He gave Hawkins his life, for God's sake, and there was only a piddling insurance policy on it! Hawkins wasn't big on employee benefits. He gave the bare minimum. Brad earned that money, Lauren. And he wanted you to have it."

Lauren swallowed hard, trying to ingest all that Matt had told her. "Did he really? Or did you tell me that just to make me feel better?"

"He said it. Believe me—ah, hell." Matt flopped back in the chair. "Believe what you want. The fact is that you've put the money to good use. No one can ever take it away from you."

They were back to square one. "Someone's trying. Is it this fellow, Hawkins?" she asked nervously.

"He claims not."

"You *spoke* to him?"

Matt was out of his seat, pacing again. "What did you think I went to San Francisco for?"

"I didn't know! I assumed it had something to do with your own work. You didn't volunteer any details!"

"I went to confront Hawkins."

"And?"

"He says he's innocent."

"Do you believe him?"

"I'm not sure." Matt stopped his pacing and stared at her. "On the one hand, he wouldn't dare try anything. I wasn't the only friend Brad had. If Hawkins tries to pin something on Brad, even posthumously, any number of us will cry foul. Hawkins can't risk that. There's too much that can be pinned right back on him."

"On the other hand..."

He took a deep breath. "On the other hand, I wouldn't put it past him to try something on the sly. He and Brad had reached a stalemate. Each knew what the other was doing, so it was a form of mutual blackmail. Hawkins didn't dare fire Brad for fear he'd squeal. But Brad's gone now. It's possible that Hawkins thought he'd go after some of that money—"

"By terrorizing *me?*"

"Sick minds work in sick ways. Besides, Hawkins wouldn't do it himself. He'd hire someone. If he's discovered that you've invested the money between the shop and this place, he may be out for his own private form of revenge."

"So we're back where we started."

"Not...quite," Matt stated with such quiet thunder

that Lauren's pulse skipped a beat before racing on. "There are still certain allegations you've made that have to be resolved. Y'know, you're right." He cocked his head and eyed her insolently. "I may well be the man Hawkins hired, playing you now just as I've played you all along—orchestrating events, then showing up and explaining them away."

"But why *would* you?" she cried.

"You're the one with the answers." He flung himself back into the chair. "You tell me."

"I don't *have* the answers. That's what this—this is all about! I don't have *any* answers. My mind is running in circles!"

"Could be I'm getting paid a pretty penny for this."

"You don't want the money," she protested. "You're not ambitious that way! You told me so the first time we met!"

"Could be I was lying. Could be it was all an act." He jacked forward in the chair. "And since you're hurling accusations, I've got a few of my own. You were a virgin for twenty-nine years. Then you met me, and within a week we became lovers. Strange things were happening to you. You were frightened. You needed protection." He snorted. "Pretty high price to pay for it, I'd say."

She felt as though she'd been slapped. "No! I didn't—"

"Then again, maybe you were truly infatuated. I was different from the men you'd known. More physical. Brawny. But now that you've gotten what you wanted, you're scrabbling for reasons to put me off."

"No, Matt! How can you—"

"I don't meet your high standards. Is that it, Lauren?" His eyes bored into hers. "You're prepared to believe the worst because you just don't think I'm good enough for you?"

Unable to bear another word, Lauren sprang up from the sofa and rounded on him. "That's not true!" she screamed, grabbing his shoulders and shaking him. It was a pitiful gesture, since he was so much larger than she, but her fury was beyond reason. "It's not true! And I wasn't *prepared* to believe the worst!" His face blurred before her eyes. "But I had to know—had to know. I'd never been with another man, because no man had meant anything to me until you came along!" Tears trickled unheeded down her cheeks, and her hands stilled, impotent fingers clutching fistfuls of his shirt. "I've been dying, slowly dying for the past two days, grasping at straws, wondering if it was possible that—that I'd made a big mistake and given you everything and that you were really on the other side."

Her knees gave out then, and she sank to the floor between his legs. Her head was bowed. She wept softly. "It hurt so to…to think that, and I knew I had to get… get it out in the open, but that hurt, too…and…and…" Her fingers curved around his knee, gently kneading in a silent bid for forgiveness.

Matt put a tentative hand on her hair. "And what, Lauren?" he asked softly.

Her head remained down, her muffled voice punctuated by sniffles. "I love you…and I've hurt you…and somehow this new life that was supposed…supposed to be so wonderful is all messed up!"

With a low groan, he slid to the floor. His thighs flanked hers as he took her into the circle of his arms. "Oh, baby. Sweetheart, shhh." He rocked her tenderly. "You've just said the magic words. Nothing's messed up. Everything's suddenly clear."

She shook her head against his chest, too upset to comprehend.

He spread a large hand over the back of her head, buried his face in her hair and pressed her closer. "It's all right," he whispered between soft kisses. "Everything's going to be all right."

Lauren let her tears flow. They were a purging of sorts. It wasn't that she agreed with Matt or understood things as he seemed to, but being held in his arms this way, absorbing his strength and incredible tenderness, she felt herself slowly emerging from the hell she'd been living for the past few days.

He rubbed her back, caressing her gently. He whispered soft words of endearment and encouragement; with each one the darkness receded and she moved closer to the light. The warmth of his body thawed her inner chill. She fed on his strength like a creature starved for it.

Then he tipped her chin up and kissed her, and the last of her anguish broke and dissipated like a fever at the end of a long illness. She felt suddenly free, light-headed and very much in love. Shaping her hands to his cheeks, she gave herself up to his kiss; but because she offered as much as she received, Matt was as aroused as she by the time they finally parted, panting.

While she strung slow kisses along the line of his jaw and his chin, she worked at the buttons of first her shirt, then his. His hands were already in full possession of her breasts before she'd finished the latter, and when she came to her knees to press closer, the squeeze of her thighs against the mounting ache between them was a necessity.

From numbness such a short time before to this rich blossoming of the senses, Lauren reeled. Everything about Matt turned her on, from the vitality of the thick, sun-burnished hair through which her fingers wound to the musky scent of the rough, sweat-dampened skin beneath her lips to the virile cords of muscle straining against the rest of her body.

"I love you," she whispered against his mouth. "I love you, Matt." Her hands slid from his head down his chest, savoring the journey. But urgency was quickly mounting. She released the snap of his jeans, then the zipper, and worked her way beneath the waistband of his shorts until her fingers found what they sought. He was thick and hard, needing her in the same way that she needed him.

He gave an openmouthed moan and whispered her name, then set her back and shoved his jeans lower. "Hurry," he rasped as Lauren rocked back on her bottom and tore her own jeans off in jerky movements. He reached for her with urgent fingers, bringing her close until she straddled his thighs.

"Love me, Matt. Please, love me…"

"God, yes…"

His hands covered her buttocks, urging her downward even as she guided him inside her, and there was nothing then but paradise. His hands on her body, stroking…inflaming…lifting. His tongue wet and greedy on her throat, her collarbone, her breasts. Her own hands clutching his bronzed flesh, molding…straining…her mouth rapacious, her hips meeting his every thrust with matching ferocity.

They brought each other to near-peak after near-peak of exquisite sensation, and when the final climax hit, their cries were simultaneous, prolonged and distinctly triumphant.

For long moments, Lauren was aware of nothing but

the state of heavenly bliss in which she floated. Then came Matt's ragged breathing. It took her a minute longer to realize that her own throat was contributing to the rasping sound.

Very gradually the gasping eased, then ended, yet neither of them made a move to leave the other's arms. Their bodies remained joined, and Matt defied the limpness of his limbs to hold her even closer.

"I love you, Lauren," he murmured hoarsely. "Please, please don't doubt me again. I think it would—" His voice broke. "It would destroy me."

Her face buried in the warm crook of his neck, she whispered his name over and over again. Her arms, too, had taken on a strength that denied passion's drain, and she held him with no intention of ever letting go. "I'm sorry" came her muffled cry. "I shouldn't have suggested those awful things."

"No, it's good you did. You were right. They had to come out in the open." He tipped her head back and looked into her eyes. "We need the truth, sweetheart. Both of us. There are so many things we can't figure out, but the situation becomes only more complicated if we can't be honest about ourselves and our feelings." With one arm supporting her back, he gently smoothed damp tendrils of hair from her cheeks. "I have insecurities. Lots of them. They hit me like a ton of bricks when I first met you, and they've kept me a little off balance ever since."

"You didn't need to worry about *anything!*"

"But I did. At the start I worried that you'd associate me only with Brad and that you'd transfer the rift between you and him to me. I worried that you'd turn down your nose at my occupation, that you'd categorize me and put me in a slot and wouldn't like the things I

BARBARA DELINSKY   409

suggested we do. Then, when I began to realize how I felt about you, I was afraid you wouldn't feel the same." He slid his cheek against her temple. "And all the time I was worried about what was happening to you. I imagined Hawkins might be behind it, and I was reluctant to tell you the truth. Maybe I wouldn't be able to protect you or catch the bastard before he really hurt you."

"You'll be dead long before I will if you keep up that worrying," Lauren quipped softly, "and *then* where will I be?"

"Do you love me?"

"I do love you."

"And you're not bothered by who I am and where I come from?"

"Only that you come from the opposite coast, and that's much too far away."

A tremor shot through his body and he gave her a bone-crushing squeeze. "God, you're wonderful. You're beautiful and bright and warm and giving. What did I ever do to deserve you?"

Lauren was thinking the very same thing, but with the pronouns reversed. "I love you," she whispered. She'd never tire of telling him so, and with that knowledge and the intimate closeness of his body, her insides began to quiver. She tightened her lower muscles and was rewarded by the faint catch in Matt's breath; then, as he grew inside her, she began to move.

It was much, much later, after they'd finally sought out her bed, that she turned in his arms. "Matt?"

His eyes were closed. She was wondering if he was asleep when she heard his low "Hmm?"

"Do you realize what we did?"

He shifted his hips and smiled smugly. "Mmm-hmm."

"But without anything." After that first night, Matt had taken the responsibility of protecting her. "Aren't you worried?"

"You told me to stop worrying."

"But if we make a baby…"

His eyes opened slowly, but the smugness remained on his face. "If we make a baby, we'll have it. It'll be beautiful and bright and healthy."

"But the planning, the logistics…"

The light in his eyes grew brighter. "I love you, Lauren. If a baby comes out of that love, I think I'd be the happiest man alive."

With a soft sigh of elation, she nestled more snugly against him. "Oh, Matt, I love you so." Basking in a special glow, lulled by the strong and steady beat of his heart, she fell into a deep and untroubled sleep.

COME MORNING, LAUREN and Matt awoke together, showered together, dressed together, cooked and ate breakfast together. Neither seemed to tire of touching the other, or smiling, or whispering those three precious words.

It was only when they were getting ready to drive into Boston that Lauren permitted herself to think beyond the fact of their newly shared love. Matt sat sideways on the sofa, sorting through papers in his briefcase. Curling an arm around his neck, she slid onto his lap.

"We can't go to the police," she began quietly. "You're right. If they start looking into things and somehow come upon Brad's dealings, his memory will be sullied. I'm not sure my parents would care, but I would. So that leaves us back where we began. What should we do?"

Matt finished straightening a pile of letters, set them

in the briefcase and snapped it shut. "I think maybe it's time to call in some help. Not the police—someone private." He slipped an arm around her waist. "That way we can control what comes out. Hawkins may be behind this, or it may be someone totally unrelated to him."

"In which case the motive is still a mystery."

"We need a fresh ear, someone who might ask questions we haven't thought of or see things from a new angle." He paused. "Should I get a name and make a call?'

"Yes. We have to do something. I don't want to live with a shadow hanging over me, especially not now."

Matt was in total agreement. Through one of the corporate powers he'd been dealing with in Boston, he contacted a reputable private investigator by the name of Phillip Huber and set up a meeting for the following morning. In the meantime, he stayed as close to Lauren as he could, returning to the shop between business meetings of his own, taking her to lunch, then dinner. When they finally arrived back in Lincoln, it was late. Given the minimum of sleep each had had—not to mention the strain of jet travel on Matt, about which Lauren teased him unmercifully—they were both tired.

Absently she picked up the mail and flipped through it. Gas bill. MasterCard bill. Advertisements. She lifted the next piece of mail, a disconcertingly familiar gray envelope, and stared at it.

Susan Miles. Addressed directly to the farmhouse.

Fingers trembling, she tore open the flap, pulled out the stationery and unfolded it. A separate piece of paper floated to the floor, but once again, the stationery itself was blank. Stooping, she lifted the paper that had been enclosed. Roughly cut at the edges, it was a picture of a gleaming fox fur coat, apparently taken from a magazine. The model had been unceremoniously decapitated.

"Matt?" she called faintly, then louder: "Matt!"

He appeared at the top of the stairs, his shirt unbuttoned, its tails loose. Lauren's anxious expression brought him trotting down immediately.

She spoke quickly. "Last Friday and again on Saturday we received a letter at the shop addressed to a Susan Miles. Neither Beth nor I know anyone by that name. We assumed it was simply a mistake. Now there's a letter addressed to Susan Miles *here*." She held out the piece of stationery and watched him turn it from front to back.

"It's blank."

"So were the other two. The only difference is that this one came with a magazine clipping." She offered it as well. "Just a picture of a fur coat. Nothing else."

Matt studied the clipping, frowned back at the blank sheet of stationery, then took the envelope from her hand and examined the raggedly scrawled address. "There's got to be a message here," he said at last. "We may not be understanding it, but there's got to be one. You say the other two letters were exactly like this one, but without the clipping?"

"That's right. Same gray stationery."

"Same handwriting on the envelope?"

"Yes. And the same Boston postmark. I didn't think much of the first two. They were addressed to the shop. It could have been a simple mistake. Taken with this last one, though, there has to be something more personal in it. Whoever sent them knows my home address. He's got the name wrong, but he knows where I work *and* where I live."

Much as Lauren's stomach was doing, Matt's jaw

clenched. "Right." He rubbed his forehead with his finger. "Is it possible that you've been mistaken for someone else? For this Susan Miles, perhaps?"

Lauren didn't say anything. Her heart was hammering, and the knots in her stomach had tightened painfully.

Matt's focus remained on the pieces of paper he held. "Mistaken identity...that would make sense. All along you've had no idea who would have a reason to threaten you. We know there's a chance it could be Hawkins, but if it's not, this might be something to go on. If we could identify and locate this Susan Miles..." He looked up and caught Lauren's stricken expression. "Sweetheart?" When she swayed, he held her arms to steady her. "What is it?"

"I don't believe this is happening," she whispered. Her eyes were wide, dry but filled with the horror of conviction. "I don't believe it. I knew it was too good to be true."

Matt ducked his head, bringing his face level with hers. Every one of his features broadcast love and tenderness, and his voice was filled with hope. "It's okay, sweetheart. It's good, in fact. At least it's another lead to follow, and now that we've contacted an investigator—"

She covered her face with her hands. "My parents were right. I shouldn't have done it. I played with what fate had decreed, and now I'm paying for it."

"Lauren, what—"

"My face, Matt!" she cried. "It didn't always look this way. When I was a very little girl, my bones developed improperly. I was ugly. You saw a picture! You know!"

"My God," he whispered, finally putting the last piece of the puzzle into place. "I thought it was just a bad picture. I never dreamed..." Seizing her wrists, he drew her hands from her face and clutched them to his chest. His eyes slowly toured her features. "You had surgery," he said in amazement.

She nodded. "My chin was practically nonexistent, and my jaw was so badly misaligned that I had trouble eating. That's why I was so skinny."

"And you're so beautiful now. It's incredible!" He took her chin and turned her face first to one side, then the other. "No scars," he announced excitedly. "It must have been done from the inside. When, sweetheart?"

"This past spring, right before I came to Boston. I went to a clinic in the Bahamas. The recuperative period was ten weeks. Part of that time I stayed in a rented apartment and returned to the clinic on an out-patient basis."

"Unbelievable." Done with its journey, his gaze coupled with hers. "Just this past spring. So if I'd come six months before, I'd have found you in Bennington looking exactly as I'd expected. It all makes sense now—your inexperience with men, your talk of a new life, a new look..." His eyes lit with pleasure at a new thought. "Part of Brad's money went toward this, didn't it?"

"Some. Insurance paid for most of the surgery, since it had become a legitimate medical problem."

"And you feel better?"

"Physically *and* emotionally." She hesitated. "What about you, Matt? How do you feel?"

"How do I feel?" he echoed, puzzled.

"About what I did. Having plastic surgery and all."

"I think it's marvelous! If you'd looked this gorgeous much earlier, you'd have been snapped up before I could have found you."

"But what do you think about the surgery itself? Does it…bother you?"

"Of course not! Why would it bother me?"

"It bothers my parents. They were against my doing it."

"Hell, it's no different from a kid wearing braces on his teeth to correct a bite problem that would become troublesome in time. Or someone having his nose fixed to correct a deviated septum."

Lauren blushed. "I had that done, too."

"You did!" He grinned. "What did it look like before? The picture I saw was a head-on shot."

"It was crooked," she admitted sheepishly. "And lousy for breathing. I used to snore something awful."

"You sure don't now. I love your nose." He ran a finger down its smooth slope. "It looks so—so natural. The whole thing looks so natural! I'd honestly decided that the picture was just a bad one. Either that, or you'd simply come into your own as you'd grown older."

"Then Brad didn't say anything specific?"

Matt's voice mellowed. "No. It wasn't often that Brad spoke of home, but when he mentioned you, there was always a certain tenderness in his voice. In spite of the rift, you had a special place in his heart. He worried about you. Wow, if he could only see you now!"

"Yeah," Lauren drawled wryly. "I've got a new face that apparently looks so much like someone else's that an enemy of that someone else is out for blood."

"Hey, we don't know that!"

"Well, maybe not blood, but something, that's for sure." She sent a pleading look to the ceiling. "I don't believe this. I just don't believe it. It's like something only Beth could have dreamed up, but she didn't." She arched a brow at Matt. "You do agree that the mistaken-identity theory is the strongest one we've had?"

"Mmm. Not that I'm ruling out Hawkins. But, given the letters for Susan Miles, this theory is more plausible."

"What could the newspaper clipping mean?"

"I don't know. If the letters were real letters with writing and all, it wouldn't be so bad. But three blank sheets of stationery—that's odd."

Lauren sighed. "So, we look for Susan Miles."

"It's the way to go. Seems to me that'd be right down our investigator's alley."

IT SHOULD HAVE BEEN. Lauren and Matt met with the detective at a small coffee shop in Boston early the next morning. They told him everything, from a detailed account of each of Lauren's mysterious incidents to their theories involving, alternately, Brad's boss and Lauren's new face.

Phillip Huber went off in search of Susan Miles. Unfortunately, after a full day of poring through State House and registry records, he could find no evidence of anyone by that name living in the area.

The next day he went through the records of the local and state police, and the day after that he made use of his considerable network of contacts to broaden the search to include the rest of New England and New York.

By Thursday night, Lauren and Matt were no closer to finding Susan Miles than they'd been at the start, and by Friday afternoon, the search was temporarily abandoned.

LAUREN LEFT THE SHOP shortly before four, intent on getting to the bank and back before Matt came for her.

He'd been her shadow for most of the week, and she'd loved it. But that day he'd had business to attend to, so she set out on the errand alone.

With the luxury of Jamie's working full-time, Lauren was taking off early. It was a beautiful day. She and Matt planned to return to Lincoln to change, then drive one town over, rent a canoe and explore the Concord River.

She walked at a confident pace, buoyed by the anticipation of the outing, lulled into security by the peaceful week it had been. Since Monday, when the letter for Susan Miles had arrived at the farmhouse, there had been no incidents. Of course, Matt had been close at hand, a visible deterrent to mischief, and Phillip Huber had taken his turn when Matt had been busy.

Lauren had barely turned down the side street on which the bank was located when a car slid smoothly to the curb. Its door opened, and she was jostled inside by a burly hulk that had come from nowhere on her opposite side. Before she knew what had happened, she was seated in the back seat of a car that would have been roomy except for the two giants who crowded her between them.

She tried to squirm, but she was solidly pinned. "What—what is this?" she cried between attempts to free herself.

"Sit still, pretty lady," the man on her left said. "You know what it is."

"I—do—not." She was trying to elbow herself out of the human vise, only to find that the vise had tightened. "Let me out of this car!" she gritted. She began to pound at the thighs flanking hers but succeeded only in having her wrists immobilized by a single beefy paw on either side. "You can't do this!"

"We've just done it," the same man pointed out. His voice was calm, matter-of-fact, infuriating.

"Well—" she kicked out "—I'm not—" she writhed lower in the seat "—having it!" She managed to hike herself forward but was pitched back by the arm of steel that crossed her collarbone and tightened. She bit at the arm and heard a low grunt. Before she could struggle free, she was slapped viciously across the side of her head. Sharp pain radiated through her entire skull, rendering her utterly dazed. She sagged limply against the seat and fought to catch her breath.

"That's better," the man on her left said. "Now sit there and *don't move*."

She couldn't have moved if she'd tried, and she couldn't even try. The blow had robbed her of what little strength had remained after her futile attempt to escape. Her head lolled against the upholstered seat, and for long moments she could do nothing but hope to regain her equilibrium. Her jaw hurt something fierce, and she felt a momentary flash of hysteria. If they'd broken her jaw after all she'd gone through to set it right, after all she was going through because she *had* set it right…

"You've got the wrong girl," she managed to mumble through stiff lips.

"Mmm" came a hum from her left. "Somehow we knew you'd say that."

"You do." Gingerly she worked her jaw. It was sore, but at least it functioned. "I don't really look like this… I had repair work done to correct a problem…"

"We know the problem."

The one on the left was apparently the designated speaker. She dared a glance at him. He was dark-haired, dark-eyed, dark-looking in every respect. His eyes were focused straight ahead, following the course the driver was taking.

"If you know the problem," Lauren ventured, "then you know this is all a mistake."

"The problem is that you didn't want to be found." He looked at her then, and she cringed under his scrutiny. "It's subtle, I have to say that much. You're clever. Didn't do anything drastic, thought we'd be off looking for someone *completely* different. Or maybe you just thought what you had was too beautiful to tamper much with. You always were a haughty bitch."

"You've got the wrong woman," Lauren pleaded in a shaky voice. "As God is my witness, I'm telling the truth. The surgery I had was to correct a problem I've had from childhood. You can contact the clinic. My doctor will tell you."

The man was looking forward again, a smug look on his face. "We've already been to the clinic. That was a fancy job you did with the records, and if we were stupid we might have been put off. But we're not stupid, Susan. I think it's about time you realize that."

"I'm not Susan! I know you think I'm Susan Miles, because that's the name on those envelopes, but *my* name is Lauren Stevenson! Lauren Stevenson, from Bennington, Vermont. I have family and friends still there—you can check."

"Lauren Stevenson." He rolled the name around on his tongue in a way that made her want to vomit. "It's as good an alias as any."

"It's *not* an alias!"

Dark eyes glittered dangerously back at her. "Keep your voice down. I have a headache."

"I'll talk as loud as I want—" she fairly shouted, only to have her words cut off by the human mitt that clamped over her mouth. It had come from the right, but the voice, as always, came from the left.

"I'll gag you. Is that what you want?"

"No," Lauren answered the instant the mitt had left her mouth. She had to be able to communicate if she was to get anywhere.

"Then keep your voice down. And talk with respect." The last had been tacked on almost as an afterthought, but the man appeared to find immense satisfaction in it.

She wasn't about to argue. Physically, she was outsized and outnumbered. All three men—one on either side of her, plus the driver—were huge. Their sedate business suits did nothing to disguise the bulk of their physiques. Intellectually, though, she had to believe she was at least on a par with them, if not above. Yes, she was terrified, and terror had a way of fudging the workings of the mind. But if she could stay cool and somehow control her fear, she had a chance.

In keeping with that, she considered her captor's command. If it was a respectful tone he wanted, a respectful tone he'd get. Far more could be accomplished with sugar than with vinegar.

"Who are you?" she asked quietly, directing her efforts solely to the man on the left.

"Now, that is an insult if I ever heard one. You know who I am."

"I don't."

"I sure know you." He tilted his head to the side and studied her lazily. "You're looking good, Susan. Hair's a little shorter. Face looks good. Makeup's different. Easing up on it, are you?"

"Where are you taking me?"

He gave a careless shrug. "I'm not sure."

"What are you going to do with me?"

"I'm not sure."

"You must have a plan."

"Oh, yes."

She waited, but he said nothing more, so she dropped her gaze to her lap. "The plan is to make me nervous. Just as you've been doing for the past two weeks."

He puckered his lips, then relaxed them in acknowledgement of her perception. "Very good."

"But you do have the wrong person," she argued, albeit in a respectful tone. "The first few things you did didn't even make me nervous, because I had no reason to suspect there was anything to them."

"You wised up."

"Not really. It was the mail for Susan Miles that pulled it all together. Up until then I couldn't imagine what anyone would have against me." The issue of Chester Hawkins was irrelevant. "That's when I realized it had to be a case of mistaken identity."

"Sure," he drawled.

Lauren felt a movement in the arm that was pressed against her right side, and she looked sharply toward the hulk connected to it. The man was laughing. Silently, but laughing nonetheless. On the one hand, she was livid; on the other, she was more frightened than ever. They were obviously prepared for her denials, which practically defeated her efforts before they'd begun, but she wouldn't give up. There had to be *some* way out of this mess—if only she could find it!

CHAPTER NINE

FOR THE FIRST time since her abduction, Lauren looked beyond the confines of the car to the outside world. If she'd expected to see narrow, unfamiliar streets, she was mistaken. The car was on Storrow Drive, taking the very same route out of the city that she traveled every day.

She wished she knew what her wardens were up to, but she hadn't gotten that far yet, so she thought of Matt. Surely he'd have arrived at the shop. Surely he and Beth would be getting nervous when she didn't return from the bank. The bank!

"I have money," she exclaimed in a burst of hope. "If it's money you want, I'll give you all I've got." She fumbled in her purse for the envelope containing the cash and checks she'd been on her way to deposit, but her offer was immediately denied.

"We don't want money. The boss pays us plenty."

"Who's the boss?"

"Come on, Susan. We're not really as dumb as you'd like to think."

"I don't think you're dumb at all," Lauren declared quietly. "You've just made an innocent mistake. I'm not Susan, and I don't know who 'the boss' is. And *because* you're not stupid, you'll realize that I'm telling you the truth before you do anything drastic. If you go ahead with whatever you're planning, sooner or later someone *will* call you stupid—because you'll have done whatever you're planning to do to the wrong person."

He shot her a sidelong glance. "You've gotten quick with words. You never used to talk this much."

"Maybe Susan Miles didn't, but I always have. Look, there are any number of people—people who've known me for years—who can vouch for my identity."

"Like the medical records in that clinic did?" His question dripped of sarcasm.

"If you don't believe the records, that's not my problem."

"But it is. Seems to me it's very much your problem."

He was right. She had to take a different tack. "Okay. So you don't believe the records and you won't believe my friends. You tell me. Who am I supposed to be? Just who *is* this Susan Miles?"

"You want to play games? I'll play games. Susan Miles was the boss's best girl. He gave her everything any woman could want—" his eyes pierced Lauren's and his voice grew emphatic "—like a safe full of jewels and a closet full of furs. Where are they, Susan? We haven't been able to find them yet. Did you sell everything to bankroll that little shop you've got, or the house?"

"Jewels?"

"And furs."

"That clipping," she murmured, horrified. "Matt was right. There was a message in the clipping, but we just didn't get it."

The man on her left said nothing.

"I don't have jewels *or* furs. I bought the shop and the house with a legacy from my brother, who died a year ago." In other circumstances she'd never have volunteered that information, but these were unusual circumstances, to say the least.

"A legacy from your brother. Touching, but not terribly original, although I suppose it is different from the dead-uncle or maiden-aunt story, or that of the parents who were tragically killed in an automobile accident."

"My parents are alive and well and living in Bennington, Vermont. Check it out in a phone book. Colin and Nadine Stevenson."

The man on her left was silent.

"How *else* would I get money to open that shop? I've never had anything of my own like that before."

"Oh, please."

"I did?"

"How quickly you forget."

"What was it? What did I own?"

"A charming little boutique in Westwood Village. Actually, you were running it into the ground. After you died, the boss put one of his own men in charge, and it's begun to turn a pretty profit."

"I *died?*" Lauren felt as if she were in the middle of a slapstick comedy, only nothing was funny. She was totally bewildered. "But if I died, what am I doing here and why are you after me?"

The man on her left seemed to weary of her questions. "You didn't die," he growled. "You just made it look like you'd died. You took off with the jewels and furs, changed your face, bought your shop and your house and thought you could get away scot-free." His expression grew even darker. "Well, let me tell you, no one does that to the boss and gets away with it. And no one does it to *me!*"

"What did I do to you?" she whispered fearfully.

"You made a fool of me. I was the one who reported that you burned to death in that car."

"Oh."

"Yes, 'oh.' It's been a sweet pleasure putting you through hell these past couple of weeks. What was it like, Susan, knowing someone was on to you?"

"I *didn't*. I told you—"

"I'll bet you didn't believe it at first. You always were arrogant, with your pretty little nose stuck up in the air."

"It's not my nose—"

"When you finally admitted to yourself that you'd been found out, did you think of running? It wouldn't have done you any good. We'd have been right on your heels." He sniffed loudly. Lauren decided he had a deviated septum of his own. "I've enjoyed it. And the best is yet to come. What I've got planned for today will singe your hair. I mean *really*, this time. Think about *that* while we take our little drive."

Their "little drive" had already taken them to the outskirts of Lincoln. Lauren stared out the window and swallowed hard. *Singe?* She began to shake. What was he planning? Did he intend to kill her? She had to escape. And soon. But how?

They turned off Route 2 and began the drive down the street she took each night. She would have stiffened in her seat, or sat straighter, but she had precious little room to move in and barely more strength. Her arms and legs were beginning to ache from a combination of tension and the steady pressure applied from both sides. Her face hurt. Her stomach was knotting.

"Where are we going?" she asked in a small voice.

"Don't you recognize the streets?"

At that moment they turned down the very road that would lead to her house.

"Thought you might want to take a last look."

"A...last look?"

The man on her left said nothing.

"This is a mistake. It's all a mistake. I really am Lauren Stevenson. *Really.*"

"Sure."

She took a quick breath. "Look, you can come inside the house and I'll show you everything. I have identification—a birth certificate, college diplomas, even pictures of my family." Her captor's snort told her what he thought of the validity of that identification. She barely had time to wonder how one could possibly forge family pictures when another thought hit her. "I have a passport! Picture and all!" It didn't take a snort from her left for her to realize she'd struck out again. The passport would do her no good. If there'd been various point-of-entry stamps recorded over a period of time, she might have proved that Lauren Stevenson had existed long before Susan Miles had supposedly died. But Lauren's passport had been issued shortly before her trip to the Bahamas. Ironically, she hadn't needed it; it had never even been stamped. And yes, the picture was of her "before" face, but the files in the clinic had contained a similar picture, which these men had written off.

"So much for identification," she muttered under her breath. Then her head shot up. "My car! The registration!" Her face dropped again. "I reregistered it when I came to Massachusetts."

The man on her left seemed to be enjoying himself. "Keep thinking, pretty lady. See if you can come up with something we haven't already looked over. Don't forget, we've been through most of your belongings."

Lauren's nostrils flared, and for a minute she forgot herself. "You know, it wasn't so bad that you sampled my perfume and fiddled with my shoes. If that's what turns you on, okay. But my *underwear?* I mean, there's kinky and then there's—ahh!" Her arm had been wrenched up sharply against her back. She twisted to ease the pain. "Please," she gasped out in a whisper. "Please—that hurts!"

"I don't have to take your smart mouth. You're not calling the shots around here—*I* am!"

"Please," she begged, then gasped again when her arm was released. She hugged it close and alternately rubbed her elbow and her shoulder.

By this time the car was approaching the farmhouse. Lauren held her breath as she peered out the window, praying that Matt might be there, though she knew he wouldn't be. He was in Boston, waiting for her, maybe out looking for her by now.

The driver slowed in front of the garage, shifted into reverse, backed the car around and headed for the street again.

"Weird place," the man on her left said. "Pretty run-down. I really thought you had more class."

Lauren bit her lip and said nothing. She gazed longingly out of the window, hoping to see a neighbor walking along the side of the road, in which case she'd force some sort of ruckus inside the car that would attract attention. But she saw no one. The road was as quiet and peaceful as it had always been.

To her amazement, they drove on into the center of town. She marveled at the gall of her keepers, until she realized that she couldn't have made a stir if she'd tried. Large hands suddenly manacled both of her arms, just as burly legs had gripped her calves. She might have bucked in the middle, but no one outside the car would have noticed. And if she yelled—

"Don't even think it," the man on her left advised. "Mouse here has a mean right hook. It'll be even meaner the second time around."

"But if you're going to kill me anyway, why would it matter?"

He grinned. "The pain, Susan. The suffering. It'll be bad enough for you as it is. If you want it worse, well, then, go ahead and scream."

Lauren didn't scream. But she did decide that this man's grin had to be the ugliest thing she'd ever seen. And she vowed that if she ever escaped, she'd take great pleasure in personally wiping it from his smug face!

They passed the police station, and she stifled a cry. They passed the market, and she bit her lip. "You won't get away with this. There are two good men who are probably on our trail right now."

"Two good men? Well, I know about the dick you hired. I suppose he's a good man, but he won't find a thing. As for Kruger, haven't you figured that out yet?"

"Figured what out?"

"He's one of ours."

She didn't even blink. "You're lying."

The man on her left shrugged. "Suit yourself. Cling to romantic illusion if you want."

"You can say anything else and it might make me nervous. But Matt—one of *yours?* Not by a long shot."

"What do you think his quickie trip to the coast last weekend was for, if not to check in with the boss?"

"I know what his trip was for, and it wasn't your boss he was checking in with."

"You're awfully sure of yourself."

"Where Matt's concerned, yes."

"Why? What proof do you have that he's not with us?"

She knew she'd be wasting her breath to mention

things like love and trust. "He has the proof. Or, if you want to be crude, it was on my sheets the morning after we first made love. I was a virgin. If Matt had been with you, he'd have known something was strange. Unless, of course, your boss is some kind of eunuch."

"A virgin," the man on her left mused. "Kruger didn't mention that to us."

"Of course not. He doesn't know you from Adam."

When he shrugged again and simply repeated, "Suit yourself," Lauren knew she'd scored a point.

That was the last bit of satisfaction she was to have in a while. They left Lincoln behind and drove along back-country roads with no obvious destination, at least none obvious to Lauren. Her mind jumped ahead, touching on possible stopping places and possible forms of punishment in store for her, then recoiled in fear, seeking refuge in more purposeful thoughts.

"Did she have any birthmarks?" Lauren asked suddenly.

The man on her left frowned at her.

"Susan Miles. Did she have any distinctive birthmarks? There had to be *some* way I can prove I'm not her."

"Birthmarks. That's an interesting thought. I could ask the boss about it. Do *you* have any distinctive birthmarks?"

"No."

"Are you sure?"

"Yes."

"Maybe we should pull over to the side of the road. If you strip, I can check you out."

He was goading her. She looked away. "I don't have any birthmarks," she muttered half to herself as she shriveled into the seat. Her arms and legs had been released once they'd left Lincoln proper, but she might as well have been shackled for the little freedom she'd gained. Shoulders hunched, she tried to minimize contact with the bodies on either side by making herself more narrow. It was a token gesture; the more she narrowed, the more the two men spread.

They drove on and on. She lost track of their direction, and much of the scenery was unfamiliar. With each mile, though, she grew more edgy. They couldn't drive forever. Sooner or later they'd have to stop. And what then?

"Y'know," the man on her left offered, "you really blew it. You had it all. The boss adored you—"

"Who is he?"

"Oh, Lord."

"What's his name? If he's the one who's behind all this, don't I have a right to know his name?"

"You don't have *any* rights, pretty lady. You gave them up when you double-crossed him."

"I didn't double-cross anyone!"

His nonchalance faded. "I'd watch my tone if I were you. It's getting uppity, and if there's one thing Mouse can't stand, it's uppity women. Right, Mouse?"

Mouse grunted.

"I'm sorry," Lauren said as conciliatorily as she could. "I didn't mean to sound uppity. It's just that you assume I know everything, but I don't, and I feel as if this whole thing has to be an awful joke, except no one's laughing, and I'm sitting here trying to figure out a way to prove to you who I am, but my mind is getting all foggy and…and…" She'd begun to shake. Tucking in her chin, she closed her eyes. "I don't feel very well."

"Throw up in this car, lady, and I'll make you lick it up."

She swallowed hard against the rising bile and took several deep breaths through her nose. The strain was getting to her. Her insides continued to shake; she wrapped her arms around her middle as though to hold them still, but it didn't work. She was hot and tired and positively terrified.

"It's amazing," the man on her left said. "You're quite an actress, after all. Funny, you should be such a flop in Hollywood."

"I thought you said Susan had a boutique," Lauren murmured weakly.

"Yeah. But she was like everyone else in that town. Between running the boutique and pleasing the boss, she read for every bit part she could. Had a couple of walk-ons." He sent her a look of ridicule. "She wasn't much of an actress, at least not on the silver screen. What she's doing now is remarkable."

"I have never been, nor had the slightest desire to be, an actress."

"Sure."

Lauren didn't have the strength to argue further, and they didn't stop driving. Dusk fell over the landscape. She thought she'd explode if something didn't happen soon. Once she cast a glance over her shoulder. The man on her left picked up on it instantly.

"Sorry. No one's following."

She grew defensive. "Aren't we stopping for dinner or something?"

He simply laughed.

"Or the bathroom? Don't any of you need one?"

"We're like camels. You'd better be, too. No, we're not stopping. Sorry, but you'll have to think of some other way to escape."

She tried. Oh, Lord, she tried. But, imprisoned in

the car between two dark-suited sides of beef, she was hamstrung. There was no hope for escape unless they stopped, and it terrified her to think of where that would be and what they had planned for her then.

Just as she was beginning to bemoan the darkness, she noticed that the car was heading back toward the city. Of course. It made sense. Psychological torture. The purpose of the long ride had been to set her further on edge.

"Look, you've accomplished what you've wanted," she confessed without pride. "I'm thoroughly frightened. You can drop me off anywhere. I'll even take my chances and thumb a ride home."

"Is that what you thought, that we'd just let you go? Susan, Susan, how naive you are."

"What are you planning?"

The man on her left made a ceremony of debating whether or not to tell her. He moistened his lips, scratched the back of his head, then shrugged. "I guess it's time you knew. We're gonna do what we thought had been done months ago."

Lauren's heart was slamming against her breast. "What was that?"

"Your car plunged off the road and burst into flames. There was nothing left but ashes. The ashes were supposed to be you, so the boss gave you a fine burial." He sighed. "In this case, the burial came before the death, so we're kinda doing things ass-backward. But you will burn, Susan. Take that as a promise. You will burn."

Where Lauren got the breath to speak was a mystery. Perhaps the source was her desperation. "It's a threat, and you won't get away with it."

"Oh, we'll get away with it, all right. We're not novices at this type of thing."

"You're killers, then. Hit men. Is your boss connected with the mob? Well, let me tell you, if the mob kills its own, that's one thing. But I've got nothing to do with the mob or your boss or Susan Miles or you, and that makes me an innocent victim. I swear, you won't get away with it!"

The man on her left laughed. "Ah, pretty lady, that's priceless. Tell me, what do you intend to do once you're dead? Haunt us?" He laughed again.

Lauren gritted her teeth, no mean feat since they were chattering. "You'll get yours. So help me, you'll get yours."

When his laugh only came louder, she lapsed into silence. She'd save her strength, she decided. At some place, at some time, she'd glimpse a chance to escape. She'd need every resource she had when that time came.

Unfortunately, she couldn't seem to glimpse that chance to escape. After they had arrived back in Boston, the car drove down Atlantic Avenue, parallel to the harbor. It turned into a darkened path, continued to the end and stopped.

"Let's go," the man on her left said.

Before he'd even left the car, the man on her right had seized her. His arms were like cords of steel around her legs and shoulders. She was literally crunched into a ball with her face smothered against his chest. As she was carried from the car, she called on those resources she'd saved to try to free herself, but her bonds only tightened. Her scream was a pathetic sound muffled against the man's shirt, and she grew dizzy from the lack of air.

Terror was a driving force, though. Frantically she fought against the arms that held her. Futilely she tried to turn her head and gasp for air. While the doomed battle waged, she was carted up a flight of stairs, then another and another. Her captors' footsteps hammered against the wood planks, each forceful beat driving another nail into her coffin.

Then she was released, dumped unceremoniously onto the floor of a cavernous room. Gasping and trembling, she pushed herself up and looked around. It was dark, but she knew she was in a warehouse—a rank and decaying, abandoned warehouse.

The two men loomed over her. Their bodies were straight, their legs planted firmly apart. Their stance was aggressive, but it couldn't have intimidated her any more than she already was.

The man who'd been on her left abruptly hunkered down. She inched back on the floor, but she couldn't escape his hand when he took a strand of her hair between his fingers. He spoke with lethal quiet. "Your final resting place, pretty lady. Take a look around. Try to find a way out. It'll keep your mind busy."

"Where are you going?" she whispered.

"I've got a call to make."

"To whom?"

He let the strand of hair sift through his fingers. "Who do you think?"

"Your boss?" A sudden flare of fury gave her voice greater force. "You tell him for me that he's an idiot! You tell him that he's murdering the wrong woman and that he'll pay—"

When the man raised his hand, palm up, she ducked her head and shrank back. But he didn't hit her. Instead, he slowly lowered his hand until it gently brushed her cheek. "Such a pretty face," he murmured. "Such a shame—"

Her lips moved in a mere whisper. "You know I'm telling the truth. You do."

"I know you'd like to think that. It's okay. Hold on to the hope if you want. It won't be much longer. We'll be back soon."

"And then?" The devil made her ask that. Her eyes were wide with pleading.

"Then," he answered quietly, ever calmly, "we will sprinkle you with gasoline and set you on fire." She gasped and began to shake her head, but he went on. Too late, she realized she'd played into his hands by asking what he planned to do. Clearly, he took pleasure in her horror. "We'll watch you burn, Susan. This time there will be no doubt that you've died."

"Someone…will find me."

"I think not. Y'see, there's a contract out on this building. The man who owns it wants to build condominiums here, like those others along the waterfront, only he's a little strapped for money." The man glanced at his watch. "Roughly two hours from now, one of Boston's best torches will set fire to this place. It'll go up so quick that by the time the fire department gets here, the floor you're on will have long since fallen through. Your ashes will be hopelessly scattered. There's no way anyone will know you've been here, much less be able to prove you died here."

"Please," she cried, feebly grasping the lapels of his jacket, "please don't do this."

"Are you sorry, Susan? Do you finally regret what you've done?"

Lauren was weeping softly. "I haven't done anything…you *have* to believe me…*I'm not Susan Miles!*"

The man threw back his head, took a deep breath and

stood up. Together with his sidekick, he made the long walk across the rotting floor. At the door, he looked back.

"You can scream as much as you want. No one will hear you. And Mouse will be right outside this door in case you decide you want to take a walk." He glanced at his buddy. "I think he'd like to get his hands on you again. Right, Mouse?"

Lauren never heard Mouse's answer. She found herself alone, trembling wildly and feeling more frightened than ever. For long moments of mental paralysis, she remained where she was. Then the bottom line came to her. It was do or die. Life or death. Scrambling to her feet, she began to explore her prison, seeking any possible hole or loose plank or trapdoor that might offer escape.

THE BOSS WAS LOUNGING by the pool when his houseboy brought out the cordless phone. He took it, nodded at the boy in dismissal, then put the instrument to his ear. "Yes?"

"We have her. She's safely tucked away. And she's dying just thinking about dying."

"Good. When will you do it?"

"Soon. Uh—did you get the pictures I sent?"

"This morning."

"What do you think?"

"With her hair that way and the clothes, she looks a little younger, more innocent, but it's Susan, all right."

"Are you sure?"

There was a pause. "Aren't you?"

"I thought I was until we picked her up today. Somehow, close up, she seems different."

"That was her intent."

"No. Not just in looks, but in character. The woman we've got does seem more innocent. Susan would have tried a come-on. She'd have promised us all kinds of little favors if we let her go. This one hasn't done that— like it's never occurred to her that she's got a market-able commodity. She's terrified, but half of it seems to be that we won't believe her story. Either Susan has suddenly become one hell of an actress, or we've been tricked."

The boss lit a cigarette and took a long drag. "You think it's someone else?"

A pause. "I'm not sure."

"Is it possible that Susan could have set up someone else to smoke us out?"

"Possible, but not probable. This one claims she had her face fixed to repair a medical problem, just like the clinic records said. If she's telling the truth, it'd be just too convenient that Susan would have happened to find her, looking so similar and all. And if she knew about Susan, she'd have squealed by now. She's scared, really scared."

"So it wasn't a setup. It has to be Susan."

"Or someone who looks like her."

Silence dominated the next half minute. Then, "It's not like you to get cold feet."

"That's what I've been telling myself, but something just doesn't feel right. If we do have the wrong woman, we'll be in trouble."

"I thought you had it arranged so that no one would know."

"I do. It's foolproof."

"So what's the problem? If it's really Susan, she'll be getting her due. If it's not Susan, but someone she set up to take the fall for her, let her take the fall. That'll get Susan shaking all the more."

"And if it's simply a case of mistaken identity?"

"I can't believe that. The resemblance is too strong."

"But we'll never know. That's the problem. Once this one's dead, we'll never know for sure whether we've taken care of Susan or not."

"Damn it, what do you suggest?"

"I suggest...that we let this one escape and then continue to follow her for a while. If she suddenly runs from Boston and tries to change her looks again and sets herself up somewhere else, we'll know for sure that she's Susan. She won't have a head start on us this time. We'll be watching her constantly."

"I don't like this. I want Susan dead."

"So do I. But I want to make sure it *is* Susan who's dead."

"I thought this was all clear-cut. You'd found her. You'd been tormenting her. You've got her set to fry. It's all very neat. I don't like waffling."

"It's your decision, Boss."

The silence this time was the lengthiest yet. It ended with a low growl of frustration. "Ah, hell. Let the girl go. Then follow her. Do you understand? *Follow her.* If you lose her, so help me, you'll die right along with her!"

"Right."

"And let me know what's happening."

"Right."

LAUREN WAS AMAZED by the simplicity of her escape, although she assumed anything would have seemed simple in comparison to what she'd been through and the fate she'd so vividly been made to envision. After a lengthy search of the room, she'd found old planks sealing up a shaft. She'd pried them off—most had crumbled in her hands—and discovered a door leading to what was a cross between a dumbwaiter and a freight elevator. After climbing onto the platform, she'd pulled and tugged on a fraying cord of rope until she'd lowered the platform to its base. Then she'd shouldered her way through the rotting wood of the door and burst into a run along the street floor of the warehouse. Moments later, she was in the summer night's air.

Smelling vaguely of dead fish and other refuse, the air was the sweetest she'd ever breathed. But she didn't pause to savor it. She continued running out to Atlantic Avenue, veered left around the corner and didn't stop until she'd reached the first of the waterfront restaurants. She barged inside and made her way to the maître d's desk.

"I need a phone," she gasped, hunching her shoulders against the pain in her chest.

The maître d' smiled politely and gestured. "Right over there, in front of the rest rooms."

"No! I don't dare!" She shot a glance at the phone by his hand. "You've got one here. I'm being followed, and if I go back there, they're apt to catch…me again and I can't risk it…because they want to kill me and I…have to make this call. Please?" Her breath was coming in agonizing gulps, but she was beyond caring.

"This phone is reserved for—"

"Please!" she whispered. "It's critical!"

"I could call the police for you."

"Let me…please?"

Whether he acquiesced because, in her disheveled state, she didn't look like a troublemaker, or because he had a hidden streak of protectiveness in him, Lauren would never know. As soon as he reached to turn the

phone her way, she snatched up the receiver and began
to punch out the number of the shop. It was the closest place Matt might be, unless he was out searching.
She had to try three times before her shaking fingers
hit the right buttons.

"Lauren! My God, where *are* you?" Beth exclaimed.
"We've been looking all over for you! Matt's half out
of his mind, and the police won't do anything about a
missing person for at least twenty-four—"

"Where is he? I need him, Beth. Where is he?"

"You sound awful!"

"Where's Matt?"

"He's out looking for you. He calls in here every
few minutes. We've got Jamie stationed at your house."

Lauren's fingers had a death grip on the ridge of
wood running around the top of the maître d's desk.
"I'm at Fathoms. The restaurant. On Atlantic Avenue.
Tell him to come *right away*."

"Where have you been? Are you all right?"

"Just tell Matt. I have to go." Lauren set the receiver
back in its cradle, looked up at the maître d' and said,
"You can call the police now." Then her knees buckled
and she sank to the floor in a dead faint.

By the time she came to, she was lying on a couch
in the manager's office. It took her a minute to get her
bearings; then she bolted up, only to be restrained by
two firm but gentle pairs of hands.

"It's all right, miss. You're safe. The police are on
their way."

She recognized the maître d' but looked warily at
his companion.

"I'm the manager, and you're going to be just fine."

"Matt…Matthew Kruger…he'll be looking for me."

"It's all right," the manager assured her. "The police will be here any minute. We won't let him get to you—"

"No! He's my—my—he's okay. He's not one of them. I need him."

The two men exchanged a glance before the manager spoke again. "Then we should let him in?"

"Yes!"

He nodded toward the maître d' who turned and left. When the door opened several minutes later, two uniformed officers entered. By this time, Lauren was sitting upright, sipping shakily from a glass of water. One of the officers sat down beside her on the couch; the other knelt before her and began to ask questions. Lauren barely heard the questions, much less her answers. At the slightest movement or sound, her eyes flew toward the door.

After what seemed forever, but was probably no longer than fifteen minutes, Matt burst in. His eyes were wild, his tanned skin was pale and his entire body was trembling, but that didn't stop him from catching Lauren when she rocketed into his arms or from crushing her tightly to him.

Brokenly, he whispered her name. He took her weight when her legs seemed to dissolve from under her and melded her body to his. She was crying softly, clinging to his neck, unable to say anything for a very long time. At last he lifted her and carried her back to the couch, which the seated officer had vacated for that purpose. Taking her onto his lap, Matt began to stroke her hair, her back, her arms.

"It's all right, sweetheart. Everything's going to be all right. I'm here. Shh." His breath was warm on her forehead, her ear, her cheek.

"Oh, Matt...you have...no idea..."

Framing her head with his hands, Matt examined her closely. "Are you all right?" His gaze focused on the faintly discolored side of her face, and his voice came out in a croak. "What happened to your cheek?"

"He hit me. It was Mouse, but he wasn't the one in charge."

Matt looked up quickly at the manager. "Can we get some ice for this?"

The man nodded and hurried out, but Matt's attention was already back on Lauren. "Can you talk about it, sweetheart? From the beginning?" His thumbs stroked the tears from beneath her eyes. "The officers will listen. You'll have to go through it only once."

Nodding, Lauren slowly launched into her tale. It was interrupted from time to time—when the ice arrived; when she began to cry again; when Phillip, who'd been out searching for her, too, joined them—but she managed to get through it all before she collapsed, emotionally drained, against Matt.

It was Phillip, soft-spoken and dependable, who turned to the officers. "You'll look for the car?"

"You bet," the older of the two answered. "And if the warehouse hasn't already been torched, we'll search it." He grimaced and rubbed his neck. "I'm afraid we don't have much to go on. Dark blue Plymouths are pretty common. But we'll check out the local rental agencies and the hotels. Three oversize men might be remembered, particularly if they've been here for a while. Of course, they could be staying somewhere other than at a hotel."

Matt was cradling Lauren against his chest. "We'd be grateful for anything you can do. And we'd like to be kept informed."

"Can we reach you at—" The officer flipped back

several pages in his notebook and read off Lauren's Lincoln address.

Matt caught Phillip's headshake. "No. They know the house. I can't take the chance they won't return. We'll be at the Long Wharf Marriott. You can either call us there or leave a message at the print shop."

With a nod, the policemen left, followed several minutes later by Phillip. Matt studied Lauren with tender concern. "Feel up to moving, sweetheart?"

When she nodded, he helped her to her feet, then wrapped an arm around her waist and guided her out. Less than half an hour later, they were in a spacious hotel room overlooking the harbor. Despite her exhaustion, Lauren insisted on taking a shower. She felt dirty all over. With her eyes closed or open, she could smell the men who'd abducted her.

She scrubbed herself until her skin was pink, while Matt stood immediately outside the shower. He helped her dry off, tucked her in bed, then sat down beside her. If she'd ever doubted his love, she doubted no more; it was indelibly etched on every one of his features.

"Want some aspirin?"

She shook her head and managed a wan smile. "We don't have any, anyway."

"I could call down for some."

"I'm okay." She reached for him and whispered, "Just hold me, Matt. Just hold me."

He did. After a time, he moved back to shed his own clothes, then climbed under the sheets with her and held her for the rest of the night.

Come morning, Lauren had recovered to the point where she could think more clearly. Matt had been at that stage from the moment she'd fallen asleep in his arms.

They were sitting cross-legged on the bed, dressed only in white terry velour robes. She'd begun to gnaw on a strip of bacon when she set it back down. "I've been thinking, Matt. Theoretically, those guys are still after me. But something's odd. I escaped too easily."

Matt wasn't eating, either. "I know."

"It took me a while to find that shaft, but the one who went to make a phone call hadn't returned. No one heard me tearing off the strips of wood. No one heard the elevator. No one chased me down the street. Considering the way they manhandled me earlier and spelled out exactly what they planned to do to me, it just doesn't make sense."

"Maybe the terror they put you through was the end point of the exercise."

She thought about that for a while as she leaned against the headboard and sipped her coffee. "I suggested that to him, and he denied it. Maybe I managed to convince him that I wasn't Susan Miles, or at least plant some doubts—"

"In which case he *let* you escape. If only we knew for sure whether your escape was deliberate or accidental. I have no intention of assuming that you're off the hook until I have proof of it, which means either finding those thugs or—"

"Finding Susan Miles."

"Right. If we could find her and convince her to go to the police, they could question this boss of hers. At least then he'd know he had the wrong woman in you, and we could breathe freely."

Lauren sat forward and reached for the bacon. Matt's presence, his commitment to her cause, the fact of the two of them working together to resolve the problem— all gave her a sense of optimism that, in turn, awakened her appetite. "So," she said between bites, "we have to find Susan Miles, which may be easier said than done. No doubt she's using a different name, and she's probably had plastic surgery to alter her looks, so that's where we'll begin."

He nodded. "The clinic in the Bahamas."

"Right. That's where the boss found out about me, though how he knew to check out that particular clinic is a mystery. I wonder if Susan had been there before, or if she'd mentioned it to him at some point."

"If that was the case," Matt reasoned, "I doubt she'd be stupid enough to go back there when she was trying to flee him. On the other hand, the boss may have had some information we don't. Airline tickets, hotel reservations, something. I think we should fly down and talk with your doctor. Can they spare you at the shop?"

"They'll have to. The shop means a lot to me, but my own health and safety mean more. Between Beth and Jamie, things will run smoothly."

Matt popped a cube of cantaloupe into his mouth. "That Beth is a character. You wouldn't believe some of the stories she came up with to explain your disappearance. She even dared to hint that Brad had come back from the dead and taken you off to some hideaway to heal old wounds!"

"Did she really say *that?*" Lauren grimaced, then sighed. "She's got an unbelievable imagination. I think she's incurable."

"I think she's also incredibly devoted and loyal. She refused to budge from that shop yesterday because she wanted to be there if you called, and when you finally did, she all but sent out the cavalry to find me. She called Jamie to pass on your message in case I contacted the farmhouse first. She got in touch with Phillip—he has a phone in his car—and sent him looking for me. She was ready to tell the police I'd stolen her car so they would go out in pursuit. You're lucky to have her for a friend, Lauren."

Lauren reached out and touched his cheek. There was warmth in her fingers and love in her eyes. "I'm lucky about a lot of things. Very, very lucky."

THE POLICE WEREN'T so lucky. They had nothing to report to Matt except the fact that shortly before they'd arrived to search it the night before, the warehouse had gone up in flames. The fire marshal's office was investigating arson, but that case had little to do with Lauren's, and there was no sign whatsoever of either the dark blue Plymouth or the three oversize thugs.

Accompanied by a pair of officers from the Lincoln police department, Lauren and Matt returned to the farmhouse at noontime on Saturday, packed their bags and headed for the airport. Matt took a few minutes to phone Phillip to keep him abreast of their plans. Then he and Lauren were airborne, en route to the Bahamas.

To the best of their knowledge, they hadn't been followed.

CHAPTER TEN

UPON LANDING, Matt took Lauren directly to one of the plush hotels on the island. It had become clear to him in the course of the flight that she was suffering a delayed reaction to what had happened the day before. She'd been shaky and restless, unable to do more than pick at the meal that was served. She'd dozed off, then awakened with a start to a fit of uncontrollable trembling. He'd teased her, saying that *he* was the one who was supposed to be nervous, but his fear of flying took a back seat to her upset. He'd known that what she needed most was a peaceful restorative night.

First thing the next day, though, they went to the clinic. Purposely, they didn't call in advance. They knew that the boss's men had been there, and they weren't sure how they'd be received. Lauren was convinced that the doctor would not have willingly colluded with thugs, but Matt reserved his own judgment until their meeting.

Richard Bowen was in surgery. They insisted on waiting in the room just outside his office and caught him the minute he returned. Richard was surprised and pleased to see Lauren, doubly pleased to find her with Matt. After the brief introductions, he ushered them into his sanctuary. Neither Lauren nor Matt missed the subtle blanching of his face as she explained what had happened.

"They made it very clear that they'd seen your files," Matt concluded for her when he sensed that Lauren wasn't sure exactly how to confront the doctor. She obviously liked and trusted him, and she was loath to toss accusations his way. Matt had no such qualm. "Did you show anyone those files, or know that they'd been seen?"

To Lauren's relief, Richard was not offended and deeply shared their concern. "My files are confidential. The only way I'd have shown them to anyone would have been if Lauren had specifically requested it."

"Then how—" Lauren began, only to be interrupted.

"About a month ago there was a break-in here. My file cabinets were forced open and the files rifled. Records of hundreds of patients were left scattered all over the office. Nothing was taken that I could tell. Until now I've had no idea what the burglars were after."

"And Susan Miles?" Matt prompted. "Have you treated a patient by that name?"

Richard widened his eyes for an exaggerated second. "Treated, no. Spoken with, yes. Oh, yes. She came by to see me last fall, maybe early winter. She wanted to discuss having some minor work done. It never got past the discussion stage, so I don't have a file on her, but I'll never forget her face. She was stunning. A real beauty." He cast an apologetic glance at Lauren. "Yes, Lauren, you do look a lot like her now."

"Did you do it intentionally?" Matt growled. It was obvious that Richard Bowen had been taken with Susan Miles's looks. For him to try to form another woman in her image might have been conceivable, if infuriating and possibly unethical.

Richard chuckled. "I'm a plastic surgeon, not a miracle worker. It's only in the movies that one face can be completely altered to look like another. No, in Lauren's case, it was pure coincidence. The hair's the same in texture and color, and the figure is complementary, now that Lauren's put on weight. The eyes were alike all along. But, if I remember correctly, and I'm sure I do, Susan Miles wore much more makeup. As for the rest—the nose, the cheekbones, the jaw—they all just came together. You have to understand that in cases like Lauren's, the end results are sometimes a mystery even to the doctor until everything's done. Reconstructive work can go this way or that in the healing process." He smiled ruefully at Lauren. "Yours went the way of Susan Miles."

"From what you say, I should be happy about that," Lauren mused, "but given all that's happened…"

"There are differences," Richard pointed out, "but mostly I think they come from within. The woman I spoke with had a harder edge to her. She was very much like so many of the others I treat, women whose inner tension does things to their faces that no amount of plastic surgery can correct."

"Then she didn't really need plastic surgery?" Lauren asked. She looked at Matt. "Maybe she was planning on disappearing even back then."

Richard spoke before Matt could comment on that supposition. "There were a few things that could have been touched up, but basically they could have gone another five or ten years without attention. People would have thought her beautiful if she'd done nothing."

"Did you tell her that?" Matt inquired. Richard gave him a wry, what-do-*you*-think look. "But she didn't come back."

"No. I never saw her again."

Lauren sat forward. "We have to find her. We know

she came from the L.A. area and had a boutique there. Did she say anything to you—drop any names—that might give us a clue?"

Richard sat back in his chair and frowned, trying to absorb all that Lauren had told him. "I don't think so."

"She was probably with a man," Matt offered. "A very wealthy and powerful man."

"Wealthy and powerful men are a dime a dozen on the islands. She did say that she was here on a pleasure trip and had heard about the clinic from a friend."

"No name?" Matt asked.

Richard shook his head. "Fully one-third of my patients have been from the West Coast. They like coming here for the ambience, and for the distance. They can go on an extended vacation far from home, then return looking positively marvelous with no one the wiser." His frown deepened, and he chafed one eyebrow with the knuckle of his forefinger. "I can picture her sitting here talking with me. I'm sure I asked her where she way staying—it's standard small talk in a place like this—and I don't think it was one of the large hotels, because I would have formed a mental image of her there. Maybe a smaller—no—" He hesitated, concentrating. "A boat. I think she mentioned something about the marina."

Matt grunted. "There have to be dozens of marinas. She didn't say which one?"

"If she did, I don't remember."

"Then it'll be like finding a needle in a haystack, and we don't even know which haystack to search."

"How about other clinics on the islands?" Lauren asked.

"There are none I'd recommend, and I doubt a

woman like that would go to a second-rate place." Richard held up a hand. "No conceit intended."

"None presumed," Matt offered in his first show of faith. "Can you tell us anything else about her—how she wore her hair, any distinctive jewelry or style of dress?"

Richard closed his eyes as he called back the full image from his memory bank. "Her hair was pulled away from her face in a chic kind of knot. She was wearing gold jewelry—large hoops at the ears, a chain around her neck. She had several rings, maybe one with a stone, and she was wearing white silk slacks and a blouse. Oh, and high-heeled sandals. I noticed that because her toenails were polished to match her fingernails, and the pink was the same color as the sash around her waist."

"You were very observant." was Matt's wry comment.

Richard laughed good-naturedly. "It's my business to be observant when it comes to women's looks, and this woman was well worth the look. I remember thinking how elegantly she'd coordinated everything. She was stunning. Truly stunning."

Matt pushed himself from his chair. "The description may prove to be helpful somewhere along the line. I hope." It went without saying that they were still at the very start of that line. He held out a hand for Lauren. "Come on, sweetheart. We'll have to rethink our strategy."

Richard walked them to the door. "I'm really sorry I have no more information. If only—" His brow rippled. "Wait a minute. There is something. I mean, it'd still be a long shot, but—"

Matt and Lauren had turned hopeful faces his way. "What is it?" Lauren asked, holding her breath.

"She smoked. I remembered thinking that in time her face would show it. It does, you know."

"But where does that get us?" Matt prodded.

"She was using a little green box of matches. Not a matchbook, but a little green box. I remembered thinking, 'Ah, she's been to Terrance Cove.' It's one of the more showy restaurants around here. Just the place for the wealthy and powerful."

Matt and Lauren exchanged a look of excitement. "Let's try it, Matt," she said. "We've got nothing to lose."

It was Matt who turned to shake Richard's hand and thank him. Belatedly, and purely on impulse, Lauren gave the doctor a hug. "You've been great, Richard. How can we ever thank you?"

His grin was crooked. "You can find Susan Miles and get both of you out of danger. Her friends don't sound very charitable."

Lauren agreed, then slid her hand into Matt's.

A taxi took them to Terrance Cove, which, fortunately, had just opened for lunch.

"What are you going to say?" Lauren asked. "If Susan Miles was with the boss, who presumably made the reservations, the people at the restaurant would have no way of knowing, much less remembering, her name."

"But the face," Matt cooed. "Ah, the face. Susan Miles had a memorable face. And, sweetheart, you've got that face. *I* always knew it was memorable, but then, I'm slightly biased."

Lauren pinched him in the ribs, but she was buoyed. She held her head high when they entered the restaurant, and tried to look every bit the boss's woman while Matt did the talking. His story sounded conceivable enough.

"My fiancée is looking for her identical twin

They've been separated for two years, and we just got word that she was here last winter. Her name is Susan Miles." He looked at Lauren affectionately. "And this is her face. Does it look at all familiar? Ring any bells? Susan might have had her hair pulled back, and she was probably wearing more makeup and jewelry. But the similarities are marked." He paused. "She might have been with a rather impressive man, and if we can find him, we can get a lead on her."

The maître d' stared at Lauren long and hard. "I'm sorry," he said in crisply accented English. "I don't recognize her. But I only work afternoons. The man who was working evenings last winter was recently retired. He is living in Miami with his daughter and grandchildren."

"It's very important that we reach him," Lauren urged. "We have no other leads. Do you have an address or a phone number?"

The man seemed to waver. His indecision came to an end when Matt pressed a folded bill into his hand. "Wait here, please. I'll see what I can do."

As soon as he had disappeared, Lauren leaned close and whispered to Matt, "Why does that always work?"

He whispered back, "It doesn't, at least not always. I was prepared to give him another. He sold himself cheap."

"That was quite a story. *Identical twin?*"

"Beats the other explanation."

Neither of them commented on the fiancée part of the tale.

Within minutes the man returned with a small index card on which he'd printed the name of the former employee and his Miami address. Matt pocketed the card, and he and Lauren headed back to the hotel.

"To Miami?" Lauren asked.

"To Miami."

"When?"

Matt glanced at his watch. "As soon as we can get a flight."

They both knew that the personal visit was a must. They could easily get the man's phone number and call him, but Lauren's face was the key. So they put back the few things they'd taken out of their suitcases, returned to the airport they'd landed at less than twenty-four hours before, and caught the first plane to Miami.

The flight was short and uneventful. As always, they were watchful, alert to any face that would be familiar, or threatening, or in any way suggestive of a tail. As always, they saw none.

After the plane had landed, they took a taxi straight to the address printed on the index card—a modest house on the outskirts of the city. Various bicycles and toys littered its driveway. Instructing the driver to wait, they approached the door.

It was opened by a gentleman in his early seventies. The children crowding behind him called him "Papa," but his actual name was Henry Frolinette.

Matt repeated the story they'd given the maître d' at Terrance Cove, stressing simultaneously their regret at disturbing him and the urgency of their mission. The man nodded, looked closely at Lauren and nodded again.

"I don't know the name," he admitted, "but I do remember the face. They came to the restaurant more than once."

"They," Matt echoed. "Then she was with the man."

"Oh, yes. A dapper sort, and a generous spender. There were usually eight or ten in his party, though the

individuals differed—except for the woman. Miss...
Miles, you say?" When Lauren nodded quickly, he went
on. "Miss Miles was always with him. And Mr. Prinz
always picked up the check for the entire group. He paid
in cash, too, I might add."

Lauren's gaze met Matt's. "Prinz," she breathed.

Matt was already looking back at Henry. "Do you
know his first name?"

"Oh, yes. He's been quite a presence in the islands
over the years. Theodore Prinz, from Los Angeles. Not
that everyone speaks highly of him, mind you. There
have been rumors about the nature of his work. I never
believed them, personally. He is a good-looking man,
very well behaved and dignified, and he was always
more than gracious to me."

Unfortunately, Henry Frolinette was unable to give
them any specific information on Susan Miles. Lauren and Matt discussed it that night over dinner at the
beachfront hotel they'd checked into.

"At least we have the boss's name," Lauren mused,
"but that's about all. I suppose we could show up on
his doorstep and tell him he's made a mistake, but—"

"He wouldn't believe us, and we'd only be putting
ourselves right back in his hands. No, if anything's
going to stick, we have to find Susan Miles. If Henry
had been able to pinpoint a marina, maybe we could
have gone back and found someone who might give us
a clue to where she went when she left Prinz. But to use
Theodore Prinz's name alone would only be asking for
trouble. Word is bound to get back to him, and if he's
half as powerful as I suspect, we'd be playing with fire."

"So?"

"We call Phillip, who can use his contacts to get the
lowdown on Prinz. If Prinz is involved enough with that

boutique to have his own man running it, the name of
the place will be sandwiched in there with the rest of
the information. At least, it will be if Phillip is worth
his salt, and from what I've seen, he is."

Lauren didn't understand. "But what good will it do
to know the name of the boutique? We can't show up
there, any more than we can show up at Prinz's home.
If we start asking questions of nearby shopkeepers,
they're apt to call Prinz. Besides, I'm sure he had his
men question everyone in sight when he started looking for Susan himself."

"True. But what if we go further back? What if Phillip can get hold of the original papers for that shop?"

"What if Prinz bought it for her in the first place?"

"Maybe he did and maybe he didn't. If he didn't,
there might just be some information—even data on
loan applications—that could lead us to where she came
from—or even to a friend or a family member whom
she might have contacted when she relocated."

"But wouldn't Prinz have done that?"

Matt's eyes were filled with excitement, and his
voice held a kind of restrained glee. "Prinz went forward. He obviously felt he knew Susan well enough to
anticipate what she'd do. He must have known of her
visit to the clinic when they were in the Bahamas. That's
why his men went there right away. They found what
they were looking for, so why look further?"

"But you'd go backward," Lauren stated with sudden comprehension. And admiration. "Cautious Matt.
Wants to know the ingredients before he takes a taste."

"It makes sense, doesn't it?"

"Sure does. And in spite of the danger, you're enjoying yourself."

"Sure am. I read somewhere—maybe not in a

Spenser novel, but somewhere—that private investigators often locate people who've been missing for years by staking out the graves of their parents. Unless this Susan Miles is truly made of ice, she's been in touch with someone from her past, and more likely than not, that someone is a family member." He straightened in his seat and sighed. It was as though he'd suddenly set down the mystery novel he'd been reading and returned to reality with a jolt. "All *we* have to do is find that family member."

"WHAT'S HAPPENING?"

"They flew back to Boston. Looks like she's not trying to disappear. Kruger's with her constantly. They're staying in a hotel in town, but that may be because workmen have started tearing up her farmhouse."

"Tearing it up?"

"Remodeling. At least, that's what it says on the side of the truck parked out front. I don't think she's planning to abandon the place, Boss."

"Then she's not Susan."

"Looks that way. She's still pretty nervous, y'know. Looks all around her whenever she goes out, and, like I said, she doesn't go anywhere alone. More than that, the police are in and out of her shop."

"Susan wouldn't have dared call the police."

"Right."

"So. She's not Susan. Do you think she's given up the search for Susan?"

"I don't know. Word has it that the detective's been doing some research."

"About what?"

"The boutique."

"You have to be kidding! How did they find out about that?"

"I told her."

"Not smart. Not smart at all."

"It was when I had her in the car. I thought she was Susan then."

"They'll get my name."

"They've already got it."

There was a pause, then an arrogant "No problem. The boutique's on the up-and-up. You'll just have to be doubly careful with Susan's demise."

"What about Lauren Stevenson? And Kruger? And the dick, for that matter? If they do manage to find Susan for us and then something happens to her, they'll know who to blame."

"But Susan's death won't be traceable to us. It could be an accident; it could be part of a larger scheme. If it looks like someone else kills her, that's not my worry. And if a whole bunch of people shoot each other to bits, so much the better. I don't care how you do it, but keep us clean. I pay you good money to handle things like this. Do what you have to. Don't bore me with the details. I want Susan dead!"

"WE'VE HIT PAY DIRT!" Matt exclaimed with a broad grin as he set down the telephone. He was seated at the desk in the back room of the shop, and Lauren was propped expectantly at its edge.

"What did he say?" The call had been from Phillip. She'd known that much, but had been unable to follow the conversation, which had been distinctly one-sided in favor of the detective.

"He said," Matt began slowly, savoring the suspense, "that Susan bought the boutique herself and she financed it with a loan from a local bank. The loan application listed two people as references, neither of whom are named Miles, but both of whom are from Kansas City."

"Kansas City. Where she grew up?"

"Either that, or where she was living before she hit L.A. It doesn't really matter. At least we have contacts." He patted the scrap of paper on which he'd jotted the two names.

"But what if these contacts are somehow related to Prinz? What if one or the other of them was the instrument of Susan's introduction to him?"

Matt was shaking his head. "According to Phillip, neither of the names has shown up in any of the information he's gathered on Prinz. There's still that possibility, but I think it's remote. And even if it's not, neither one has any direct association with Prinz now, which means that we'll be safe." He lifted the receiver again and called the airport. Within hours, he and Lauren were headed for Kansas City.

"Poor Matt," Lauren mused when they were airborne again. "For someone who hates flying, you've done your share in the past few days."

He leaned close to her, denying the steel arm between them. "It's worth it. Every hateful minute."

Lauren smiled and whispered, "You are a wonderful man."

"Nah. I'm just along for the ride."

"That's one of the reasons I love you." She kissed his too-square chin. "You didn't ask for any of this."

"But I asked for you," he murmured deeply. "All my life I've been asking for you, and now that I've found you, I'll take any ride, as long as you're along." He sought and captured her lips, kissing her thoroughly.

"And when this is all over," he whispered against her mouth, "we are going to take a vacation to beat all vacations. We'll fly somewhere and stay put for two weeks, just the two of us. Sun and sand and moonlit nights…"

"Sounds wonderful, but you'll have used up all your vacation time by then."

"So I'll take more."

"And if your boss objects?"

"I'll quit."

She grinned. "Mmm. I'd like that. San Francisco's too far away."

"My thoughts exactly." He kissed her again, softly, deeply. His mouth was just leaving hers when the flight attendant came by with lunch.

Beneath the lighthearted teasing, Lauren had been very serious. San Francisco *was* too far away. But she couldn't think about the future. Not yet. There was still too much to be done to ensure that she had a future at all.

BRIGHT AND EARLY the next morning, Lauren and Matt showed up in the office of one Timothy Trennis. The office was done in obvious taste and at obvious cost; the man was in his early forties, neatly dressed and pleasant-looking. When he saw them, his mouth dropped open. His eyes were riveted to Lauren's face.

"Susan?" he asked uncertainly.

"Almost," Lauren said gently, "but not quite. I am looking for her, though. We thought maybe you could help us."

Timothy continued to stare at her, then slowly shook his head. "The resemblance is remarkable. It's been a long time since I've seen Susan. I could have sworn—"

He seemed to catch himself, and his cheeks reddened. "But you'd know, wouldn't you?"

Lauren nodded. "It's very important that we reach her. Do you have any idea where she might be?"

"Is she in trouble?" he asked with genuine concern.

Lauren looked hesitantly at Matt, who took over. "She may be if we don't find her. Someone else is looking for her. It's critical that we find her first."

"It's that Prinz guy, isn't it?"

"Do you know about him?" Lauren asked.

Belatedly, Timothy gestured for them to sit. When they'd done so, he lowered himself into a chair near his desk. "Susan and I dated for a time. I always knew she had greater ambitions—ambitions that went beyond Kansas City, I mean. When she decided to move to Los Angeles, I wasn't surprised. We kept in touch for a while, so I knew she was seeing Prinz. I made it my business to find out about him, and when I tried to caution her subtly, she pretty much severed all contact between us."

"When was the last time you heard from her?" Matt asked.

Timothy thought about that for a minute, making rough calculations in his mind. "It had to have been more than three years ago."

"And there's been nothing since then?"

Timothy shook his head.

"Is there someone she *might* have contacted? Someone she's kept in touch with—family, maybe?"

"If there is, I don't know about it. Susan rarely talked about family. There was an older sister, and her mother. The father died when she was a child, and the mother remarried. Susan detested her stepfather. She left as soon as she could."

"Do you know where the mother lives?" Lauren asked.

"Susan grew up in a small town in Indiana. Whether the mother's still there is anyone's guess. I don't even know her married name."

"How about the sister?" Matt queried.

"The sister was older by five or six years, took off after high school and got married. Susan never mentioned her. I simply assumed they'd lost contact, too."

Matt looked at Lauren. "Another strikeout." He fished the scrap of paper from his pocket. "What about, uh, Alexander Fraun? Do you know him?"

Timothy nodded. "Susan worked for him. He owns a pair of dress shops in the area. Nice-enough fellow. You could try him. He may have information I don't." As Lauren and Matt stood up to leave, he added, "I hope you find her. I always wished her happiness."

Lauren smiled warmly. She liked this man and felt he'd given them the first positive picture of Susan Miles to date. "We'll tell her that when we find her," she said. *When*, not *if.* Pessimism had no place here; there was too much at stake for all of them.

"THEY'RE IN KANSAS CITY."

"Kansas City? Clever. Susan was from Kansas City. They *are* looking for her."

"Will they find her?"

"In Kansas City? No. She wouldn't go back there. It's too obvious." There was a pause. "It is possible, though, that she's contacted one of her old friends there." A smug smile. "And if that's the case, Kruger and the girl will find out. They're doing our legwork for us."

"Seems to me I'm doing it anyway, following them around like this."

"You're not stupid enough to let them see you, are you? After that little kidnapping stunt, the girl would recognize you instantly."

"Don't worry. We've got Jimbo tailing them close, and she never saw him, so we're safe."

"But you're not far."

"No, sir."

"Good. I don't trust Jimbo to do the heavy work."

"Neither do I, and I have a personal investment here, too. Susan's kept us running in circles. That kind of thing inspires revenge."

"Mmm. I like that. Very good."

ALEXANDER FRAUN WAS harder to reach. When Lauren and Matt arrived at the address Phillip had given them, they were told that Fraun was at the other store. When they arrived at that one, they were told that he'd gone to a luncheon meeting and would be back at the first store that afternoon.

They went to lunch themselves, then returned to the first store to await the elusive Mr. Fraun. Shortly before two o'clock, he entered the small outer office in which they sat. He had started to pass through into his own office, after glancing briefly their way, when he did a double take on Lauren and came to an abrupt halt.

"Susan?" he asked uncertainly.

"Almost," she said gently, "but not quite." She felt she was living a broken record and quickly moved to free the needle from its cracked groove. "My name is Lauren Stevenson. And this is Matt Kruger. We're looking for Susan and thought you might have some idea as to her whereabouts."

"Come into my office," the man said with a broad wave of his hand. He was as different from Timothy

Trennis as night from day. Not only was his office a disaster area, but the man himself looked as though he'd seen better days. Lauren estimated that he was in his late fifties. His bald pate was scantily covered with strands of gray that had been called to the rescue from somewhere just above his ear. He had chipmunk cheeks and a multitiered chin, both of which coordinated perfectly with his girth. There was something about him, something strangely genuine, that made Lauren like him on the spot.

"Now," he said, scooping a pile of ancient magazines from the torn vinyl sofa so that Lauren and Matt could sit down, "what's this about Susan?" He propped himself on the edge of the desk. The wood groaned.

"We're trying to find her," Matt explained. "We were told she worked for you once."

"What do you want with her?" Fraun shot back with such suspicion that Lauren, for one, wondered if Prinz's men had reached him first.

Matt did the talking, apparently taking the man's suspicion for protectiveness. He explained just why he and Lauren were anxious to find Susan.

Fraun shifted his gaze back to Lauren. "You look just like her. For a minute when I walked in, I thought she'd come back."

"We know that she went to Los Angeles when she left here," Lauren offered, "but we were hoping that you might have heard from her."

"She's not still there?"

Lauren shook her head.

The wrinkles on Fraun's brow echoed higher on his bald head. "I thought she was. Last thing I heard from her, she had her own boutique." He smiled. "Susan was good. She had a way with color and style." He gave his head a little toss. "She was wasted here. I told her so. I mean, my goods are nice enough, but she needed high fashion to make the most of her talents."

"When was the last time you heard from her?" Matt asked.

Fraun suddenly scowled at him. "How do I know you're on the up-and-up? How do I know you two haven't come to do her harm?"

Lauren, too, saw protectiveness this time. As briefly but meaningfully as she could, she told him where she'd come from and where she worked, then did the same for Matt. "We don't wish Susan any harm. We have no reason to do her harm. If Matt and I can locate her, Susan and I stand to benefit—Susan, because she'll be aware of the danger and be able to do something about it; me, because if Susan does something about it, I'll be out of danger, too."

Fraun tugged a slightly warped pad of paper from beneath a haphazard pile of letters. "I'm going to write down your names and addresses. That way, if anything happens to Susan, I'll know who to call."

"Then you know where she is?" Lauren asked in excitement.

"Driver's licenses, please."

Lauren and Matt exchanged a glance and dug into their respective pockets for identification. Only when the man had taken notes to his satisfaction did he put down the pad and face them.

"No, I don't know where Susan is," he admitted. "The last time I heard from her was nearly two years ago. She sounded fine then. Why did she leave L.A.?"

"We're not sure," Matt answered. "But we do know she left. We'd hoped she'd contacted you, or someone else she knew before."

"You could try Tim—"

"We already have. He suggested we try you."

Fraun sighed and gave a shrug that made his belly shake. "I don't know what to tell you. I can't believe Susan's in trouble. She was always honest, and a hard worker."

"She probably still is," Lauren speculated. "It's just that she had the ill fortune to get mixed up with a man who's probably neither of those things. Can you think of anyone she may have contacted? Timothy said she wasn't close to her family, but there's always a chance she could be in touch with one of them."

Fraun shook his head. This time his jowls shimmied. "Tim was right. She wasn't big on her family. She did mention the sister from time to time."

"Do you know her married name," Matt asked, "or where she's living?"

"Nah— Wait just a minute." He bounced off the desk and tugged at the drawer of a file cabinet. It resisted his efforts, yielding at last, but with reluctance. Lauren understood why. The drawer was nearly as overstuffed as was the man rummaging through it.

"How can you find anything in there?" she asked on impulse.

"I find. I find. It just takes a little time."

It took a good fifteen minutes, during which Lauren and Matt sat by helplessly, glancing from each other's faces to the man at work to the calamity of his office.

"Here we go!" Fraun exclaimed at last. He held up a sheet of paper that had a permanent press running diagonally through it. "Susan's original employment application. You see," he cried victoriously, "it sometimes pays not to clean out drawers." Holding the paper at arm's length, he ran his eyes down the form. "Aha!

Person to call in case of emergency: Mrs. Peter—Ann—Broszczynski. Relationship: sister." Proudly, he offered the form to Lauren. "St. Louis. Think you can get there?"

Lauren looked from the form to Matt and grinned. "You bet we can." When she returned her gaze to Alexander Fraun, she realized that, with a beard and a little more hair, he would have reminded her of Santa Claus.

ANN BROSZCZYNSKI WAS not living at the address listed on the employment application, which was understandable, Lauren and Matt told each other, since the application had been filled out seven years before. The people presently living at that address didn't know what had become of the Broszczynskis, but the telephone company did.

A phone booth with its book miraculously attached and intact gave them the information they needed, and a taxi delivered them to the right address. It was another apartment, but a nicer one, more a garden complex. Lauren felt a certain pleasure that Susan's sister had moved up in the world.

The door was answered by a teenage girl who reminded Lauren of the guard at the garage where she parked. Definitely a music fan. If the net of lace banding her curly hair, the penciled mole just above her lip, or the abbreviated top and minuscule straight skirt hadn't given her away, the fingerless lace glove on her hand would have.

"Mmm?" the girl mumbled.

"We're looking for Ann Broszczynski," Lauren explained. "Is she in?"

The girl tilted her head back and hollered to the ceiling, "Mom!" A minute later she stepped aside to make room for the woman who approached.

Ann Broszczynski was a clean and attractive representative of middle America. She wore jeans, a sleeveless blouse and an apron, the latter serving at the moment as a towel for her wet hands. Her hair, a little lighter than Lauren's, was shoulder-length and swept behind her ears. Even devoid of makeup, her face was lovely.

It was also momentarily stricken. Her eyes were huge. She opened her mouth, then closed it and stared at Lauren in puzzlement.

Lauren smiled. "I look a lot like Susan, I know, but my name's Lauren Stevenson. This is Matt Kruger. We wonder if we could talk with you for a few minutes."

"Are you friends of Susan's?" the woman asked, more wary than curious, a fact that Lauren attributed to the distance between the sisters.

"Indirectly, yes," Lauren answered. "May we come in?"

Ann didn't budge. "Susan and I don't see each other," she returned a little too quickly. "We go our own ways."

"I know that. But we need to talk with you. No one else has been able to help us."

"Why do you need help?" Ann shot back.

Matt, who'd been silent up to that point, suddenly understood the problem. "We don't wish Susan any harm, Mrs. Broszczynski. If anything, the contrary is true, which is why we're here. Susan is in danger. Apparently you know that, or at least you know she's living somewhere new under an assumed name and that there's a potential for danger if she is discovered. What you don't know is that Lauren was mistaken for Susan by Theodore Prinz's men. For weeks they've put her through hell, using one scare tactic after another. Last week they abducted her and came very close to killing her. It was during the time she was being held that she learned about Susan." He spoke with soft urgency. "We need to find your sister. She must be told that she's being hunted. We have to convince her to go to the police. Between her testimony and Lauren's, we know that something can be done about Prinz."

Ann was pale. She gnawed at her lower lip and clutched the folds of the apron in her fists.

"May we come in?" Lauren asked again, this time pleadingly.

After another moment's hesitation, the woman nodded. Shooing her daughter away, she led them into a small, modestly furnished living room. None of them sat; the air was too tense for that.

"I'm not sure if I know what you're talking about," Ann burst out. "I'm not involved in Susan's life."

"We realize that," Matt said quietly, intent on convincing her of the legitimacy of their mission. "We've just come from Kansas City, where we spoke with both Timothy Trennis and Alexander Fraun. Do those names ring a bell?"

After a pause, Ann nodded.

"Do you trust them?" he asked. When, after another pause, Ann nodded again, he went on. "Alexander Fraun was the one who found your name on Susan's old employment application. He was obviously fond of Susan and wouldn't have given us your name unless he trusted us." Though he raised a hand to emphasize his point, his voice remained soft. "We wouldn't be bothering you if we had anywhere else to turn, but no one seems to know where Susan is or what she's doing. Prinz doesn't seem to be aware that Susan had any family, which may explain why no one has reached you sooner. But it's simply a matter of time before he gets to you, and then to Susan, because it may well be that you're the only one who knows Susan's new name and address." He paused, gentling his voice all the more. "Will you tell us, Ann? We only want to help."

"I wish my husband were here," Ann wailed softly, hands tightly clenched before her. "I'm no good at things like this."

"You're Susan's sister. It's your decision, more so than your husband's."

"But things are so tenuous between Susan and me," she argued. "For years we had very little contact. She was in one world, I was in another. There was no middle ground between us. I don't want to do something that will anger her, or worse, put her in danger."

"Then you have to tell us where she is," Lauren urged. "*None* of us will be safe until we find her and convince her to go to the police with us. For all we know, Matt and I are just one step ahead of Prinz's men right now."

Ann pondered Lauren's words nervously, her gaze shifting from one spot in the room to another. Then she brightened. "Why don't you let *me* call Susan? I can tell her everything you've told me—"

"Do you think she'll believe you—or that we're legitimate?" Matt cut in. "She'll run, Ann. She's done it before, and she'll do it again if this isn't handled right. She needs to *see* Lauren and the physical similarity between them in order to believe what's happened."

Ann looked from one face to the other. "You're asking an awful lot."

Lauren nodded. "We know."

"If you turn out to be the bad guys—"

"We're not! You can call the police back home, either in Boston or Lincoln. They'll verify everything that's happened to me."

"And Fraun took precautions of his own," Matt added soberly. "He has our names and addresses. He knows where to send the police if anything happens to Susan."

"I'll never forgive myself if she's hurt because of me!"

Matt put every ounce of feeling into a single, last-ditch plea. "*No* one will be hurt if we reach her in time. But time is of the essence, and we can't reach her if we don't know where she is."

Ann worried the issue for several minutes longer, her eyes filled with concern, her lips clamped tightly together. Her gaze slid from Lauren to Matt and back to Lauren, asking questions for which there were, as yet, no answers.

Just as Lauren was about to scream in frustration, Ann straightened her shoulders, took a deep breath, let it out in a sigh and surrendered.

CHAPTER ELEVEN

A SINGLE LONG shadow stretched across the grass behind him as Ted Prinz stood in his garden staring out over the hills. Absently he lit a cigarette and dragged deeply on it. Pensive, he narrowed his eyes through the tunnel of smoke.

So Susan was in Washington, D.C. That made sense. He could picture her trying to hook up with a politician who had enough clout to protect her.

He grinned. She'd never make it. His men would make sure of that. At this very moment Kruger and the girl were being staked out at the Hay-Adams House. When they moved, his men would, too.

And Susan would regret the day she'd been born.

"WHADDYA THINK?" Matt asked, looking at his watch. "Should we make a stab at it tonight?"

Lauren pressed a hand to her chest. "My heart is pounding. I can't believe we've found her."

"Don't believe it until you see it. There could be a catch yet."

But Lauren was shaking her head. "Ann said she'd spoken to her just last week. Oh, she's here all right. I can *feel* it."

Slinging an arm around her shoulder, Matt tugged her close. "My eternal optimist." He popped a kiss on her nose. "So. What will it be? Tonight, or tomorrow morning?"

Lauren pondered the choice. "If we go tonight, it'll have to be to her apartment. Ann said it's a nice place, which means there will be security guards—"

"Who call up to announce your arrival and get permission to let you in. Susan doesn't know us. She'll never allow it. No, I think we'll have to take her by surprise. Any advance announcement of our presence will put her on guard and, in turn, put us at an immediate disadvantage."

"On the one hand," Lauren mused, "I hate to wait. The sooner we get to her, the sooner we'll all breathe freely. But another twelve hours, after all this time... it can't hurt."

Matt nodded his agreement. "We know where she works. If we surprise her there tomorrow, she won't have a chance to turn us away sight unseen. And if she gets scared and tries to run, we can stop her."

"But we need time with her, time to explain what we're about." Lauren ran her tongue back and forth over her lower lip, then expressed her thoughts aloud. "She's a beauty consultant, Ann said. That figures. From what we've learned, she has a way with makeup and color and style. What if I call first thing in the morning and make an appointment? If we just drop in, she's apt to be with a client. On the other hand, if I can guarantee us a piece of her time..."

A slow grin spread over Matt's face. "Smart girl. I *knew* there was a reason why I brought you along."

Lauren grabbed his ears, tugged him down and kissed his yelp away. She lingered to savor his returning kiss, her fingers tangling in his sun-kissed hair. At last she dropped her arms to his waist and pressed her cheek to his chest.

They were silent for a time, enjoying the closeness. But Lauren's thoughts of the day to come refused to stay in abeyance for long. "Poor Susan. If she only knew tonight what was in store for her tomorrow."

"Save your sympathy, sweetheart," Matt murmured. "Susan Miles may still put us through an ordeal. Confronting her is one thing, convincing her that we're on the level is another, but selling her on the idea of going to the police may be a different can of worms entirely."

MICHELE SLOANE, AS Susan now called herself, had set up her business in fashionable Georgetown. Lauren got the phone number from directory assistance and started calling at eight-thirty in the morning on the chance that the shop opened early for the prework set. It wasn't until nine that she got through.

Luck was with her. Michele had a cancellation and could see her at eleven-thirty.

The minutes ticked by with agonizing slowness as Lauren and Matt pushed their breakfasts around their plates in the hotel dining room. Then, to expend nervous energy, they went out for a walk. But while the White House, the Mall and the Lincoln Memorial should have inspired awe, they were too preoccupied in anticipation of the coming meeting to award these sights their due.

Ten o'clock came and went, then ten-thirty. Back in their hotel room, Lauren began to pace the floor. By eleven she was ready to jump out of her skin, but it wasn't until eleven-ten that she and Matt left the room, rode the elevator in silence, walked calmly through the hotel lobby and climbed into the cab that the doorman had whistled up. They'd calculated well for the traffic.

It was eleven-thirty on the dot when the cabbie pulled up at the address they'd given him.

For a minute Matt and Lauren stood before the stately brownstone on the ground floor of which was Susan's shop. The sign on the front window, a contemporary logo in burgundy, read "Elegance, Inc." Smaller letters, far below, advertised fashion advice and salon services.

Taking a collective breath for courage, they crossed the sidewalk, descended three steps to the door and entered the shop. An aura of quiet dignity surrounded them instantly. The reception area was done in shades of a soothing pale gray and peach. Soft pop music hummed in the background, low enough to create a modern mood yet be unobtrusive.

A woman sat in a chair reading a magazine, apparently awaiting her appointment. Lauren and Matt made their way directly to the receptionist.

"May I help you?" she asked politely.

"Yes. My name is Lauren Stevenson. I have an eleven-thirty appointment with Michele Sloane."

The receptionist consulted the large book open before her, put a tiny dot next to Lauren's name, then smiled up at her. "Why don't you have a seat? Michele is just finishing up with another client. She'll be with you in a minute."

Lauren thanked her and settled into one of a pair of chairs farthest from the receptionist. She crossed her legs, folded her hands in her lap and leaned closer to Matt, who'd taken the chair immediately on her left.

"When was the last time you were in a place like this?" she whispered in an attempt at levity.

His soft grunt was the only answer she got, the only thing that betrayed his mood. He looked self-confident and composed. Taking her cue from him, she breathed deeply and straightened her shoulders. They were so close, so close....

Moments later another woman entered the shop, checked in with the receptionist and was sent directly through to one of the back rooms. Lauren stared after her, noting a long hallway sporting two doors on the side she could see. She assumed another two doors were on the opposite side.

Just then, from that blind side came the soft murmur of conversation. It was immediately followed by the appearance of two women, but Lauren's eyes homed in on only one of them.

Susan Miles was everything she'd been built up to be. She was indeed stunning. Very much Lauren's own height and build, she wore a pale yellow dress whose shoulder pads gave a breadth that narrowed, past a hip belt, into a pencil-slim skirt. Chunky beads hung around her neck. A coordinated bracelet ringed her wrist. Whether she wore earrings was not immediately apparent, for her chin-length hair was a mass of thick waves that framed her face in haphazard tumble.

The entire look was chic without being ostentatious. Lauren, who mere moments before had felt sufficiently confident in her own stylish tunic and slacks, was envious.

She was also puzzled. Susan Miles looked very much like her, yet very different. Apparently the receptionist had missed the resemblance. Now, studying Susan, Lauren could understand why.

Susan's hair was far lighter than Lauren's, for one thing. It had obviously been colored, though there was nothing obviously doctored about the blond, sun-streaked tangle. It blended perfectly with Susan's skin tone and makeup and looked completely natural.

Makeup. Yes, another difference. While Lauren wore it lightly and for simple enhancement, Susan's makeup sculpted her face, shading and contouring with a skill that was remarkable. Plastic surgery? Lauren doubted it. Yet there was something about the nose…a small bump…

The woman who'd been with Susan left. Susan bent over the desk to examine the appointment book, then followed the receptionist's finger to Lauren and Matt. She smiled as she straightened and approached them, but her smile wavered as she neared. Lauren thought she saw a faint drain of color from Susan's face. The smile remained but was more forced.

Lauren stood up, finding solace in the warmth of Matt's body by her side. If Susan was playing a part, she herself was doing no less. She held out her hand, willing it not to shake. "Michele?"

Susan met her clasp. "Yes. You're Lauren. And…" Her gaze slid to Matt.

"Matt Kruger," he said with a smile.

Susan nodded, but she was already looking back at Lauren. She folded her hands at her waist, hesitated a minute too long, then cleared her throat. "Well. You're here for a consultation. Why don't you come back to my office?"

They followed her down the hall to the last door on the right. The office they entered was simply decorated and furnished, exuding the same quiet dignity as the front room had. Large semiabstract watercolors—one of a woman's face—hung on the walls. Had it been another time, Lauren would have paused to admire the pictures themselves, if not their matting and framing, but she was too busy trying to organize her words and thoughts to handle anything else.

They were all three seated—Susan behind her desk, Matt and Lauren in comfortable chairs before it—when Susan spoke. "What can I do for you?" she asked. Her tone was thoroughly cordial, even warm. The wariness in her eyes was subtle enough to go unnoticed by any but the most watchful of observers. Lauren and Matt were that.

Lauren went straight for the heart. "You've noticed the resemblance, haven't you?"

Susan frowned. "Resemblance?" Her expression was one of confusion, but it was studied. A second, almost imperceptible drain of color from her face betrayed her.

"I have a problem," Lauren explained softly, her eyes never once leaving Susan's. "I was hoping you could help me. Several months back I had plastic surgery, reconstructive work, actually, to correct a long-standing medical problem. The work was extensive, and when it was done, I looked like a new person. But after I returned to the States—the clinic where I had the surgery was in the Bahamas—I ran into trouble. Things started happening. Odd things. Dangerous things." She gave several examples, then paused, looking for a reaction in Susan. But the latter, aside from her underlying pallor, remained composed, so Lauren went on.

"Matt and I put two and two together when I began to get letters addressed to Susan Miles. We realized that I was being mistaken for someone else, but we couldn't find a Susan Miles in the area and we didn't know what to do next. Then, just about a week ago, I was abducted, forced off the street into a car by two men who firmly believed I was Susan Miles."

Susan blinked. That was all.

"They drove me around for hours, finally brought me to an abandoned warehouse and told me their plan.

They meant to set me on fire and watch me burn. They had every intention of seeing me dead, as their boss wanted me to be." Lauren paused again, this time out of necessity. Her voice began to shake, whether from remembered terror or the utterly bland look on Susan Miles's face, she didn't know.

Matt came to her aid. "Lauren managed to escape. But we don't know if they're still out looking for her or if they actually let her go because she managed to convince them she wasn't Susan. The police have nothing to go on, at least nothing that's leading them anywhere, and Lauren can't live under guard indefinitely. We realized then that our only hope was in finding Susan."

For the first time, Susan stirred. She propped her elbow on the arm of her chair and rested her chin on her knuckles. Her fingernails were beautifully shaped and painted a sheer pink noncolor. "I'm not sure I understand. I'm a beauty consultant, not a detective. Why have you come to me?"

Lauren resumed speaking, more calmly, now, and briefly sketched the course of their search. She concluded with a soft "Ann Broszczynski sent us here."

Susan's eyes were blank and she was shaking her head, but her knuckles had curved into a fist. "None of those names mean anything to me. Ann—whoever she is—must have been wrong. I have no idea why she sent you here."

"I think you do," Matt challenged. "You saw the resemblance to your old self the minute you looked at Lauren, and we saw the resemblance the minute we looked at you."

A hoarse laugh tripped from Susan's throat. "This is ludicrous! I don't know why I'm even sitting here listening to you." But she didn't move. "Do you really expect me to swallow the story you've told? I'm sorry. Even if I believed it, which I don't, I don't know why someone would have sent you to *me*. And as far as the resemblance is concerned, you're mistaken—"

"No." Matt spoke softly, trying his best to understand her fear as he tamped down his own impatience. "We're not here to hurt you. You have a problem, and because of that, Lauren has a problem. I, for one, don't think it's fair that she's been saddled with it. She did nothing but try to correct a medical deficiency, and now she's being punished. We know that Theodore Prinz is at the root of the problem. We also know that unless you agree to go to the police and testify along with Lauren, he'll snake his way free." Susan's telephone chirped melodically. Matt ignored it. "It's only a matter of time before he finds you—Ann realized that—and he may well kill Lauren along the way."

When the phone on the desk chimed a second time, Susan picked it up. Her every movement was carefully controlled. "Yes?... She's back?... No, no, don't let her go. I'll be there in a second." Replacing the receiver, she rose from her seat and headed for the door. Matt was instantly on his feet, but she held him off with a hand. "There's a problem at the front desk. I have to see to it, but I'll be back. Please don't go anywhere. I'd like to hear more about this Theodore Prinz."

With that, she left the office. The door had no sooner closed behind her than the phone rang again, that same soft tinkle. Matt stared at it and frowned. When he made a move toward it, Lauren was one step ahead. Their lines of sight merged on the keyboard. A red dot flashed beside the bottommost number, one that was separate from the others, one totally apart from that marked "X" that would connect the interoffice line.

"Damn it," Matt barked, heading for the door, "she's gone! That wasn't the receptionist. It was someone on her personal line, someone who's calling back now to find out what in the hell she was talking about." He was in the hall, looking first one way, then the other, with Lauren by his side. "I'll take the back, sweetheart. It probably leads to an alley. No, you take the back. I'll circle around and head her off." He burst into a run toward the front of the shop.

Brushing past the white curtain at the end of the hall, Lauren raced through the back room, threw open the door and dashed up the steps. Yes, there was an alley, a long, long alley strewn with trash cans and miscellaneous other debris. Susan Miles was about halfway down its length and running.

"Michele!" Lauren screamed as she, too, broke into a run. "Wait!"

Susan wasn't waiting. She was running as if the devil himself were at her heels, and would have long since made it to the end of the alley had it not been for the dodging the obstacle course demanded.

"Michele! Wait! It's dangerous!"

But Susan had no intention of stopping. Had it not been for Matt's timely appearance at the end of the alley, she'd have escaped. As it was, when she saw him, she whirled around, saw Lauren, whirled again and made for the nearest doorway. Matt reached her before she made it.

Capturing her bodily, he swung her up and wrestled her back until he'd pinned her to the nearest brick wall. "I am *not* going to hurt you, Susan," he gritted out between breaths, "but neither…neither am I going to let you get away. Not…after all we've been through to find you, not after all Lauren's been through *because* of you."

Lauren came to a breathless halt just as Susan sagged lower against the wall. Matt simply shifted his grip, veeing his hands under her arms and propping her right back up. She'd tricked him once. Lauren agreed with his caution.

"It wasn't my fault," Susan gasped. Her composure had vanished. There was near panic in the eyes that skipped from Matt's face to Lauren's and back. "I'd been with Ted for two years before I discovered who he really was. I wanted to leave him then, but he wouldn't hear of it. For a year, a whole year, I tried, but he threatened awful things and I kept giving in until I hated myself nearly as much as I hated him. I was desperate... so desperate that I tried to kill myself."

"A suicide attempt?" Matt drawled. "We knew about the accident, but that's a new twist to the story."

"Why else would I drive over a cliff? You thought I wasn't in the car when it went over the edge? I was. *I was*. But I was thrown free when the car began to roll." Trembling, she shoved the hair from her forehead. Just below her hairline was a three-inch scar. "I broke an arm and several ribs, but I could breathe and think and feel, and it was then that I realized I'd been given a second chance. So I let them think that I'd died, and I ran. Don't ask me what hospital I went to—it was in some godforsaken town in northern Arizona."

"How did you get there?"

"I hitchhiked."

"Talk of ludicrous stories!"

"It's the truth. At the time, nothing was more dangerous than staying where I was."

"Why didn't you go to the police? If Prinz threatened you—"

"Ted *owns* the police, or half of them, and what he doesn't own he has connections to. I know what I'm talking about. I've seen him buy his way out of serious investigations. That was what tipped me off in the first place!"

Lauren entered the conversation at that point. She was beginning to feel sorry for Susan. While she understood Matt's anger, she wanted to put the other woman at ease. They still needed her cooperation. "Okay," she said gently. "You felt you couldn't go to the police. Where did you go? What did you use for money? The two men who kidnapped me mentioned furs and jewels."

"I had both. Ted had given them to me. As far as I was concerned, I'd earned them."

"But how did you get them? You'd have to have gone back to Los Angeles."

"A friend did it." Susan's voice softened. "He was a little old man who used to sell flowers on a street corner not far from the boutique. I liked him. He reminded me of my father—or what my father would have been like if he'd lived beyond forty," she added in a whisper. "Sam was kind and gentle. I knew he'd do anything for me." She averted her gaze. "Maybe it was wrong of me, or arrogant. I knew Sam was dying. He'd told me that he'd been given six months to live. I figured that he wouldn't mind the risk, that he'd take pleasure in helping me out." Her eyes met Lauren's. "And he did. He told me so in a note he stuck inside the pocket of one of the coats."

"An old man, breaking into your apartment and stealing your things?" Matt was clearly skeptical.

"He didn't steal them," Susan shot back. "He simply returned to me what was mine. As for breaking into my apartment—he had friends who would have done anything for him, just as I would have."

"But you never got the chance," Matt concluded sarcastically, only to be instantly corrected.

"I did. After I sold the very first ring, I sent him a large chunk of the money. I know he received it, because I called him to make sure." Susan took a ragged breath. "Whether he lived long enough to enjoy it, I'll never know. I've tried to call him again, but there's been no answer. He may be using the money to travel, or he may be...well, I'll never know."

Matt stared at her. "Prinz's men may have had him killed."

"Do you think I don't know that?" Susan cried. "I've *seen* Ted in action—"

"Isn't it about time you did something about it?"

The air between the two sizzled. Lauren set about diffusing it. "We're getting ahead of ourselves. Did you come directly to Washington from Arizona?"

Susan was leaning against the brick on her own now, Matt having released her and stepped back. She took several calming breaths. "I made a few stops. I wasn't sure where I wanted to settle. But each time I stopped, I felt I was still too close to Ted, so I kept going. When I reached Washington, it was either stay or swim. So I stayed."

"What about your nose?" Lauren frowned as she leaned to the side for a profile view. "We assumed you'd have plastic surgery to change your looks. Prinz's men assumed the same, which was how they got onto me."

"I figured they'd think that, so I avoided it." Susan gave a self-conscious half shrug. "My nose had been broken in the accident, and I didn't trust the doctors in that hospital to do more than tape it up. When the bandages came off, I saw the bump. It was subtle enough to change my profile just that little bit. I told myself it'd give my face character." She snorted. "Obviously it didn't fool you."

"We started with an advantage." It was Matt speaking, more gently now. "We had your name and knew where to find you. Even before you walked into that reception area, we were primed to see Susan Miles."

With an air of helplessness, Susan raised her eyes to the sliver of sky above. "Well, you saw her. And you have her cornered. I suppose I knew that someday someone would find me. In some ways, it's a relief that it's you."

"Then you do trust us?" he asked.

Her gaze met his. "Trust? Maybe that's going a little too far."

Lauren grasped her arm. "But you do believe that what we've told you is the truth."

Susan studied her for a long time. "The resemblance…it's amazing. What did you look like before?"

Dropping Susan's arm, Lauren glanced awkwardly at Matt, who nodded. "I was awful." Lauren proceeded to paint a brief, if blunt, picture of her former self. "Richard took care of it all, bless him." She winced. "Then again…"

Matt curved his hand around her neck. "No, no, sweetheart. From a purely medical standpoint, it is a blessing, what he did. And as for this other, we'll work it all out. Susan will go to the police with us—"

"Whoa. I never said that."

"But you have to!" Lauren cried. "It's your only chance. Sooner or later those guys will find you—"

A deep voice cut her off with an ominously sarcastic "Hel-lo, hel-lo."

All three heads jerked around. Lauren and Susan gasped in tandem. Matt grew rigid.

"What have we here?" drawled the man whose face and voice Lauren would never in a million years forget. He stood several yards away, a human wall with a gleaming gun in his hand. "Matthew Kruger, Lauren Stevenson...and if it isn't the elusive Miss Susan Miles."

"What do you want, Leo?" Susan demanded. Her eyes were hard, glittering more with disgust than with fear.

Leo grinned, that ugly grin Lauren remembered so well, and looked first at Mouse on his left, then at another thug on his right. The eyes he refocused on Susan were nearly black. "You know what I want. I want you."

"I'm not available."

"Seems to me you are." He cocked his head toward Lauren and Matt. "These two don't want you, that's for sure. You've been a thorn in their sides."

"I'd pick her any day—" Lauren began, only to be silenced by the restraining hand Matt put on her arm, and by his own retort.

"You've got the three of us, and you know damn well that if you so much as touch Susan, we'll go straight to the police. Do you plan a triple murder?"

"Wouldn't bother the boss any. I have his okay."

"Think, Leo, think," Susan urged. "There are too many people involved now. If you do something to Matt and Lauren, someone *else* will go to the police. This isn't another one of your little in-house jobs. If you kill one of your own, you're doing us all a favor. But to kill me—and these two, who are totally innocent... The police will get you one day, Leo. And if you think Ted will come forward on your behalf, you're crazy."

Leo laughed. "The police won't get me. I'm good at what I do. We'll have it arranged so it looks like you shot the others, then killed yourself. Very clean."

"Very simpleminded," Susan retorted. When Leo made a move toward her, she slipped into a half crouch, arms raised. "I think it's only fair to warn you that I've learned karate."

Lauren and Matt glanced at each other, then at Susan. Leo threw back his head and laughed louder. "Talk of simpleminded. That threat's the oldest in the book, and in your case it's empty. You haven't had the time to learn enough karate to protect yourself."

"I'm a quick study."

"Against a gun?"

Susan had no answer for that, and Matt and Lauren said nothing. They were concentrating on the gun, measuring the distance between Leo and his accomplices, peripherally evaluating the potential weaponry within reach.

"Gotcha there, don't I?" Leo said. He took a step back. "Okay, I want the three of you to start moving. Straight to the car at the head of the alley." He gestured at Susan with the gun. "You first."

Lauren swallowed hard. She had no desire to be in a car with Leo and company. She knew the helplessness of that. No, if a move was to be made, it had to be now.

Matt's hand remained on her arm, but it was steadily tightening. He agreed with her. She waited for his signal.

Slowly Susan moved forward. She hadn't taken two steps, though, when her ankle turned and she buckled over.

"Ah, hell," Leo moaned. "That's the corniest move I've ever seen. It won't get you anywhere, Susan, and if you think I'm going to carry you, you're nuts."

"These heels," Susan gasped. "They're too high."

Matt's hand tightened all the more on Lauren's arm. They both knew from personal experience how well Susan could maneuver, high heels or no. Internally coiled and ready, they watched her unstrap the thin buckles and remove the shoes.

"Come on, come on. We haven't all day—" Leo's words were abruptly cut off by a totally unexpected, lightning-quick move. As Susan straightened, she hiked her slim skirt high on her thighs, spun around and delivered a kick that would have made her instructor proud.

The gun went flying, as did Matt, who barreled into Leo's midsection, knocking the burly man to the ground. Susan, meanwhile, turned her attention to the other men, throwing strategically placed kicks with such speed that they barely knew what hit them. When Mouse doubled over in pain, she whirled around and into his pal, and by the time she was done with him, she was aiming lethal chops at Mouse again.

Lauren came to her aid. Grabbing a heavy shovel from its resting place beside a nearby trash bin, she slammed it repeatedly against the back of whichever man Susan wasn't battering. Each slam vented a little more of her anger, and she might have actually enjoyed herself if she hadn't shot a glance at Matt.

He and Leo were fighting hand to hand, tumbling on the filthy pavement, each landing his share of punches.

Dropping the shovel, Lauren scrambled along the alley, returning seconds later to put an end to the fray. *"That's it!"* she screamed. *"Enough!"* She stood a safe distance back with her feet planted firmly, both hands curved around Leo's gun. The fact that she didn't know how to use it was secondary to the proprietary air with which she held it. Her chest was heaving, the only part of her that betrayed any weakness.

Later she realized that if she'd had to shoot, she'd never have been able to separate Matt from Leo, so fast were they shifting. But her strident yell brought all heads up in surprise. Matt took advantage of the precious seconds to free himself and stumble to her side. He grabbed the gun and turned it on the trio.

"Susan! That's enough!" he ordered. She'd been poised to deliver another side-handed slice to Mouse's head, and only with reluctance did she lower her arm and move back.

Matt motioned with the gun toward the three. "Okay, up! And if you think I don't know how to use this, think again. I'm an avid hunter." His knees were bent; both hands were on the gun, holding it aimed and steady. Not once did his eyes leave the men. "Lauren, go back inside the shop and call the police—"

The sound of shoes clattering on the pavement interrupted him, and seconds later the police themselves rounded the corner and entered the alley with their guns drawn. Slowly Matt straightened. He didn't lower his arm until each of Prinz's men had been handcuffed.

"Mr. Kruger?" one of the officers asked. He was the only one not in uniform and was obviously the man in command. "I'm Detective Walker. Phil Huber gave me a call and told me to keep an eye out. He sensed there might be some trouble."

"How did you know where to come?" Matt wondered. His voice shook. He shot a glance behind him to make sure Lauren was safe.

Walker smiled and cocked his head toward Susan,

who stood warily at the side. "Miss Miles's receptionist gave us a call when she found out that something had gone awry with your, uh, beauty consultation. Sorry we didn't get here sooner." He studied Matt's face. "We might have spared you a little of that."

Gingerly Matt fingered his cheek, then his mouth. In the next instant, he reached out for Lauren and hauled her close. She was eager to support him; he'd fought valiantly and had to be uncomfortable.

"Those three thugs intended to kill us," he said.

Lauren pointed. "Those *two* were the ones who kidnapped me back in Boston."

"No doubt," Matt added, his eyes filled with venom, "the third is another of Prinz's men."

"His name is Hank Ober, but he's called Rat," Susan stated stiffly. "The one with the ugly nose is Leo Charney, and the other, Mouse, is Malcolm Donnia." She watched as the three men were hustled off. "What will you do with them?"

The detective faced her. "Book them for attempted murder."

"Then what?"

"They'll be arraigned, and if they can post bond, they'll be released until their trial."

"*Released!* Do you know what they'll do once they hit the streets? They'll disappear. But before they do that, they'll finish off one or another of us, if not all three!"

"Susan…" Matt took her shoulder with his free hand. "That won't happen. The police won't *let* it—"

"The police! If they're not already in Ted's pocket, they will be soon!"

"Just a minute now," Walker growled. He took a menacing step closer. "I have never been, and will never be, in anyone's pocket, and I can safely vouch for three-quarters of my men."

"And the other quarter?"

"They won't be allowed anywhere *near* this case. The Ted Prinzes of the world would like to believe they can buy their way out of trouble, but it won't work here."

"You know of Ted?" Susan asked, wavering.

"Every major law-enforcement officer in the country knows of him. It will be one of the greatest thrills of my career to nail him, but I can do that only if you're willing to testify."

"You have to, Susan," Lauren begged. "Once and for all, it has to be put to rest."

Matt echoed her sentiment. "Lauren's right. If the three of us work together, we can do it. Lauren and I alone…well, it'll be tougher."

"He'll still come after me. It won't matter if he's in prison."

Walker spoke up. "He won't *dare* come after you. Nor will he send anyone else. He knows we'll be watching his every step. I've seen how these men work, Susan. Revenge may eat them alive, but in the end they opt for survival. Prinz will be signing his own death warrant if he comes near you again. He'll know that. Believe me, he'll know it."

Susan swallowed and looked from the detective to Matt and Lauren. "I want to believe. Really I do."

"Trust him," Matt urged. "Trust *us*. But then, you already do, don't you?"

"What makes you think that?" she returned, but there was a softness in her tone.

Matt smiled, then winced when his bruised lip protested. He soothed the spot with his finger. "You really do know karate, but you don't try it on me. One kick, and you'd have escaped. The fact that you didn't try it had to mean something." He ventured a second smile, this one more carefully. "How *did* you learn it so quickly?"

Susan shrugged and gave a tentative grin of her own. "Like I told Leo, I'm a quick study."

Matt chuckled softly. Reaching out, he drew Susan to his side at the same time that his arm tightened around Lauren. "You'll work with us, Susan, won't you?"

Susan moistened her lips, but it was Lauren she was looking at. "After all you've gone through for me, I guess I'll have to." She jerked her head toward Matt. "Where did you even find this big lummox, Lauren? Do you think maybe he has an identical twin stashed away somewhere?"

Lauren grinned up at Matt. "I don't think there's another man like him on the face of the earth. He's pretty special, isn't he?"

Purpled cheek, bruised lip, battered ribs and all, Matt sucked in a deep breath and threw back his head. "Ahhhh. Paradise. One pretty lady on the left, one pretty lady on the right...if only my buddies at the beer hall could see me now!"

"THE BEER HALL? You never talked about a beer hall. For that matter," Lauren said, scowling, "you never said you were an avid hunter." They were back in the hotel room after spending the afternoon at the police station. Lauren had insisted that Matt take a long, hot bath to soothe his aching body, but now she had him in bed, exactly where she wanted him.

Matt looked up at her through one half-lidded eye. "Where did you think construction workers went for fun?" He steeled himself against an attack that never came.

"Did you get drunk?" Lauren asked.

"On occasion."

"What were you like...drunk?"

He shrugged the shoulder she wasn't leaning against. "I don't know. I was too far out of it to tell."

She grinned. "And the hunting?"

"Wooden ducks at an amusement park. We should go sometime. I'll win you a huge stuffed teddy bear."

Lauren settled onto him, gently and with a sigh. "Thanks, but I've already got one." She rubbed her ear against the tawny hair on his chest and stilled only when he began to stroke her back.

"You're pretty special yourself," he murmured. "The way you thought to go for that gun, and then the way you held it...I thought for a minute that *you* were the one with experience."

"All a bluff. I've never held a gun in my life."

"Not even a water gun?"

"Nope. My parents were pacifists. Dead set against weapons of any kind. That's one of the things that drove them crazy about Brad. He used to make guns out of whatever toys he had handy. Some of them were pretty creative."

"Lauren?"

She took a deep breath, inhaling the clean, male scent of his skin. "Mmm?"

"What will your parents say about me?"

"That depends," she said softly and raised her head. "It depends on what I tell them first."

"How about you tell them that I love you and want to marry you?"

"How about I tell them that you're fearless and

strong, or that you've got brains as well as brawn, or that you saved my life?"

"I didn't save your life. You escaped from the warehouse on your own. Then, today, you were the one who saved all of our lives."

"You saved my life."

"How did I save your life?"

"You gave it deep, deep, lasting meaning. A good job is fine. So's a good house, even a pretty face. But the thing that really pulled it all together was you. I love you, Matt. Love is what counts. Always has been, always will be."

Matt cleared his throat, but his voice still came out hoarse. "How about you tell them that I love you and want to marry you?"

"They'll hit the roof, but you know something?" Lauren asked, pushing her chin out. "I don't care! If they love me—and I'm sure they do—they'll come around in time. So. Any other questions?"

"Just one. Aren't you worried about where we'll live?"

She turned the tables on him. "Are you?"

"No."

"Why not?"

"Because I've already decided that if my boss won't open a permanent Boston office, I'm quitting. I've made enough contacts here to get another job. And I love the farmhouse in Lincoln." He paused, narrowing his eyes. "But you knew that. You've known all along. You're too smart, that's what you are. You've got me wrapped around your little finger. Y'know, maybe I ought to re-think this. If I'm going to be led around by the nose for another fifty or sixty years—"

Lauren's lips silenced him, and within seconds he

was fully involved in the nonverbal give-and-take of love. Belying the punishment he had taken that day, he rolled over to cover her with his body. Hands buried deep in her hair, hips poised above hers, he whispered thickly, "…for another fifty or sixty years, I'll love it… every…sweet…minute."

* * * * *